How I Made It to Eighteen

a mostly true story

How I Made It to Eighteen

a mostly true story

Tracy White

ROARING BROOK PRESS
NEW YORK

FOR MY MOM WHO I'VE ALWAYS
LOVED AND NOW FINALLY LIKE.

Copyright © 2010 by Tracy White
Published by Roaring Brook Press
Roaring Brook Press is a division of Holtzbrinck Publishing
Holdings Limited Partnership
175 Fifth Avenue, New York, New York 10010
www.roaringbrookpress.com
All rights reserved

Distributed in Canada by H. B. Fenn and Company Ltd.

Cataloging-in-Publication Data is on file at the Library of Congress
ISBN: 978-1-59643-454-7

Roaring Brook Press books are available for special promotions and premiums.
For details contact: Director of Special Markets, Holtzbrinck Publishers.

First Edition June 2010
Book design by Danica Novgorodoff
Printed in the United States of America
10 9 8 7 6 5 4 3 2 1

This book is only mostly true because

I've skipped over things, moved events around, embellished, and occasionally just plain made things up. Also I wanted to respect the privacy of people and places so names and recognizable details have been changed. The technical term for this is dramatic license. I used it.

The 100% true big picture facts: I did a lot of drugs. I had body image issues. I had a nervous breakdown. I checked myself into a mental hospital. I stayed longer than I'd orignally intended. I got better. Eventually.

From the desk of Tracy White

The Friends

MARIA

EIGHTEEN. OPINIONATED. FEARLESS. CARING. GIRLFRIEND TO OLIVER. VEGETARIAN.

DETAIL ORIENTED. MIND READER. WICCAN. LIBRA. MAJORING IN SOIL SCIENCE — YEAH, YOU CAN MAJOR IN DIRT. I WANT TO UNDERSTAND HOW OUR ENVIRONMENT AFFECTS THE FOOD WE EAT. GROWING UP IN NEW YORK MADE ME WANT TO GO LIVE ON A FARM. I HATE ALL THE CONCRETE.

I'M THE FUNNY ONE. I HAVE A TOUGH EXTERIOR BUT I GET HURT EASILY, SO BE KIND. I DO CARE WHAT YOU SAY AND HOW YOU SAY IT. I TRY TO BE MYSELF IN EVERY SITUATION FOR BETTER OR FOR WORSE.

LIFE IS A JOURNEY NOT A DESTINATION.

VIOLET

ALMOST OLD ENOUGH TO VOTE. I'M A VIRGIN AND WILL STAY THAT WAY TILL I'M MARRIED. DON'T TELL ME IT'S UNREALISTIC. I KNOW WHAT I'M DOING. WHEN I GIVE MYSELF TO SOMEONE IT WILL BE FOR ALL THE RIGHT REASONS.

I WANT TO BE A PHOTOJOURNALIST SO I CAN TRAVEL ALL OVER THE WORLD. MY FAVORITE FOOD IS A CHICKEN TIKKA TACO — I INVENTED IT.

I'M A GO-GETTER. I'M AN ALCOHOLIC. I WAS A CUTTER FOR FIVE MONTHS. I THINK I AM A CARING PERSON BUT THAT'S MY OPINION. MY ELBOWS ARE TICKLISH. I HATE COOKED ONIONS BECAUSE THEY FEEL LIKE DEAD WORMS IN MY MOUTH.

I AM MORE THAN THESE WORDS.

LOLA

I'M EIGHTEEN. I'M IN LOVE BUT IF I TALK ABOUT IT I'LL JINX IT. I CURRENTLY GO TO COLLEGE IN CANADA AND, YES, IT IS COLD IN THE WINTER.

I HAVE A CAT NAMED KITTY. I HAVE NATURALLY STRAIGHT HAIR BUT I WISH I HAD CURLS, OR EVEN SOME WAVES.

I KNOW WHAT I WANT. SOME PEOPLE THINK I'M A BITCH, AND WHEN I AM IT'S FOR A GOOD REASON. I'M OBSESSED WITH WORKING OUT, BUT I WANT TO BE AN ACTOR SO I NEED A GOOD BODY.

I AM A LOYAL FRIEND.

ASHLEY

SEVENTEEN. TENNIS PLAYER. FORMER CHEERLEADER. RELIGIOUS BUT SEX BEFORE MARRIAGE IS OK AND NOT EVERYTHING THE CHURCH SAYS IS RIGHT.

DAUGHTER OF A M.A.D.D. (MOTHERS AGAINST DRUNK DRIVING) MOM. HYPER-CRITICAL.

COLLECTOR OF JAPANESE STICKERS AND MANGA. OWNER OF ONE GUCCI BAG. INSOMNIAC. SISTER TO ONE BROTHER. BAD SINGER WHO LOVES TO SING.

CURRENTLY CONSIDERED CRAZY.

WILL STICK BY YOU IF YOU STICK BY ME.

CURRENT LENGTH OF STAY:

forty-nine hours

Golden Meadows Hospital
Restoring mental health since 1938

Regarding: Stacy Black

To Whom It May Concern:

Enclosed please find the **Med-Record** for the patient
name above. Should you have any questions please feel
free to contact this department.

Sincerely,

Medical Records Department

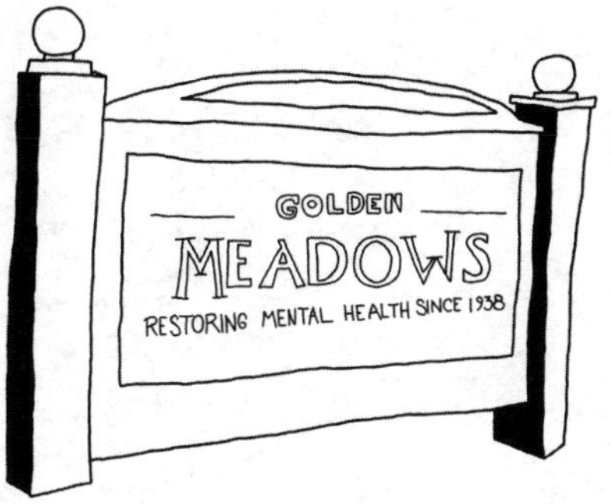
GOLDEN
MEADOWS
RESTORING MENTAL HEALTH SINCE 1938

I MISS MY LIFE.

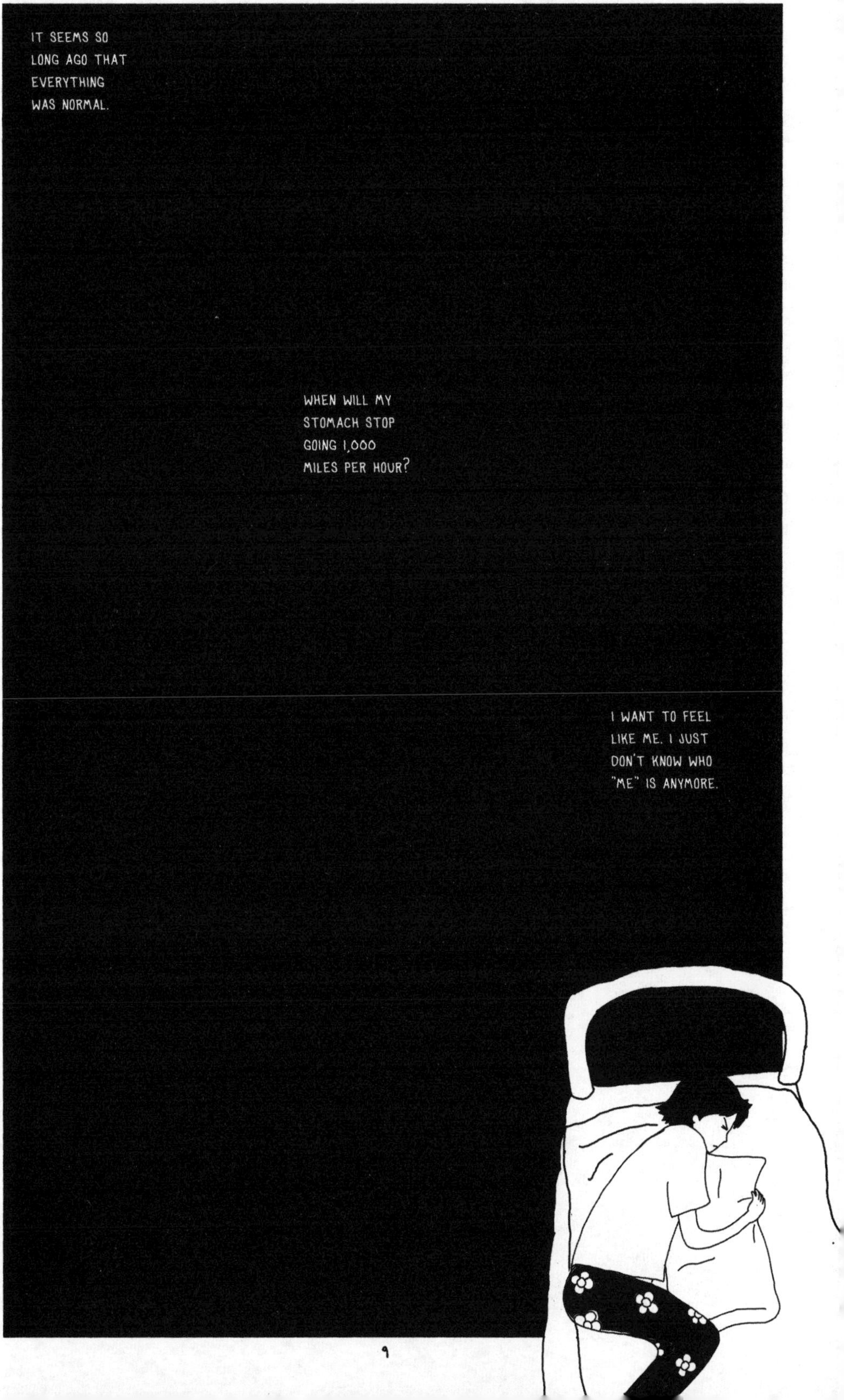
IT SEEMS SO LONG AGO THAT EVERYTHING WAS NORMAL.
WHEN WILL MY STOMACH STOP GOING 1,000 MILES PER HOUR?
I WANT TO FEEL LIKE ME. I JUST DON'T KNOW WHO "ME" IS ANYMORE.

WHATEVER THAT MEANS.

BEFORE ADMITTING MYSELF TO GOLDEN MEADOWS
I WAS BEING A RESPONSIBLE ADULT, LIVING ON MY OWN.
ZONK
SHIT.
MORNING.
ALREADY.
BEEP BEEP
3:00 PM

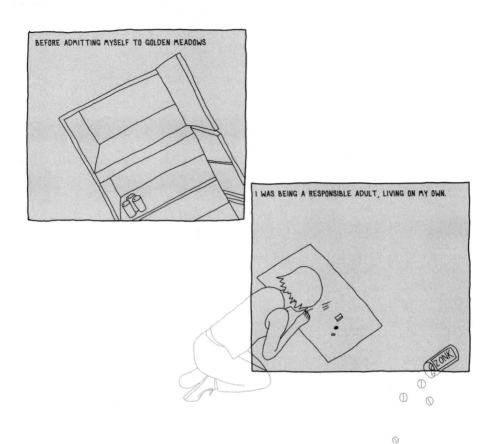

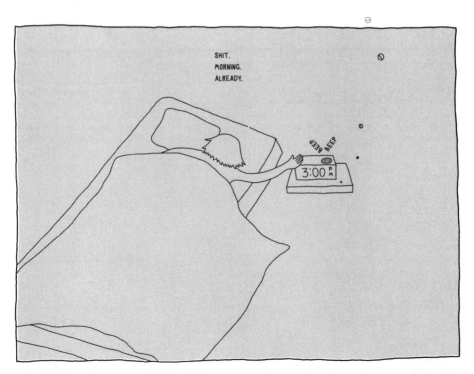

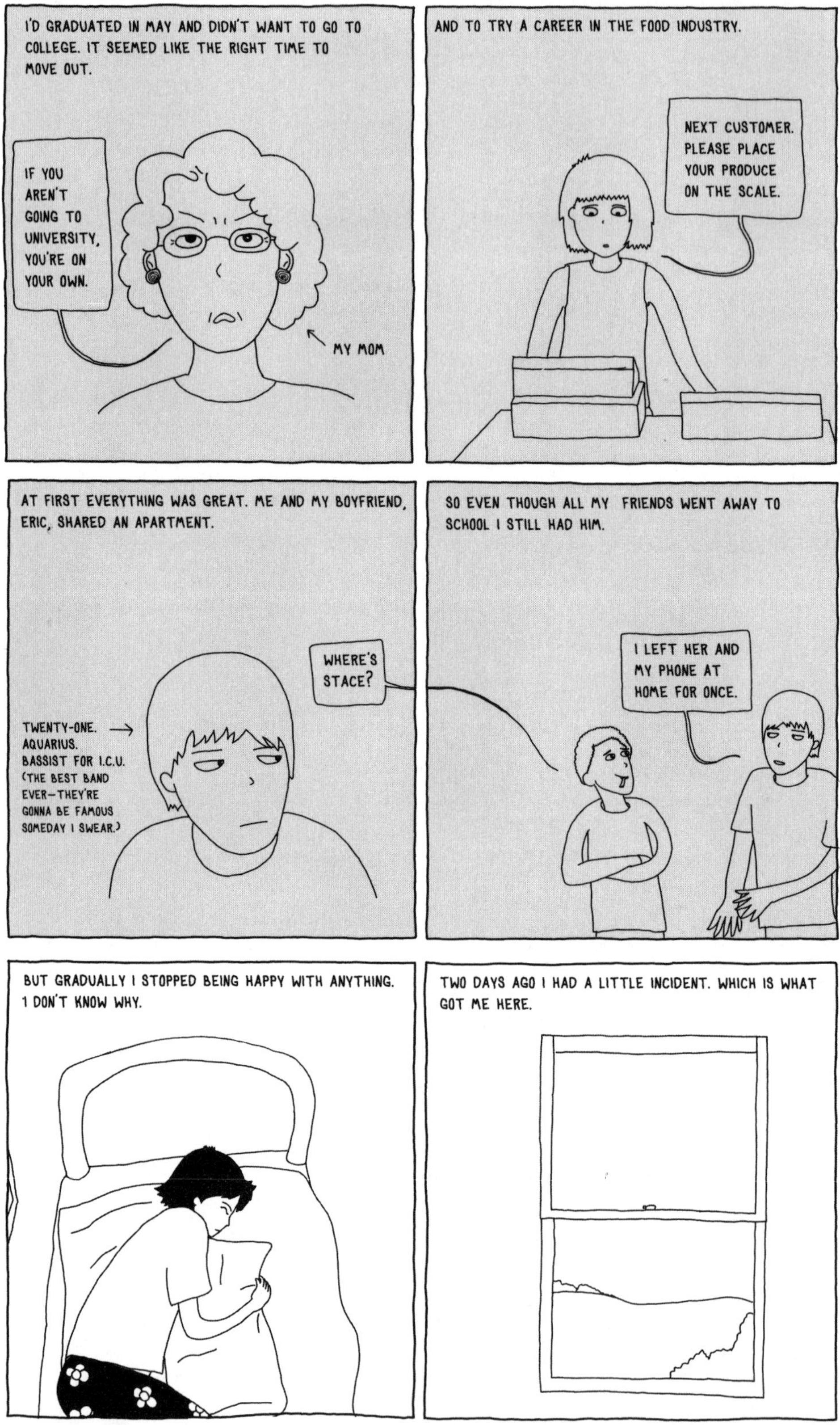
I'D GRADUATED IN MAY AND DIDN'T WANT TO GO TO COLLEGE. IT SEEMED LIKE THE RIGHT TIME TO MOVE OUT.
IF YOU AREN'T GOING TO UNIVERSITY, YOU'RE ON YOUR OWN.
MY MOM
AND TO TRY A CAREER IN THE FOOD INDUSTRY.
NEXT CUSTOMER. PLEASE PLACE YOUR PRODUCE ON THE SCALE.
AT FIRST EVERYTHING WAS GREAT. ME AND MY BOYFRIEND, ERIC, SHARED AN APARTMENT.
TWENTY-ONE. AQUARIUS. BASSIST FOR I.C.U. (THE BEST BAND EVER—THEY'RE GONNA BE FAMOUS SOMEDAY I SWEAR.)
WHERE'S STACE?
SO EVEN THOUGH ALL MY FRIENDS WENT AWAY TO SCHOOL I STILL HAD HIM.
I LEFT HER AND MY PHONE AT HOME FOR ONCE.
BUT GRADUALLY I STOPPED BEING HAPPY WITH ANYTHING. I DON'T KNOW WHY.
TWO DAYS AGO I HAD A LITTLE INCIDENT. WHICH IS WHAT GOT ME HERE.

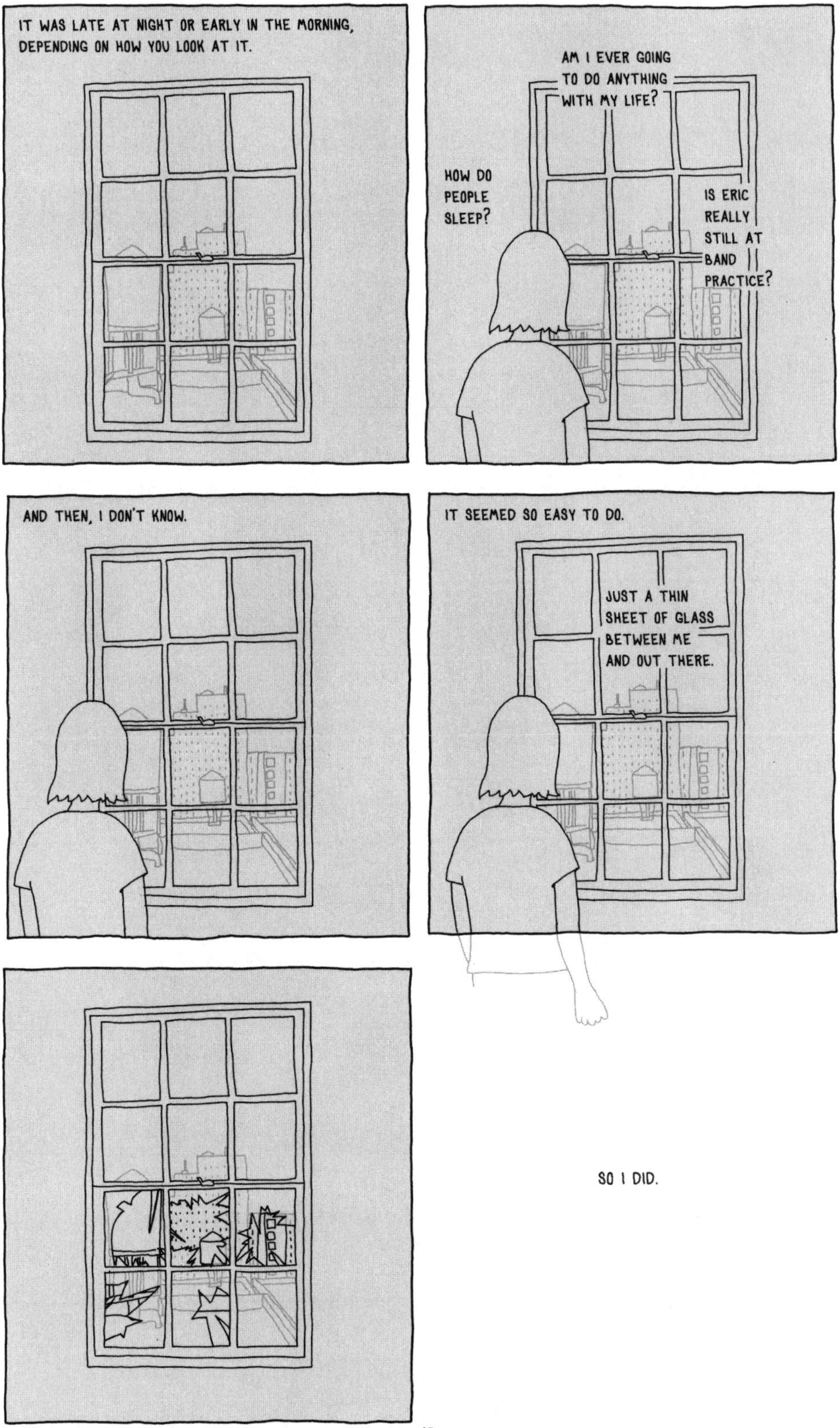
IT WAS LATE AT NIGHT OR EARLY IN THE MORNING, DEPENDING ON HOW YOU LOOK AT IT.
AM I EVER GOING TO DO ANYTHING WITH MY LIFE?
HOW DO PEOPLE SLEEP?
IS ERIC REALLY STILL AT BAND PRACTICE?
AND THEN, I DON'T KNOW.
IT SEEMED SO EASY TO DO.
JUST A THIN SHEET OF GLASS BETWEEN ME AND OUT THERE.
SO I DID.

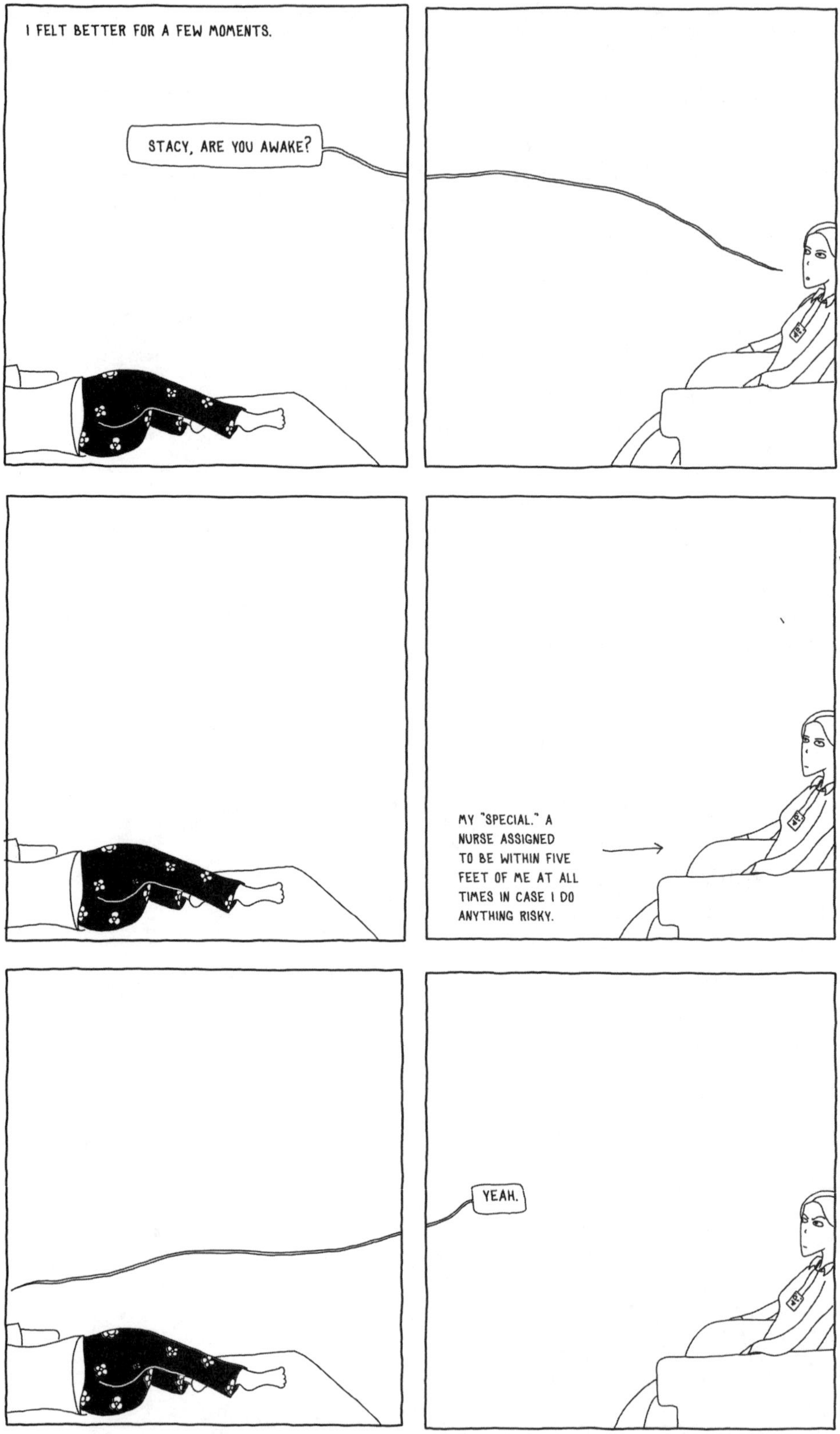
I FELT BETTER FOR A FEW MOMENTS.
STACY, ARE YOU AWAKE?
MY "SPECIAL." A NURSE ASSIGNED TO BE WITHIN FIVE FEET OF ME AT ALL TIMES IN CASE I DO ANYTHING RISKY.
YEAH.

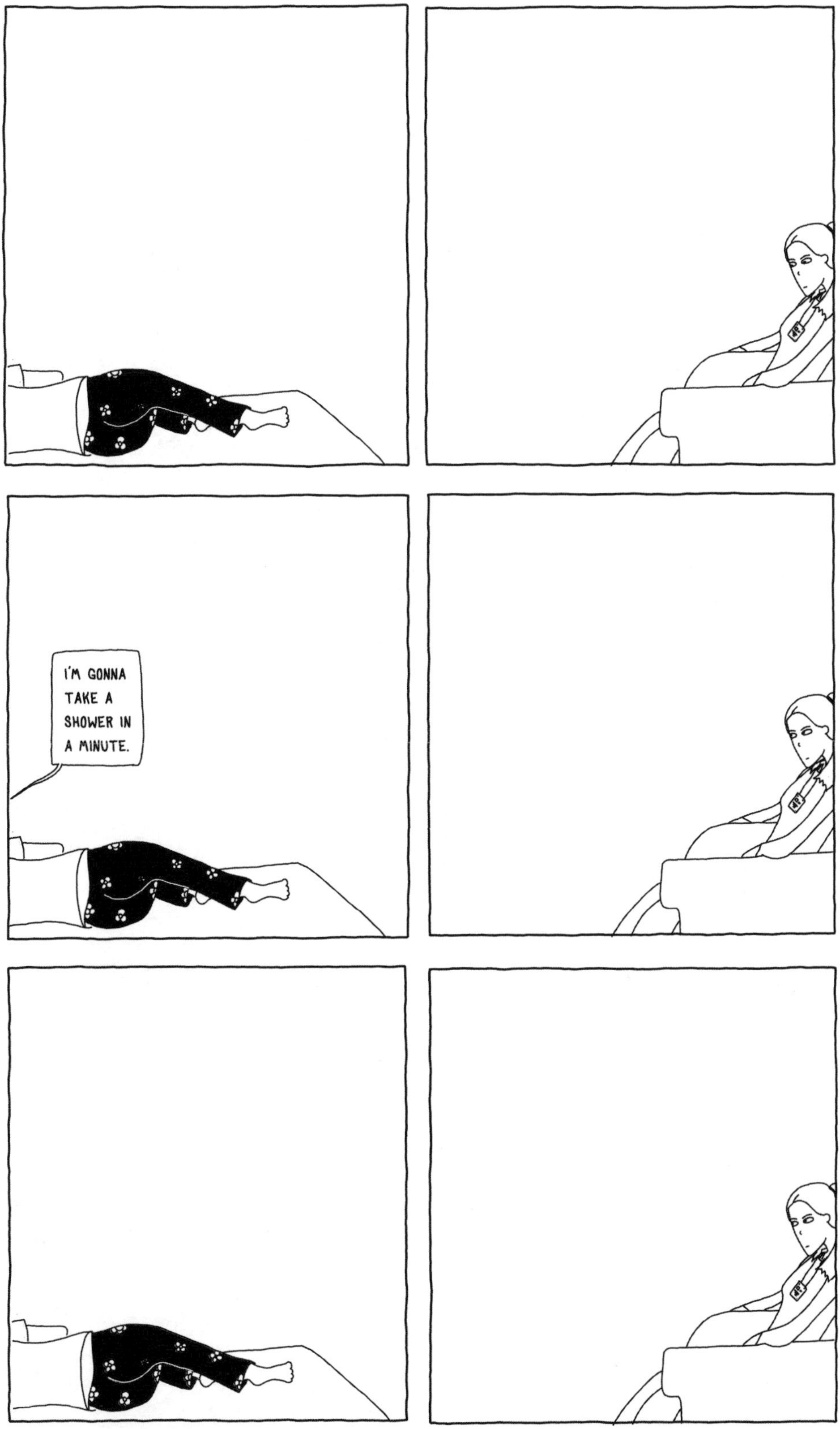
I'M GONNA TAKE A SHOWER IN A MINUTE.

NOW I FEEL
DISTANT FROM
EVERYONE
AROUND ME.

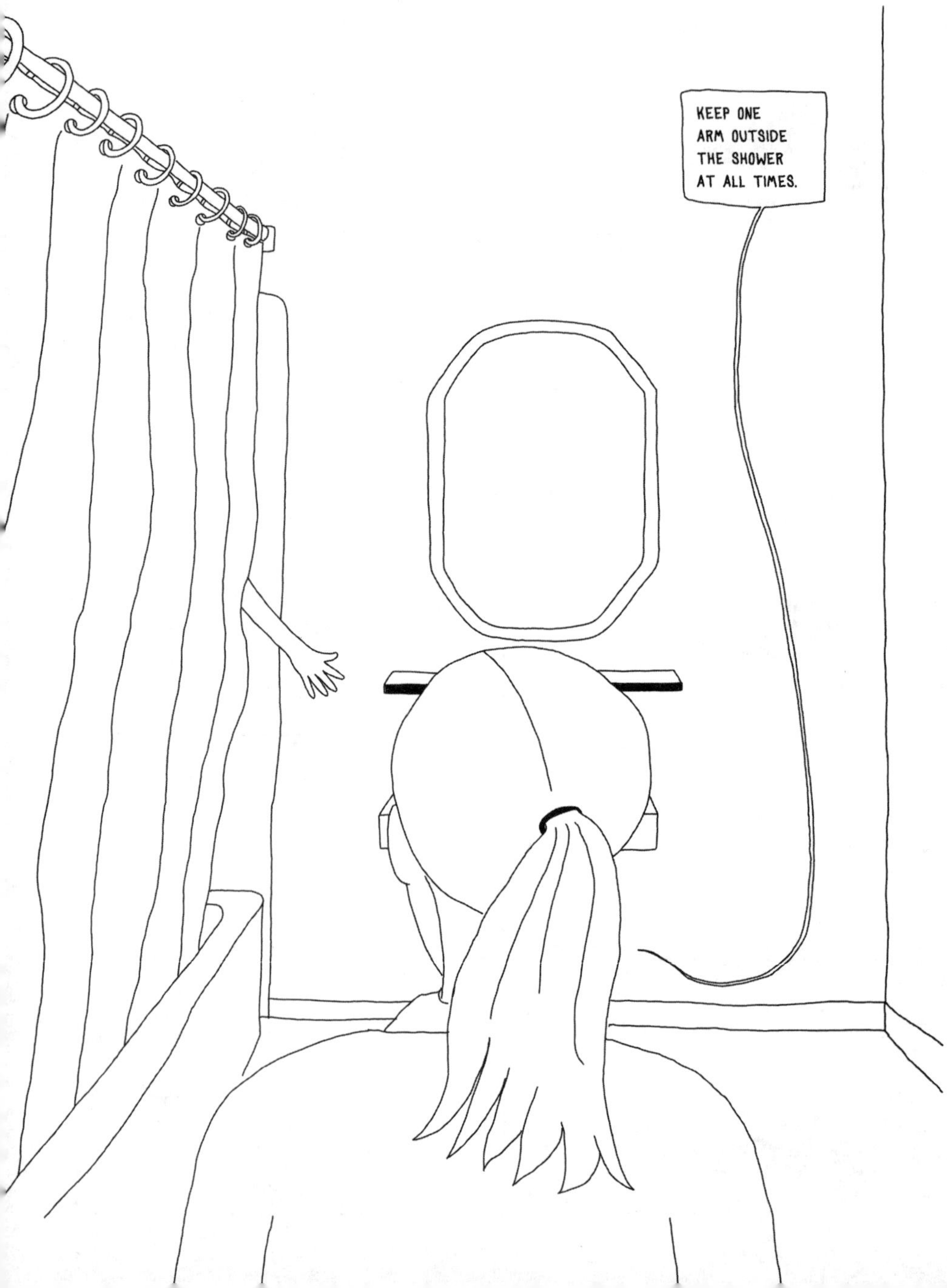
KEEP ONE ARM OUTSIDE THE SHOWER AT ALL TIMES.

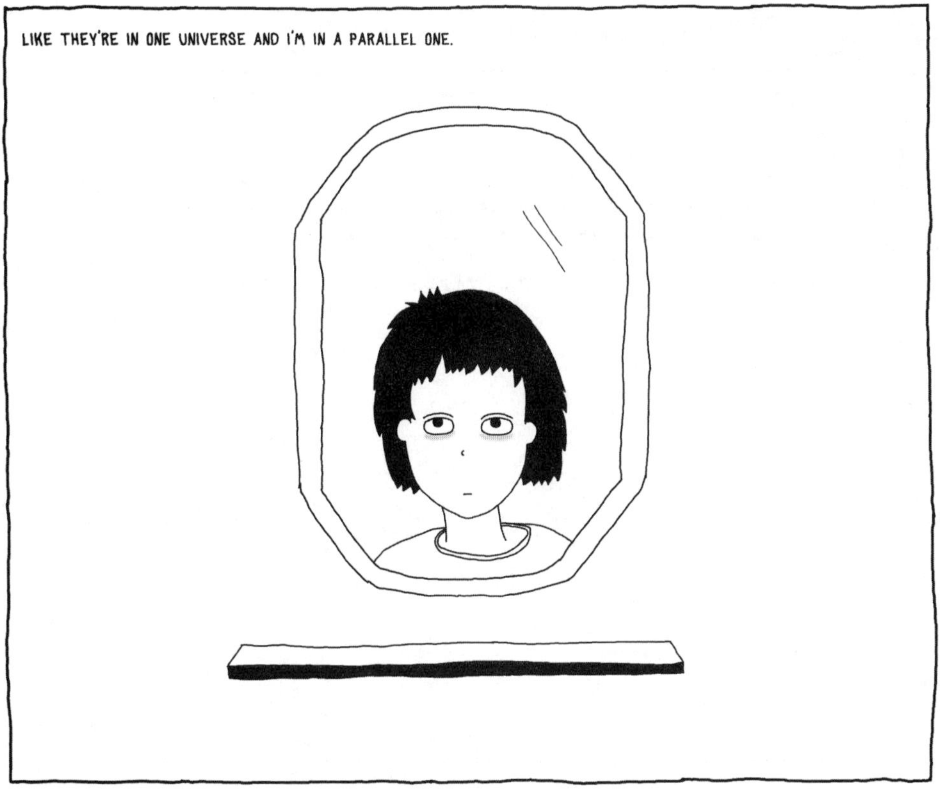
LIKE THEY'RE IN ONE UNIVERSE AND I'M IN A PARALLEL ONE.

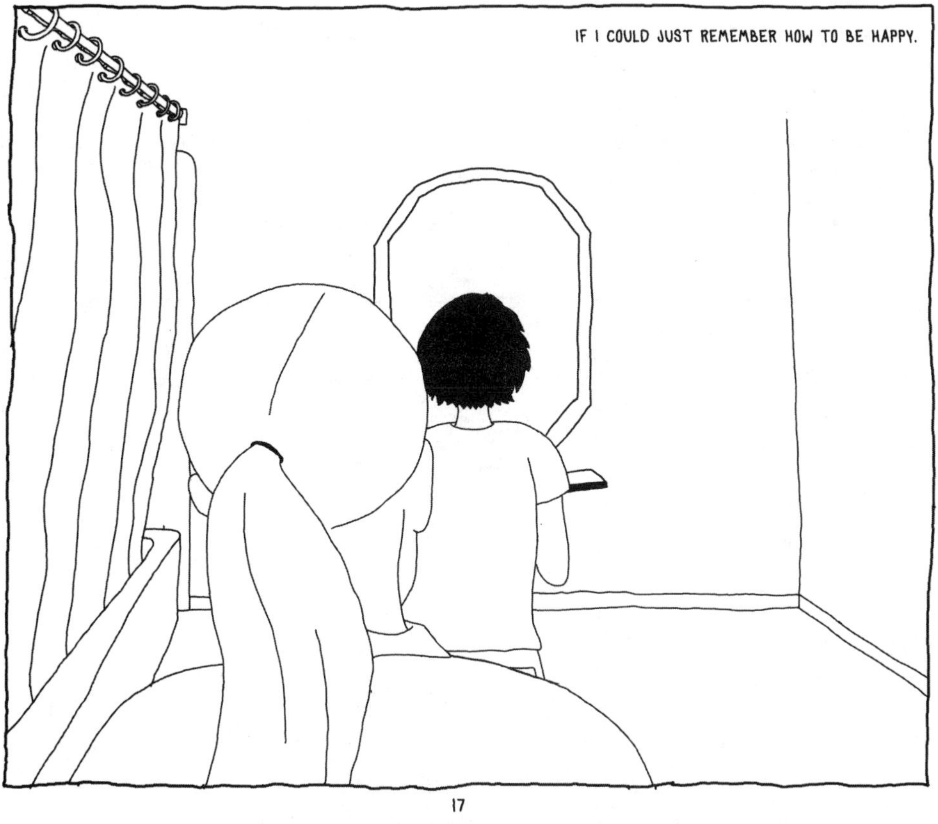
IF I COULD JUST REMEMBER HOW TO BE HAPPY.

Did you realize Stacy was depressed?

MARIA

WELL, I KNEW SOMETHING WASN'T RIGHT. HER AURA IS GRAY, NOT WHITE. I TOLD HER TO TRY MY ENERGY HEALER. SHE'S AMAZING. REALLY. ONE TIME I HAD INSOMNIA AND SHE FIGURED OUT THERE WAS A PORTAL IN MY ROOM THAT DEAD SOULS WERE PASSING THROUGH, SO SHE CLOSED IT. AFTER THAT I SLEPT LIKE A BABY. STILL DO.

I KNOW YOU'RE THINKING AURA, WHAT THE F&$K BUT WE ALL HAVE THEM. STACY'S LIGHT HAS BEEN DIM FOR A WHILE AND THAT'S A CLEAR SIGN OF DEPRESSION.

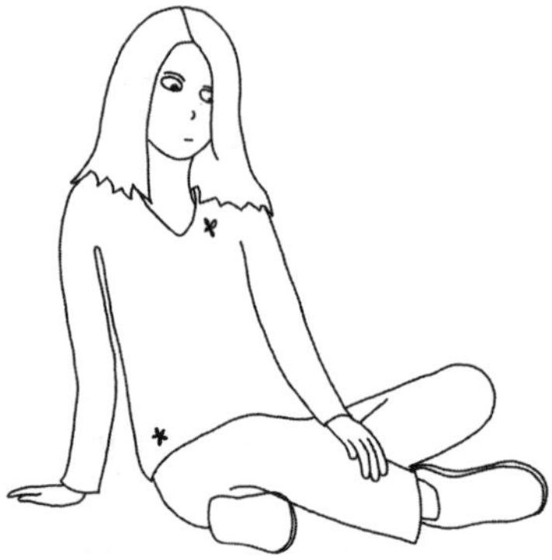

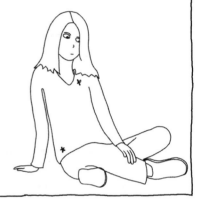

VIOLET

OF COURSE NOW I KNOW STACY WAS DEPRESSED. I MEAN, ONCE YOU HAVE HINDSIGHT EVERYTHING SEEMS OBVIOUS, DOESN'T IT?

WHEN I WAS IN REHAB THEY TOLD ME YOU DON'T DO DRUGS BECAUSE YOU'RE HAPPY. I MEAN, OF COURSE WE THOUGHT WE WERE HAVING FUN IN SCHOOL WHEN IT WAS JUST ESCAPE FROM OUR FEELINGS.

THE SIGNS WERE ALL THERE, ANGRY TOWARD HER PARENTS, WANTING TO CHECK OUT, CLEARLY IT WAS JUST A MATTER OF TIME BEFORE STACY'S SUPPRESSED FEELINGS GOT THE BETTER OF HER.

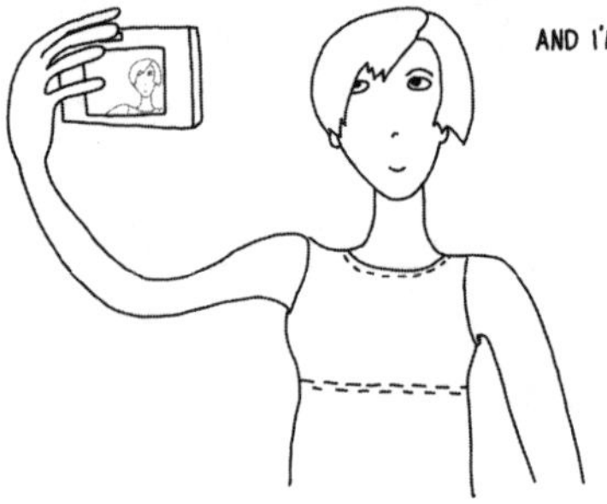

AND I'M GLAD THEY DID. SHE'S ON HER WAY TO RECOVERY.

LOLA

STACY CAME TO VISIT ME AT COLLEGE IN OCTOBER. SHE WENT TO SOME OLD
MOVIE WHILE I WAS IN CLASS AND WHEN SHE CAME BACK SHE WAS
CRYING. I TRIED TO HELP HER BUT NO MATTER WHAT I SAID SHE COULDN'T
STOP. SHE TOLD ME SHE HADN'T REALLY BEEN ABLE TO SLEEP FOR A WHILE
SO I THOUGHT THAT WAS THE PROBLEM. STILL WHEN SHE WENT HOME I
WAS SCARED FOR HER.

I WAS HOPING SHE'D HAVE IT UNDER CONTROL AND, I DON'T KNOW, I GOT ALL
CAUGHT UP IN SCHOOL. THEY GIVE US SO MUCH WORK I BARELY HAVE TIME TO
THINK ABOUT MYSELF, MUCH LESS MY FRIENDS.

THAT'S NOT AN EXCUSE. AS A PERSON WHO IS CONSTANTLY IN TOUCH WITH HER
FEELINGS (FOR MY ACTING) I SHOULD HAVE BEEN MORE AWARE OF HER DEPRESSION
AND CHECKED UP ON HER MORE OFTEN.

ASHLEY

I JUST MET STACY HERE AT GOLDEN MEADOWS. WE GOT ADMITTED IN ON THE SAME DAY. SHE WAS WEARING
THESE BIG BOOTS AND HAD BANDAGES ON ONE OF HER HANDS. SHE LOOKED SCARY. SHE HAD BLACK CIRCLES UNDER
HER EYES AND WAS THIN AND PALE.

SO YEAH, I KNEW SHE WAS DEPRESSED. I MEAN THAT'S WHY SHE'S HERE. THAT'S WHY WE'RE ALL HERE.

CURRENT LENGTH OF STAY:

sixty-one hours

"The patient is an seventeen-year-old white female. The patient has been increasingly depressed since this past summer. She complains of a full range of depressive symptomatology including feelings of hopelessness, helplessness, and worthlessness. The patient has insomnia, her appetite has fallen off, and she admits to suicidal ideation but denies intent. No compulsive phenomena were observed. She was oriented to person, place, and time. Her insight regarding her difficulty is intact to the extent she realizes she needs help. The patient appears undernourished and exhausted. She was referred to Golden Meadows by Dr. Andrew Norris, the patient's GP."

From the admissions records of case #17281
Golden Meadows Hospital

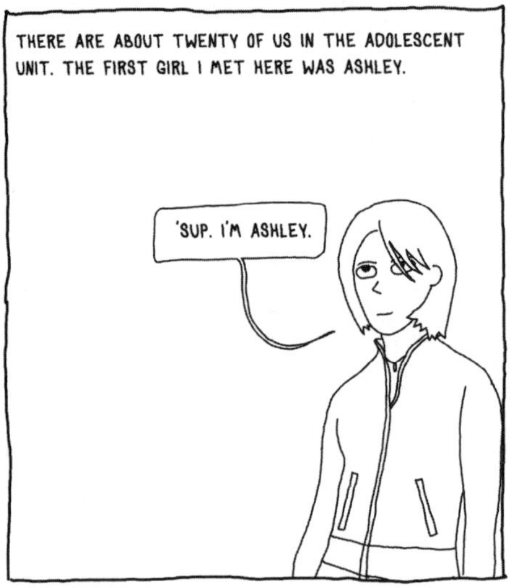
THERE ARE ABOUT TWENTY OF US IN THE ADOLESCENT UNIT. THE FIRST GIRL I MET HERE WAS ASHLEY.
'SUP. I'M ASHLEY.

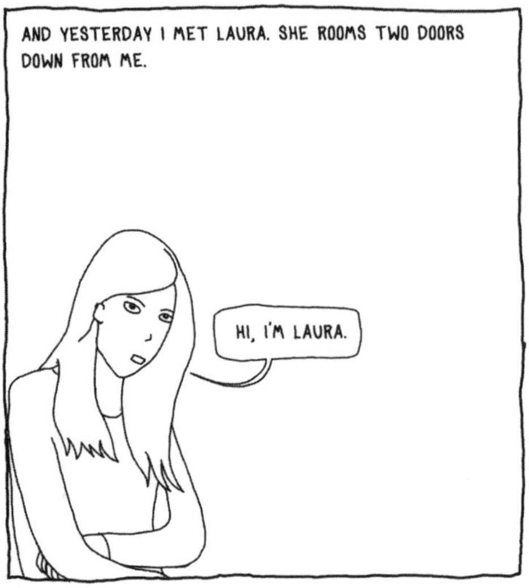
AND YESTERDAY I MET LAURA. SHE ROOMS TWO DOORS DOWN FROM ME.
HI, I'M LAURA.

EVERYONE'S HERE FOR A DIFFERENT REASON.

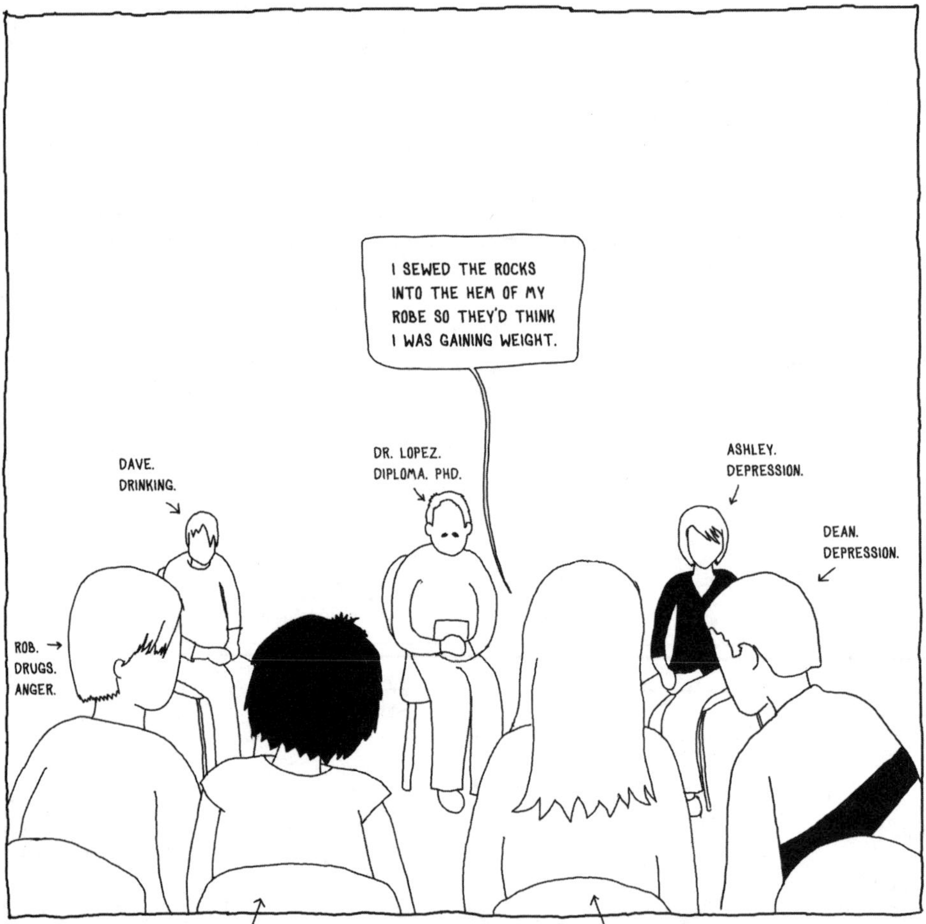
I SEWED THE ROCKS INTO THE HEM OF MY ROBE SO THEY'D THINK I WAS GAINING WEIGHT.
DAVE. DRINKING.
DR. LOPEZ. DIPLOMA. PHD.
ASHLEY. DEPRESSION.
DEAN. DEPRESSION.
ROB. DRUGS. ANGER.
ME. A MESS.
LAURA. ANOREXIC.

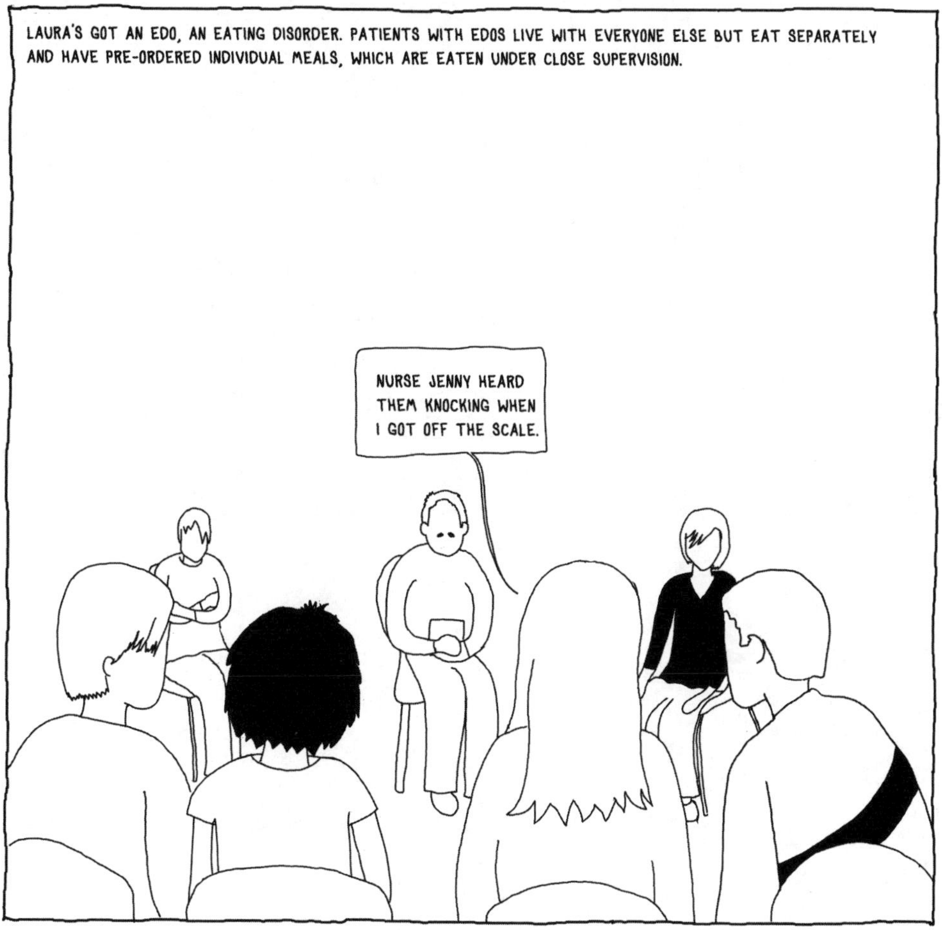
LAURA'S GOT AN EDO, AN EATING DISORDER. PATIENTS WITH EDOS LIVE WITH EVERYONE ELSE BUT EAT SEPARATELY AND HAVE PRE-ORDERED INDIVIDUAL MEALS, WHICH ARE EATEN UNDER CLOSE SUPERVISION.
NURSE JENNY HEARD THEM KNOCKING WHEN I GOT OFF THE SCALE.

I'D HATE PEOPLE WATCHING EVERYING I ATE.
AT LEAST I'M NOT THAT FAR GONE.

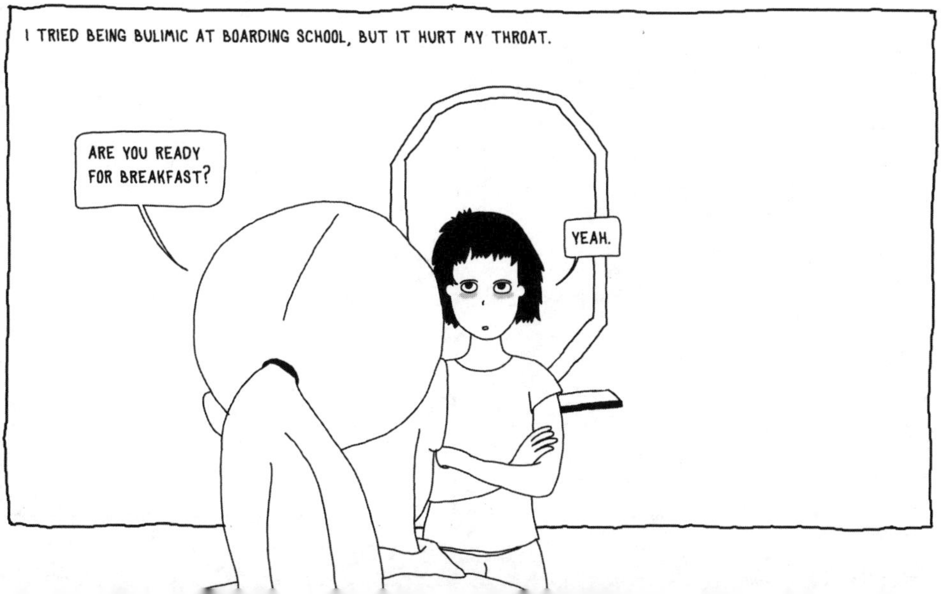
I TRIED BEING BULIMIC AT BOARDING SCHOOL, BUT IT HURT MY THROAT.
ARE YOU READY FOR BREAKFAST?
YEAH.

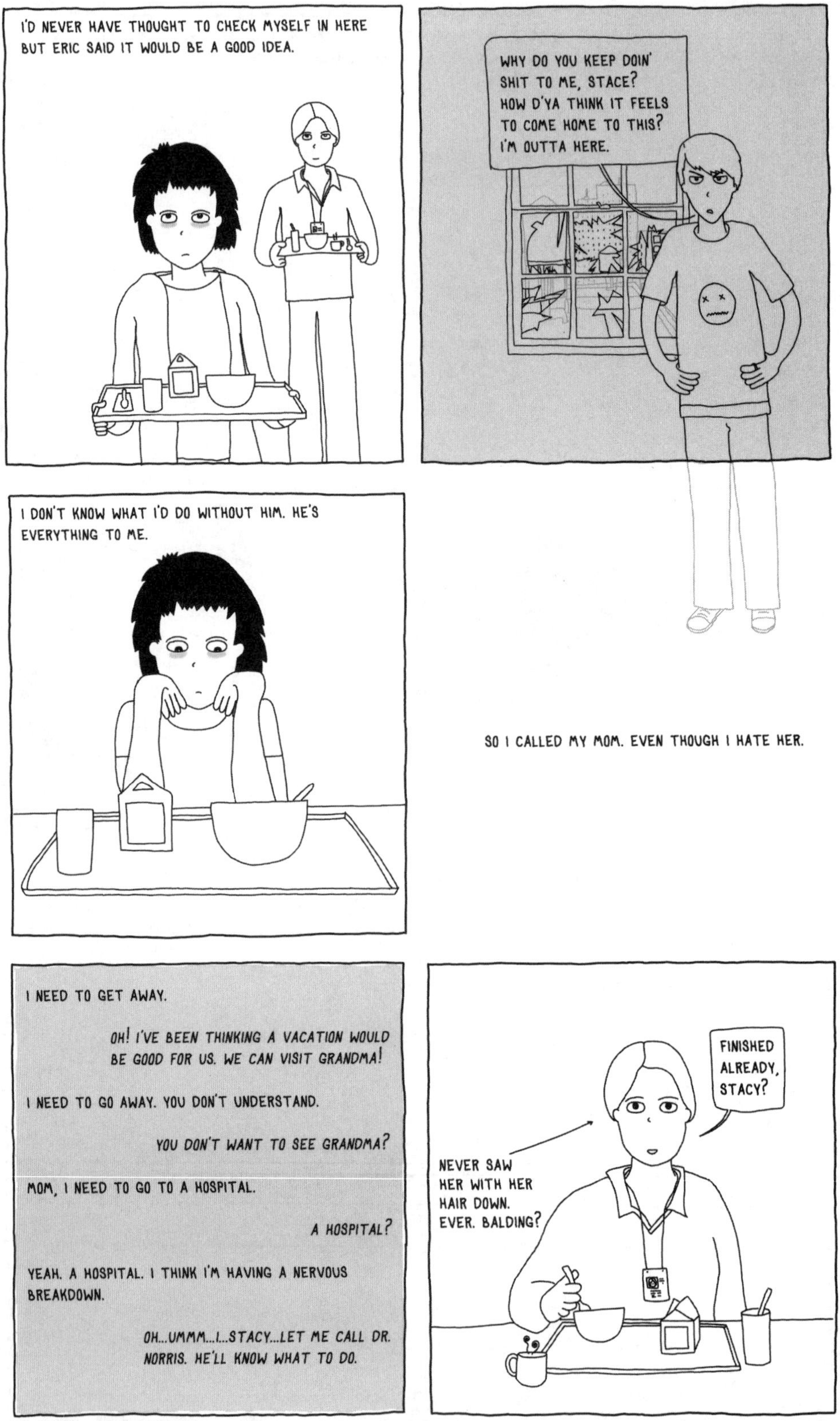
I'D NEVER HAVE THOUGHT TO CHECK MYSELF IN HERE BUT ERIC SAID IT WOULD BE A GOOD IDEA.
WHY DO YOU KEEP DOIN' SHIT TO ME, STACE? HOW D'YA THINK IT FEELS TO COME HOME TO THIS? I'M OUTTA HERE.
I DON'T KNOW WHAT I'D DO WITHOUT HIM. HE'S EVERYTHING TO ME.
SO I CALLED MY MOM. EVEN THOUGH I HATE HER.
I NEED TO GET AWAY.
OH! I'VE BEEN THINKING A VACATION WOULD BE GOOD FOR US. WE CAN VISIT GRANDMA!
I NEED TO GO AWAY. YOU DON'T UNDERSTAND.
YOU DON'T WANT TO SEE GRANDMA?
MOM, I NEED TO GO TO A HOSPITAL.
A HOSPITAL?
YEAH. A HOSPITAL. I THINK I'M HAVING A NERVOUS BREAKDOWN.
OH...UMMM...I...STACY...LET ME CALL DR. NORRIS. HE'LL KNOW WHAT TO DO.
NEVER SAW HER WITH HER HAIR DOWN. EVER. BALDING?
FINISHED ALREADY, STACY?

DR. NORRIS= FAMILY DOCTOR

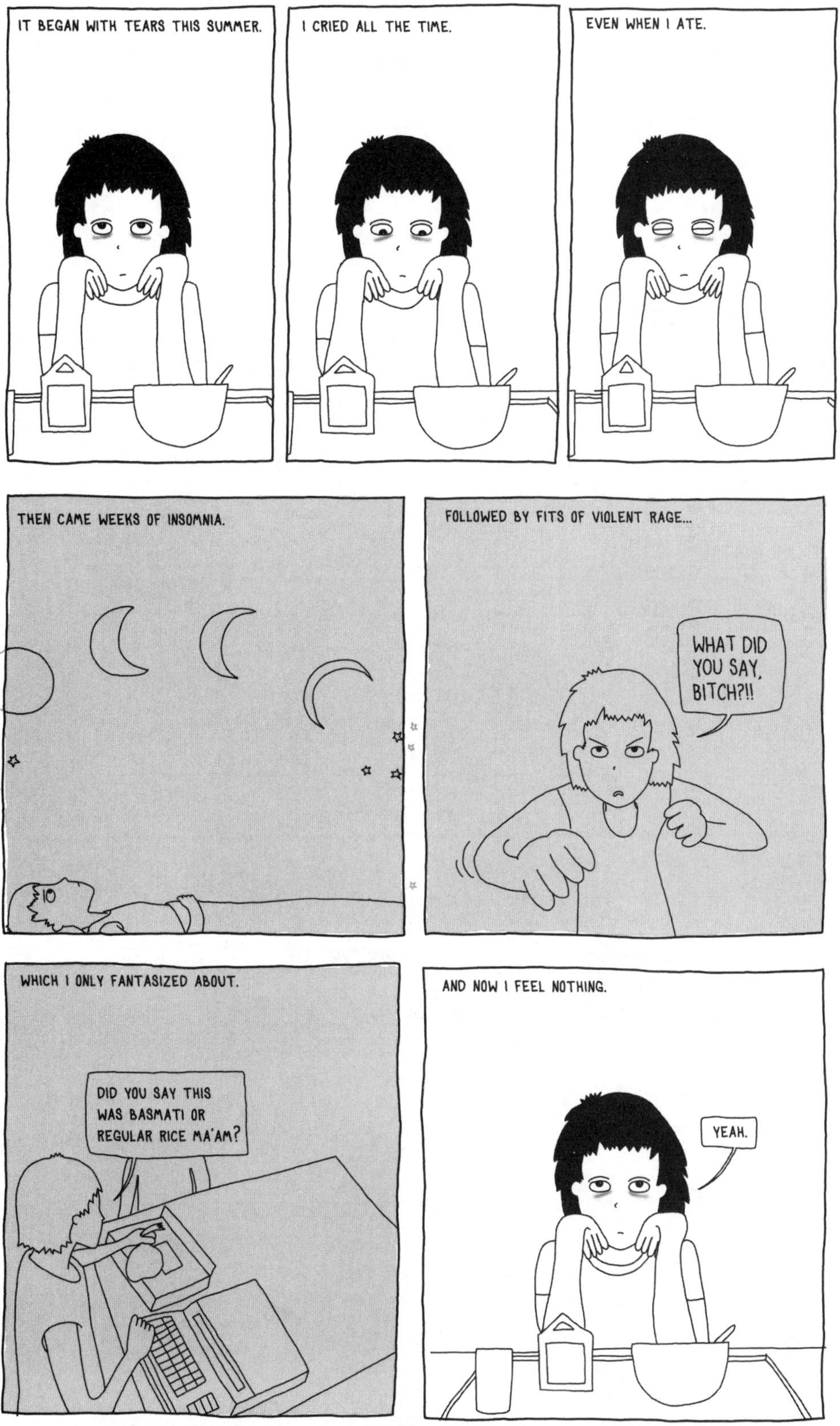
IT BEGAN WITH TEARS THIS SUMMER.
I CRIED ALL THE TIME.
EVEN WHEN I ATE.
THEN CAME WEEKS OF INSOMNIA.
FOLLOWED BY FITS OF VIOLENT RAGE...
WHAT DID YOU SAY, BITCH?!!
WHICH I ONLY FANTASIZED ABOUT.
DID YOU SAY THIS WAS BASMATI OR REGULAR RICE MA'AM?
AND NOW I FEEL NOTHING.
YEAH.

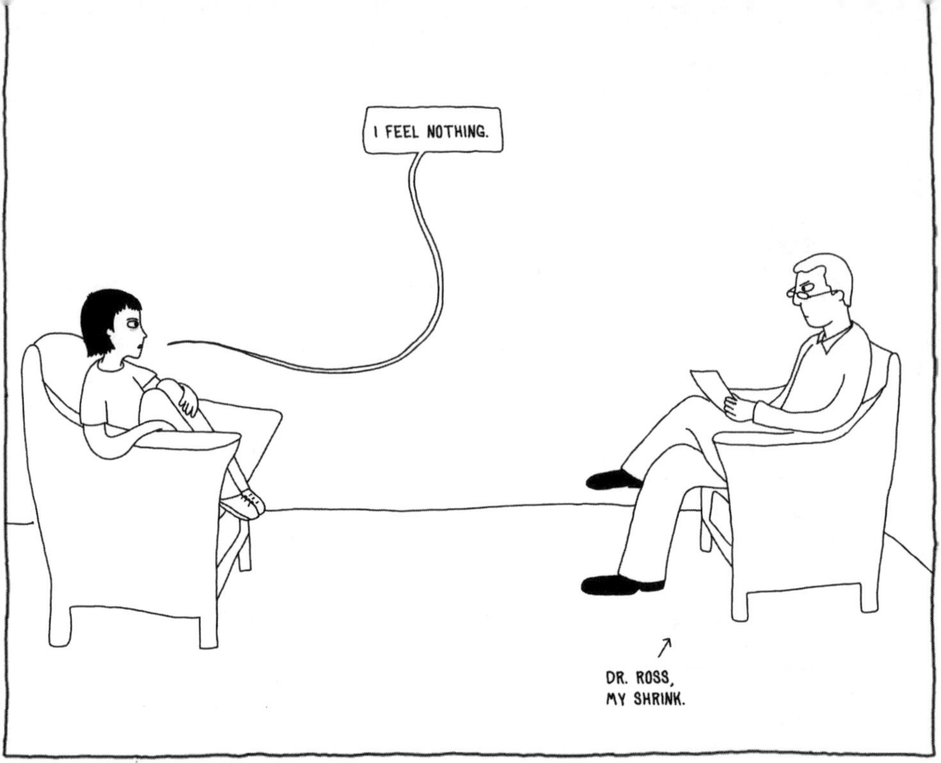
I FEEL NOTHING.
DR. ROSS, MY SHRINK.

I'M PRETTY SURE I KNOW WHY I'M SO FUCKED.

I NEVER MET A DRUG I DIDN'T LIKE.

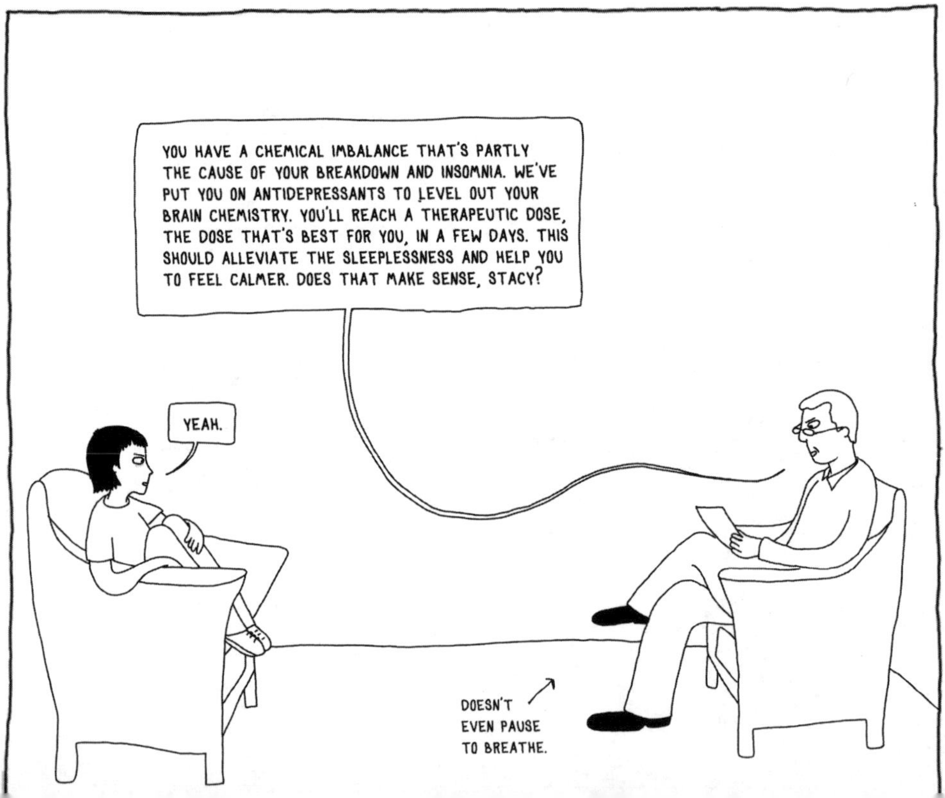
YOU HAVE A CHEMICAL IMBALANCE THAT'S PARTLY THE CAUSE OF YOUR BREAKDOWN AND INSOMNIA. WE'VE PUT YOU ON ANTIDEPRESSANTS TO LEVEL OUT YOUR BRAIN CHEMISTRY. YOU'LL REACH A THERAPEUTIC DOSE, THE DOSE THAT'S BEST FOR YOU, IN A FEW DAYS. THIS SHOULD ALLEVIATE THE SLEEPLESSNESS AND HELP YOU TO FEEL CALMER. DOES THAT MAKE SENSE, STACY?
YEAH.
DOESN'T EVEN PAUSE TO BREATHE.

I STARTED DOING DRUGS FOUR YEARS AGO.

TIME FOR MEDS.

NURSE "I'M YOUR PAL" VAL.

THEY'RE GREAT IF YOU'RE SHY BECAUSE ON THEM YOU'RE NOT. OR I'M NOT...

I COULD GO OUT AND ACTUALLY FEEL CONFIDENT. THAT'S HOW I MET ERIC...WENT UP TO HIM WITH NO FEAR AT A PARTY.

TOO BAD I DON'T GET THE GOOD ONES.

THEY BASICALLY SHUT OFF THE PARANOID PART OF MY BRAIN SO I CAN TALK LIKE A NORMAL PERSON.

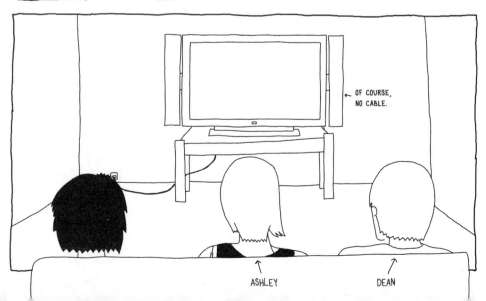

← OF COURSE, NO CABLE.

ASHLEY

DEAN

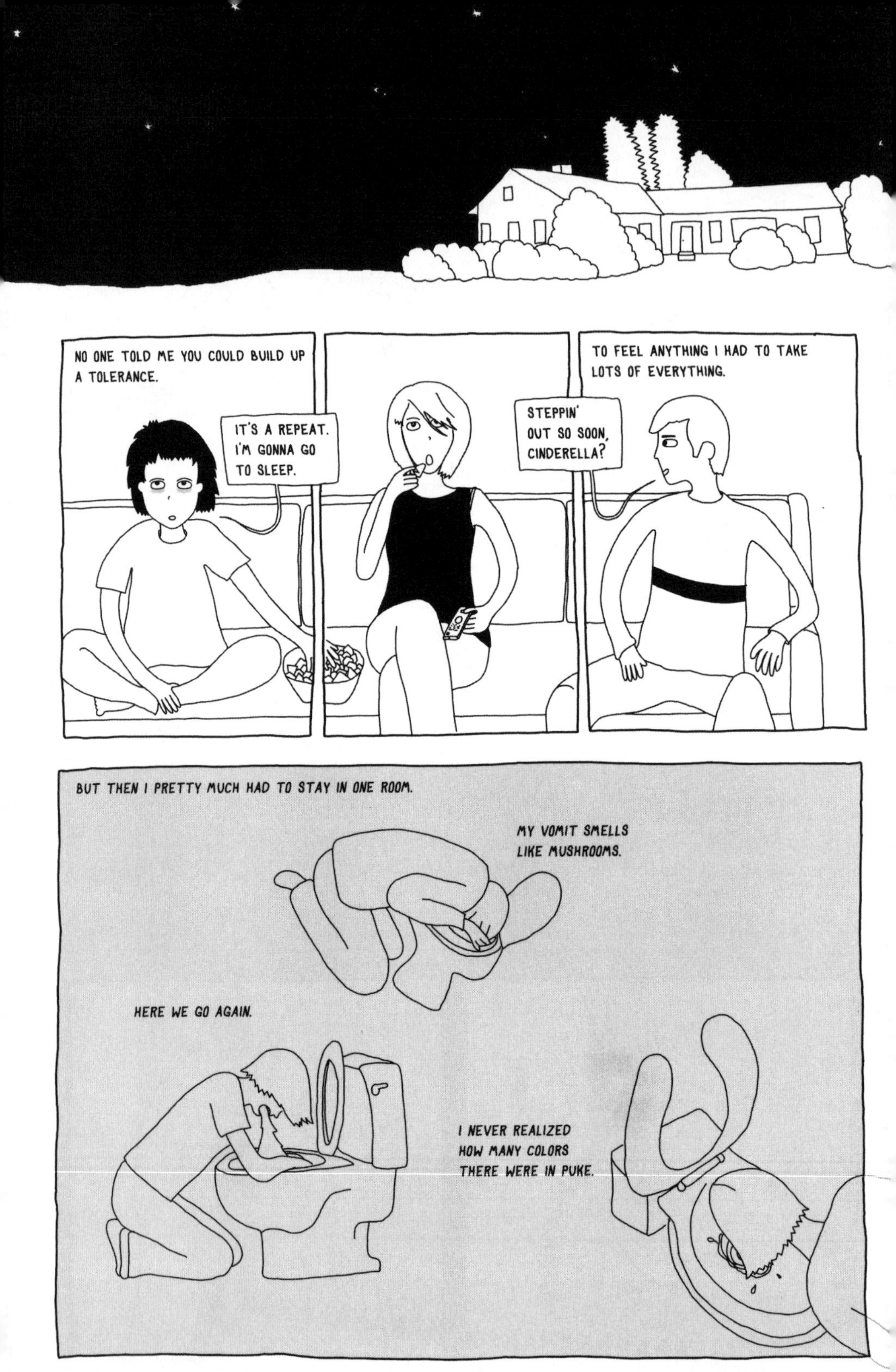
NO ONE TOLD ME YOU COULD BUILD UP A TOLERANCE.
IT'S A REPEAT. I'M GONNA GO TO SLEEP.
TO FEEL ANYTHING I HAD TO TAKE LOTS OF EVERYTHING.
STEPPIN' OUT SO SOON, CINDERELLA?
BUT THEN I PRETTY MUCH HAD TO STAY IN ONE ROOM.
MY VOMIT SMELLS LIKE MUSHROOMS.
HERE WE GO AGAIN.
I NEVER REALIZED HOW MANY COLORS THERE WERE IN PUKE.

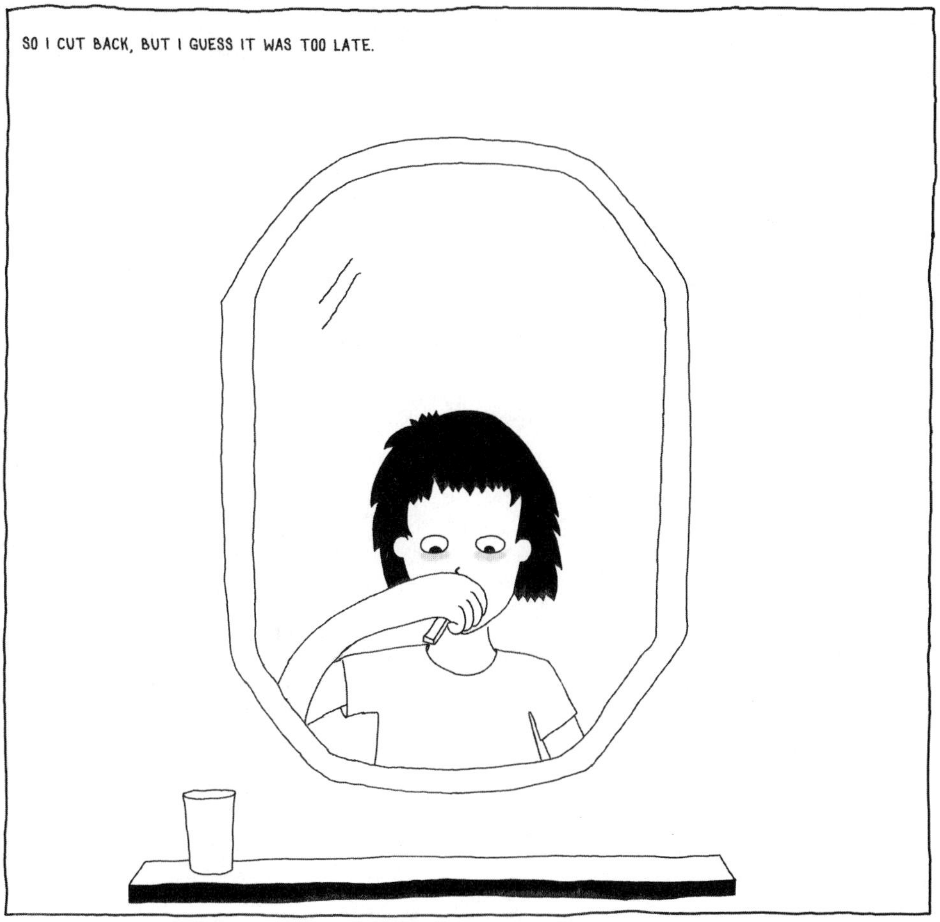
SO I CUT BACK, BUT I GUESS IT WAS TOO LATE.

I WONDER HOW MANY DOCTORS IT'LL TAKE TO PUT ME BACK TOGETHER AGAIN.

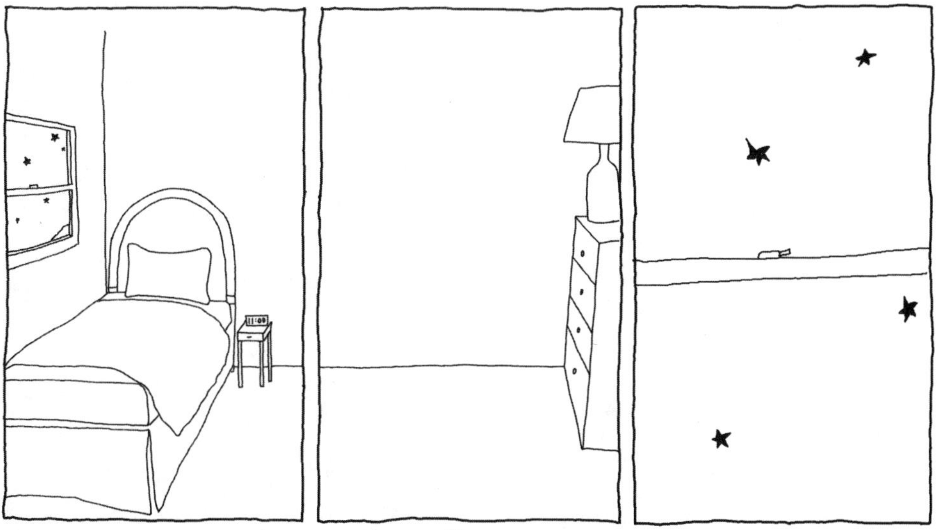

Do you think Stacy is in the right place?

MARIA

THE HOSPITAL'S THE BEST THING FOR HER, SHE'LL END UP DEAD OTHERWISE. STACE DOESN'T HAVE A STOP MECHANISM WHEN IT COMES TO PARTYING. HER MOM CALLED ME AND SAID, "STACY'S IN THE HOSPITAL AND SHE'S NOT IN GOOD SHAPE AND YOU'VE ALWAYS BEEN A GOOD FRIEND TO HER. WHAT DO YOU THINK, WHY DID THIS HAPPEN?"

I WASN'T SURPRISED. SHE GAVE ME STACY'S PHONE NUMBER AND I CALLED BUT STACY HASN'T TAKEN MY CALLS OR RETURNED THEM OR WHATEVER, AND I'M NOT GONNA SPEND ALL THAT MONEY TO SEE HER IF SHE DOESN'T WANT TO SEE ME. GAS IS EXPENSIVE AND I LIVE IN ALBANY. SHE ALMOST GOT ME KICKED OUT OF SCHOOL WHEN SHE CAME TO VISIT BECAUSE SHE SOLD SOME DRUGS ON CAMPUS FOR SPENDING MONEY. WHEN I TOLD HER NOT TO GIVE ANY TO MY BOYFRIEND SHE DID ANYWAY. I ASKED HER WHY AND SHE SAID, "BECAUSE HE WANTED SOME." NOT THE RIGHT ANSWER.

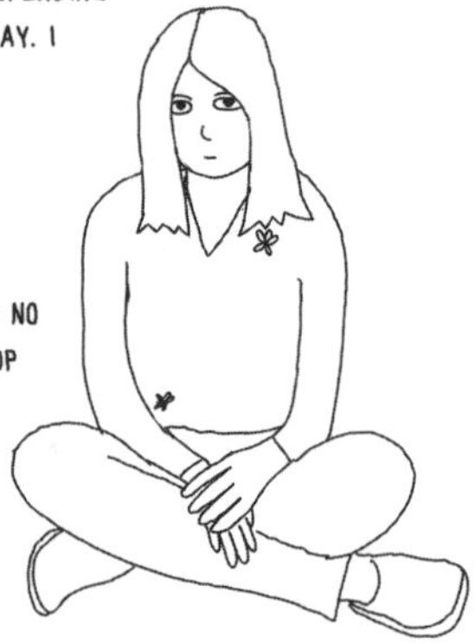

I'M STILL ANGRY AT HER AND SHE'S ANGRY AT ME BECAUSE I TOLD HER MOM I WAS WORRIED ABOUT HER DRUG USE. I MEAN, SHE'S LIKE A WALKING PHARMACY. WE HAVEN'T TALKED SINCE THEN BUT I KNEW MRS. BLACK HAD NO IDEA WHAT STACY WAS DOING 'CAUSE STACY'S A PRO AT COVERING STUFF UP AND I WAS WORRIED FOR HER.

I'VE WATCHED HER PUKE ALL NIGHT AND STILL WANT TO TAKE MORE. I'M GLAD I SAID SOMETHING AND I'M GLAD SHE'S THERE.

VIOLET

STACY AND I LOST CONTACT OVER TWO YEARS AGO WHEN MY PARENTS PULLED ME OUT OF BOARDING SCHOOL AND SENT ME TO REHAB.

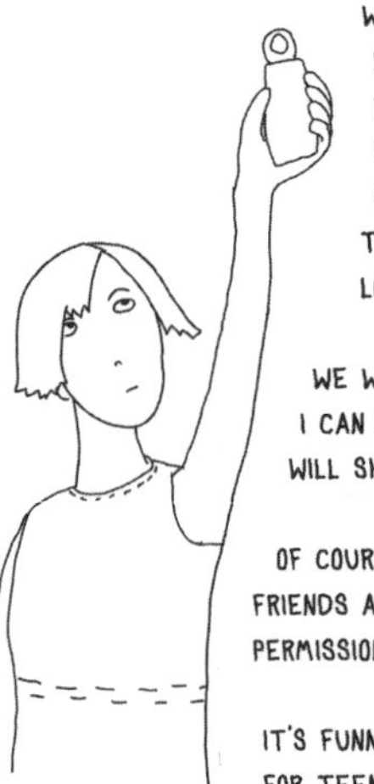

WE MET ON OUR FIRST DAY THERE. WE WERE ROOMMATES. AFTER OUR PARENTS LEFT STACY DID THIS PERFECT IMITATION OF HER MOM THAT WAS HYSTERICAL. RIGHT AWAY I KNEW WE'D BE FRIENDS. SHE'S GOT THIS REALLY FUNNY BURP — HER CALL OF THE WILD...SHE'D DO IN IT CLASS ALL THE TIME AND SAY SHE COULDN'T HELP IT BUT SHE CAN BURP ON COMMAND. SHE'LL BURP THE ALPHABET THROUGH P IN ONE GO. SOMETIMES SHE'D WAKE ME UP THAT WAY, BURP REALLY LOUDLY IN MY EAR WHILE SAYING MY NAME.

WE WERE ALSO DOING GOBS OF DRUGS. WE WERE BOTH UNHAPPY AND DIDN'T KNOW IT. I CAN SEE IT ALL SO MUCH MORE CLEARLY NOW THAT I'M IN RECOVERY AND SO WILL SHE SINCE SHE'S GETTING HELP FROM PROFESSIONALS IN A SAFE ENVIRONMENT.

OF COURSE FIRST SHE'S GOT TO ADMIT THERE'S A PROBLEM. MAYBE WE CAN BE FRIENDS AGAIN AND I BET MY MOM WILL PROBABLY DEFINITELY GIVE ME PERMISSION TO VISIT.

IT'S FUNNY. IF I HADN'T BEEN A GUEST SPEAKER AT THE GOLDEN MEADOWS OUTREACH FOR TEENS MEETING I MIGHT NEVER HAVE RUN INTO HER.

LOLA

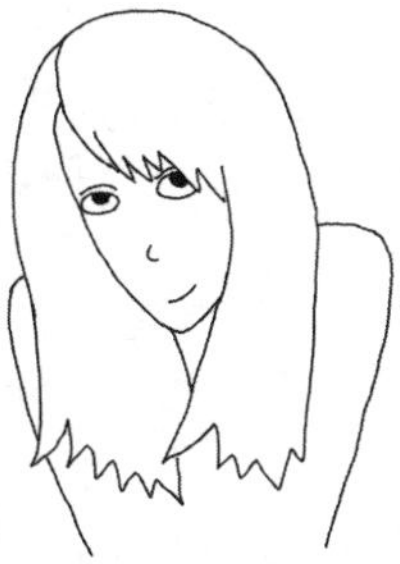

WE'RE REALLY CONNECTED. IT'S BEEN LIKE THAT SINCE WE MET IN EIGHTH GRADE. LIKE ONCE WE BOTH SCANNED OUR FACES ON THE SAME DAY AND THEN E-MAILED EACH OTHER THE IMAGES BUT WE HADN'T PLANNED IT. AND THEN I HAD THIS DREAM THAT SHE WAS USING A METAL FOLDING CHAIR TO BREAK STUFF AND SHE TOLD ME HOW SHE'D BEEN HAVING DREAMS WHERE SHE'S IN A WHITE ROOM BREAKING EVERYTHING SHE CAN GET HER HANDS ON. SEE, WE'RE THAT CLOSE AND THIS IS ALL JUST BEFORE SHE SMASHED THE WINDOWPANES.

SHE'S DEFINITELY IN THE RIGHT PLACE AND WHEN I HAVE VACATION I'LL GO DOWN TO SEE HER. I THINK SHE'S GOT A LOT OF SADNESS IN HER — LIKE HER REAL DAD DYING—SHE ALMOST NEVER TALKS ABOUT IT. SHE HASN'T EVEN BEEN TO HIS GRAVE. SAID IF SHE WENT SHE'D START CRYING AND NEVER STOP. I HOPE SHE TELLS THEM EVERYTHING AT THE HOSPITAL, AND I DO MEAN EVERYTHING. IT'D BE EASY FOR HER TO COAST THERE, SHE'S GOOD AT SEEMING FINE.

ASHLEY

WE WERE ASSIGNED TO THE SAME HOUSE AND ONE DAY DURING LUNCH I SAT NEXT TO HER. SHE JUST STARTED TALKING. I'D NEVER HEARD HER SAY A WORD SO I WAS SURPRISED BUT THEN WE BONDED OVER THE FACT THAT NEITHER OF US HAD SLEPT IN A WHILE.

I REMEMBER I GOT HERE THINKING ALL I NEEDED WAS TO REST FOR A FEW DAYS AND I'D BE OK. HA.

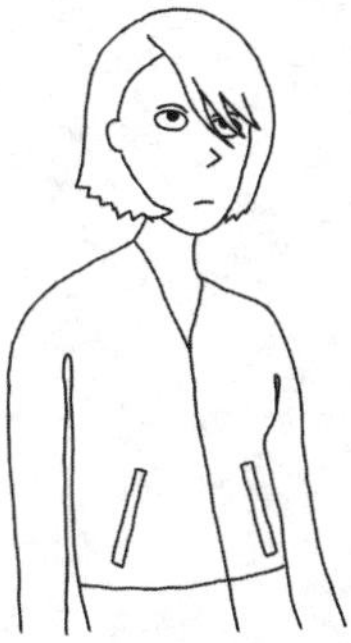

ANYWAY I TOLD HER HOW I COULD ONLY SLEEP IN MY CLOSET AND SHE TOLD ME HOW BEFORE SHE MOVED INTO HER OWN PLACE HER BOYFRIEND ERIC USED TO SLEEP IN HER CLOSET WHEN SHE WENT TO SCHOOL BUT HER MOM DIDN'T KNOW. THAT IS SO ROMANTIC.

OH—AND STACY GAVE ME A DRAWING SHE DID OF A DOG. I MISS MY POODLE DINO, AND SHE MADE A CARTOON OF HIM FOR ME FROM A PHOTO. I TAPED IT TO MY WALL.

IT MAKES ME SMILE.

CURRENT LENGTH OF STAY:

four weeks,
five days

"The patient has had an interest in sports, art, dancing, and music. The patient has some training in photography and thinks this would be a good career. She is a high school graduate and seems to have at least average intelligence. It is felt that she has the ability to go to college."

From the clinical records of Stacy Black

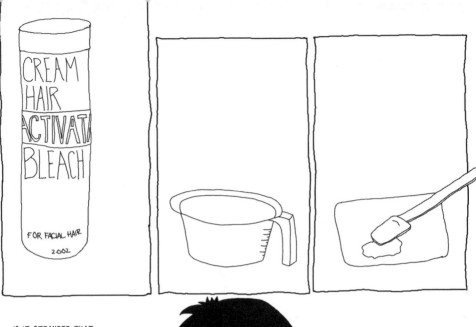

CREAM
HAIR
ACTIVATA
BLEACH
FOR FACIAL HAIR
2002
IS IT STRANGER THAT I CAN'T REMEMBER HOW TO BE HAPPY,
OR THAT I NEED TO TRY AND REMEMBER HOW?
I DON'T EVEN KNOW IF I CAN BE HAPPY ANYMORE.
BLUE
BLUE

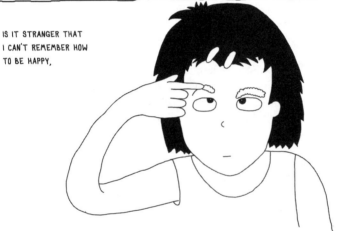

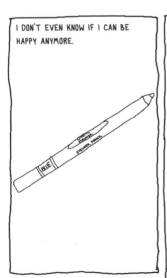

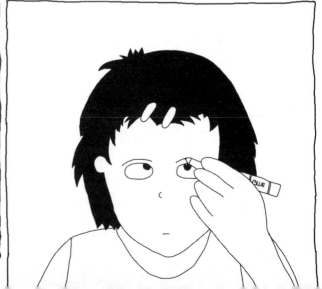

IT'S MY FOURTH WEEK HERE AT MEADOWS.

A "SHARP" CAN ONLY BE CHECKED IN AND OUT OF THE NURSES' STATION AT SPECIFIC TIMES. NOW THAT I'M OFF "SPECIALS," I CAN USE THEM.

I ONLY THOUGHT I'D BE HERE FOR THREE WHEN I CHECKED IN.

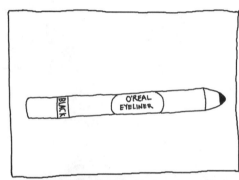

O'REAL
EYELINER

BLACK

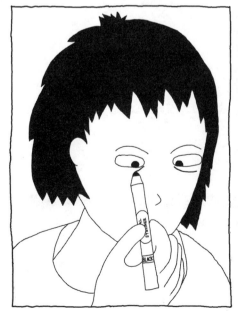

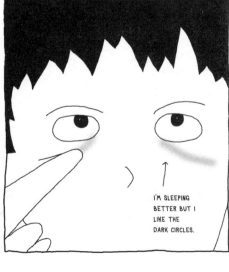

I'M SLEEPING BETTER BUT I LIKE THE DARK CIRCLES.

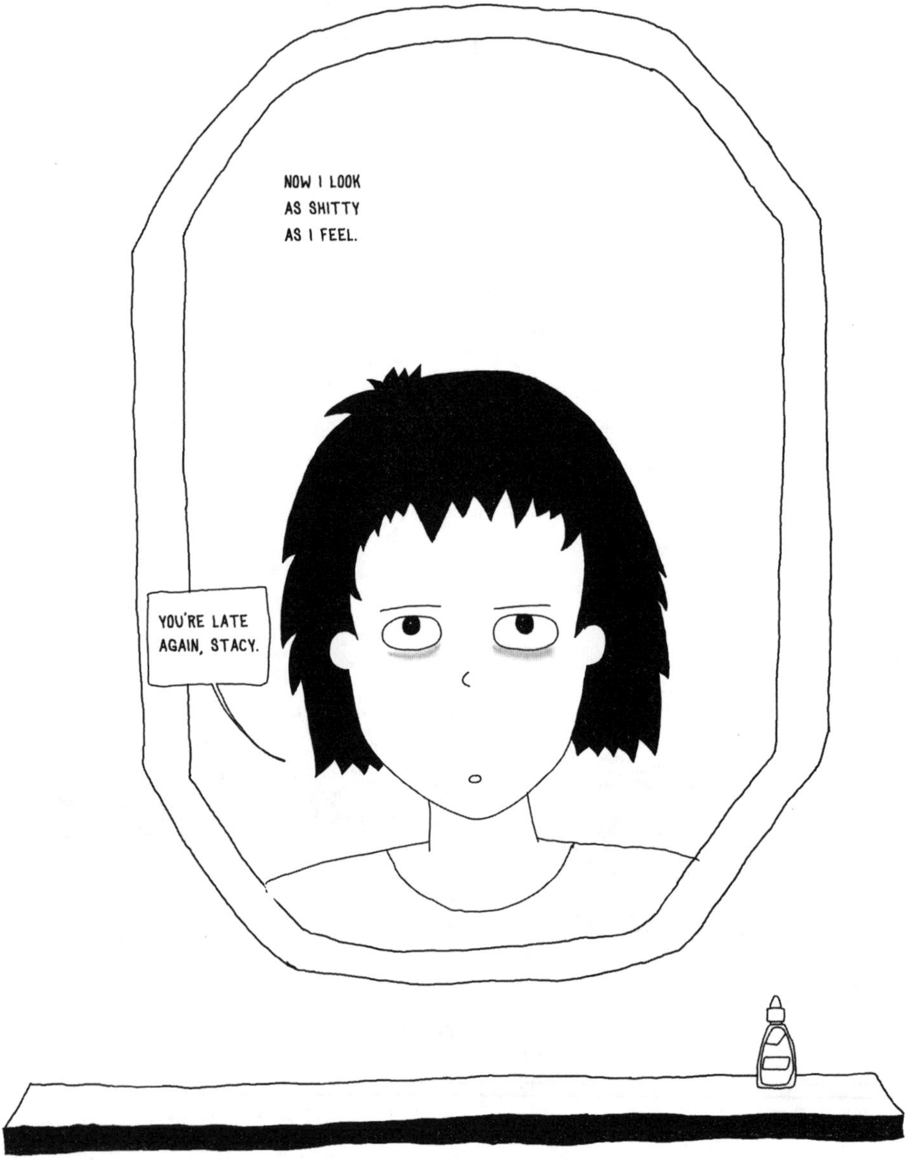
NOW I LOOK
AS SHITTY
AS I FEEL.
YOU'RE LATE
AGAIN, STACY.

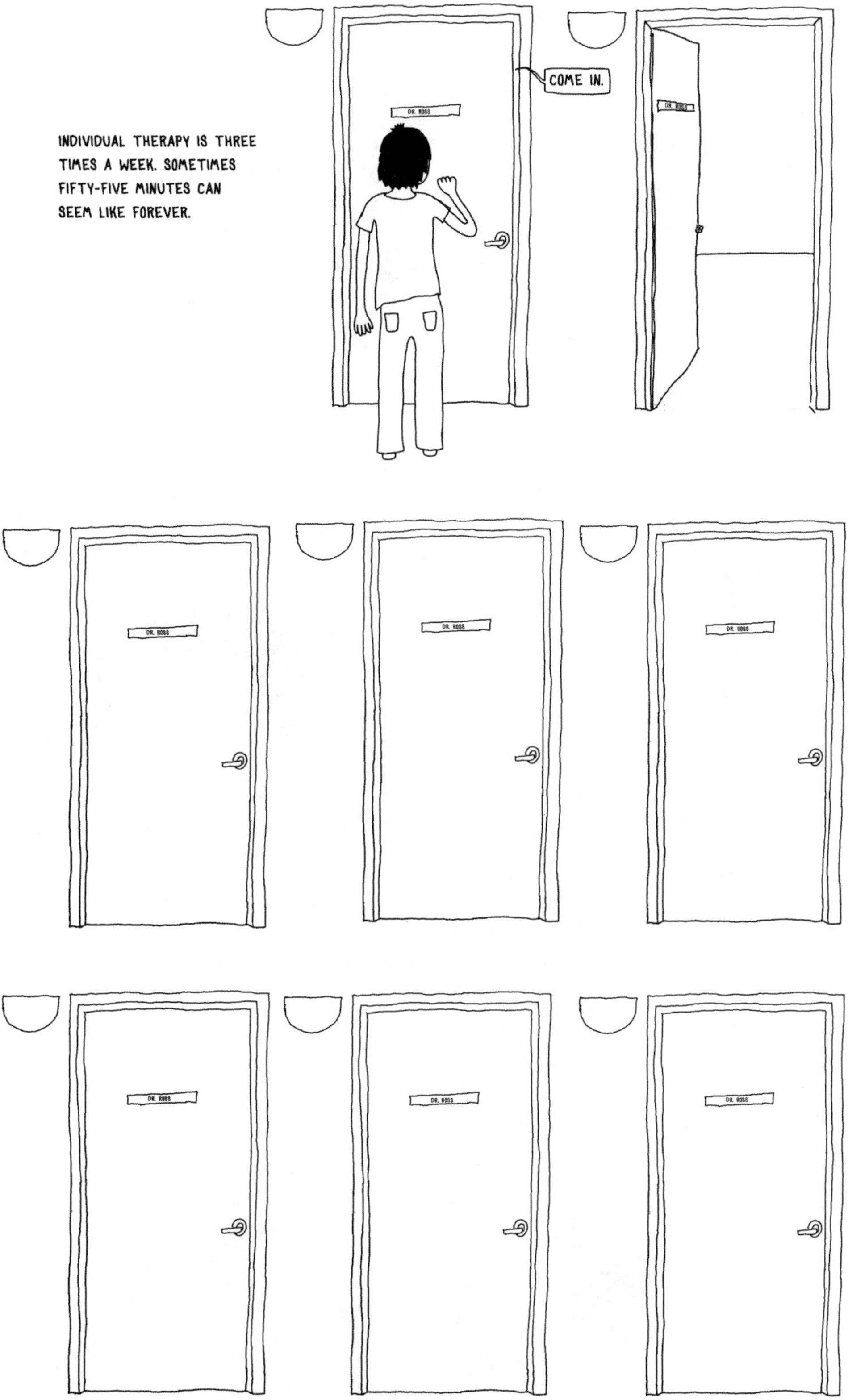
INDIVIDUAL THERAPY IS THREE TIMES A WEEK. SOMETIMES FIFTY-FIVE MINUTES CAN SEEM LIKE FOREVER.
DR. ROSS
COME IN.

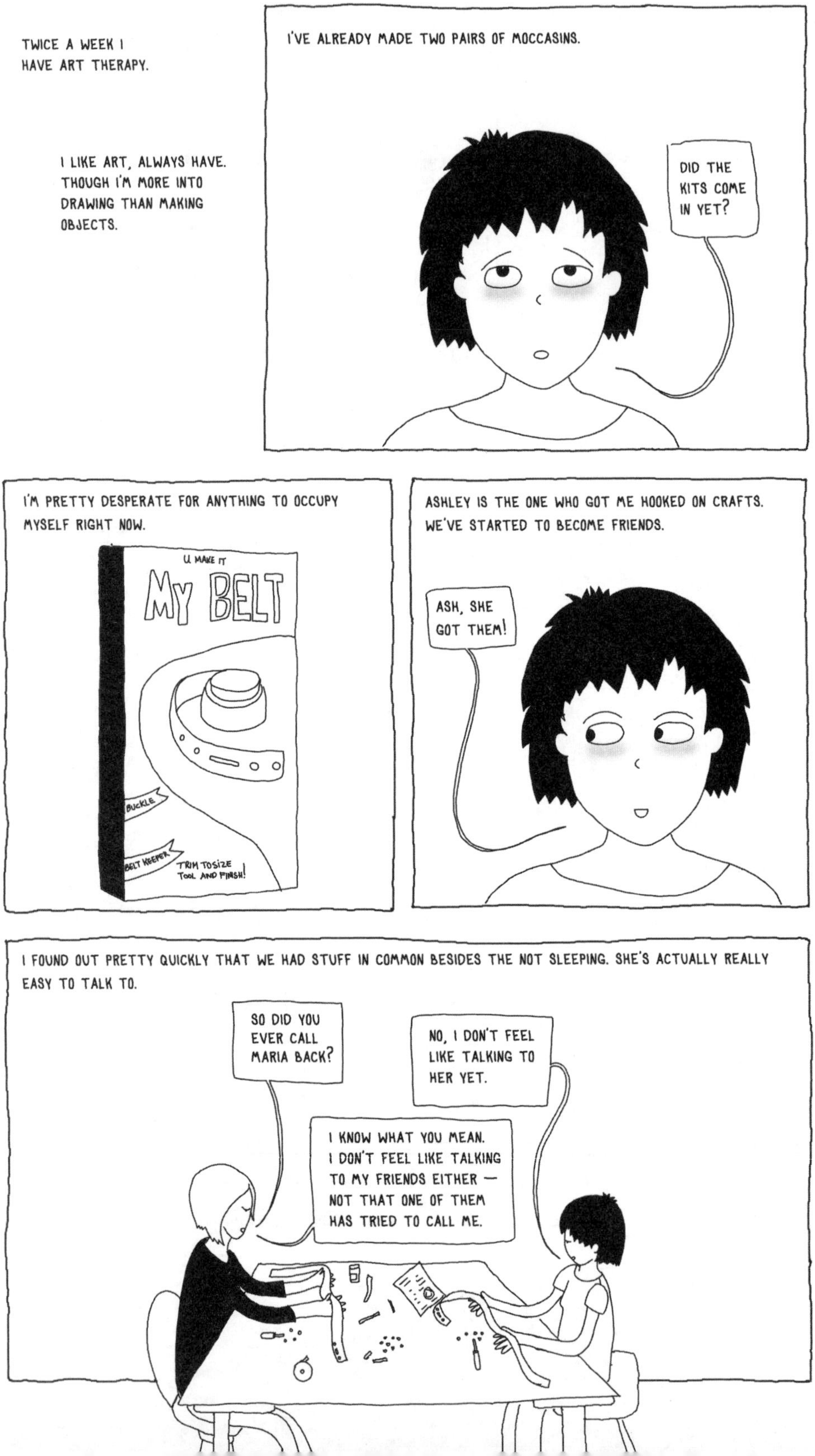
TWICE A WEEK I HAVE ART THERAPY.
I LIKE ART, ALWAYS HAVE. THOUGH I'M MORE INTO DRAWING THAN MAKING OBJECTS.
I'VE ALREADY MADE TWO PAIRS OF MOCCASINS.
DID THE KITS COME IN YET?
I'M PRETTY DESPERATE FOR ANYTHING TO OCCUPY MYSELF RIGHT NOW.
U MAKE IT
MY BELT
BUCKLE
BELT KEEPER
TRIM TO SIZE TOOL AND FINISH!
ASHLEY IS THE ONE WHO GOT ME HOOKED ON CRAFTS. WE'VE STARTED TO BECOME FRIENDS.
ASH, SHE GOT THEM!
I FOUND OUT PRETTY QUICKLY THAT WE HAD STUFF IN COMMON BESIDES THE NOT SLEEPING. SHE'S ACTUALLY REALLY EASY TO TALK TO.
SO DID YOU EVER CALL MARIA BACK?
NO, I DON'T FEEL LIKE TALKING TO HER YET.
I KNOW WHAT YOU MEAN. I DON'T FEEL LIKE TALKING TO MY FRIENDS EITHER — NOT THAT ONE OF THEM HAS TRIED TO CALL ME.

PLUS I'M SEVENTEEN AND SHE'S SEVENTEEN SO WE'RE SOME OF THE OLDEST HERE. ALMOST EVERYONE ELSE IN OUR UNIT IS LIKE FOURTEEN OR FIFTEEN. THEY ONLY THINK THEY KNOW ABOUT REAL LIFE.

ASHLEY TRIED TO KILL HERSELF.

SHE ATE AS MANY PILLS AS SHE COULD FIND.

YOU KNOW, MY FRIENDS NEVER EVEN ASKED ME WHY I WAS WALKING AROUND LIKE A ZOMBIE BEFORE I GOT HERE.

I BET ALL OUR FRIENDS ARE WONDERING IF GOING CRAZY IS CATCHING. SPEAKING OF CRAZY, DO YOU KNOW WHERE THE LEATHER CUTTERS ARE?

HA!

AND PASS THE TAPE MEASURE, PLEASE.

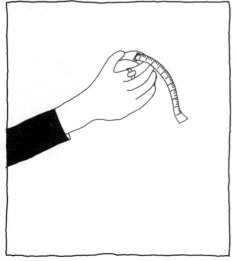

ME?

I'M PRETTY SURE IF I HADN'T CHECKED MYSELF IN HERE I'D BE DEAD.

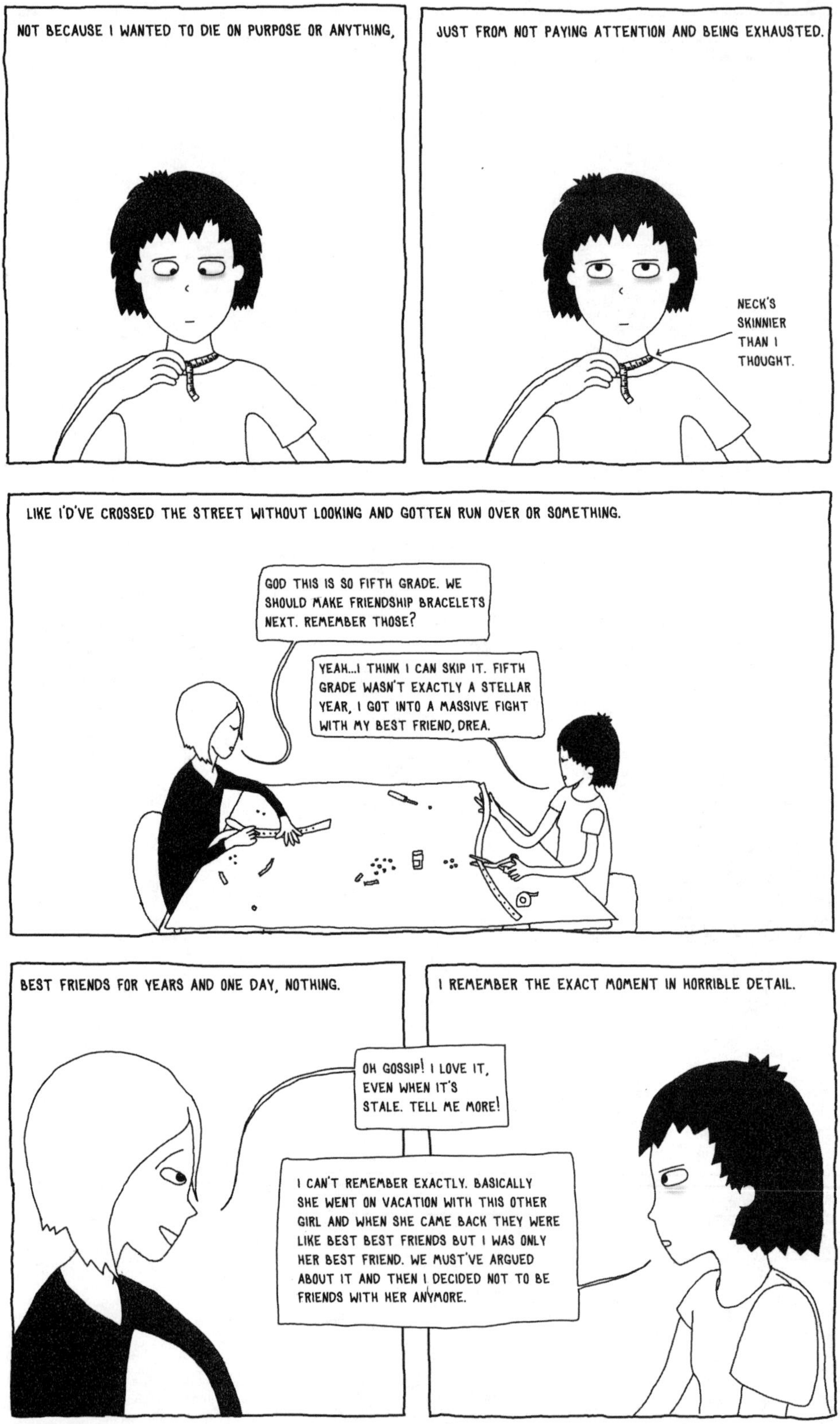
NOT BECAUSE I WANTED TO DIE ON PURPOSE OR ANYTHING,
JUST FROM NOT PAYING ATTENTION AND BEING EXHAUSTED.
NECK'S SKINNIER THAN I THOUGHT.
LIKE I'D'VE CROSSED THE STREET WITHOUT LOOKING AND GOTTEN RUN OVER OR SOMETHING.
GOD THIS IS SO FIFTH GRADE. WE SHOULD MAKE FRIENDSHIP BRACELETS NEXT. REMEMBER THOSE?
YEAH...I THINK I CAN SKIP IT. FIFTH GRADE WASN'T EXACTLY A STELLAR YEAR, I GOT INTO A MASSIVE FIGHT WITH MY BEST FRIEND, DREA.
BEST FRIENDS FOR YEARS AND ONE DAY, NOTHING.
I REMEMBER THE EXACT MOMENT IN HORRIBLE DETAIL.
OH GOSSIP! I LOVE IT, EVEN WHEN IT'S STALE. TELL ME MORE!
I CAN'T REMEMBER EXACTLY. BASICALLY SHE WENT ON VACATION WITH THIS OTHER GIRL AND WHEN SHE CAME BACK THEY WERE LIKE BEST BEST FRIENDS BUT I WAS ONLY HER BEST FRIEND. WE MUST'VE ARGUED ABOUT IT AND THEN I DECIDED NOT TO BE FRIENDS WITH HER ANYMORE.

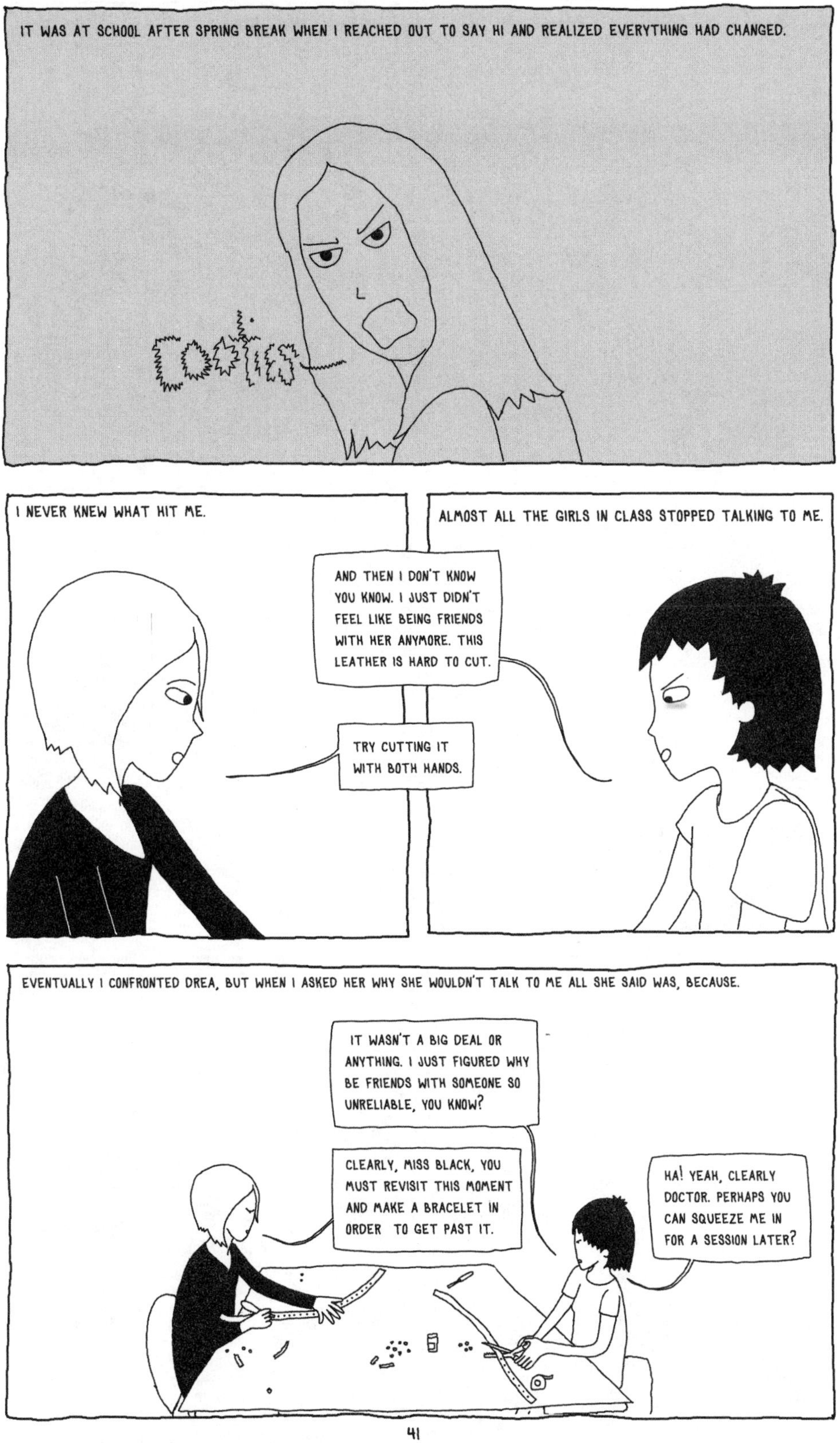
IT WAS AT SCHOOL AFTER SPRING BREAK WHEN I REACHED OUT TO SAY HI AND REALIZED EVERYTHING HAD CHANGED.
I NEVER KNEW WHAT HIT ME.
ALMOST ALL THE GIRLS IN CLASS STOPPED TALKING TO ME.
AND THEN I DON'T KNOW YOU KNOW. I JUST DIDN'T FEEL LIKE BEING FRIENDS WITH HER ANYMORE. THIS LEATHER IS HARD TO CUT.
TRY CUTTING IT WITH BOTH HANDS.
EVENTUALLY I CONFRONTED DREA, BUT WHEN I ASKED HER WHY SHE WOULDN'T TALK TO ME ALL SHE SAID WAS, BECAUSE.
IT WASN'T A BIG DEAL OR ANYTHING. I JUST FIGURED WHY BE FRIENDS WITH SOMEONE SO UNRELIABLE, YOU KNOW?
CLEARLY, MISS BLACK, YOU MUST REVISIT THIS MOMENT AND MAKE A BRACELET IN ORDER TO GET PAST IT.
HA! YEAH, CLEARLY DOCTOR. PERHAPS YOU CAN SQUEEZE ME IN FOR A SESSION LATER?

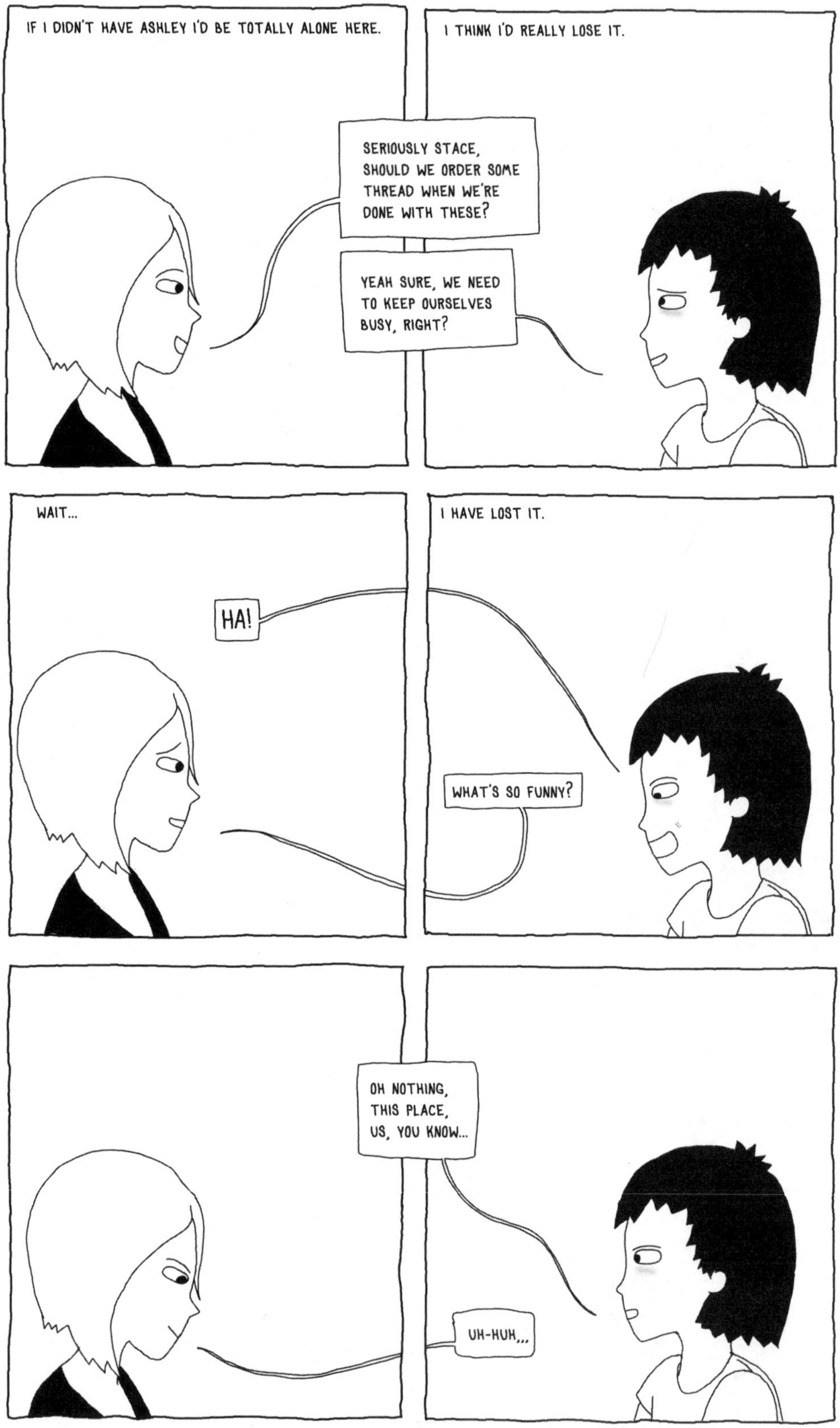
IF I DIDN'T HAVE ASHLEY I'D BE TOTALLY ALONE HERE.
I THINK I'D REALLY LOSE IT.
SERIOUSLY STACE, SHOULD WE ORDER SOME THREAD WHEN WE'RE DONE WITH THESE?
YEAH SURE, WE NEED TO KEEP OURSELVES BUSY, RIGHT?
WAIT...
I HAVE LOST IT.
HA!
WHAT'S SO FUNNY?
OH NOTHING, THIS PLACE, US, YOU KNOW...
UH-HUH,,,

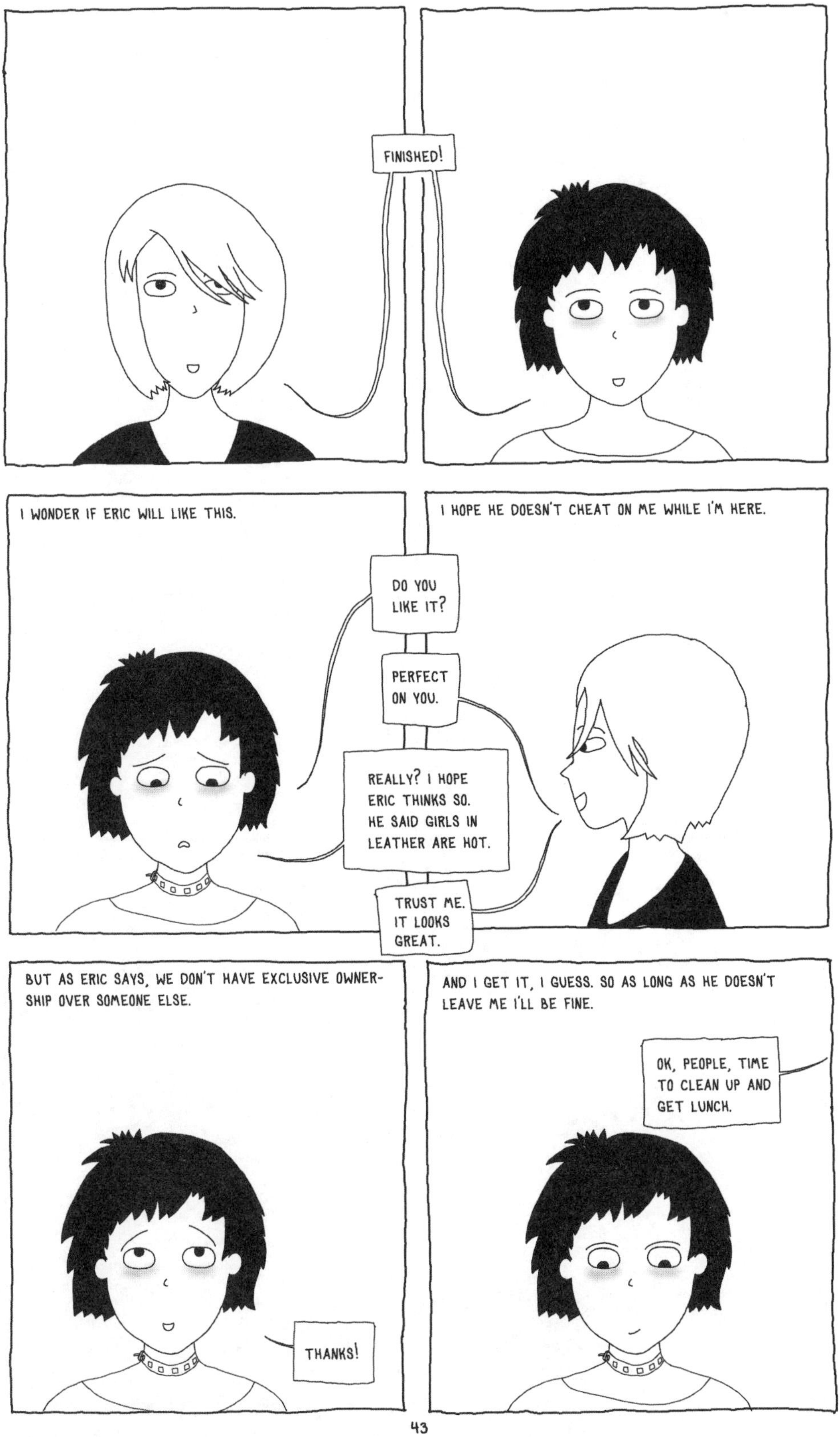

FINISHED!
I WONDER IF ERIC WILL LIKE THIS.
I HOPE HE DOESN'T CHEAT ON ME WHILE I'M HERE.
DO YOU LIKE IT?
PERFECT ON YOU.
REALLY? I HOPE ERIC THINKS SO. HE SAID GIRLS IN LEATHER ARE HOT.
TRUST ME. IT LOOKS GREAT.
BUT AS ERIC SAYS, WE DON'T HAVE EXCLUSIVE OWNERSHIP OVER SOMEONE ELSE.
THANKS!
AND I GET IT, I GUESS. SO AS LONG AS HE DOESN'T LEAVE ME I'LL BE FINE.
OK, PEOPLE, TIME TO CLEAN UP AND GET LUNCH.

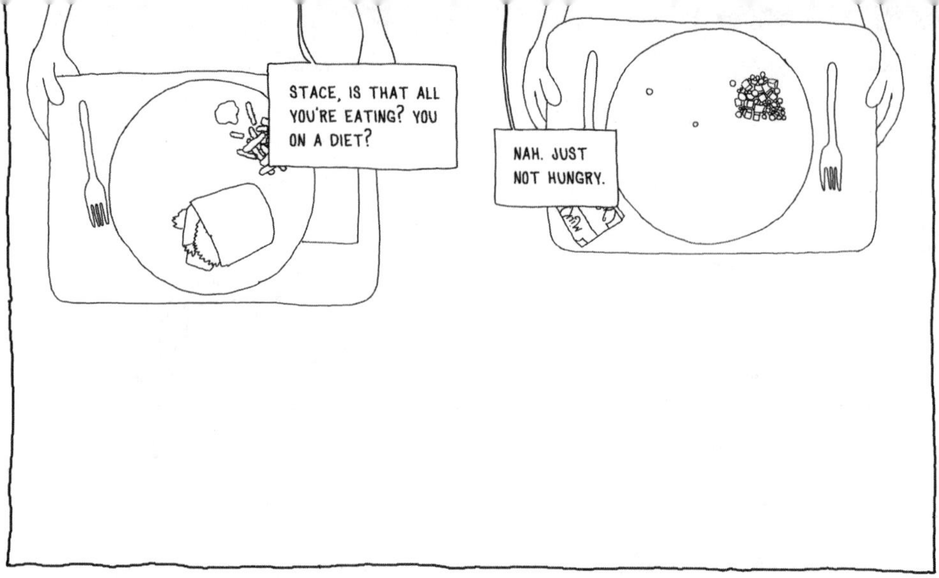
STACE, IS THAT ALL YOU'RE EATING? YOU ON A DIET?
NAH. JUST NOT HUNGRY.

I HOPE ERIC KNOWS HOW HARD I'M TRYING TO FIX MYSELF.

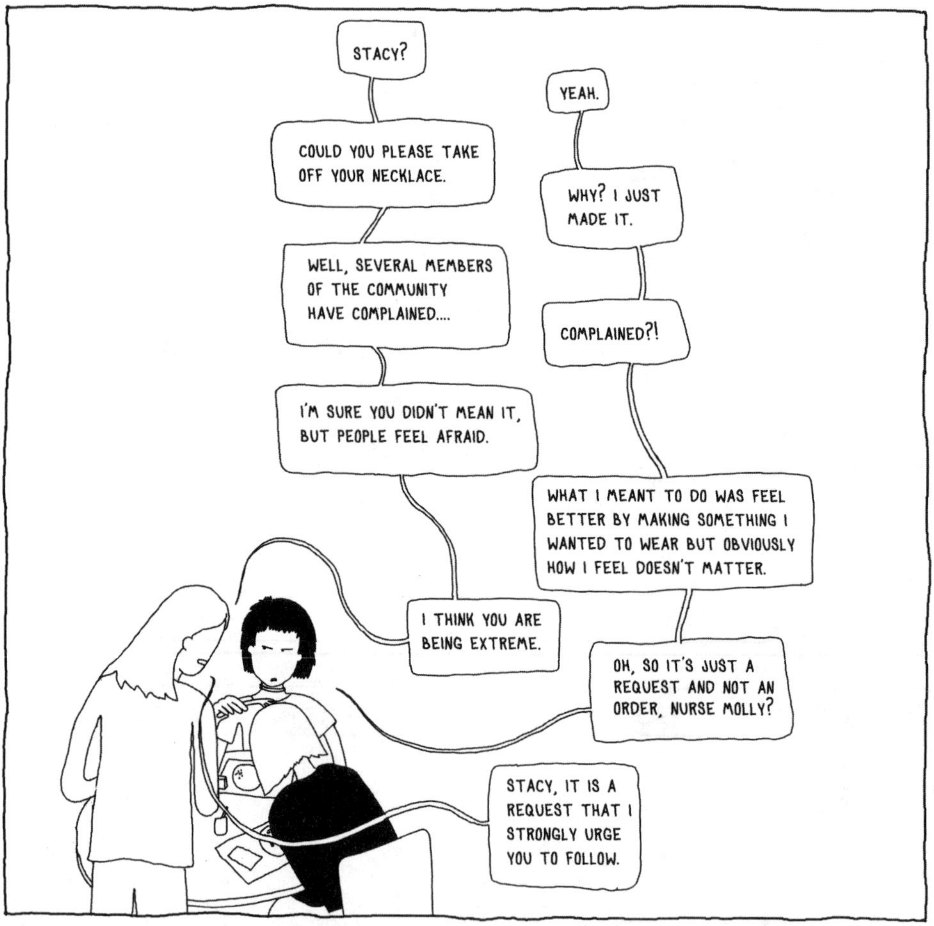
STACY?
YEAH.
COULD YOU PLEASE TAKE OFF YOUR NECKLACE.
WHY? I JUST MADE IT.
WELL, SEVERAL MEMBERS OF THE COMMUNITY HAVE COMPLAINED....
COMPLAINED?!
I'M SURE YOU DIDN'T MEAN IT, BUT PEOPLE FEEL AFRAID.
WHAT I MEANT TO DO WAS FEEL BETTER BY MAKING SOMETHING I WANTED TO WEAR BUT OBVIOUSLY HOW I FEEL DOESN'T MATTER.
I THINK YOU ARE BEING EXTREME.
OH, SO IT'S JUST A REQUEST AND NOT AN ORDER, NURSE MOLLY?
STACY, IT IS A REQUEST THAT I STRONGLY URGE YOU TO FOLLOW.

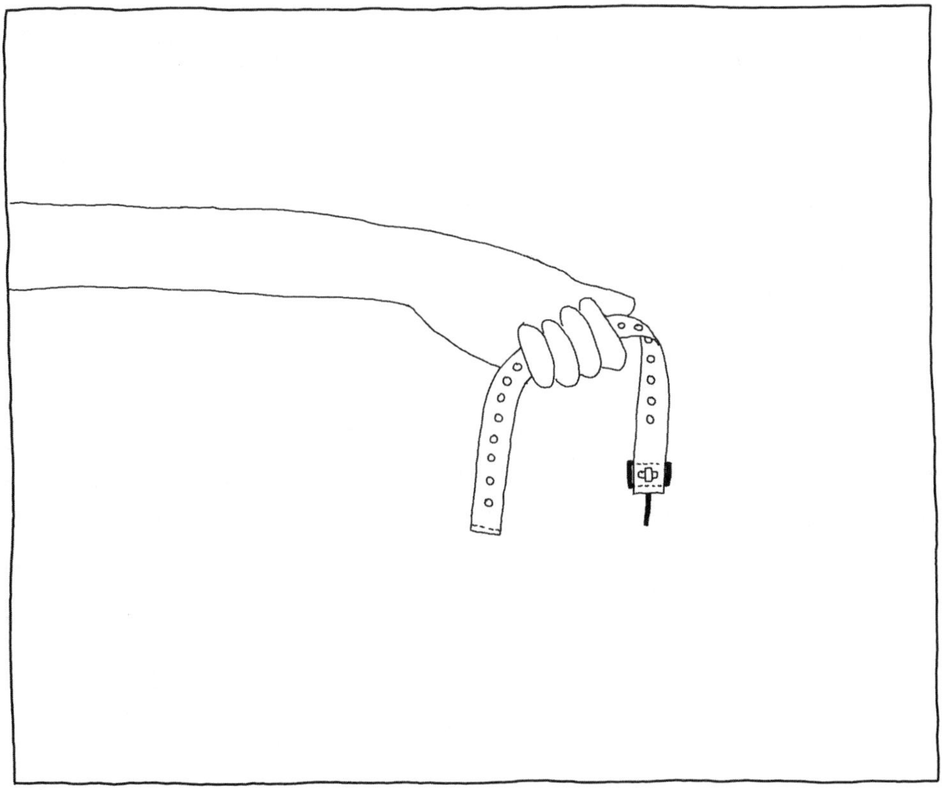

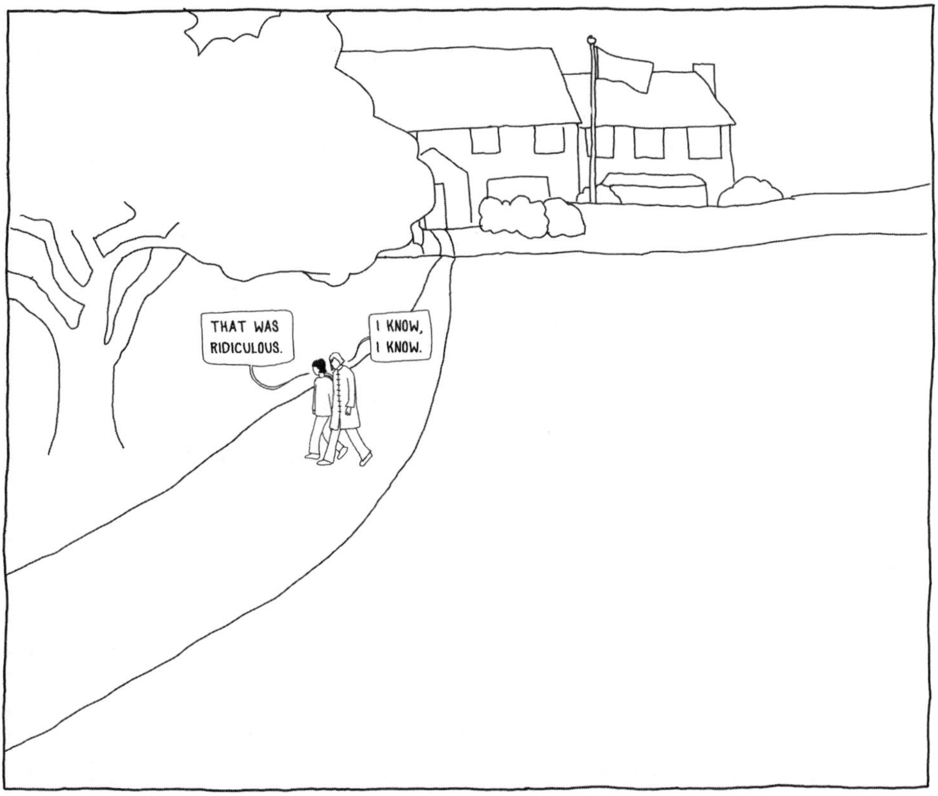
THAT WAS RIDICULOUS.
I KNOW, I KNOW.

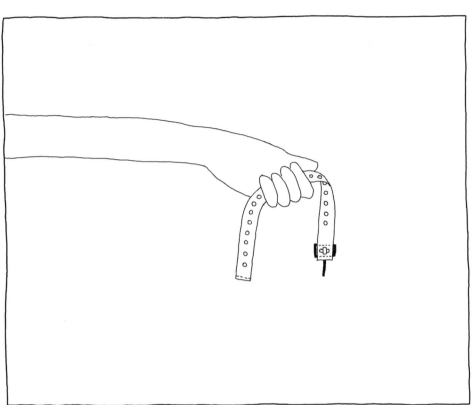

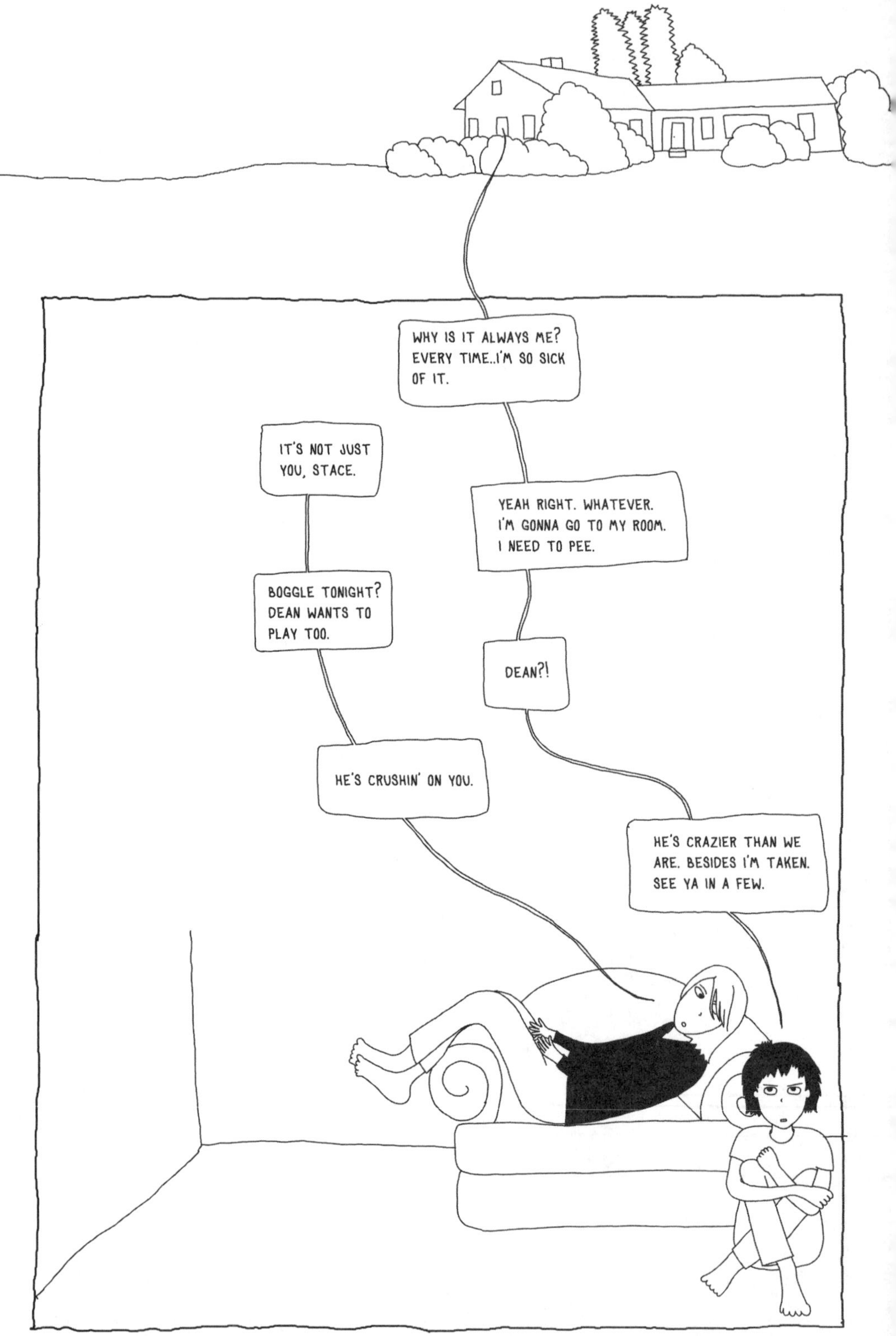
WHY IS IT ALWAYS ME? EVERY TIME..I'M SO SICK OF IT.
IT'S NOT JUST YOU, STACE.
YEAH RIGHT. WHATEVER. I'M GONNA GO TO MY ROOM. I NEED TO PEE.
BOGGLE TONIGHT? DEAN WANTS TO PLAY TOO.
DEAN?!
HE'S CRUSHIN' ON YOU.
HE'S CRAZIER THAN WE ARE. BESIDES I'M TAKEN. SEE YA IN A FEW.

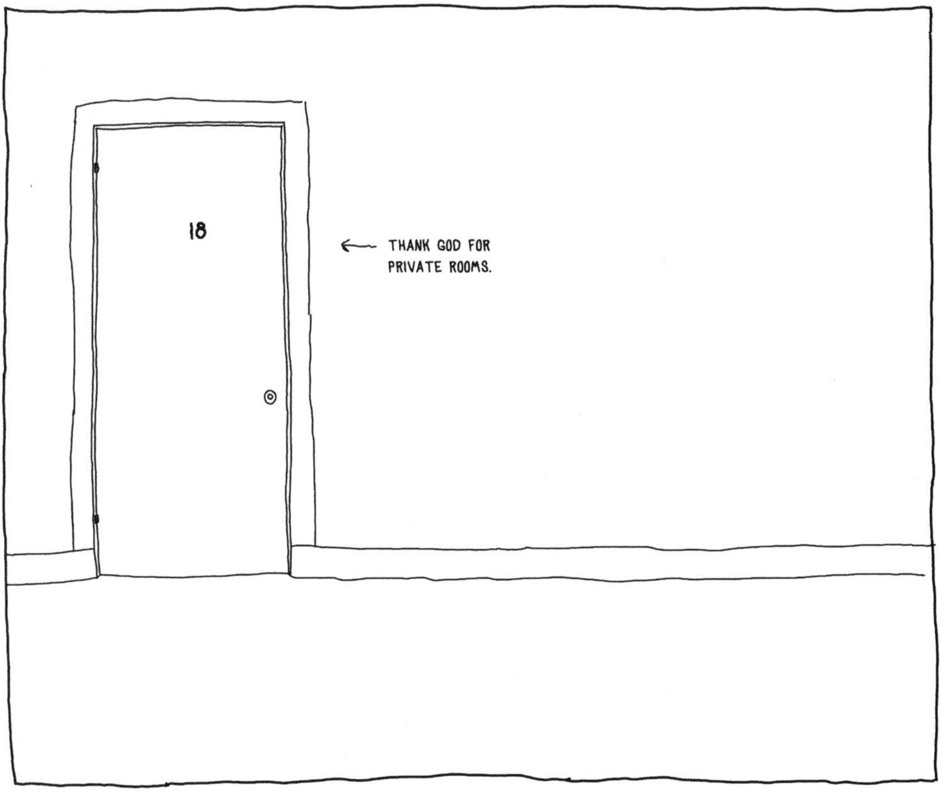
18
THANK GOD FOR PRIVATE ROOMS.

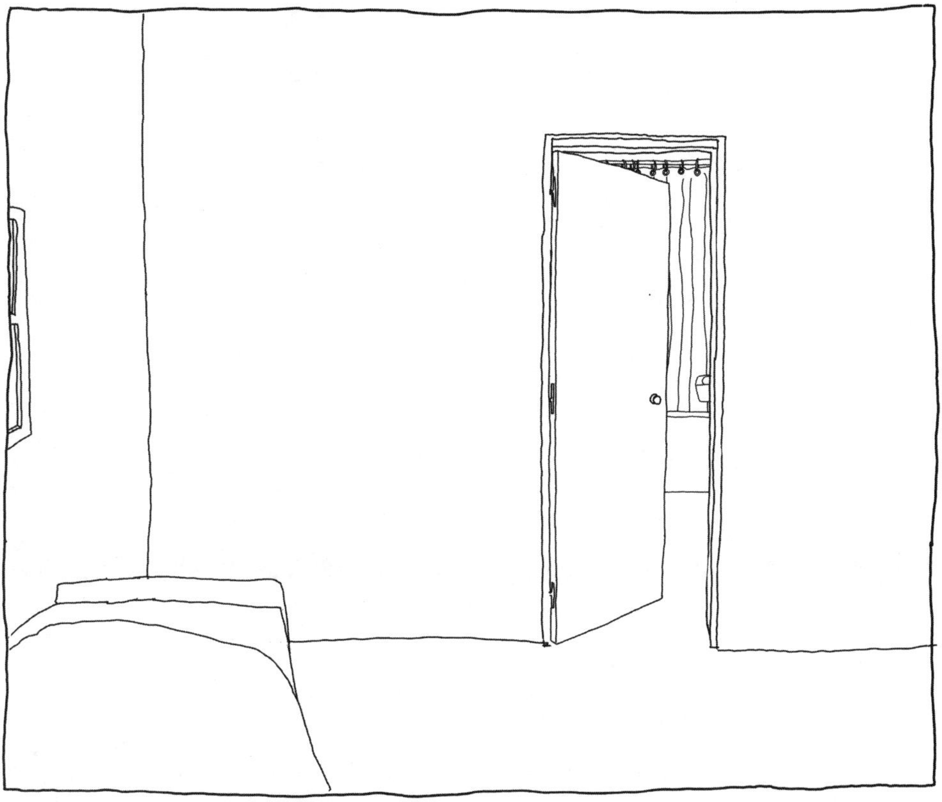

I NEED TO GET
MY LEVEL* RAISED
SOON SO ERIC
CAN VISIT.

NO ONE LOVES
ME LIKE ERIC.

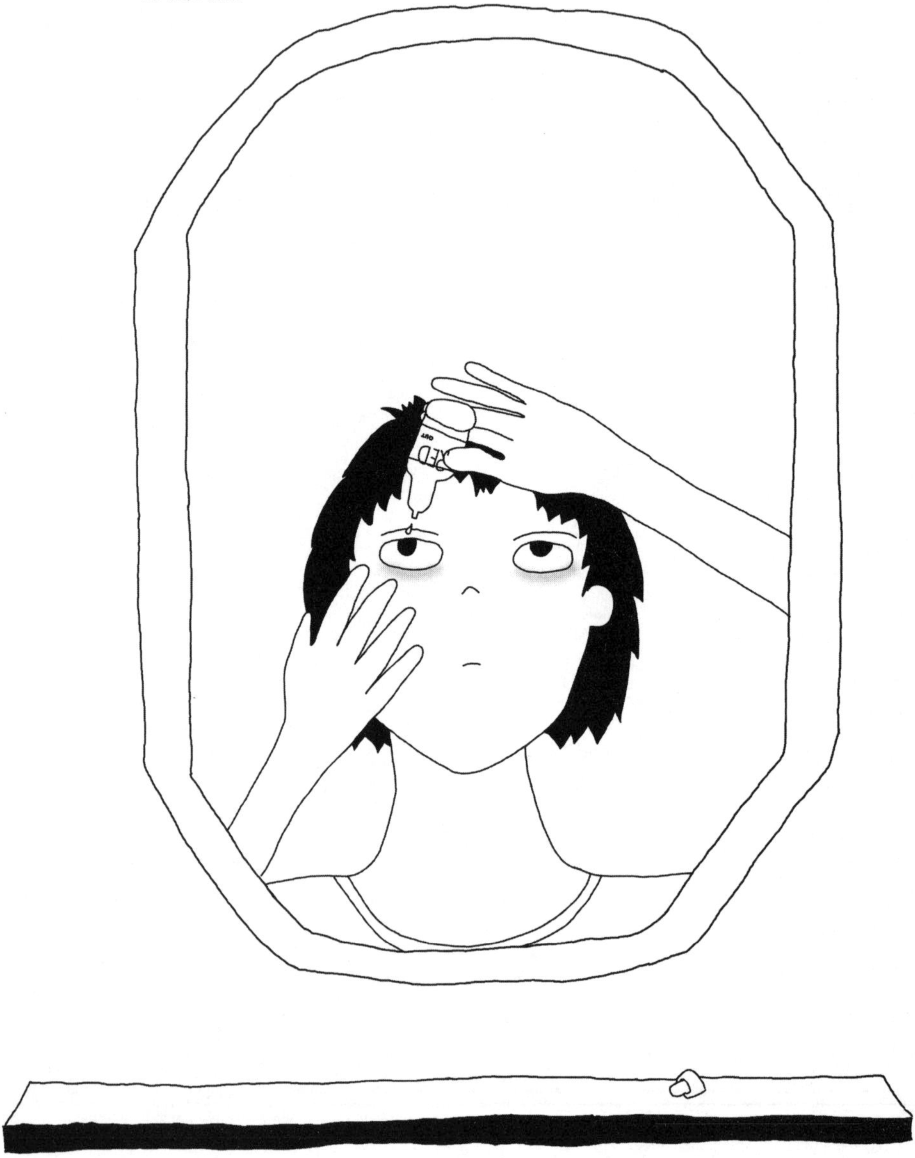

*THERE ARE FOUR LEVELS. THE HIGHER YOUR LEVEL NUMBER THE MORE FREEDOM YOU HAVE WITHIN THE HOSPITAL. PRIVILEGES ARE GRANTED ACCORDING TO INDIVIDUAL PROGRESS.

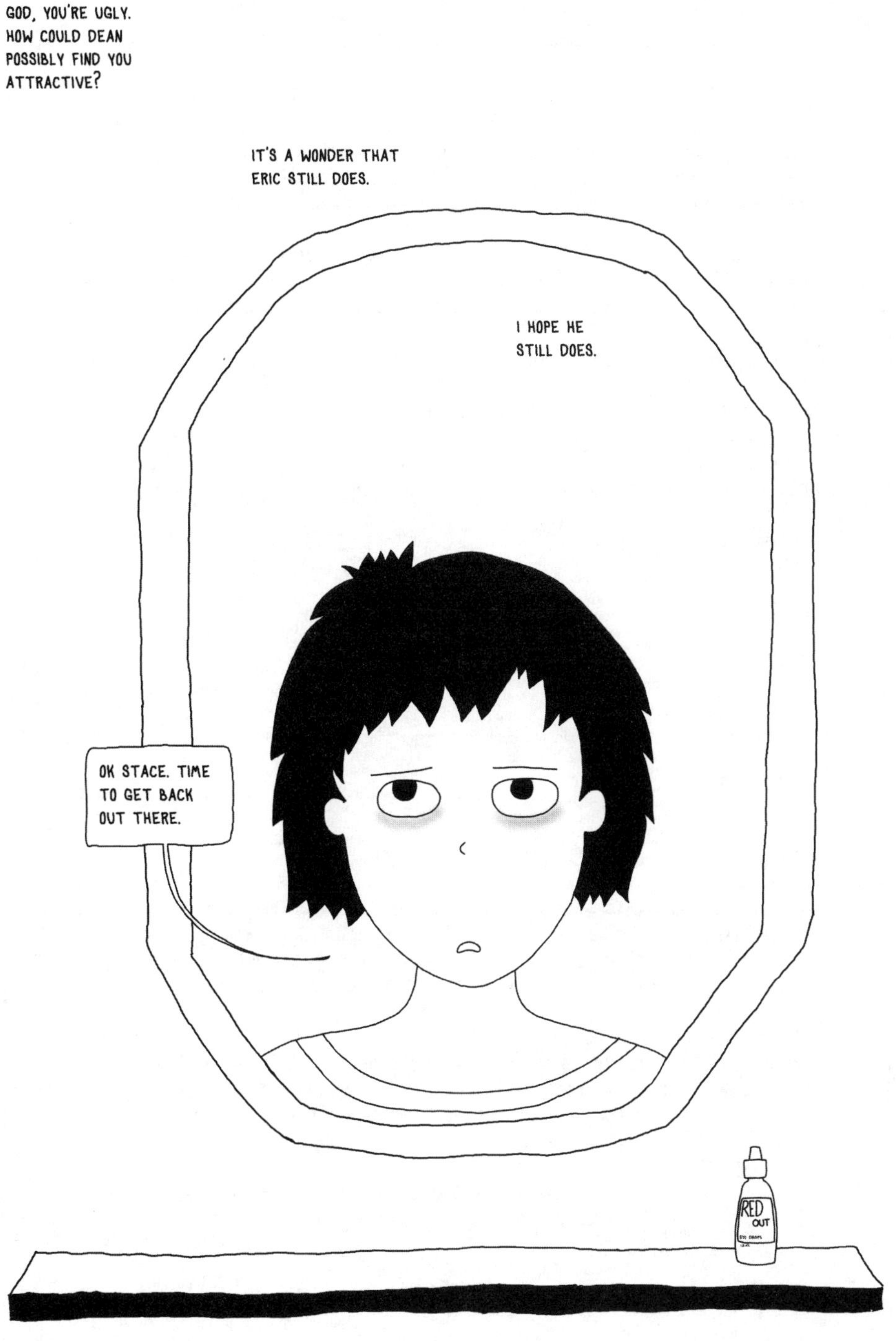
GOD, YOU'RE UGLY. HOW COULD DEAN POSSIBLY FIND YOU ATTRACTIVE?
IT'S A WONDER THAT ERIC STILL DOES.
I HOPE HE STILL DOES.
OK STACE. TIME TO GET BACK OUT THERE.
RED OUT

How did you become friends with Stacy?

MARIA

I'VE BEEN FRIENDS WITH STACY SINCE WE WERE LIKE THREE. OUR PARENTS SET UP A PLAY DATE — THEY WERE IN THE SAME MOMMY-AND-ME YOGA CLASS OR SOMETHING. WE MUST HAVE GOTTEN ALONG BECAUSE WE STARTED HAVING SLEEPOVERS. I SPENT MY ENTIRE CHILDHOOD WITH STACY.

WE WENT THROUGH A TOMBOY PHASE AND RAN ALL OVER THE PLACE, WE HAD A MAGIC PHASE AND MADE POTIONS OUT OF SOAP AND VINEGAR TO "POISON" MY BROTHER. THEN WE WENT THROUGH AN ACTING PHASE AND MADE UP SKITS FOR OUR PARENTS AND ANYONE WHO'D WATCH. AND OF COURSE WE WENT THROUGH WAY MORE.

CONTRARY TO STACY'S CURRENT BELIEF I WOULD DO ANYTHING FOR HER. THAT SAID, IT'S NOT JUST HER WHO HAS TRUST ISSUES WITH OUR FRIENDSHIP AT THE MOMENT. I REALLY MISS HER, BUT SHE WAS SO OUT OF CONTROL. I DON'T REGRET FOR ONE MINUTE ANYTHING I DID.

EVEN IF IT MEANS THE END OF OUR FRIENDSHIP.

I DON'T WANT HER TO DIE.

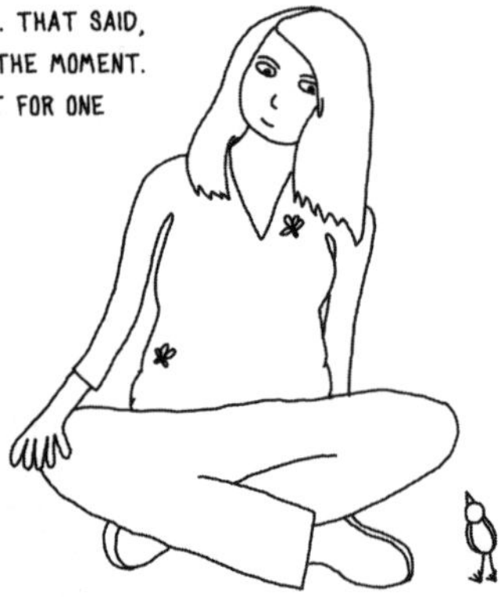

VIOLET

AT BOARDING SCHOOL WE SEEMED TO HATE AND LIKE THE SAME PEOPLE. THAT HELPED US BECOME FRIENDS. THE ENTIRE TIME I WAS THERE WE CONDUCTED THIS WAR WITH THE GIRLS NEXT DOOR TO US WHO PLAYED REALLY BAD MUSIC LOUDLY. WE'D HIT THE WALLS AND YELL, AND STACE DRILLED A TINY HOLE BETWEEN OUR ROOMS SO WE COULD SPY ON THEM. THEY NEVER KNEW. IT WAS PRETTY GREAT EVEN THOUGH THEY DIDN'T DO ANYTHING INTERESTING.

MY MOM WOULDN'T LET ME GO BACK TO SCHOOL AFTER SPRING BREAK. SHE DIDN'T LIKE THAT I WAS GROWING DREADS, PLUS SHE FOUND MY BONG. I GOT SENT TO REHAB AND MY MOM TOLD MRS. BLACK. STACY COULD NEVER CONTACT ME. SO WE STOPPED BEING FRIENDS, BUT IT WAS MORE CIRCUMSTANCE THAN ANYTHING ELSE...

THAT, AND STACE WAS STILL USING. BUT NOW SHE'S NOT AND THAT'S A REALLY POSITIVE STEP.

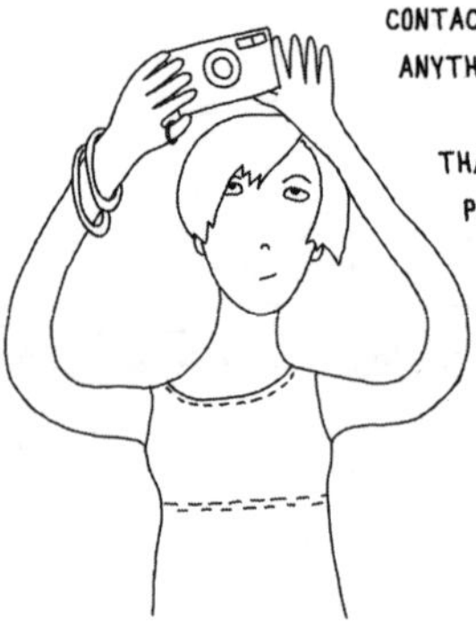

LOLA

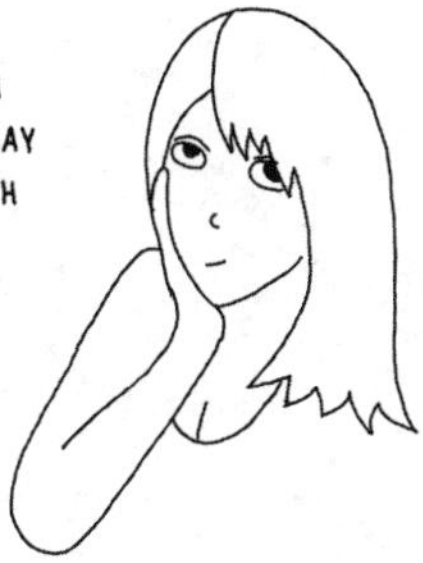

I MOVED TO NEW YORK WHEN I WAS TWELVE AND ENDED UP AT SCHOOL WITH STACY. THERE WAS ONE SPOT WHERE EVERYONE WENT TO SMOKE, SO WE'D SAY HI. THEN ONE TIME WE GOT DRUNK — SHE HAD A JUICE BOTTLE FILLED WITH A BUNCH OF ALCOHOL— AND ENDED UP SITTING IN CENTRAL PARK LISTENING TO MUSIC ON ONE SET OF HEADPHONES. WE BECAME INSTANT BEST FRIENDS.

WE SHARE ONE BRAIN, I SWEAR. WE THINK THE EXACT SAME WAY EVEN ABOUT THINGS WE MAKE UP. LIKE THE SQUISHY PEN — IT'S GOT A SOFT CASHMERE CASING FOR YOUR HAND AND FEELS GOOD AGAINST YOUR SKIN. WE HAD THIS WHOLE JOKE CAMPAIGN — SHE EVEN MADE A LITTLE ANIMATION THINGY FOR IT. STACY'S CREATIVE THAT WAY.

SHE'S ALSO A REALLY REALLY REALLY GOOD LISTENER. YOU KNOW HOW SOMETIMES YOU JUST WANT SOMEONE TO LISTEN AND NOT TELL YOU WHAT TO DO RIGHT AWAY? SHE DOES THAT. I FEEL LIKE SHE'S OLDER AND WISER THAN ME EVEN THOUGH SHE'S SIX MONTHS YOUNGER.

PLUS SHE ALWAYS HELPS ME REHEARSE LINES FOR PLAYS AND GIVES ME HONEST FEEDBACK ON MY PERFORMANCES, WHICH IS VERY IMPORTANT WHEN YOU'RE AN ACTOR — WITHOUT HONEST FEEDBACK YOU CAN'T HONE YOUR CRAFT.

THE HARDEST PART ABOUT GOING TO COLLEGE WAS LEAVING STACE BEHIND.

ASHLEY

WELL, LIKE I SAID, I JUST MET STACY IN GOLDEN MEADOWS, BUT I'M PRETTY SURE WE'LL BE FRIENDS FOR LIFE. IF YOU MEET SOMEONE WHEN THEY ARE AT THEIR LOWEST AND SO ARE YOU, WELL IT JUST MEANS YOU CAN REALLY TRUST THAT THEY WILL BE THERE FOR YOU — AND ISN'T THAT WHAT TRUE FRIENDSHIP IS ABOUT?

BEING THERE FOR EACH OTHER NO MATTER WHAT?

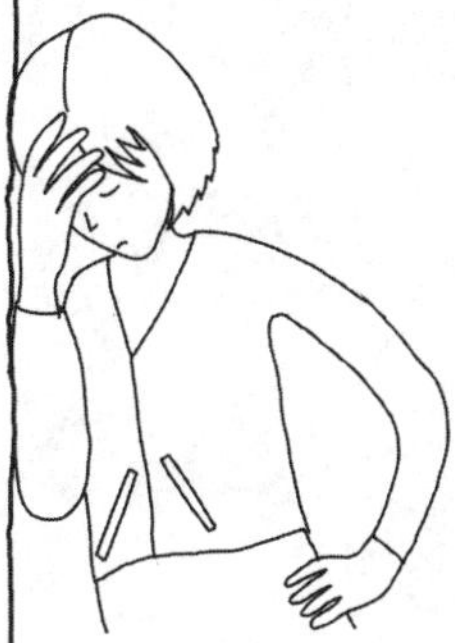

CURRENT LENGTH OF STAY:

seven weeks,
three days

"Stacy has had a reasonably productive week exploring her negativity and why she has so much trouble trusting. However the degree of participation remains problematic, as does her willingness to comply with the rules. She is so fearful of rejection that she beats everyone to the punch by various turnoffs including hostility and sarcasm. The medication that's been prescribed has made her less edgy and for the past several weeks she has been sleeping through the night."

From the individual therapy records of Stacy Black

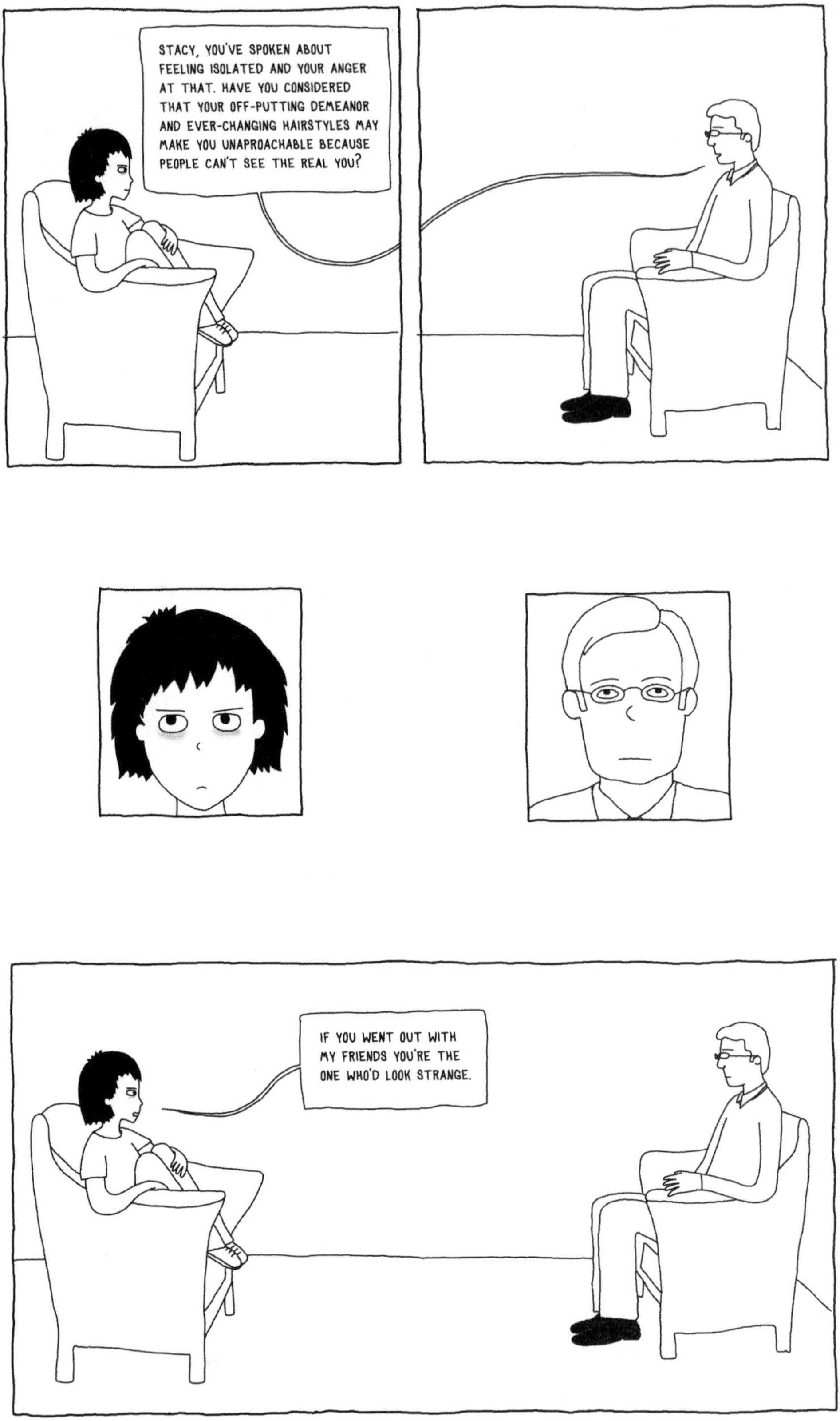
STACY, YOU'VE SPOKEN ABOUT FEELING ISOLATED AND YOUR ANGER AT THAT. HAVE YOU CONSIDERED THAT YOUR OFF-PUTTING DEMEANOR AND EVER-CHANGING HAIRSTYLES MAY MAKE YOU UNAPROACHABLE BECAUSE PEOPLE CAN'T SEE THE REAL YOU?
IF YOU WENT OUT WITH MY FRIENDS YOU'RE THE ONE WHO'D LOOK STRANGE.

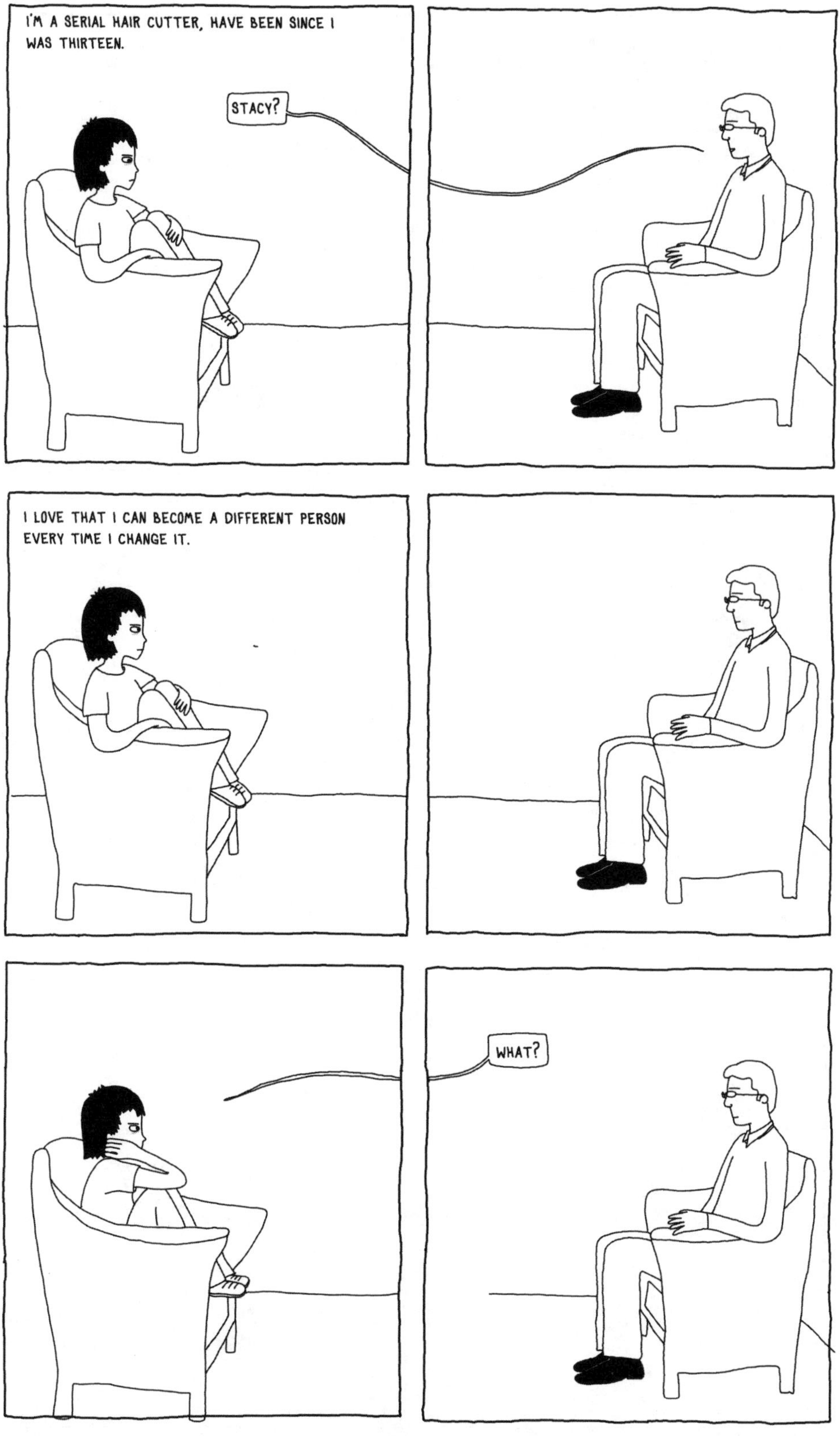
I'M A SERIAL HAIR CUTTER, HAVE BEEN SINCE I WAS THIRTEEN.
STACY?
I LOVE THAT I CAN BECOME A DIFFERENT PERSON EVERY TIME I CHANGE IT.
WHAT?

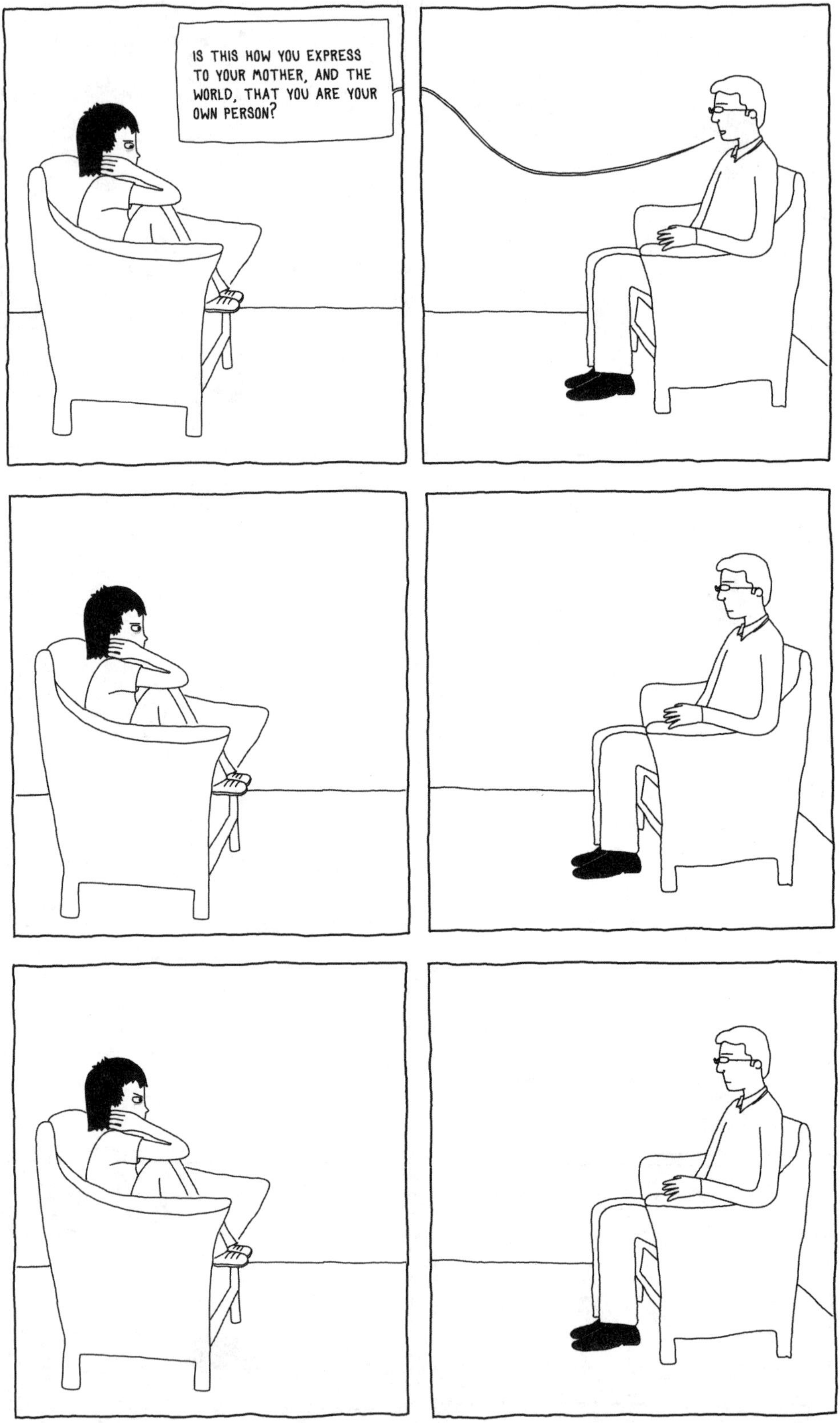
IS THIS HOW YOU EXPRESS TO YOUR MOTHER, AND THE WORLD, THAT YOU ARE YOUR OWN PERSON?

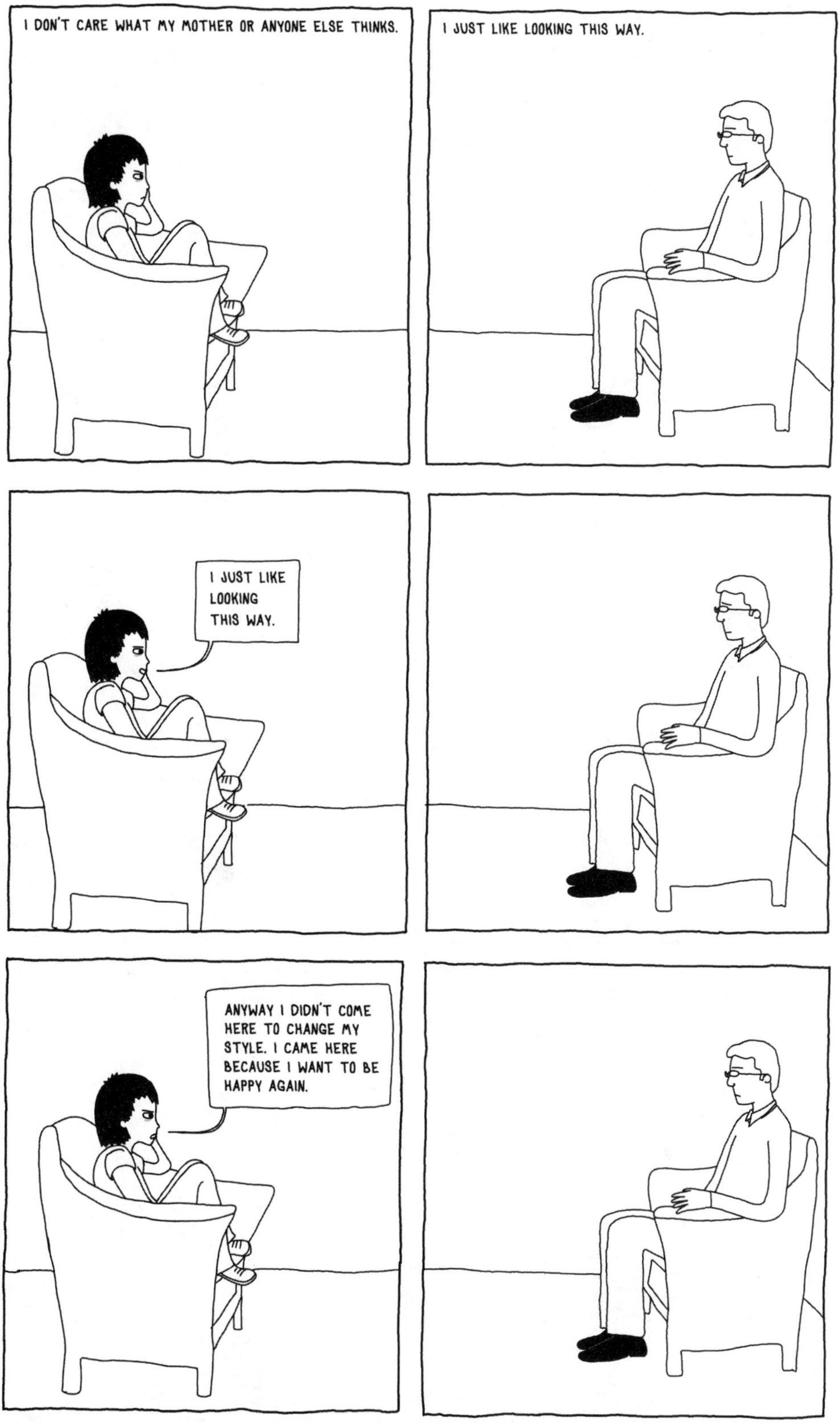
I DON'T CARE WHAT MY MOTHER OR ANYONE ELSE THINKS.
I JUST LIKE LOOKING THIS WAY.
I JUST LIKE LOOKING THIS WAY.
ANYWAY I DIDN'T COME HERE TO CHANGE MY STYLE. I CAME HERE BECAUSE I WANT TO BE HAPPY AGAIN.

IF THERE IS ONE THING I'VE LEARNED FROM MY MOM AND GRANDMA, IT'S THAT THE RIGHT LOOK IS CRITICAL.

MUST YOU ALWAYS WEAR THAT? IT LOOKS TERRIBLE.

YES, I MUST.

THE COMPANY LIKED MY PRESENTATION, MOTHER.

WELL I HOPE YOU DIDN'T WEAR THAT BLUE BLOUSE, IT'S NOT THE BEST COLOR FOR YOU.

GRANDMA CAME TO THIS COUNTRY FROM POLAND. HER NUMBER ONE GOAL WAS TO FIT IN.

WE DIDN'T WANT TO BE DIFFERENT. WE WANTED TO BE AMERICAN. THE FIRST THING I DID WAS TAKE OUT MY EARRINGS. NO ONE HAD HOLES BACK THEN. OF COURSE WHEN THEY BECAME FASHIONABLE I WORE THEM AGAIN.

MY HAIR AND CLOTHES ARE THE ONLY THINGS I LIKE ABOUT MYSELF.

IT CAN TAKE WEEKS TO PERFECT A LOOK.

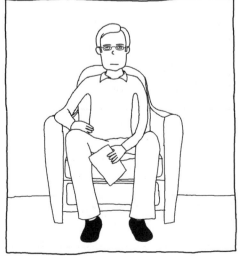

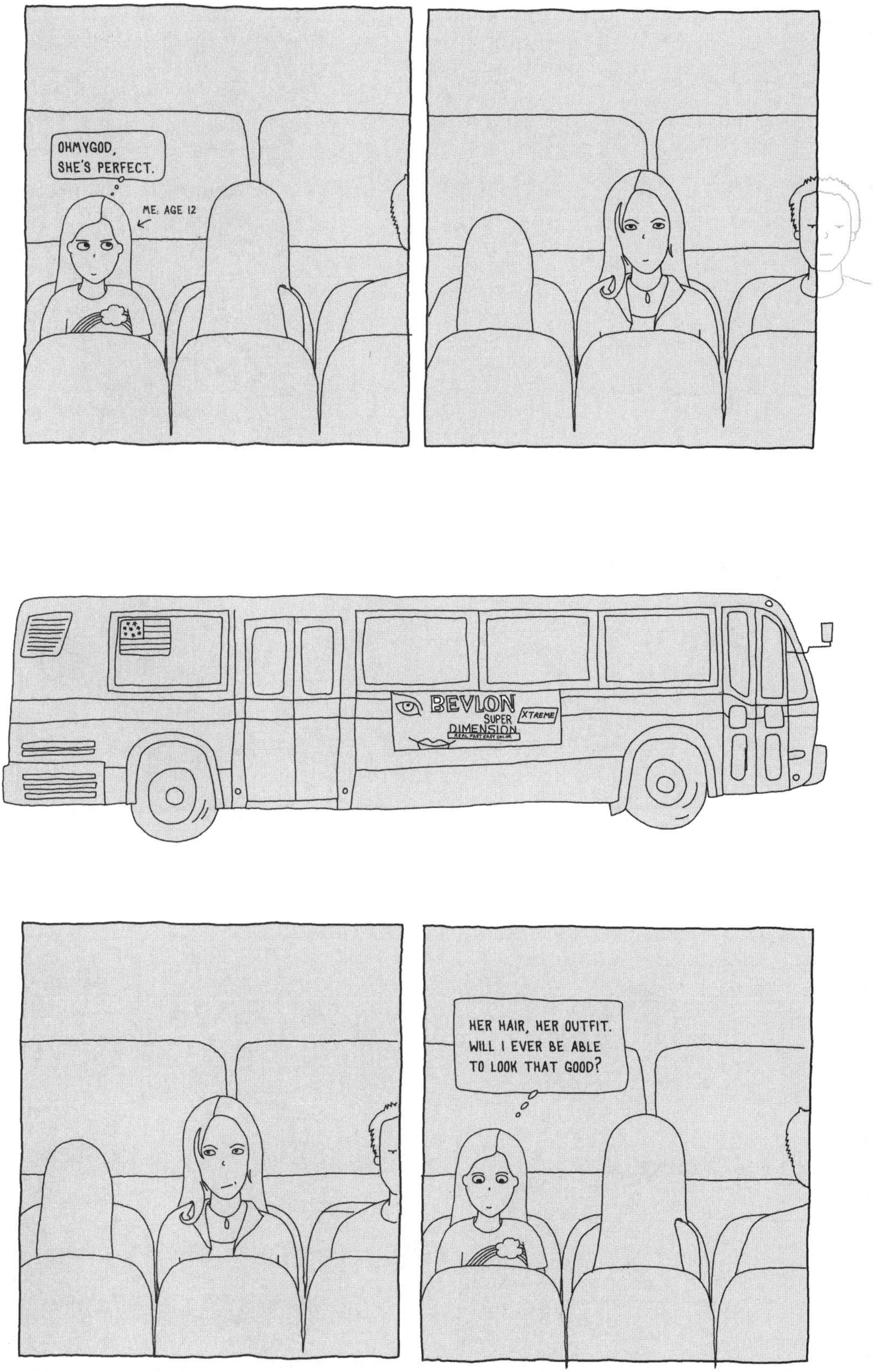
OHMYGOD, SHE'S PERFECT.
ME: AGE 12
BEVLON
SUPER DIMENSION
REAL FAST EASY COLOR
XTREME
HER HAIR, HER OUTFIT. WILL I EVER BE ABLE TO LOOK THAT GOOD?

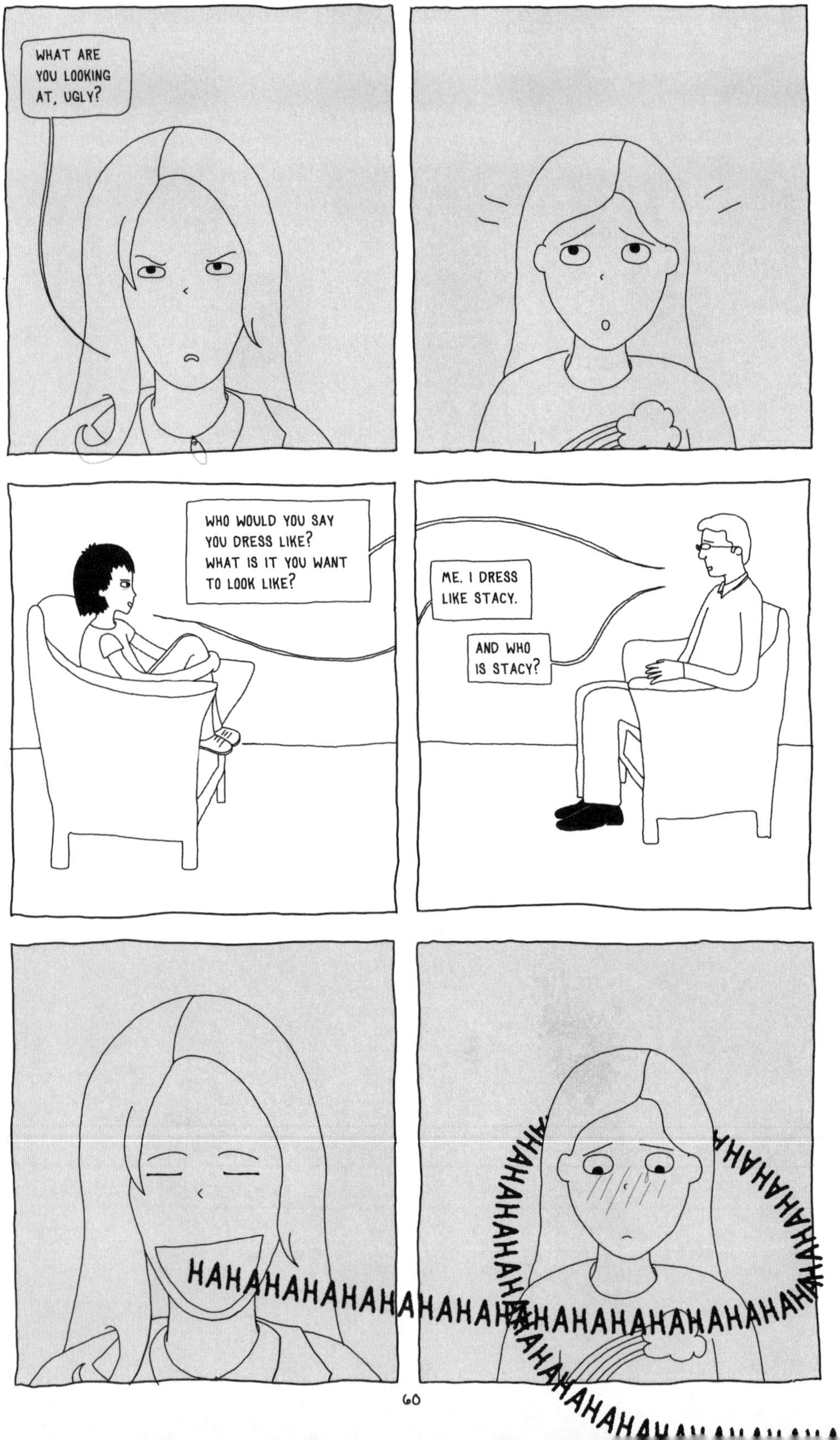
WHAT ARE YOU LOOKING AT, UGLY?
WHO WOULD YOU SAY YOU DRESS LIKE? WHAT IS IT YOU WANT TO LOOK LIKE?
ME. I DRESS LIKE STACY.
AND WHO IS STACY?
HAHAHAHAHAHAHAHAHAHAHAHAHAHAHAHA

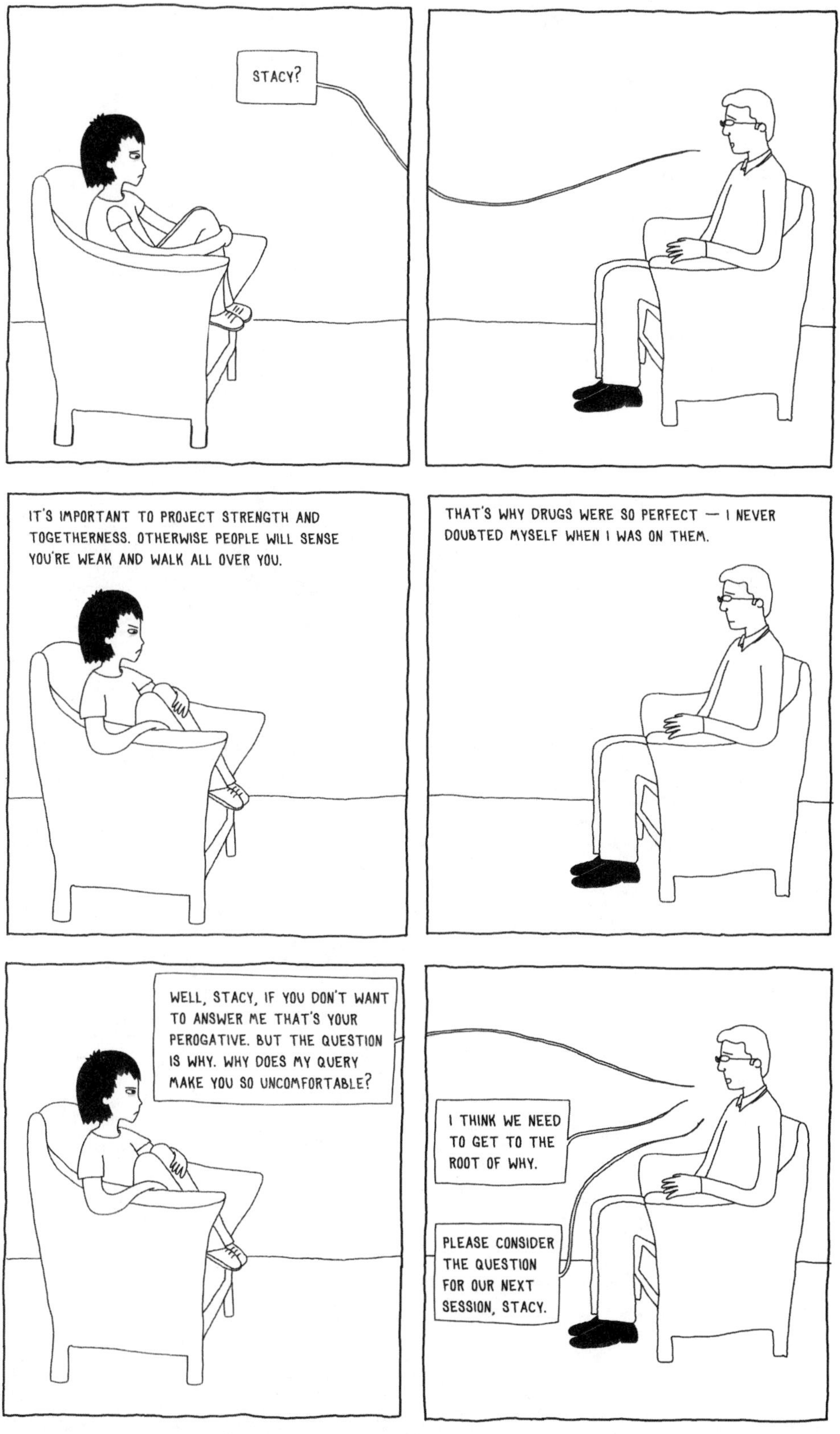
STACY?
IT'S IMPORTANT TO PROJECT STRENGTH AND TOGETHERNESS. OTHERWISE PEOPLE WILL SENSE YOU'RE WEAK AND WALK ALL OVER YOU.
THAT'S WHY DRUGS WERE SO PERFECT — I NEVER DOUBTED MYSELF WHEN I WAS ON THEM.
WELL, STACY, IF YOU DON'T WANT TO ANSWER ME THAT'S YOUR PEROGATIVE. BUT THE QUESTION IS WHY. WHY DOES MY QUERY MAKE YOU SO UNCOMFORTABLE?
I THINK WE NEED TO GET TO THE ROOT OF WHY.
PLEASE CONSIDER THE QUESTION FOR OUR NEXT SESSION, STACY.

"CONSIDER THE
QUESTION FOR OUR
NEXT SESSION, STACY."

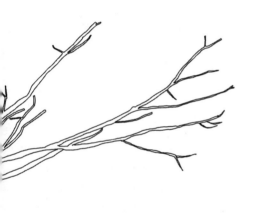

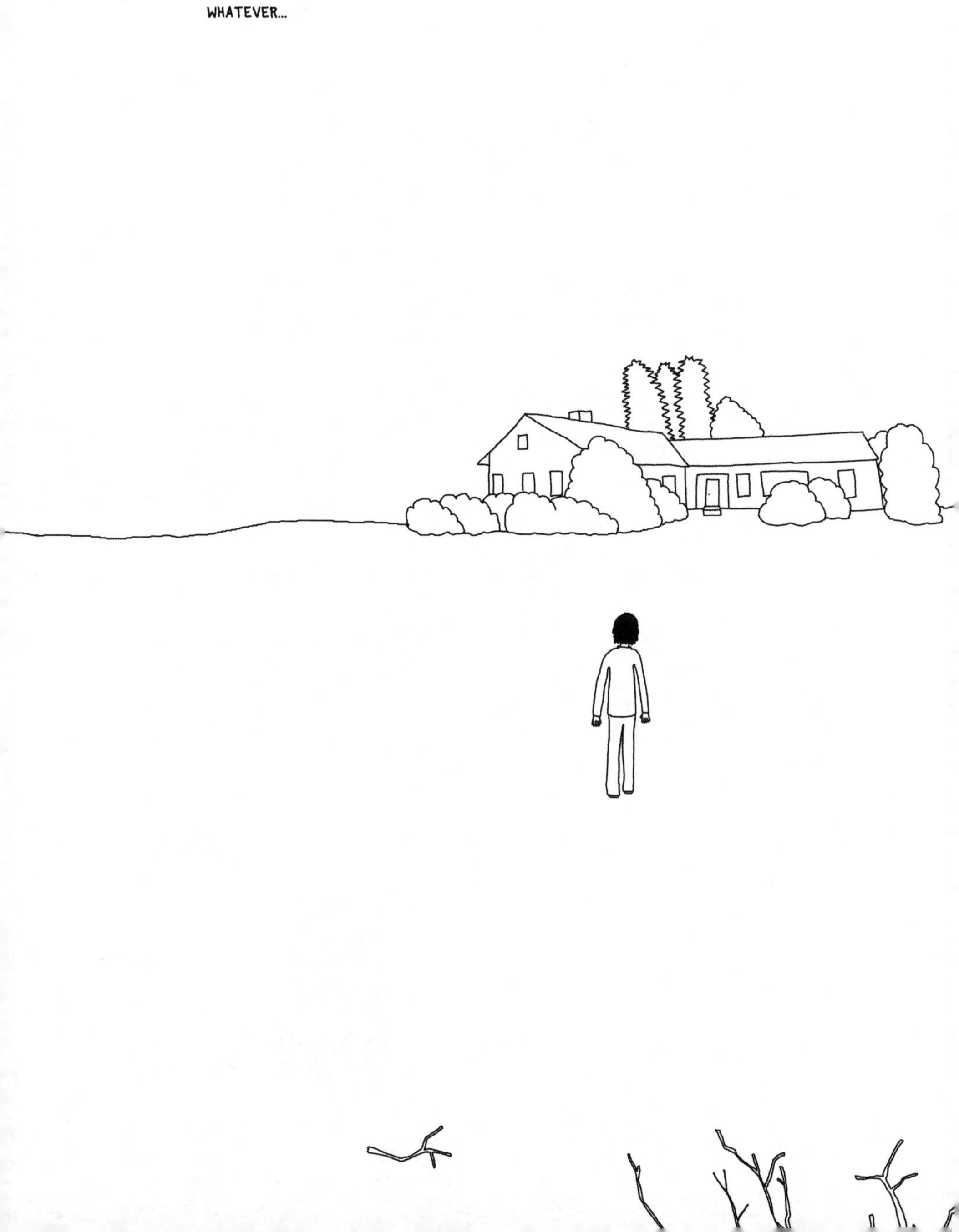
WHATEVER...

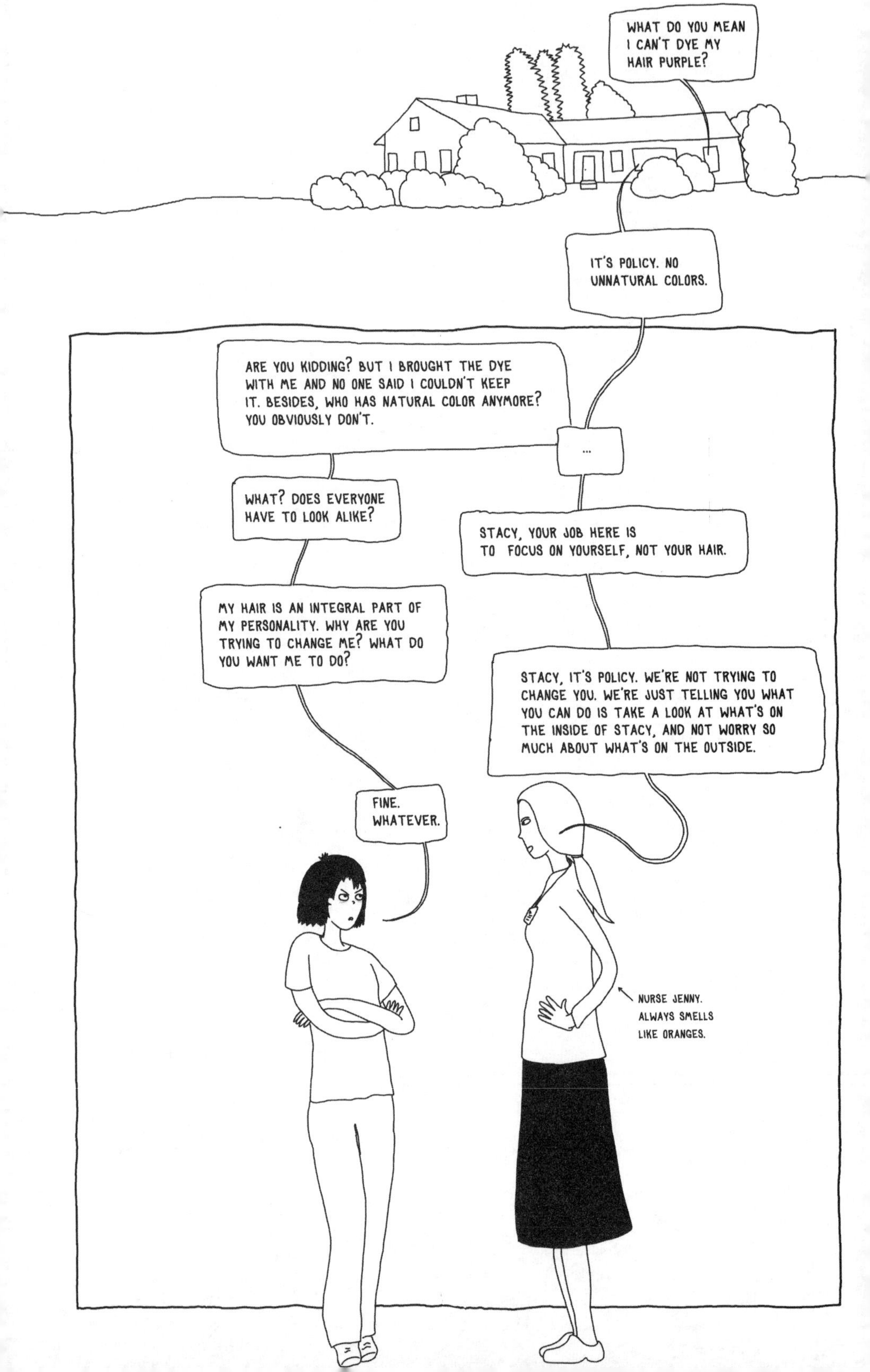
WHAT DO YOU MEAN I CAN'T DYE MY HAIR PURPLE?
IT'S POLICY. NO UNNATURAL COLORS.
ARE YOU KIDDING? BUT I BROUGHT THE DYE WITH ME AND NO ONE SAID I COULDN'T KEEP IT. BESIDES, WHO HAS NATURAL COLOR ANYMORE? YOU OBVIOUSLY DON'T.
...
WHAT? DOES EVERYONE HAVE TO LOOK ALIKE?
STACY, YOUR JOB HERE IS TO FOCUS ON YOURSELF, NOT YOUR HAIR.
MY HAIR IS AN INTEGRAL PART OF MY PERSONALITY. WHY ARE YOU TRYING TO CHANGE ME? WHAT DO YOU WANT ME TO DO?
STACY, IT'S POLICY. WE'RE NOT TRYING TO CHANGE YOU. WE'RE JUST TELLING YOU WHAT YOU CAN DO IS TAKE A LOOK AT WHAT'S ON THE INSIDE OF STACY, AND NOT WORRY SO MUCH ABOUT WHAT'S ON THE OUTSIDE.
FINE. WHATEVER.
NURSE JENNY. ALWAYS SMELLS LIKE ORANGES.

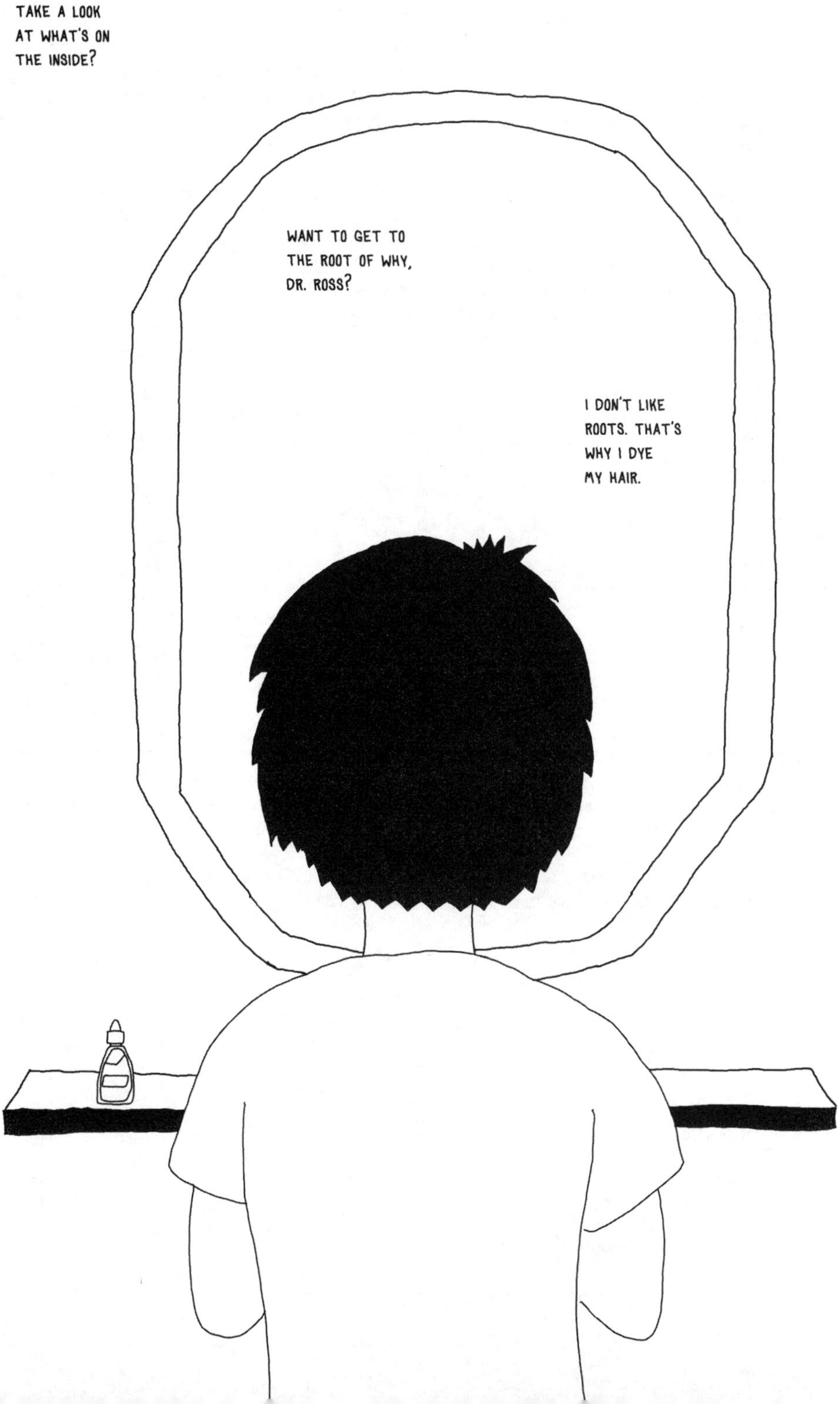
TAKE A LOOK AT WHAT'S ON THE INSIDE?
WANT TO GET TO THE ROOT OF WHY, DR. ROSS?
I DON'T LIKE ROOTS. THAT'S WHY I DYE MY HAIR.

Has Stacy always tried out different styles?

MARIA

ALWAYS. WHEN WE WERE LITTLE STACE AND I USED TO PLAY THIS GAME THAT WE WERE OLDER POPULAR GIRLS. SHE WAS GISELLE AND I WAS JESSICA. WE ATE CANDY TO GIVE US SPECIAL POWERS THAT WOULD PUT PEOPLE UNDER OUR CONTROL EXCEPT THEY WOULDN'T KNOW IT. WE'D DRESS UP AND EVERYTHING. I REMEMBER THE FIRST TIME STACY DYED HER HAIR IT CAME OUT THIS UGLY YELLOW BUT SHE WAS LIKE "I'M BEAUTIFUL NOW, I'M REALLY GISELLE."

FOR AS LONG AS I'VE KNOWN HER SHE'S TRIED OUT DIFFERENT LOOKS. SHE USED TO SAY SHE WISHED SHE WAS IN MY FAMILY AND NOT HERS BECAUSE I HAVE A NORMAL FAMILY WITH A MOTHER AND A FATHER AND A BROTHER, AND SHE JUST HAS HER MOM—WELL, AND NOW A STEPFATHER. SHE NEVER TALKS ABOUT IT BUT HER DAD WAS KILLED BY A DRUNK DRIVER WHEN SHE WAS ONE. SOMETIMES AT NIGHT WHEN WE'D HAVE SLEEPOVERS, THIS IS WHEN WE WERE LITTLE, I'D WAKE UP BECAUSE SHE WAS CRYING IN HER SLEEP, CALLING FOR HIM. SHE HAD NO IDEA AND I NEVER SAID ANYTHING.

DID I ANSWER THE QUESTION?

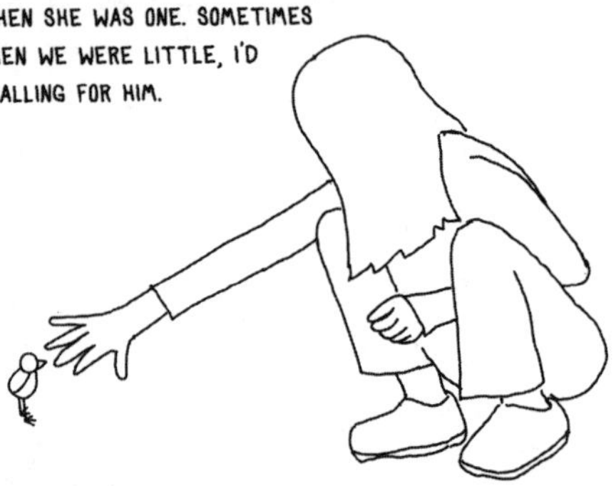

VIOLET

WELL, WE WERE BOTH INTO CHANGING OUR LOOKS A LOT AT SCHOOL. WE DYED OUR HAIR LIKE EVERY WEEK. I BLEACHED MINE SO MUCH IT STARTED TO FALL OUT SO I CUT IT OFF. BUT IT WAS WINTER AND MY HEAD WAS COLD SO STACE LENT ME THIS MULTICOLORED SCARF TO KEEP ME WARM AND THEN SHE DUBBED ME RAINBOW HEAD AND CUT AND DYED HER HAIR BLUE AND PURPLE SO WE'D MATCH.

I'VE ONLY SEEN HER A FEW TIMES RECENTLY—AND I KNOW SHE WANTS TO MAKE A STATEMENT, BUT IT'S A DISTRACTION. THAT'S WHAT THEY TOLD ME IN REHAB AND IT'S TRUE.

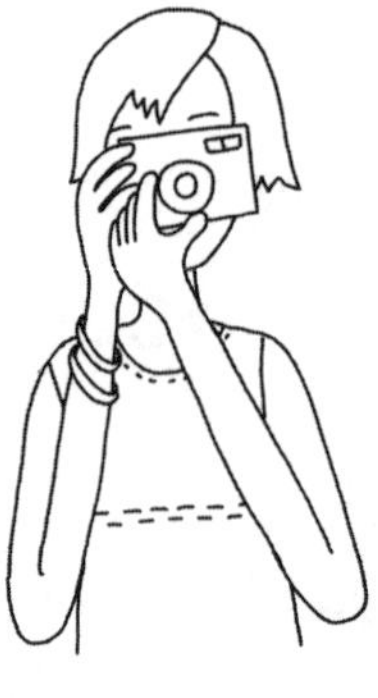

LOLA

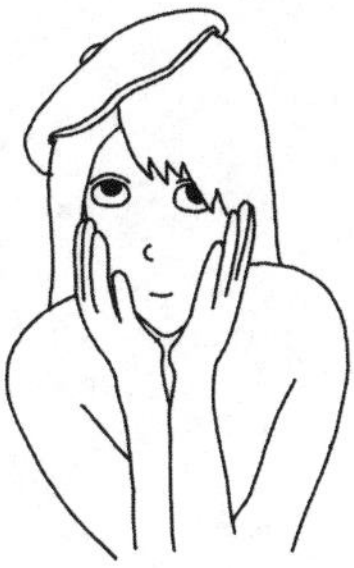

OF COURSE! BUT WHO DOESN'T?! I LOVE TO CHANGE MY STYLE. LIKE THIS SEMESTER I'M DOING A SORTA MANGA THING, BUT I'M THINKING NEXT SEMESTER I MIGHT GO MORE RETRO THRIFT.

CHANGING LOOKS IS A GREAT WAY TO EXPRESS CREATIVITY AND STACY IS ONE OF THE MOST CREATIVE PEOPLE I KNOW. YOU SHOULD SEE THE ART SHE MAKES. I THINK HOW YOU DRESS, HAIR, AND MAKEUP IS IMPORTANT AND SHOULDN'T BE UNDERESTIMATED.

OF COURSE NOT BEING OVERWEIGHT HELPS, AND IF ANYONE KNOWS ANYTHING ABOUT STAYING THIN IT'S STACY.

ASHLEY

I DUNNO IF SHE'S ALWAYS WANTED TO CHANGE HOW SHE LOOKS, BUT SINCE SHE'S BEEN AT MEADOWS SHE'S HAD A FEW STYLES, AT LEAST MAKEUP WISE. HER FASHION TASTE ISN'T FOR EVERYONE, THAT'S FOR SURE. ESPECIALLY HERE WHERE IT'S ALL AMERICAN APPAREL OR GAP.

STACY'S GREAT AND IF YOU JUST TAKE THE TIME TO TALK TO HER IT REALLY DOESN'T MATTER WHAT SHE LOOKS LIKE OR WEARS. SHE'S NOT SOME SCARY MONSTER. SHE PLAYS BOGGLE LIKE EVERYONE ELSE HERE. I'M A LABEL GIRL, SHE ISN'T. SO WHAT. I'M TELLING YOU AT THIS POINT SHE'S A BETTER FRIEND THAN THE ONES I HAVE, OR USED TO HAVE, BACK HOME WHO NOW HAVE NO IDEA WHAT TO SAY TO ME BECAUSE I'M HERE.

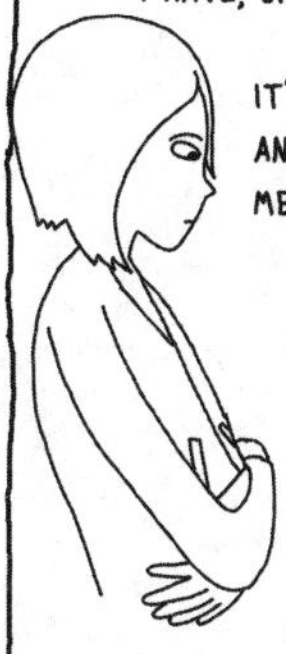

IT'S LIKE I HAVE THE PLAGUE EXCEPT I DON'T. MOST IMPORTANT OF ALL, BECAUSE I MET STACY HERE AND SHE'S MET ME AT MY LOWEST. I KNOW SHE WON'T IGNORE ME NO MATTER HOW BAD THINGS GET. I MEAN, CAN THEY REALLY GET ANY WORSE?

CURRENT LENGTH OF STAY:

seven weeks,
six days

"Pt. stated that she is a very 'negative person' and that she would like to change that negative attitude. Pt. wants to work on developing a more positive outlook but is defensive when given feedback and has trouble listening to staff. The pt. is beginning to verbalize her feelings of depression and indicated that she thinks she may have gotten mixed messages from the adults in her life."

From the nurses' notes for Stacy Black

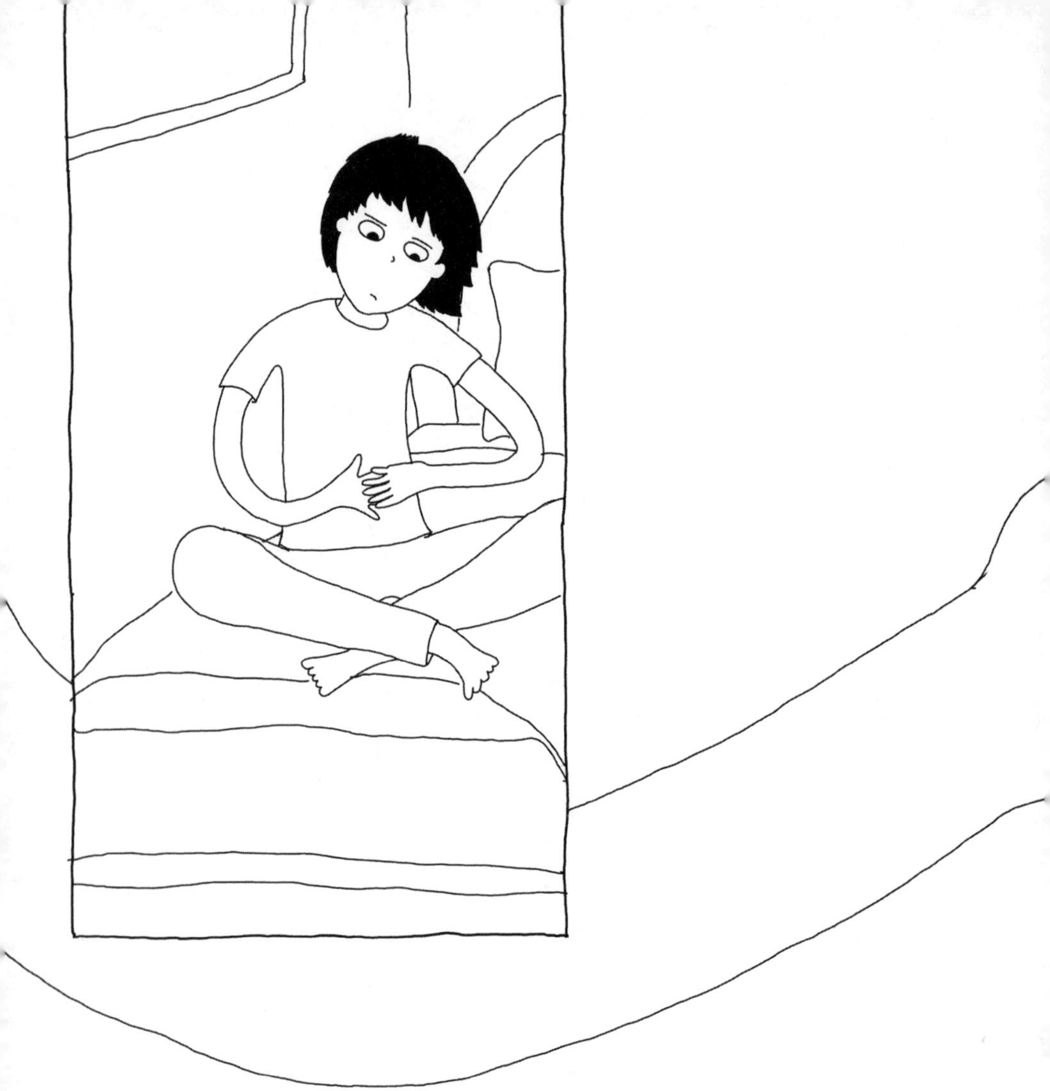

AFTER I PUNCHED OUT THE
WINDOWS IN MY APARTMENT
I TOOK A SHARD OF GLASS
AND PUSHED IT INTO MY CUTS
TO MAKE SURE THEY WERE
GOOD AND DEEP.

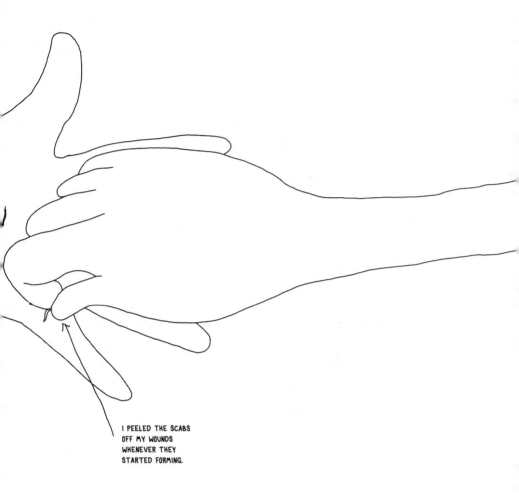

I PEELED THE SCABS
OFF MY WOUNDS
WHENEVER THEY
STARTED FORMING.

NURSE KATHLEEN SAYS I
SHOULDN'T GET SCARS
AS LONG AS I LET MY
INJURIES HEAL.

BUT I DON'T WANT THEM TO.

I WANT PEOPLE TO SEE
THEM AND WONDER WHAT
HAPPENED AND HOW MUCH
IT MUST HAVE HURT.

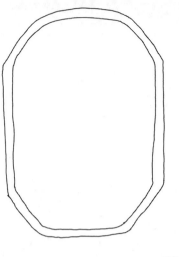

ERIC SAYS SCARS ARE WAY
MORE SIGNIFICANT THAN ANY
INK YOU GET IN A SHOP BECAUSE
IT'S PAIN NOT PAYMENT THAT
HAS MEANING.

UNDER
EYE GRAY
GOT OLD.

HE SHOULD KNOW. HE
GIVES HIMSELF SCARS
ALL THE TIME.

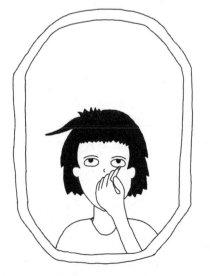

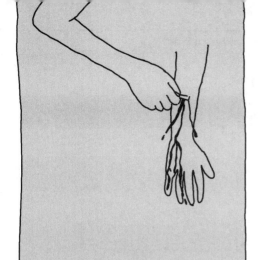

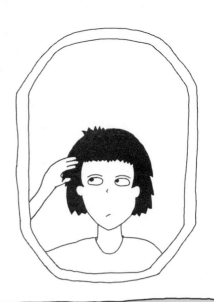

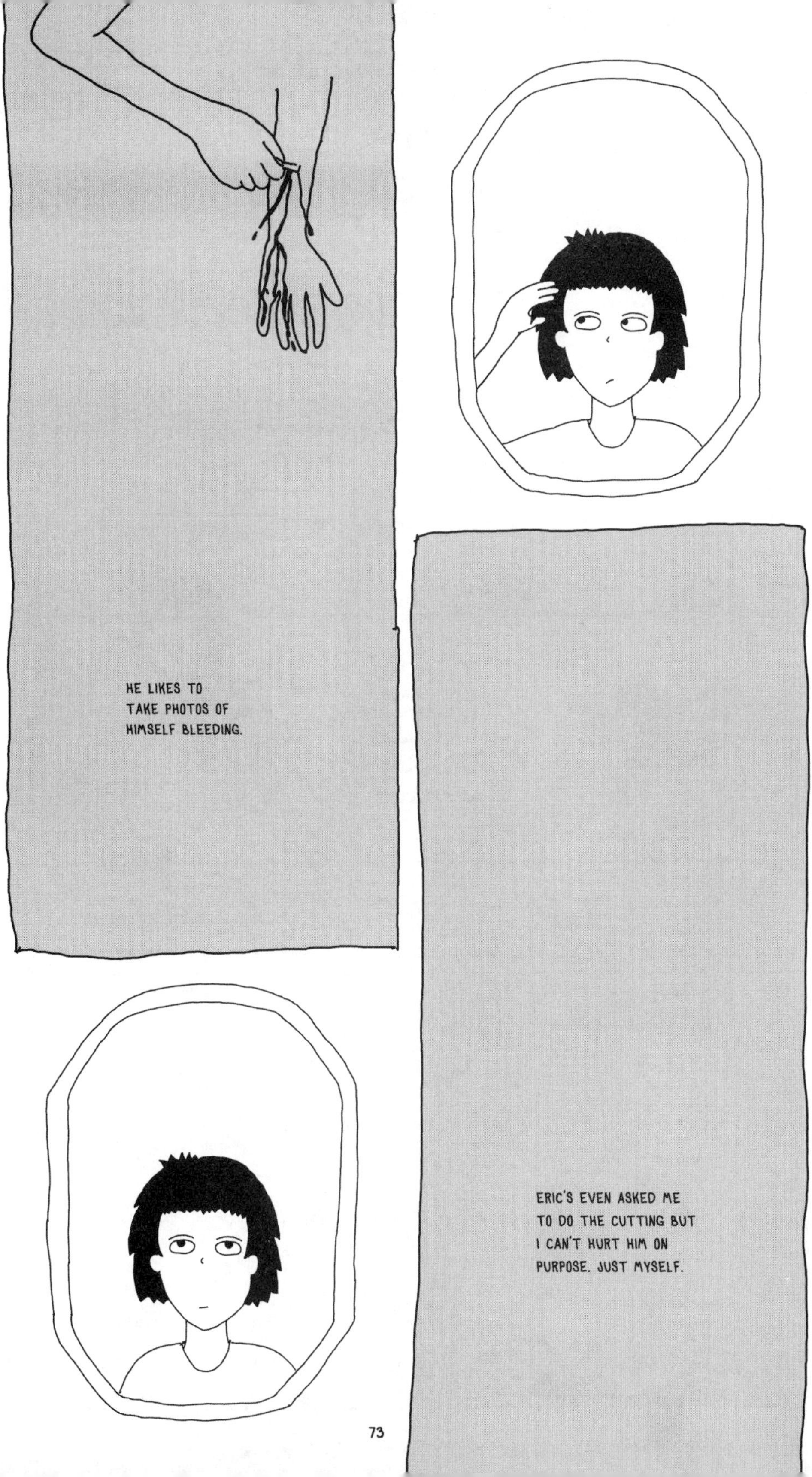

HE LIKES TO
TAKE PHOTOS OF
HIMSELF BLEEDING.

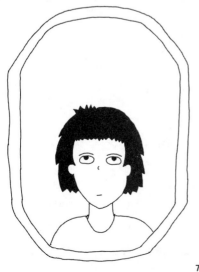

ERIC'S EVEN ASKED ME
TO DO THE CUTTING BUT
I CAN'T HURT HIM ON
PURPOSE. JUST MYSELF.

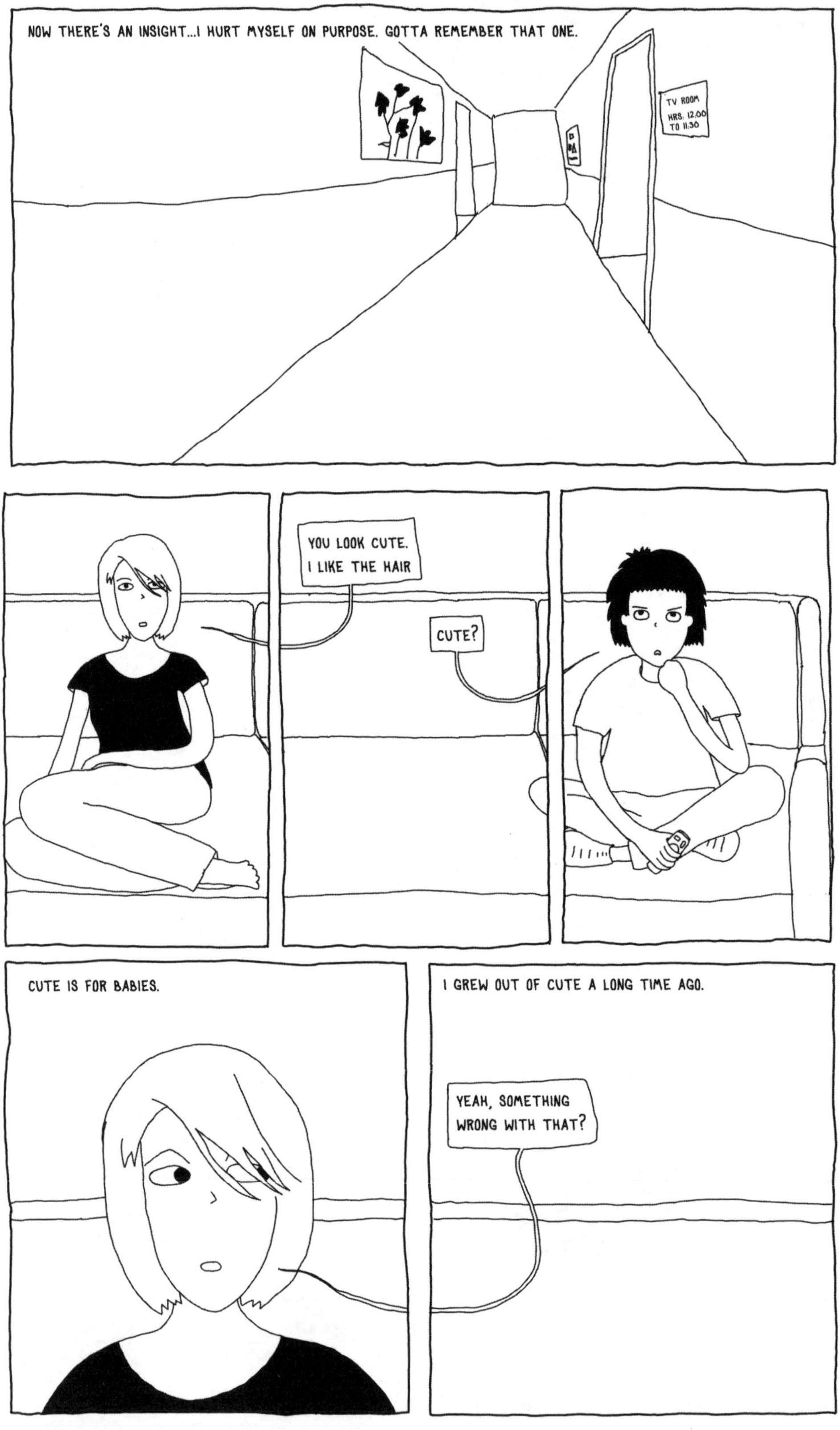
NOW THERE'S AN INSIGHT...I HURT MYSELF ON PURPOSE. GOTTA REMEMBER THAT ONE.
TV ROOM HRS. 12.00 TO 11.30
YOU LOOK CUTE. I LIKE THE HAIR
CUTE?
CUTE IS FOR BABIES.
I GREW OUT OF CUTE A LONG TIME AGO.
YEAH, SOMETHING WRONG WITH THAT?

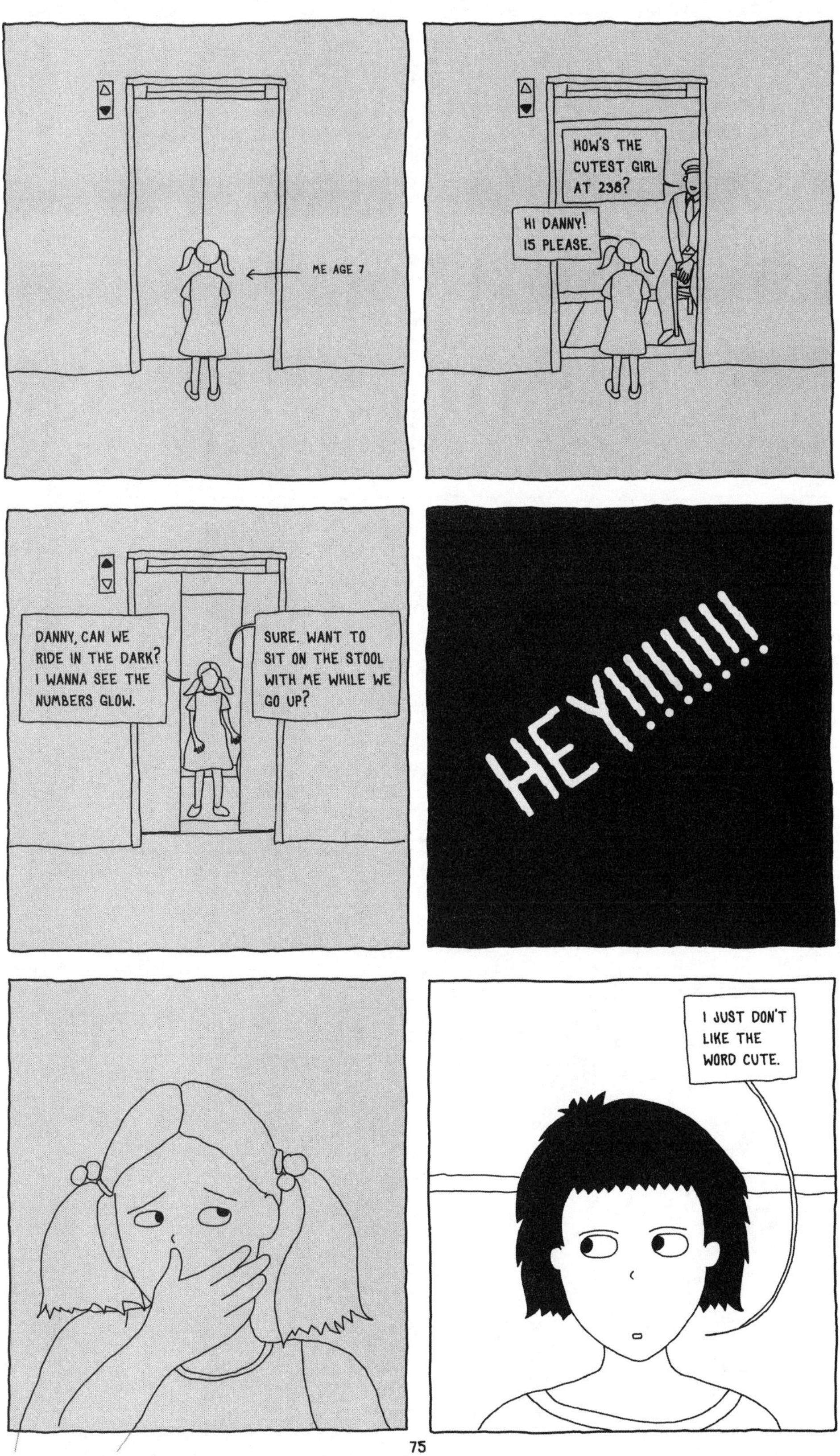

ME AGE 7
HOW'S THE CUTEST GIRL AT 238?
HI DANNY! 15 PLEASE.
DANNY, CAN WE RIDE IN THE DARK? I WANNA SEE THE NUMBERS GLOW.
SURE. WANT TO SIT ON THE STOOL WITH ME WHILE WE GO UP?
HEY!!!!!!!!
I JUST DON'T LIKE THE WORD CUTE.

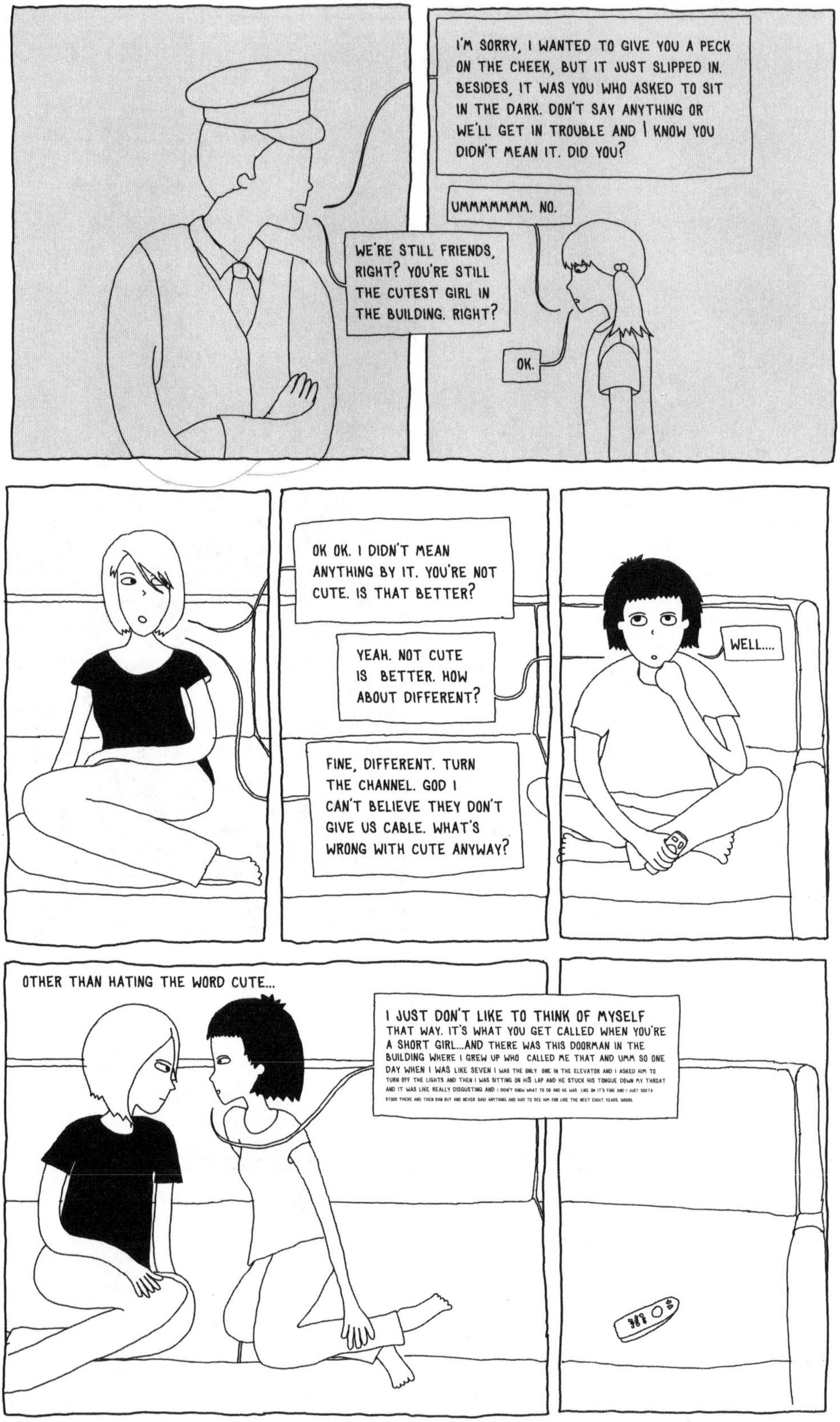
I'M SORRY, I WANTED TO GIVE YOU A PECK ON THE CHEEK, BUT IT JUST SLIPPED IN. BESIDES, IT WAS YOU WHO ASKED TO SIT IN THE DARK. DON'T SAY ANYTHING OR WE'LL GET IN TROUBLE AND I KNOW YOU DIDN'T MEAN IT. DID YOU?
UMMMMMMM. NO.
WE'RE STILL FRIENDS, RIGHT? YOU'RE STILL THE CUTEST GIRL IN THE BUILDING. RIGHT?
OK.
OK OK. I DIDN'T MEAN ANYTHING BY IT. YOU'RE NOT CUTE. IS THAT BETTER?
YEAH. NOT CUTE IS BETTER. HOW ABOUT DIFFERENT?
FINE, DIFFERENT. TURN THE CHANNEL. GOD I CAN'T BELIEVE THEY DON'T GIVE US CABLE. WHAT'S WRONG WITH CUTE ANYWAY?
WELL....
OTHER THAN HATING THE WORD CUTE...
I JUST DON'T LIKE TO THINK OF MYSELF THAT WAY. IT'S WHAT YOU GET CALLED WHEN YOU'RE A SHORT GIRL...AND THERE WAS THIS DOORMAN IN THE BUILDING WHERE I GREW UP WHO CALLED ME THAT AND UMM SO ONE DAY WHEN I WAS LIKE SEVEN I WAS THE ONLY ONE IN THE ELEVATOR AND I ASKED HIM TO TURN OFF THE LIGHTS AND THEN I WAS SITTING ON HIS LAP AND HE STUCK HIS TONGUE DOWN MY THROAT AND IT WAS LIKE REALLY DISGUSTING AND I DIDN'T KNOW WHAT TO DO AND HE WAS LIKE OH IT'S FINE AND I JUST SORTA STOOD THERE AND THEN RAN OUT AND NEVER SAID ANYTHING AND HAD TO SEE HIM FOR LIKE THE NEXT EIGHT YEARS. GROSS.

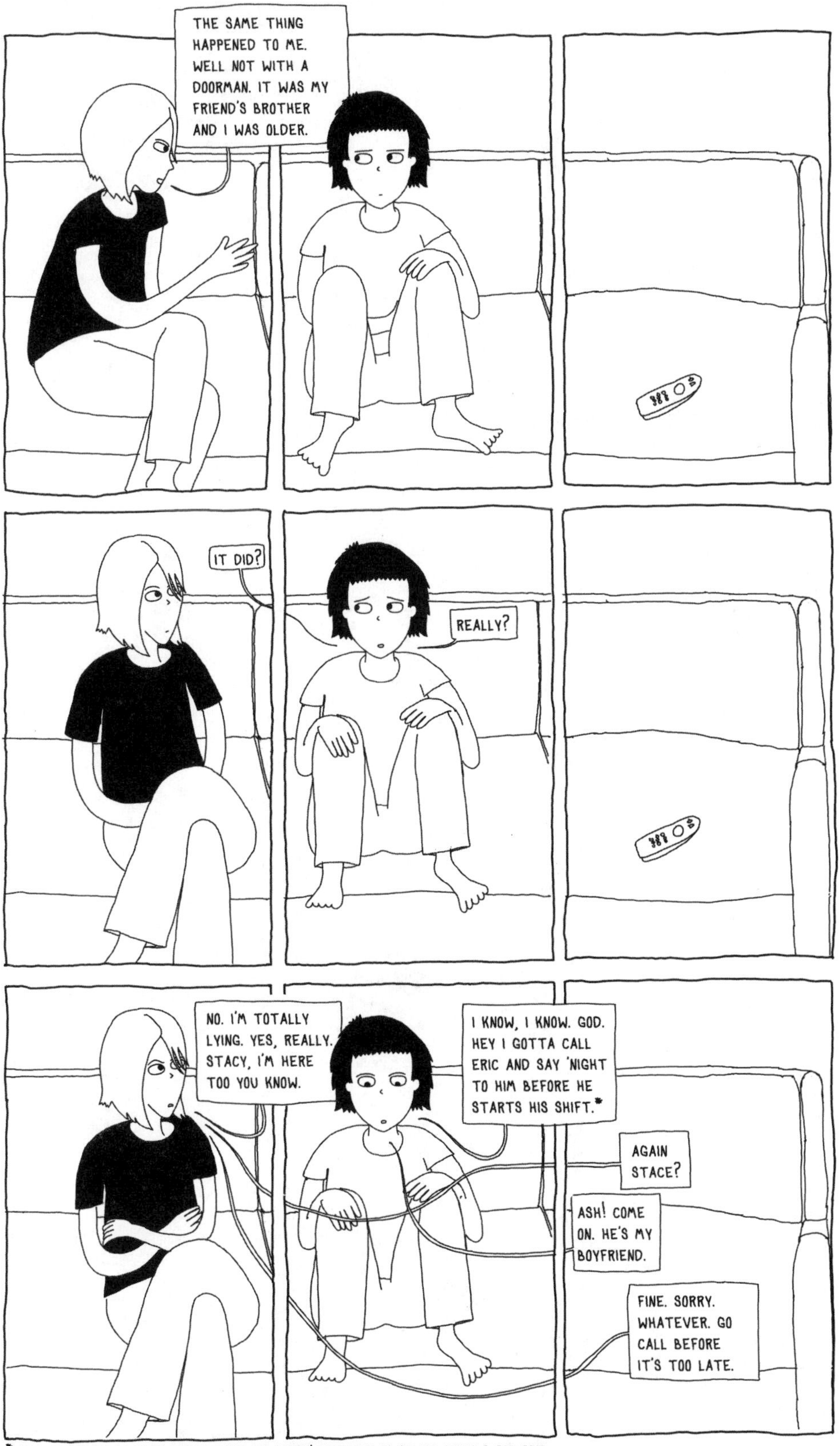
THE SAME THING HAPPENED TO ME. WELL NOT WITH A DOORMAN. IT WAS MY FRIEND'S BROTHER AND I WAS OLDER.
IT DID?
REALLY?
NO. I'M TOTALLY LYING. YES, REALLY. STACY, I'M HERE TOO YOU KNOW.
I KNOW, I KNOW. GOD. HEY I GOTTA CALL ERIC AND SAY 'NIGHT TO HIM BEFORE HE STARTS HIS SHIFT.*
AGAIN STACE?
ASH! COME ON. HE'S MY BOYFRIEND.
FINE. SORRY. WHATEVER. GO CALL BEFORE IT'S TOO LATE.

* ERIC WORKS AT A VEGAN RESTAURANT, HE DOESN'T BELIEVE IN KILLING ANIMALS FOR FOOD.

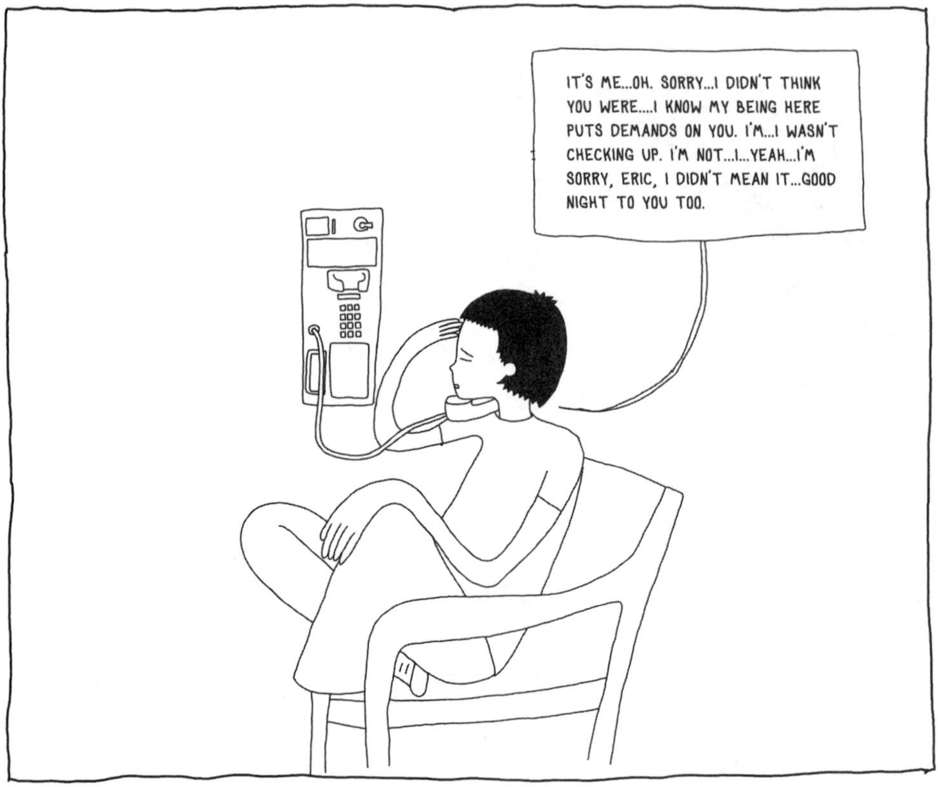
IT'S ME...OH. SORRY...I DIDN'T THINK YOU WERE....I KNOW MY BEING HERE PUTS DEMANDS ON YOU. I'M...I WASN'T CHECKING UP. I'M NOT...I...YEAH...I'M SORRY, ERIC, I DIDN'T MEAN IT...GOOD NIGHT TO YOU TOO.

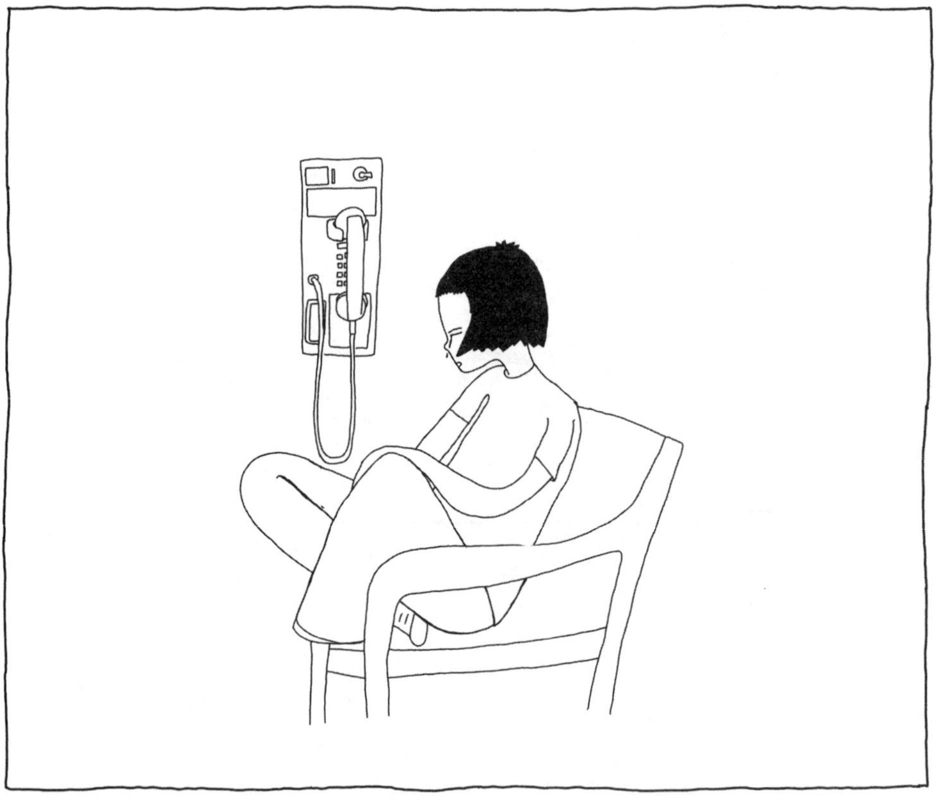

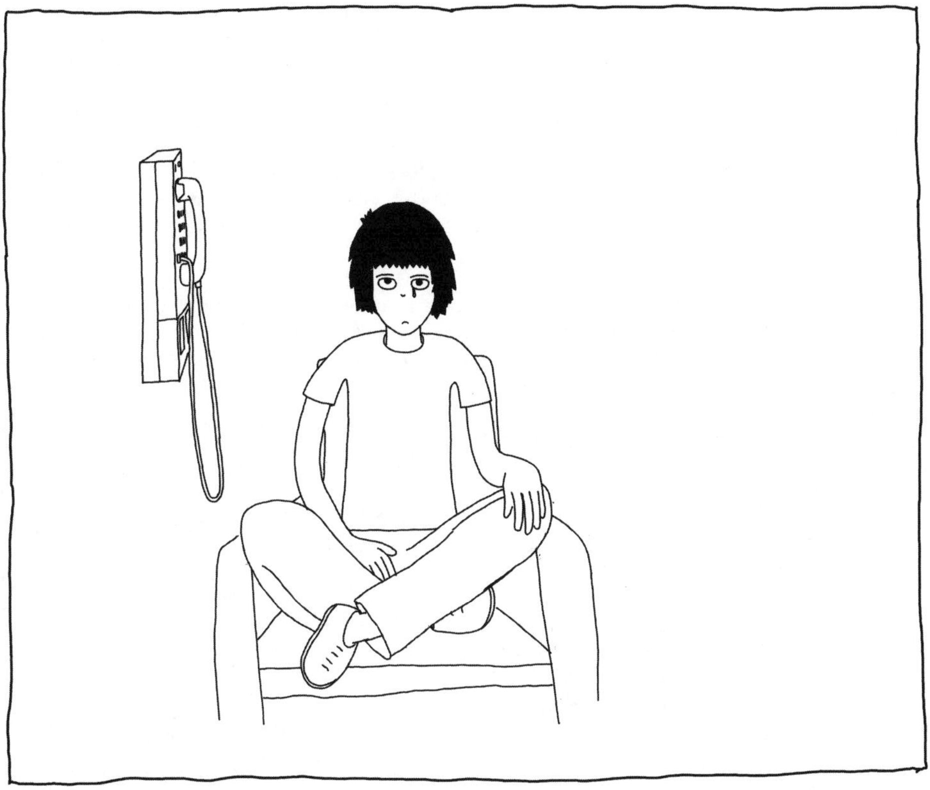

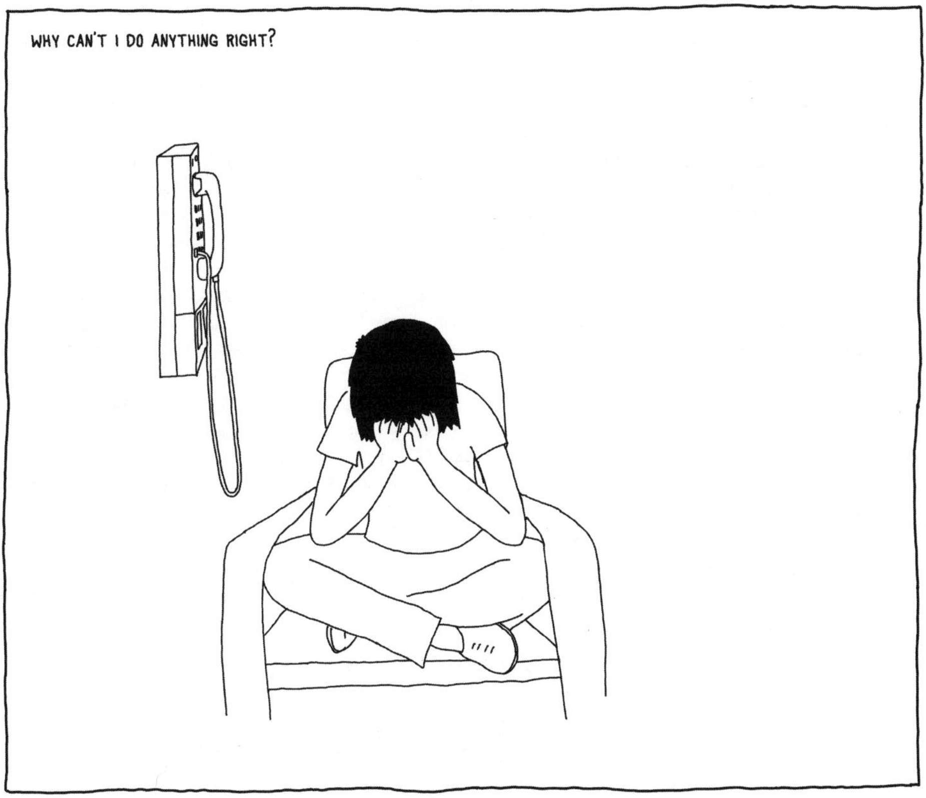
WHY CAN'T I DO ANYTHING RIGHT?

Does Stacy get along well with guys?

MARIA

STACY ALWAYS HAS GUYS AFTER HER. AND WHY NOT, SHE'S CUTE AND YES SHE HATES THAT WORD, BUT IT'S TRUE. STILL I KNOW SHE'D RATHER BE CALLED DIFFERENT OR UNIQUE OVER CUTE ANY DAY. ME? I'M HAPPY BEING CALLED CUTE. IT'S BETTER THAN WHAT I'M SOMETIMES CALLED 'CAUSE I'M FULL FIGURED NOT THIN LIKE HER.

SHE'S ALWAYS COMPLAINING ABOUT HER BODY BUT SHE CAN FIT INTO JUST ABOUT ANYTHING, INCLUDING A DRESS OF MINE SHE BORROWED THAT NOW FEELS LIKE A FAT DRESS WHEN I PUT IT ON. NEVER LEND CLOTHES TO SOMEONE SKINNIER THAN YOU. HER PROBLEM IS THAT SHE DOESN'T THINK SHE'S PRETTY AND SHE HAS NO CONFIDENCE. SHE'S SOMEHOW NEVER LEARNED TO TELL GUYS TO FUCK OFF.

TAKE ERIC, SHE NEEDS TO TELL HIM TO FUCK OFF — HE TREATS HER LIKE CRAP. I HATE ERIC. WHEN I CAME TO VISIT HER LAST WINTER I MET HIM AND HE BARELY SAID TWO WORDS TO ME. CLEARLY HE THOUGHT I WAS A THREAT TO HIS DOMINION. CLEARLY HE WANTED ME TO LEAVE. HE'D TELL STACE WHAT TO DO, AND HOW TO FEEL. YOU KNOW LIKE "STACY, WHY ARE YOU GETTING UPSET?. DON'T BE A BABY. WHY ARE YOU SO OVERLY SENSITIVE?"

STACE WAS ALL "HE'S AN ARTIST AND HE'S HAVING A HARD TIME." SHE COULDN'T SEE WHAT HE WAS DOING. I DOUBT SHE'D TELL HIM TO STOP EVEN IF SHE COULD. MAYBE SHE'LL LEARN HOW TO DO THAT IN THE HOSPITAL. HAVE SOME SELF-ESTEEM, I MEAN.

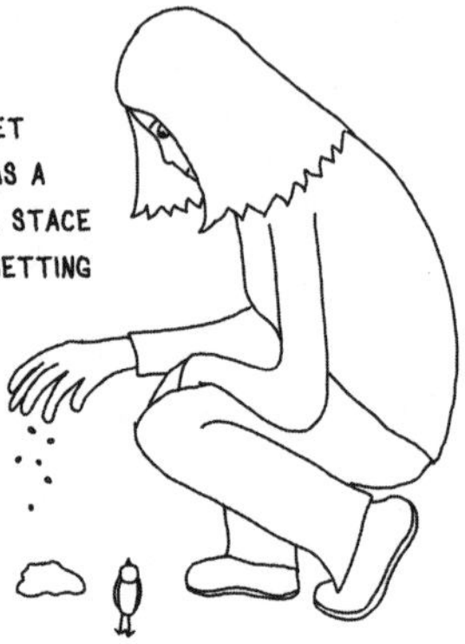

VIOLET

I HELPED STACY GET HER BOYFRIEND OUR FIRST SEMESTER AT BOARDING SCHOOL. SHE'S PRETTY SHY. PLUS SHE HAD LIKE NO EXPERIENCE. I REMEMBER THERE WAS THIS ONE GUY WHO CAME AROUND AFTER HOURS ONE NIGHT WHEN WE FIRST GOT THERE AND SINCE I WAS ON THE TOP BUNK I HEAR HIM SAY TO HER, "I FEEL LIKE I'M KISSING A SIXTH GRADER." CAN YOU IMAGINE? I MEAN THE GIRL HAD NO CONFIDENCE TO BEGIN WITH.

ANYWAY WE PLANNED OUT TO THE LAST DETAIL HOW SHE'D GET THIS OTHER GUY, ALEX, TO NOTICE HER. ON OUR WAY TO SKI TEAM PRACTICE STACY TOLD HIM WE HAD SOME VERMONT BUD — AND THEN I SAID I WAS TOO COLD AND THEY WENT OFF TO SMOKE AND WELL THAT WAS THAT...THEY HOOKED UP AND THEN THEY WERE TOGETHER.

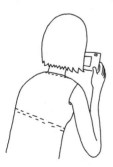

I WAS HAPPY FOR HER BUT THEN I NEVER SAW HER BECAUSE SHE WAS ALWAYS "ALEX THIS" AND "ALEX THAT" AND SHE HAD NO TIME FOR ANYONE ELSE TILL HE BROKE UP WITH HER FOR A SENIOR AND THEN SHE NEEDED SOMEONE TO CRY TO ABOUT HOW SHE SHOULDA BEEN A MORE PERFECT GIRLFRIEND. AT REHAB THEY SAY DEPEND ON YOURSELF, NOT ON ANYONE ELSE FOR YOUR HAPPINESS. MAYBE THEY'LL TELL HER THAT AT MEADOWS TOO.

LOLA

SHE'S ALWAYS SAYING THAT GUYS COME AROUND BECAUSE OF ME FIRST, HER SECOND. THEY CRUSH ON HER, BUT SHE SAYS IT'S ONLY THE SHORT ONES BECAUSE SHE'S SHORT TOO.

MY WHOLE LIFE MEN HAVE BEEN AFTER TO ME. I DON'T MEAN TO SOUND CONCEITED OR ANYTHING BUT IT'S TRUE. I'M CONSTANTLY GETTING WHISTLED AT AND HARASSED AND WHILE IT'S NICE TO GET THE ATTENTION, SOMETIMES I HATE IT. THANK GOD FOR HEADPHONES — THEY MAKE WALKING DOWN THE STREET A BREEZE.

MY MOM WAS ALWAYS VERY PROTECTIVE OF ME AND TOLD ME ALL THESE THINGS TO DO IF I FOUND MYSELF IN A "SITUATION" AND I TRY TO BE AS AWARE AS POSSIBLE. THE FIRST TIME I HAD SEX I WOULDN'T SAY IT WAS A RAPE, BUT I DIDN'T REALLY WANT TO DO IT BUT SOMEHOW COULDN'T SAY ANYTHING.

I WISH I HAD. ALL THAT ADVICE MY MOM GAVE ME WENT RIGHT OUT THE WINDOW.

ASHLEY

I DON'T REALLY KNOW HOW STACE IS WITH GUYS, JUST HOW SHE IS ABOUT ERIC. SHE'S MAD IN LOVE WITH HIM. ALMOST TOO MUCH. MAYBE. I DON'T KNOW.

SHE TALKS TO HIM LIKE FIVE TIMES A DAY, AND IN GROUP IT'S ALWAYS ERIC SAID THIS AND WHAT DO YOU ALL THINK WHEN IT SHOULD BE ABOUT WHAT SHE'S DOING AND THINKING.

BUT I HAVE TO SAY A PART OF ME IS JEALOUS. I'VE NEVER BEEN IN LOVE BEFORE.

CURRENT LENGTH OF STAY:

*eight weeks,
ten hours*

"Personality and Specific Developmental Problems: Pt. has considerable difficulty with most of the staff in terms of being able to share openly and honestly. She admittedly distances people with her negative attitude and angry persona.

Clinical Syndrome: Pt. has taken medication at bedtime for the past eight weeks. She has received considerable symptomatic relief. At this point my impression is that she was made hyper irritable by her insomnia and has been relieved of this and given some relief, at least in terms of sleeplessness."

From the weekly progress reports of Dr. Ross

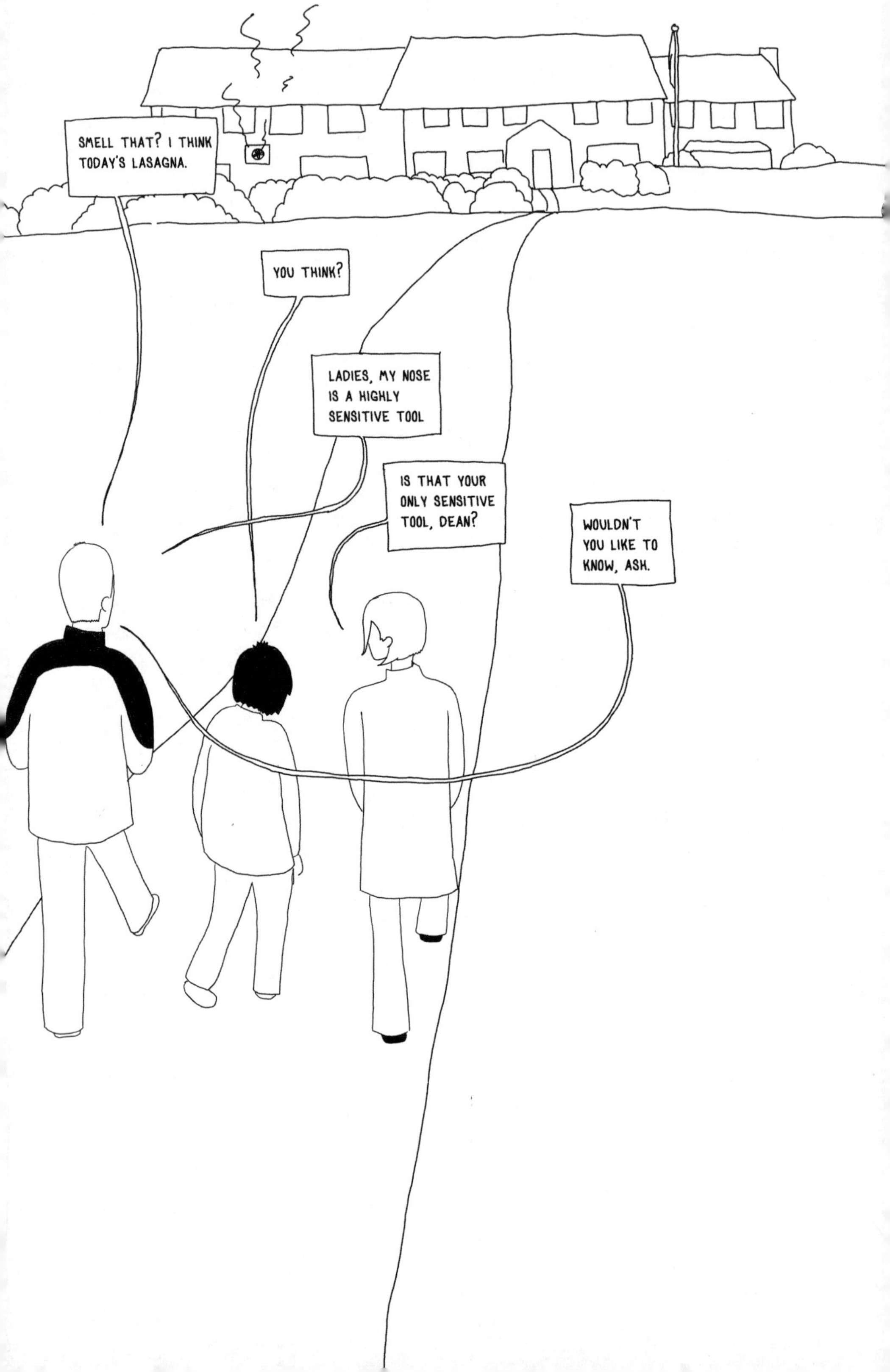

SMELL THAT? I THINK TODAY'S LASAGNA.
YOU THINK?
LADIES, MY NOSE IS A HIGHLY SENSITIVE TOOL
IS THAT YOUR ONLY SENSITIVE TOOL, DEAN?
WOULDN'T YOU LIKE TO KNOW, ASH.

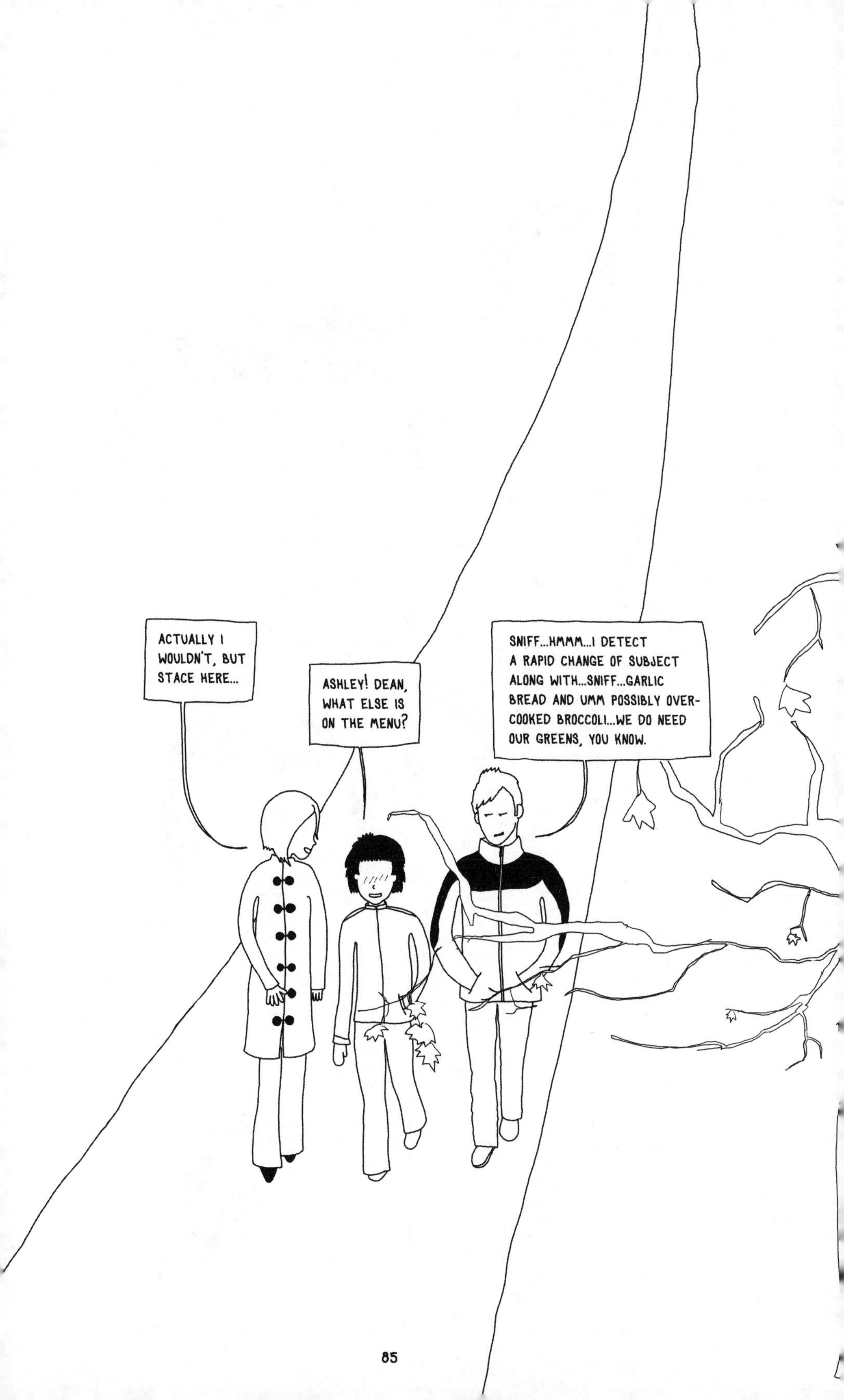
ACTUALLY I WOULDN'T, BUT STACE HERE...
ASHLEY! DEAN, WHAT ELSE IS ON THE MENU?
SNIFF...HMMM...I DETECT A RAPID CHANGE OF SUBJECT ALONG WITH...SNIFF...GARLIC BREAD AND UMM POSSIBLY OVER-COOKED BROCCOLI...WE DO NEED OUR GREENS, YOU KNOW.

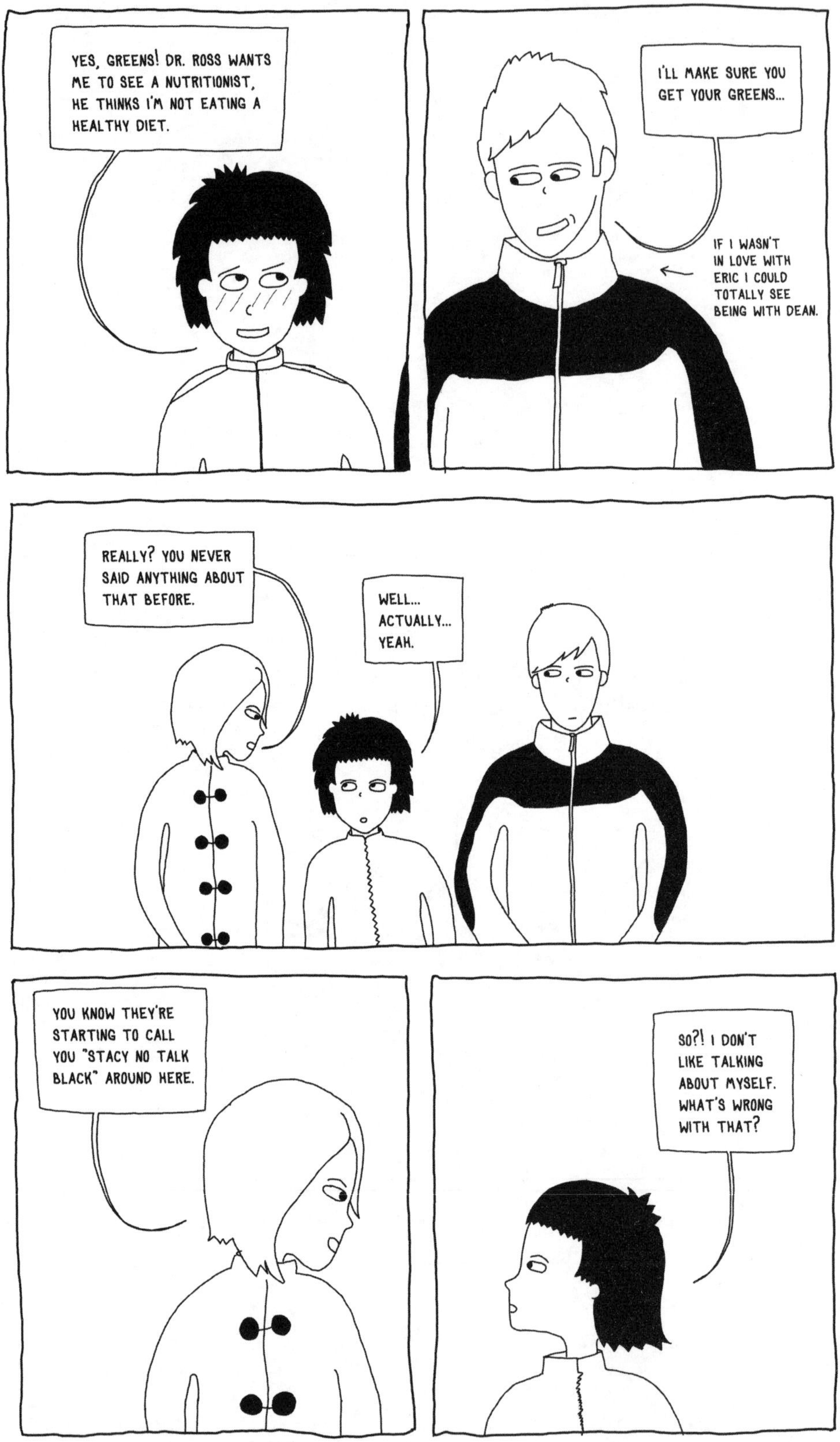
YES, GREENS! DR. ROSS WANTS ME TO SEE A NUTRITIONIST, HE THINKS I'M NOT EATING A HEALTHY DIET.
I'LL MAKE SURE YOU GET YOUR GREENS...
IF I WASN'T IN LOVE WITH ERIC I COULD TOTALLY SEE BEING WITH DEAN.
REALLY? YOU NEVER SAID ANYTHING ABOUT THAT BEFORE.
WELL... ACTUALLY... YEAH.
YOU KNOW THEY'RE STARTING TO CALL YOU "STACY NO TALK BLACK" AROUND HERE.
SO?! I DON'T LIKE TALKING ABOUT MYSELF. WHAT'S WRONG WITH THAT?

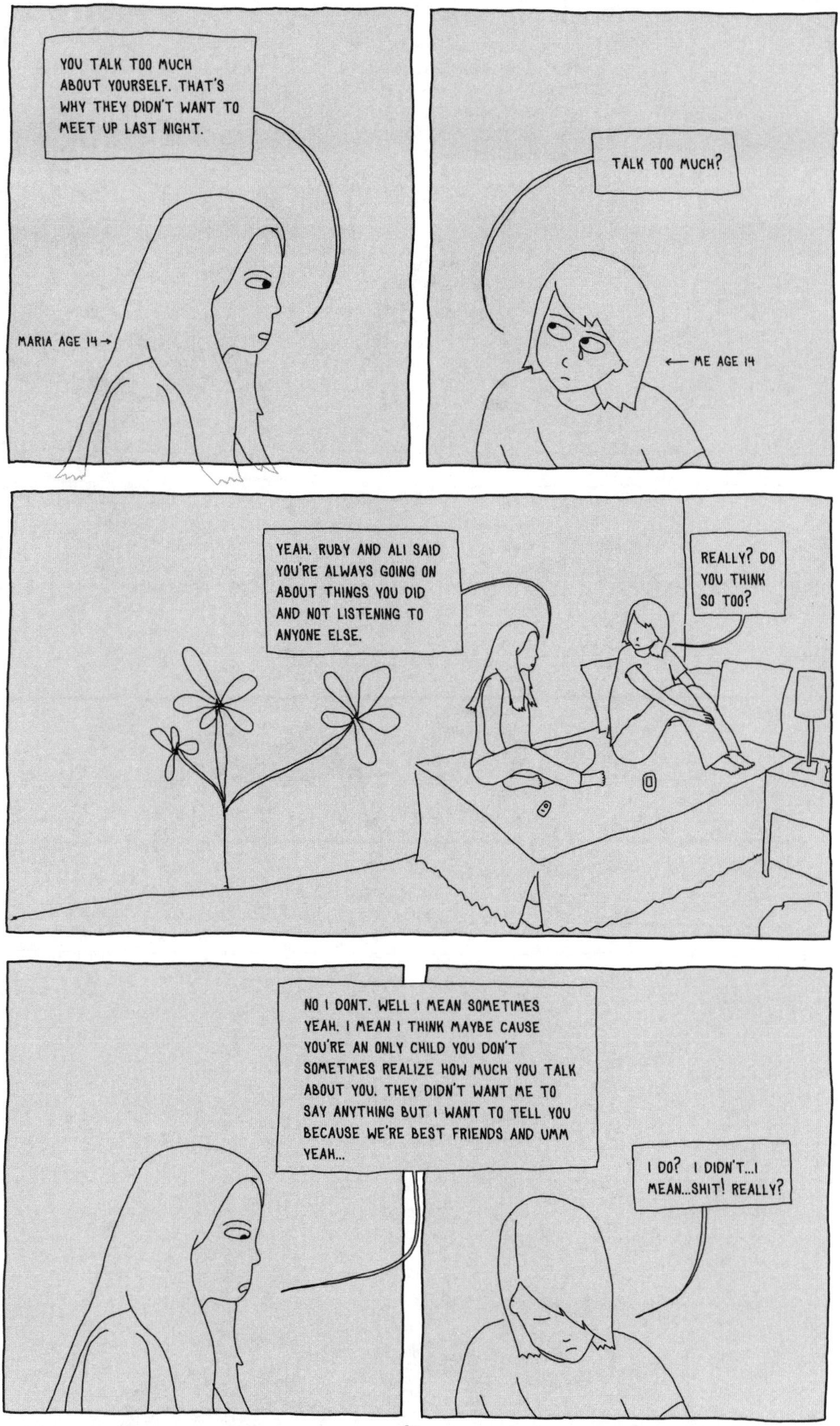
YOU TALK TOO MUCH ABOUT YOURSELF. THAT'S WHY THEY DIDN'T WANT TO MEET UP LAST NIGHT.
MARIA AGE 14 →
TALK TOO MUCH?
← ME AGE 14
YEAH. RUBY AND ALI SAID YOU'RE ALWAYS GOING ON ABOUT THINGS YOU DID AND NOT LISTENING TO ANYONE ELSE.
REALLY? DO YOU THINK SO TOO?
NO I DONT. WELL I MEAN SOMETIMES YEAH. I MEAN I THINK MAYBE CAUSE YOU'RE AN ONLY CHILD YOU DON'T SOMETIMES REALIZE HOW MUCH YOU TALK ABOUT YOU. THEY DIDN'T WANT ME TO SAY ANYTHING BUT I WANT TO TELL YOU BECAUSE WE'RE BEST FRIENDS AND UMM YEAH...
I DO? I DIDN'T...I MEAN...SHIT! REALLY?

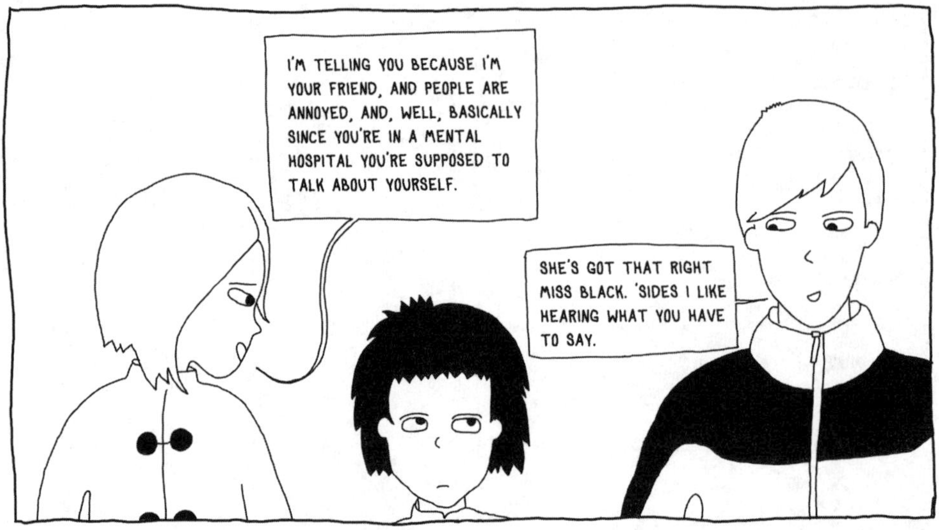
I'M TELLING YOU BECAUSE I'M YOUR FRIEND, AND PEOPLE ARE ANNOYED, AND, WELL, BASICALLY SINCE YOU'RE IN A MENTAL HOSPITAL YOU'RE SUPPOSED TO TALK ABOUT YOURSELF.
SHE'S GOT THAT RIGHT MISS BLACK. 'SIDES I LIKE HEARING WHAT YOU HAVE TO SAY.

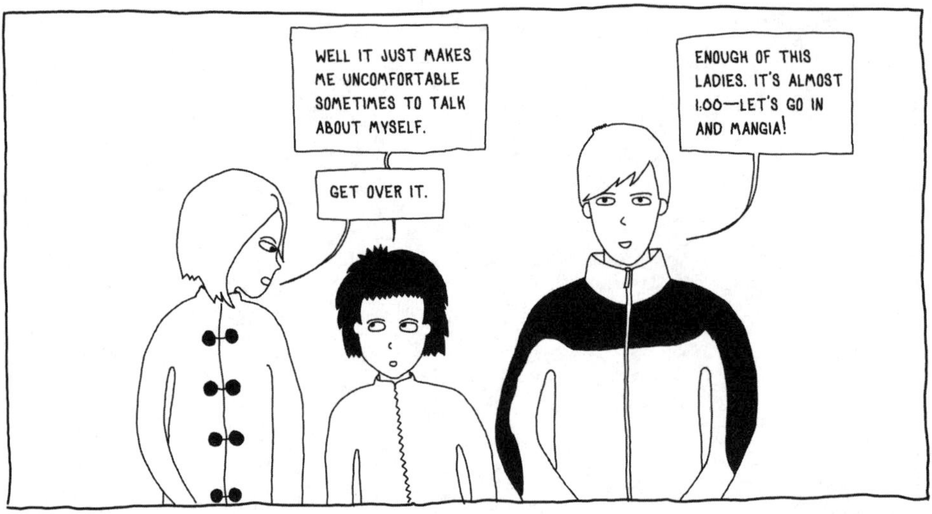
WELL IT JUST MAKES ME UNCOMFORTABLE SOMETIMES TO TALK ABOUT MYSELF.
GET OVER IT.
ENOUGH OF THIS LADIES. IT'S ALMOST 1:00—LET'S GO IN AND MANGIA!

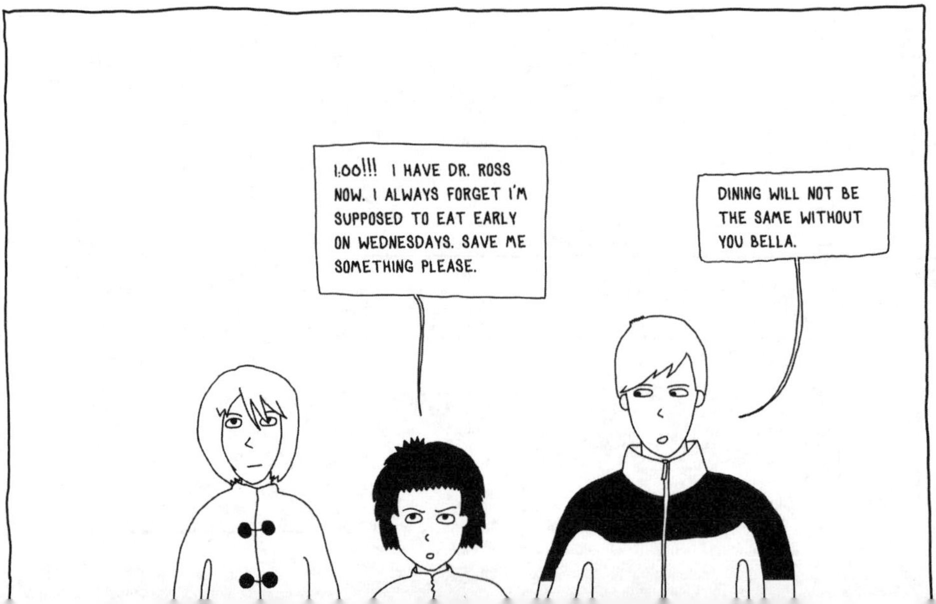
1:00!!! I HAVE DR. ROSS NOW. I ALWAYS FORGET I'M SUPPOSED TO EAT EARLY ON WEDNESDAYS. SAVE ME SOMETHING PLEASE.
DINING WILL NOT BE THE SAME WITHOUT YOU BELLA.

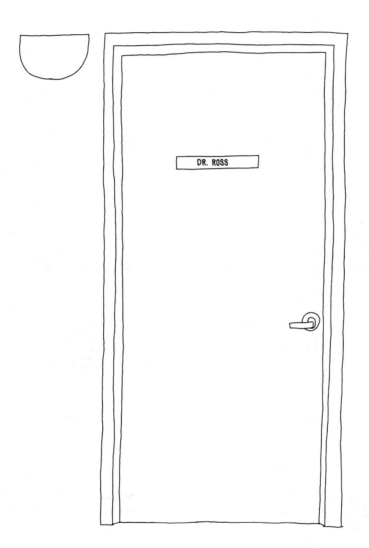

DR. ROSS

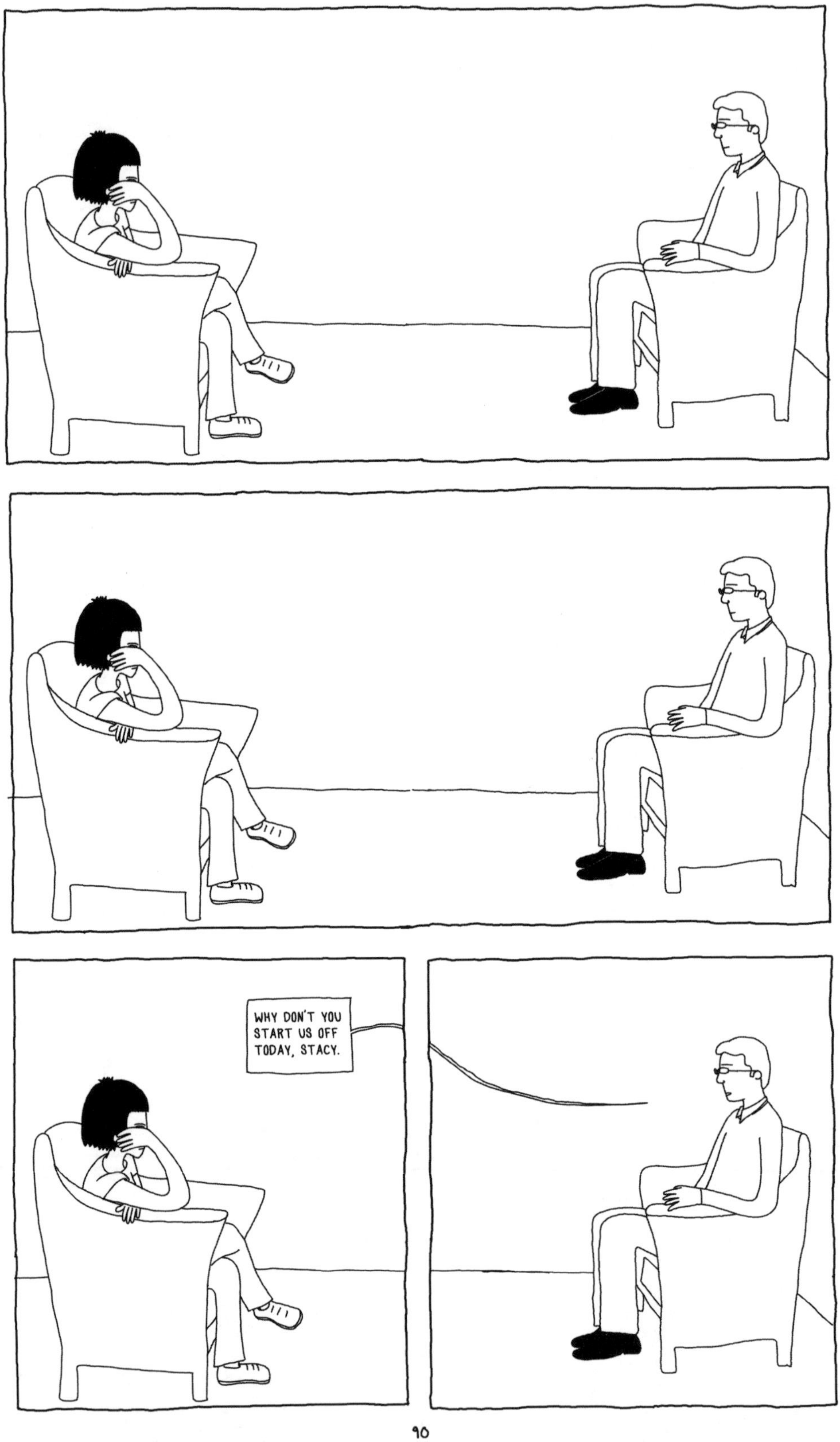
WHY DON'T YOU START US OFF TODAY, STACY.

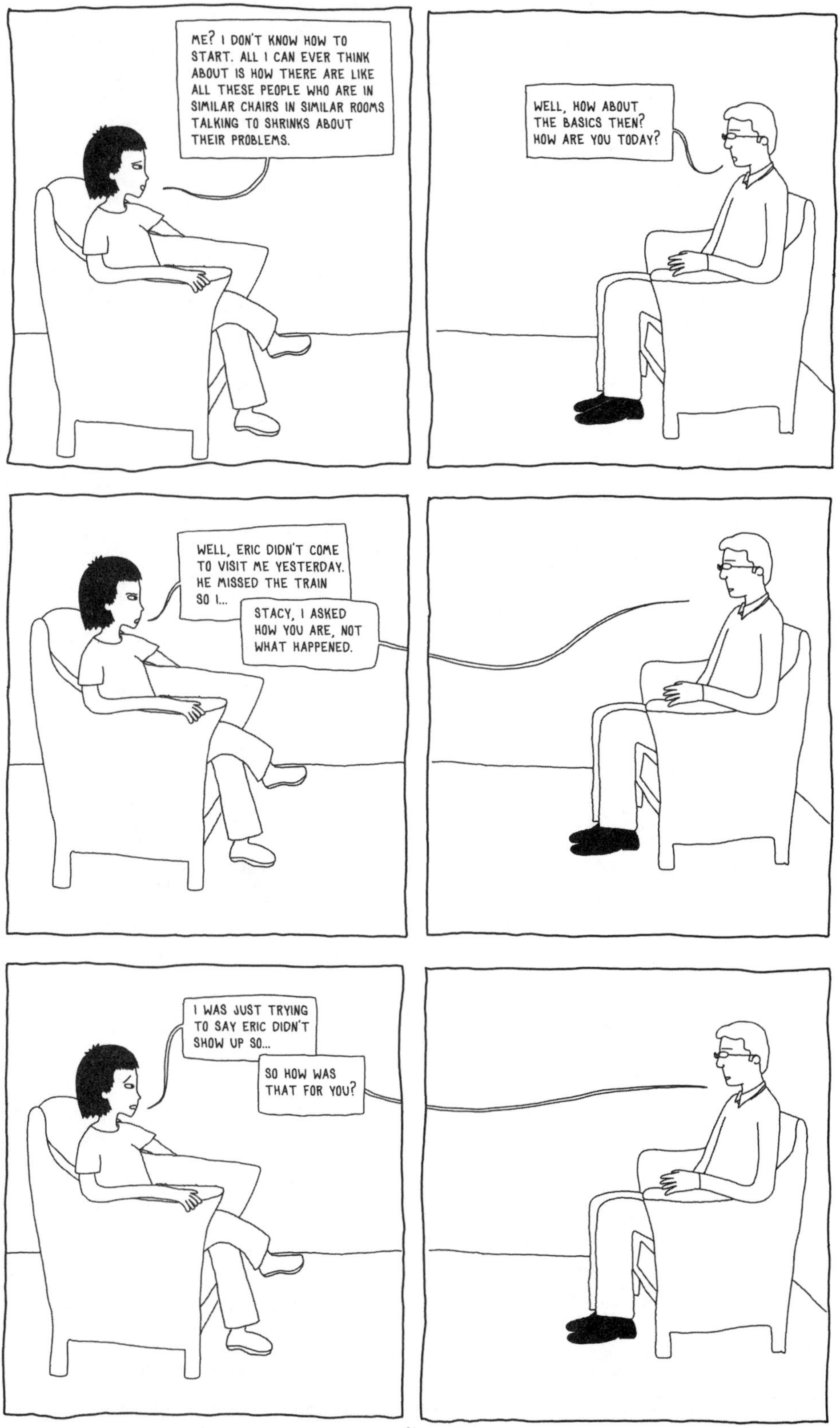
ME? I DON'T KNOW HOW TO START. ALL I CAN EVER THINK ABOUT IS HOW THERE ARE LIKE ALL THESE PEOPLE WHO ARE IN SIMILAR CHAIRS IN SIMILAR ROOMS TALKING TO SHRINKS ABOUT THEIR PROBLEMS.
WELL, HOW ABOUT THE BASICS THEN? HOW ARE YOU TODAY?
WELL, ERIC DIDN'T COME TO VISIT ME YESTERDAY. HE MISSED THE TRAIN SO I...
STACY, I ASKED HOW YOU ARE, NOT WHAT HAPPENED.
I WAS JUST TRYING TO SAY ERIC DIDN'T SHOW UP SO...
SO HOW WAS THAT FOR YOU?

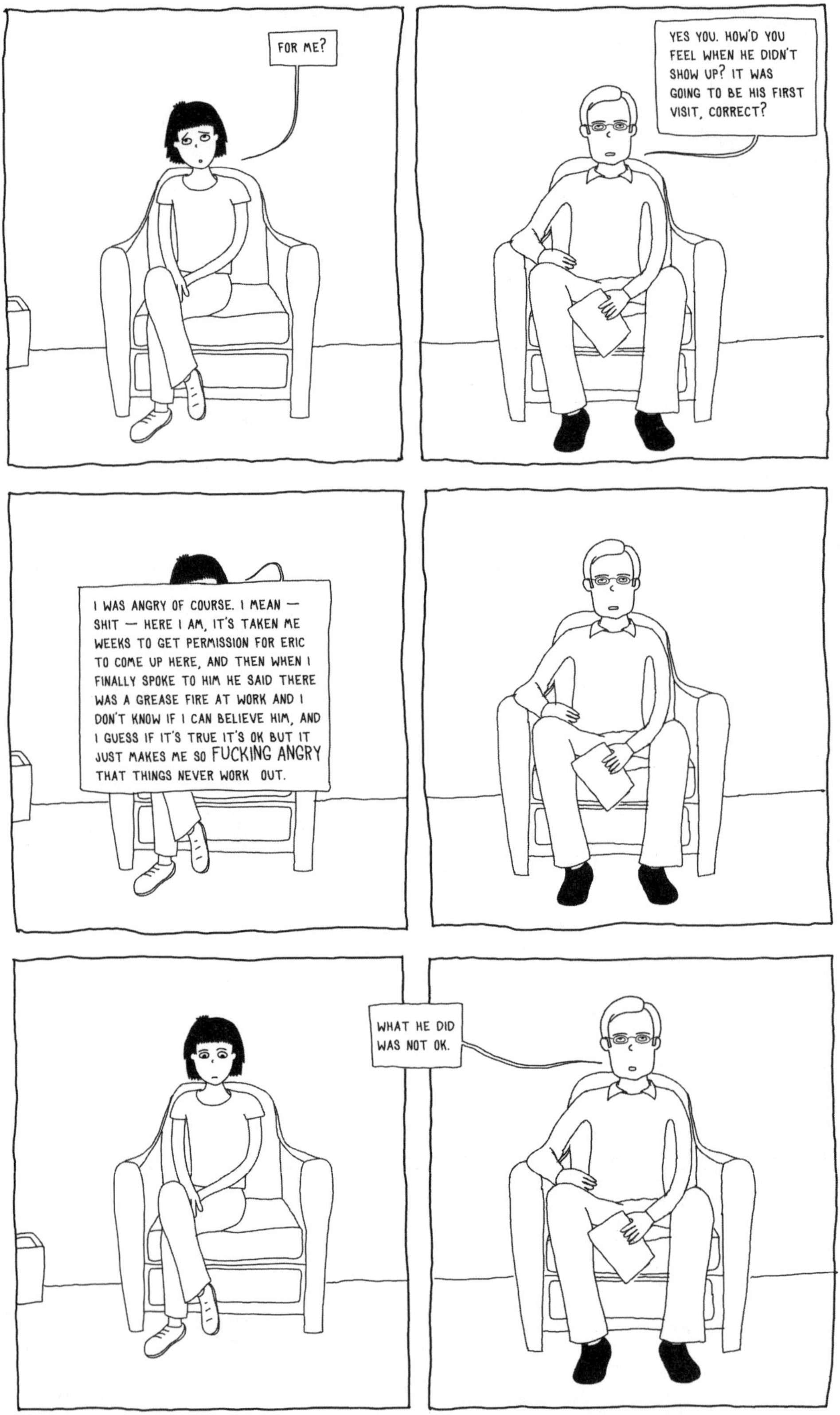
FOR ME?
YES YOU. HOW'D YOU FEEL WHEN HE DIDN'T SHOW UP? IT WAS GOING TO BE HIS FIRST VISIT, CORRECT?
I WAS ANGRY OF COURSE. I MEAN — SHIT — HERE I AM, IT'S TAKEN ME WEEKS TO GET PERMISSION FOR ERIC TO COME UP HERE, AND THEN WHEN I FINALLY SPOKE TO HIM HE SAID THERE WAS A GREASE FIRE AT WORK AND I DON'T KNOW IF I CAN BELIEVE HIM, AND I GUESS IF IT'S TRUE IT'S OK BUT IT JUST MAKES ME SO FUCKING ANGRY THAT THINGS NEVER WORK OUT.
WHAT HE DID WAS NOT OK.

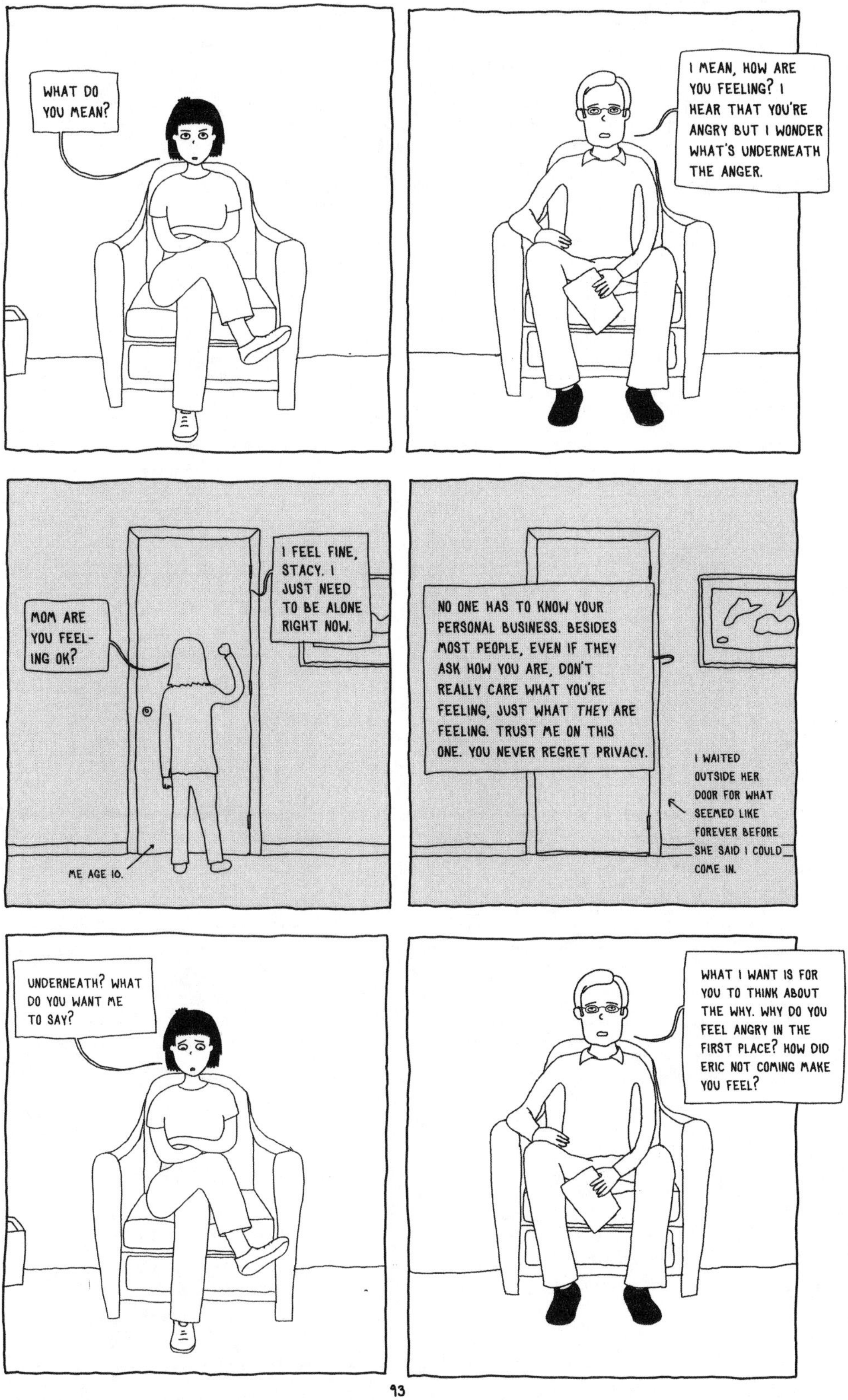
WHAT DO YOU MEAN?
I MEAN, HOW ARE YOU FEELING? I HEAR THAT YOU'RE ANGRY BUT I WONDER WHAT'S UNDERNEATH THE ANGER.
MOM ARE YOU FEEL-ING OK?
I FEEL FINE, STACY. I JUST NEED TO BE ALONE RIGHT NOW.
ME AGE 10.
NO ONE HAS TO KNOW YOUR PERSONAL BUSINESS. BESIDES MOST PEOPLE, EVEN IF THEY ASK HOW YOU ARE, DON'T REALLY CARE WHAT YOU'RE FEELING, JUST WHAT *THEY* ARE FEELING. TRUST ME ON THIS ONE. YOU NEVER REGRET PRIVACY.
I WAITED OUTSIDE HER DOOR FOR WHAT SEEMED LIKE FOREVER BEFORE SHE SAID I COULD COME IN.
UNDERNEATH? WHAT DO YOU WANT ME TO SAY?
WHAT I WANT IS FOR YOU TO THINK ABOUT THE WHY. WHY DO YOU FEEL ANGRY IN THE FIRST PLACE? HOW DID ERIC NOT COMING MAKE YOU FEEL?

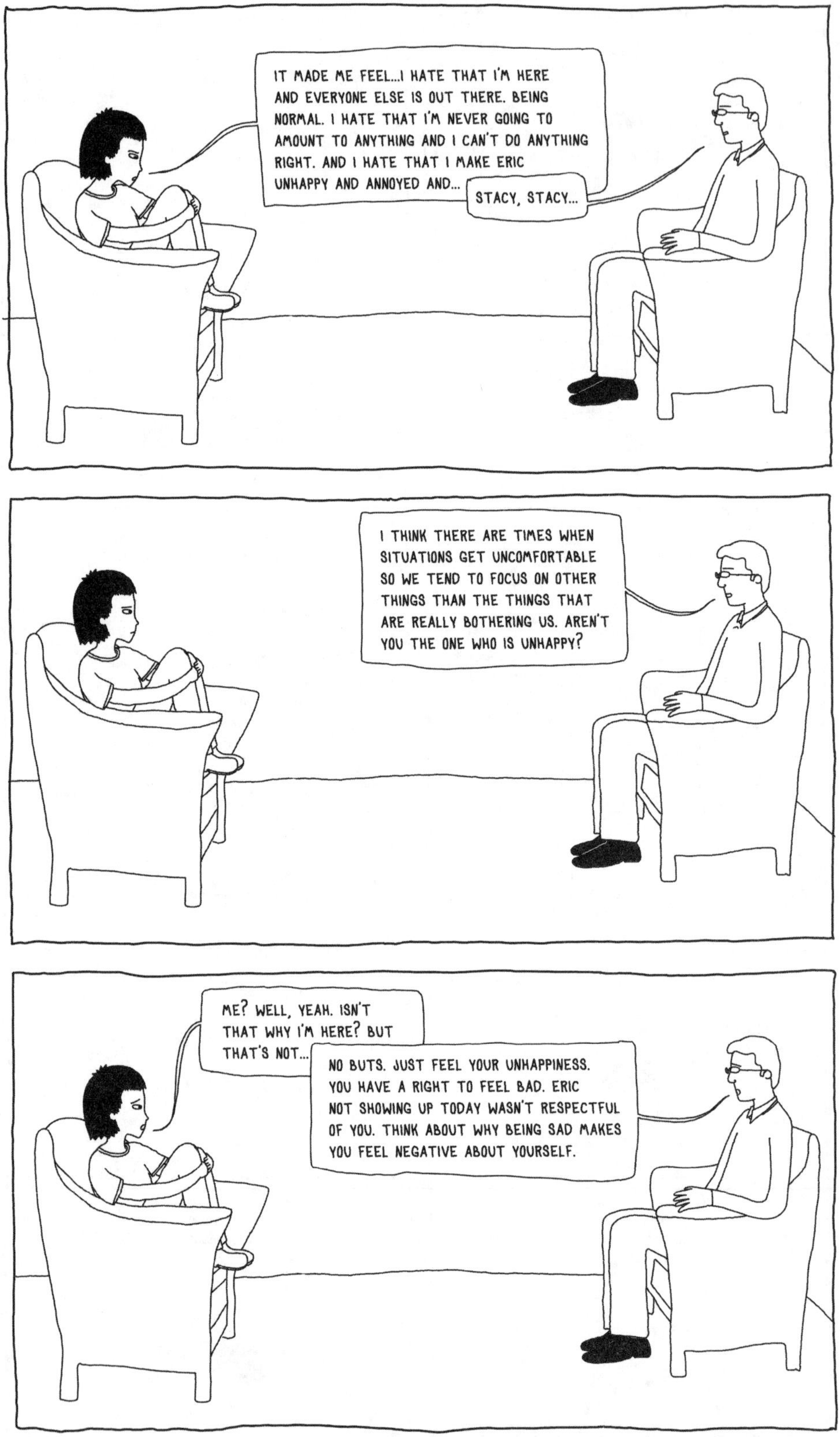
IT MADE ME FEEL...I HATE THAT I'M HERE AND EVERYONE ELSE IS OUT THERE. BEING NORMAL. I HATE THAT I'M NEVER GOING TO AMOUNT TO ANYTHING AND I CAN'T DO ANYTHING RIGHT. AND I HATE THAT I MAKE ERIC UNHAPPY AND ANNOYED AND...
STACY, STACY...
I THINK THERE ARE TIMES WHEN SITUATIONS GET UNCOMFORTABLE SO WE TEND TO FOCUS ON OTHER THINGS THAN THE THINGS THAT ARE REALLY BOTHERING US. AREN'T YOU THE ONE WHO IS UNHAPPY?
ME? WELL, YEAH. ISN'T THAT WHY I'M HERE? BUT THAT'S NOT...
NO BUTS. JUST FEEL YOUR UNHAPPINESS. YOU HAVE A RIGHT TO FEEL BAD. ERIC NOT SHOWING UP TODAY WASN'T RESPECTFUL OF YOU. THINK ABOUT WHY BEING SAD MAKES YOU FEEL NEGATIVE ABOUT YOURSELF.

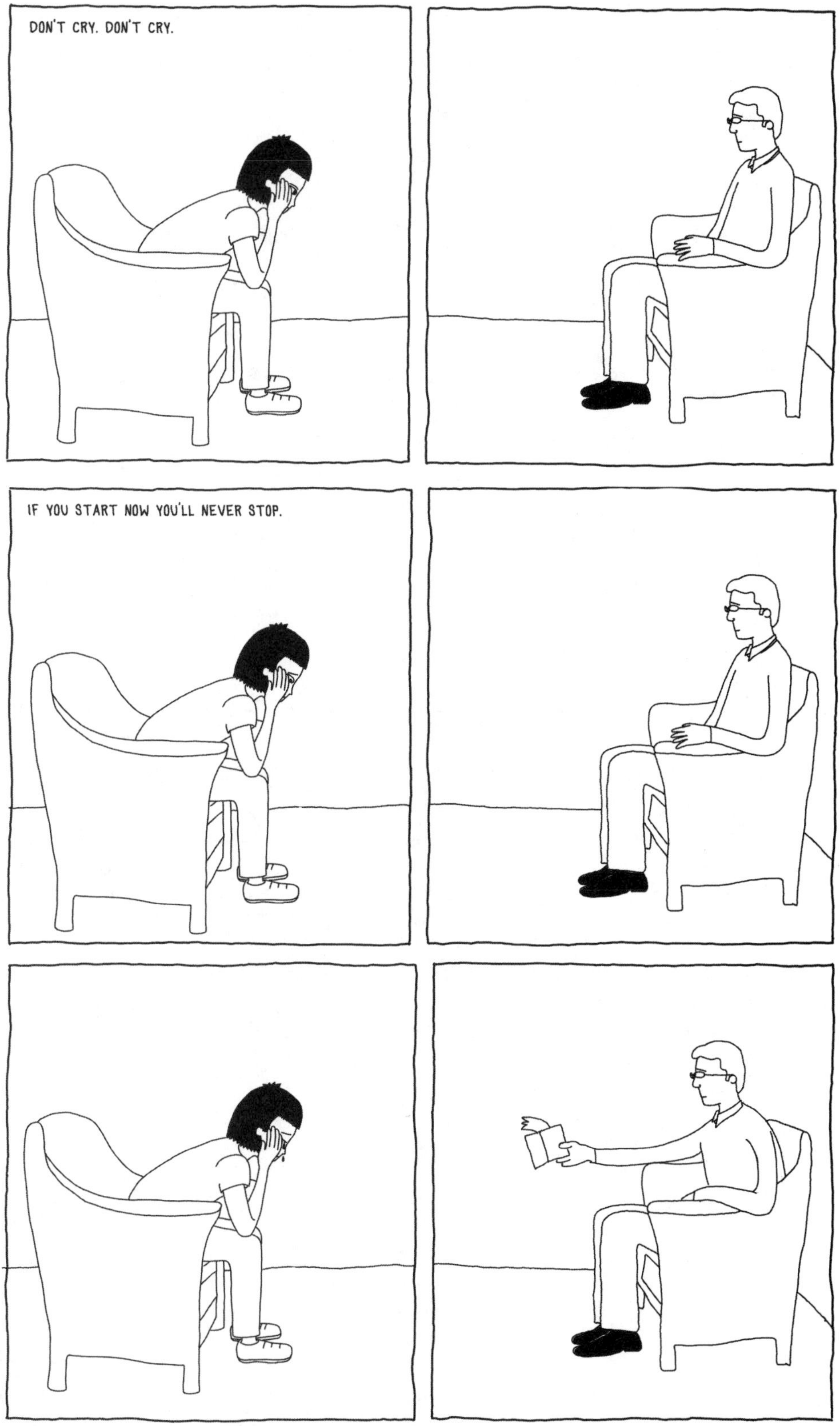
DON'T CRY. DON'T CRY.
IF YOU START NOW YOU'LL NEVER STOP.

How does Stacy deal with her feelings?
Do you think she has anger issues?

MARIA

ANGER ISSUES...UMM..WELL SHE'S ONE OF THE MOST SARCASTIC PEOPLE I KNOW, NOT SURE IF THAT COUNTS AS ANGER. SOMETIMES WHEN SHE'S DRUNK SHE CAN GET A BIT OUT OF CONTROL. NOT YELLING AT PEOPLE OR ANYTHING, MORE LIKE SHE GETS INTO THESE MOODS.

LIKE ONE TIME WE WERE STUMBLING AROUND THE CITY DRUNK AND SHE FOUND THIS PIPE AND SHE STARTED HITTING EVERY FIRE HYDRANT WE WALKED BY REALLY HARD. THINGS LIKE THAT.

NORMALLY THOUGH, STACY IS PRETTY QUIET ABOUT STUFF — SHE'S MORE PRIVATE, YOU KNOW. SHE'S NOT BIG ON LETTING PEOPLE IN. WHICH I CAN RESPECT.

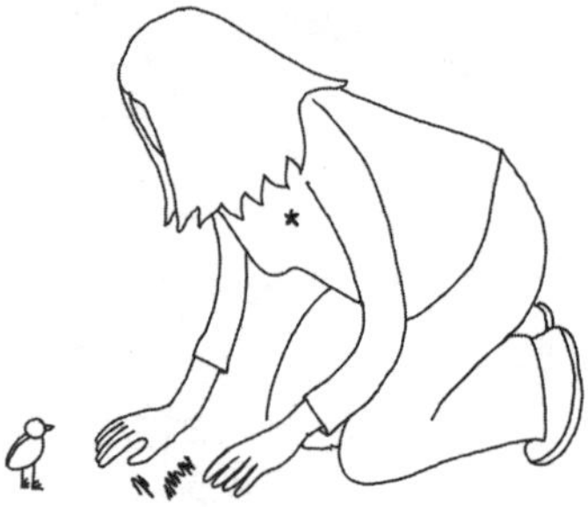

VIOLET

I NEVER THOUGHT ABOUT STACY BEING ANGRY. OR REALLY GETTING UPSET ABOUT MUCH. AT SCHOOL SHE WAS JUST SPACY STACY OR STACE IN SPACE YOU KNOW, SORTA ALWAYS FLOATING AROUND. I DON'T THINK SHE, OR EITHER OF US, REALLY CARED ENOUGH TO BE ANGRY. AND WE DEFINITELY DIDN'T THINK MOST PEOPLE WERE WORTH OUR TIME. TRUE WE'D MAKE FUN OF SOME PEOPLE BUT THEY SO DESERVED IT. WELL, WE THOUGHT THEY DID. WHEN I LOOK BACK I CAN SEE WE JUST WERE HIDING OUR TRUE FEELINGS.

I REALIZE NOW THAT EVERYONE SHOULD BE RESPECTED BUT THAT RESPECT HAS TO START WITHIN OURSELVES. NEITHER STACE NOR I EVER RESPECTED OURSELVES ENOUGH NOT TO ABUSE DRUGS OR GET INTO TROUBLE, OR FACE OUR EMOTIONS AND THAT'S THE REAL ISSUE. AT LEAST FOR ME IT IS.

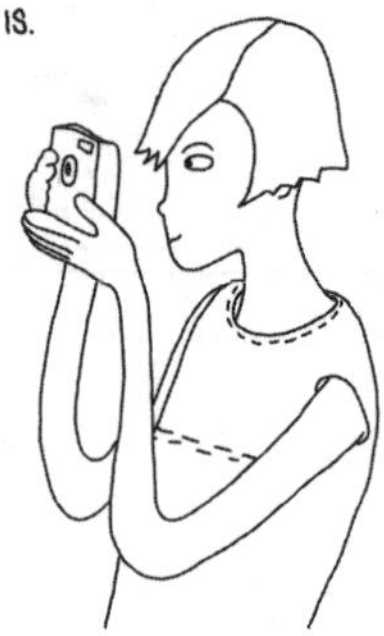

LOLA

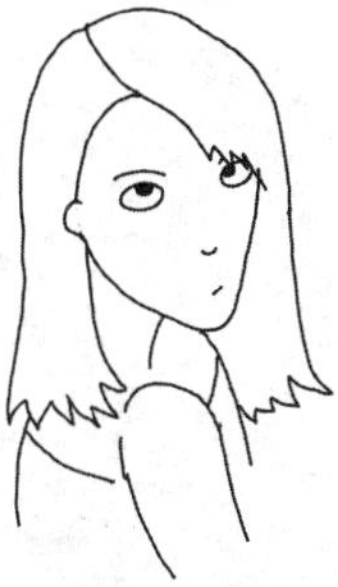

WELL, I MENTIONED THAT I HAD A DREAM, RIGHT? THE ONE WHERE I DREAMT THAT STACY WAS IN A WHITE ROOM BREAKING THINGS? I'M PRETTY SURE I VIBED OFF HER. SO YEAH, SHE'S GOT SOME PENT-UP RAGE THAT NEEDS LETTING OUT. STACY'S PROBLEM IS SHE DOESN'T KNOW HOW TO RELEASE HER FEELINGS — KEEPS EVERYTHING BOTTELED UP.

I THINK THAT'S WHY I FIND ACTING SO CATHARTIC — I GET TO PLAY ALL THESE DIFFERENT PARTS: ANGRY, SAD, AFRAID, AND I GET IT ALL OUT THERE. I HOPE AT THE HOSPITAL THEY'LL HELP HER.

I MEAN, THAT DREAM WAS SCARY AND I'VE SEEN HER DO THINGS...LIKE YOU KNOW THAT GAME WHERE YOU SPREAD OUT THE FINGERS OF YOUR HAND ON A TABLE AND THEN TAKE A KNIFE AND REALLY FAST STAB THE POINT BETWEEN THE SPACES OF YOUR FINGERS? SHE LOVES TO PLAY THAT — GOES REALLY FAST — I DON'T KNOW HOW SHE DOES IT. SHE HASN'T HURT HERSELF YET BUT I'M WAITING FOR THE DAY SHE PIERCES HER PINKY.

I ALWAYS HOLD MY BREATH WHEN SHE DOES IT.

ASHLEY

STACY IS THE QUEEN OF SARCASM. I THINK THAT'S A MANIFESTATION OF ANGER, AT LEAST THAT'S WHAT THEY SAY IN GROUP. MY GUESS IS THE ANGER'S A SHIELD. WE ALL HAVE THEM.

THE THING IS HERE IN MEADOWS WE HAVE TO LEARN HOW TO LOWER OUR DEFENSES, BUT IT'S HARD TO DO SOMETHING ONE WAY WHEN YOUR WHOLE LIFE YOU'VE BEEN DOING IT ANOTHER.

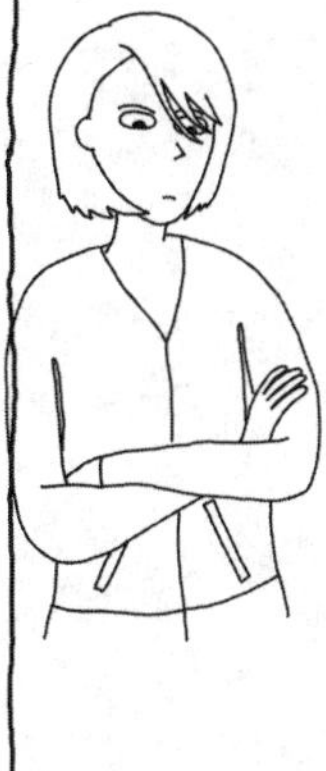

CURRENT LENGTH OF STAY:

nine weeks,
four days

"Initially [the patient's mother] has a tendency to come on in a strong, demanding manner. I found her surprsingly unaware of her daughter's difficulty, even to the extent that she said, 'I did not know there was anything wrong with my daughter.' The patient's mother seems to be expecting me to control aspects of her behavior that are ultimately not controllable. She has taken the position of not understanding that her child has a serious psychiatric condition. She also would like not to accept responsiblity for either the difficulty or its ultimate resolution."

From the family therapy files of Stacy Black

JUST BECAUSE YOU LOVE
SOMEONE DOESN'T MEAN
YOU HAVE TO LIKE THEM.

EVEN WHEN
IT'S YOUR MOM.

HERE FOR
FAMILY THERAPY
TWICE A MONTH.

BESIDES, IT'S NOT LIKE SHE WAS EVER THE WARM, FUZZY TYPE WHEN I WAS LITTLE.

LET'S GO. WE'RE GONNA BE LATE FOR DR. ROSS.

IN FACT, I'D SAY I WAS RAISED ON "THE LESS SAID THE BETTER."

HOW WAS SCHOOL?

FINE.

GOOD.

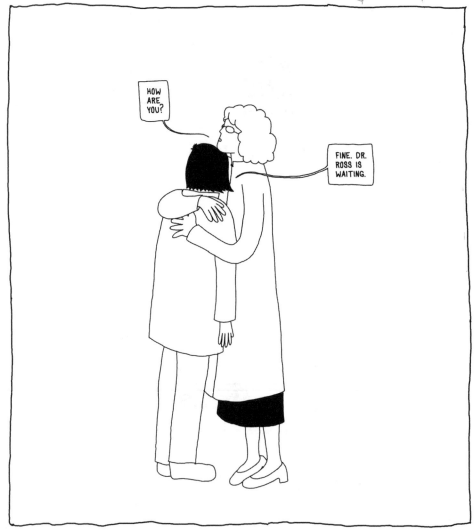

HOW ARE YOU?

FINE. DR. ROSS IS WAITING.

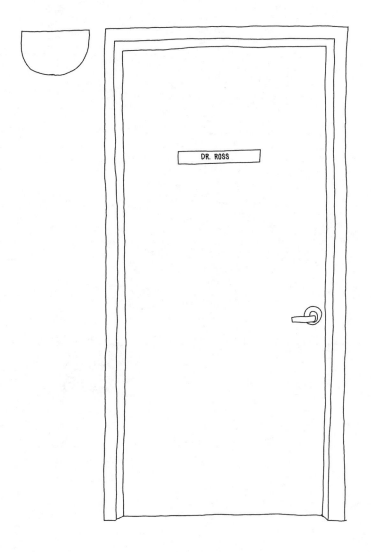

DR. ROSS

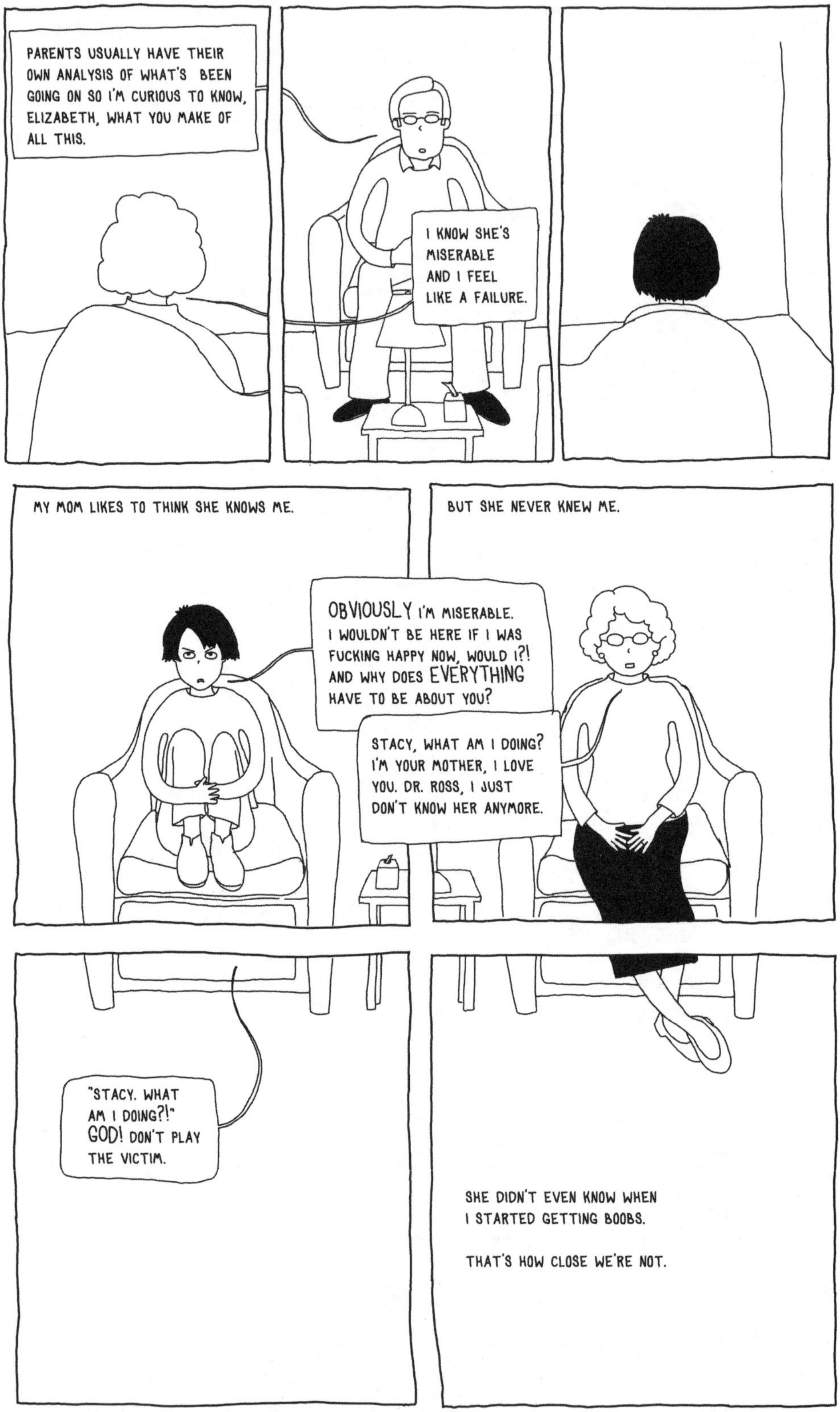
PARENTS USUALLY HAVE THEIR OWN ANALYSIS OF WHAT'S BEEN GOING ON SO I'M CURIOUS TO KNOW, ELIZABETH, WHAT YOU MAKE OF ALL THIS.
I KNOW SHE'S MISERABLE AND I FEEL LIKE A FAILURE.
MY MOM LIKES TO THINK SHE KNOWS ME.
BUT SHE NEVER KNEW ME.
OBVIOUSLY I'M MISERABLE. I WOULDN'T BE HERE IF I WAS FUCKING HAPPY NOW, WOULD I?! AND WHY DOES EVERYTHING HAVE TO BE ABOUT YOU?
STACY, WHAT AM I DOING? I'M YOUR MOTHER, I LOVE YOU. DR. ROSS, I JUST DON'T KNOW HER ANYMORE.
"STACY. WHAT AM I DOING?!" GOD! DON'T PLAY THE VICTIM.
SHE DIDN'T EVEN KNOW WHEN I STARTED GETTING BOOBS.
THAT'S HOW CLOSE WE'RE NOT.

I WAS THIRTEEN WHEN I STARTED DEVELOPING.

I WAS UNCOMFORTABLE WITH MY BODY. NOT READY.

I STILL LIKED RAINBOWS AND MARILYN MONROE.

ALMOST CAN'T TELL.

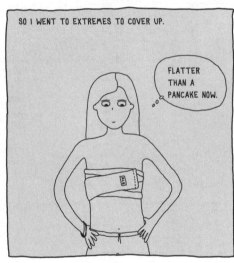

SO I WENT TO EXTREMES TO COVER UP.

FLATTER THAN A PANCAKE NOW.

IT WASN'T UNTIL MY BEST FRIEND MARIA HIT PUBERTY AND GOT HER OWN BRA THAT I GOT ONE TOO.

LOOK WHAT MY MOM BOUGHT ME.

CAN I BORROW IT?

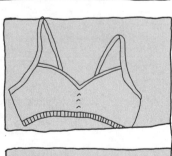

SURE!

STACY, PLEASE LET YOUR MOTHER SPEAK. GO ON, ELIZABETH.
WELL, I THINK HER FRIENDS ARE DELINQUENT DRUG ABUSERS.
I KNOW YOU MEAN ERIC. AND YOU DON'T KNOW HIM
I DON'T NEED TO KNOW HIM. I CAN SEE HIM. HE'S A DROPOUT. WHAT ARE YOU DOING WITH A GUY LIKE THAT?
DON'T YOU THINK YOU COULD HAVE DONE BETTER ON THE TEST? WHAT WILL YOU DO IN MIDDLE SCHOOL?
EIGHTH GRADE IS CRITICAL, STACY. YOU HAVE TO. APPLY YOURSELF.
WHEN I WAS SIXTEEN I WAS ALREADY IN COLLEGE.
IF YOU DON'T KEEP UP YOUR GRADES YOU'LL NEVER GET INTO A GOOD UNIVERSITY.

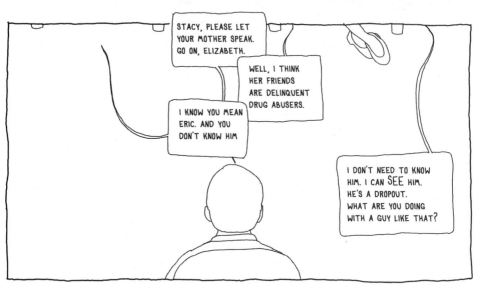

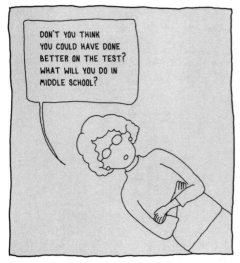

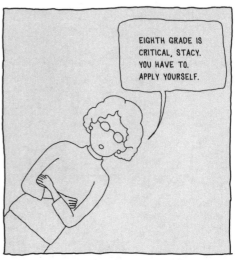

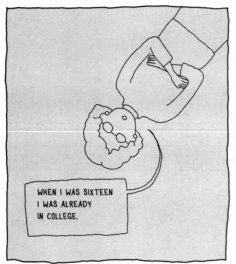

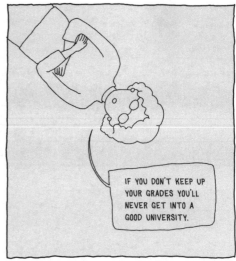

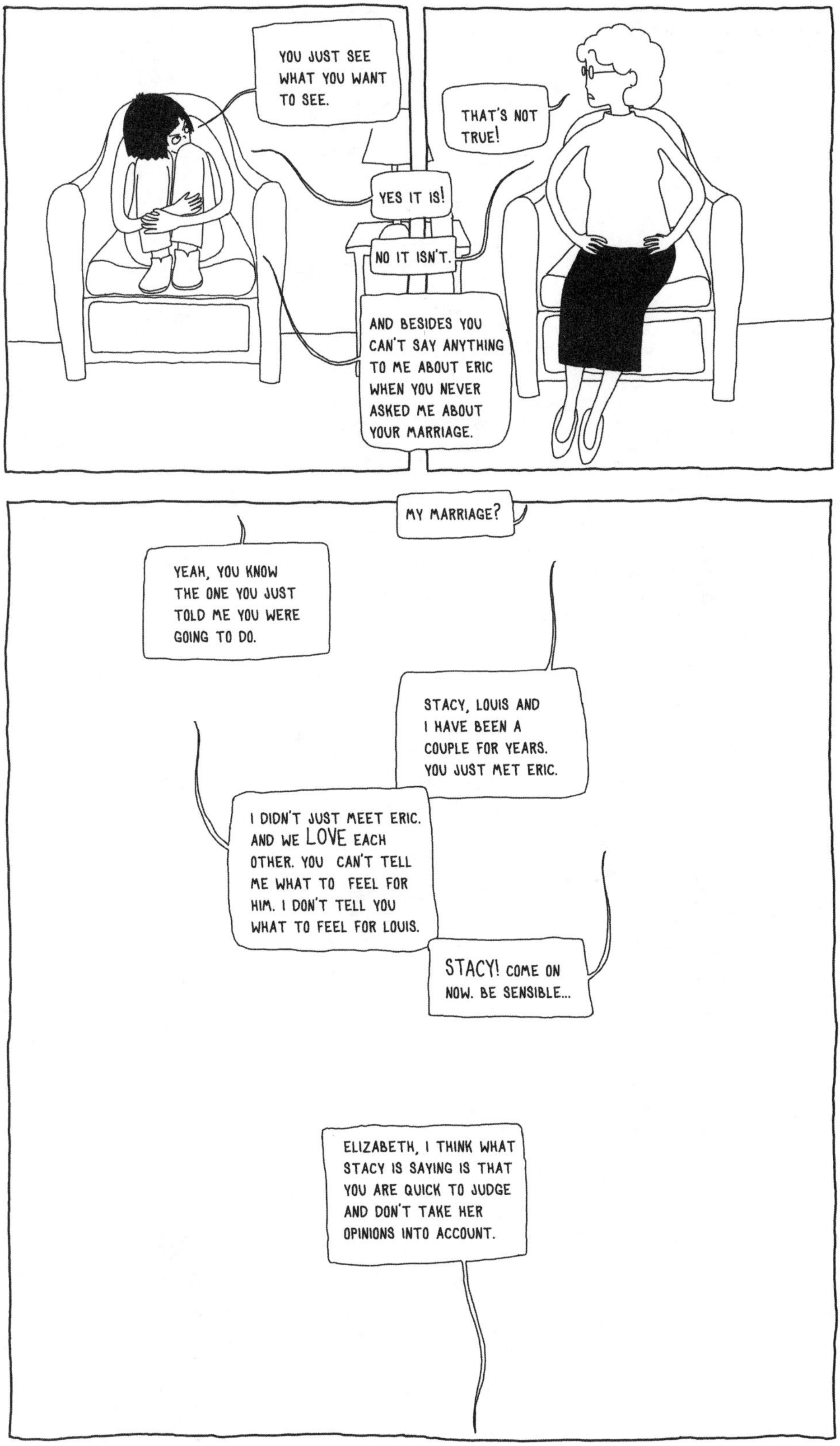
YOU JUST SEE WHAT YOU WANT TO SEE.
THAT'S NOT TRUE!
YES IT IS!
NO IT ISN'T.
AND BESIDES YOU CAN'T SAY ANYTHING TO ME ABOUT ERIC WHEN YOU NEVER ASKED ME ABOUT YOUR MARRIAGE.
MY MARRIAGE?
YEAH, YOU KNOW THE ONE YOU JUST TOLD ME YOU WERE GOING TO DO.
STACY, LOUIS AND I HAVE BEEN A COUPLE FOR YEARS. YOU JUST MET ERIC.
I DIDN'T JUST MEET ERIC. AND WE LOVE EACH OTHER. YOU CAN'T TELL ME WHAT TO FEEL FOR HIM. I DON'T TELL YOU WHAT TO FEEL FOR LOUIS.
STACY! COME ON NOW. BE SENSIBLE...
ELIZABETH, I THINK WHAT STACY IS SAYING IS THAT YOU ARE QUICK TO JUDGE AND DON'T TAKE HER OPINIONS INTO ACCOUNT.

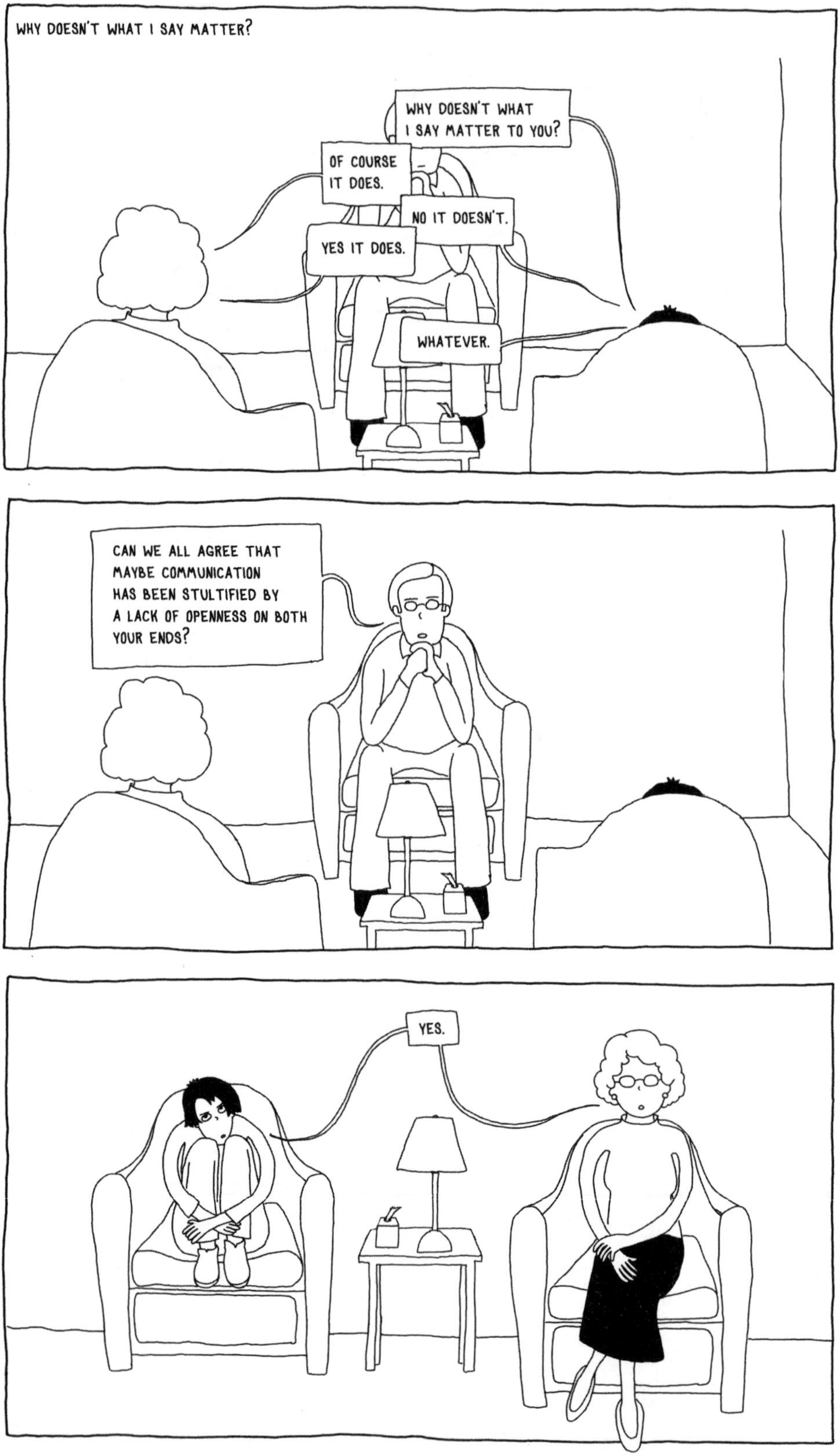
WHY DOESN'T WHAT I SAY MATTER?
WHY DOESN'T WHAT I SAY MATTER TO YOU?
OF COURSE IT DOES.
NO IT DOESN'T.
YES IT DOES.
WHATEVER.
CAN WE ALL AGREE THAT MAYBE COMMUNICATION HAS BEEN STULTIFIED BY A LACK OF OPENNESS ON BOTH YOUR ENDS?
YES.

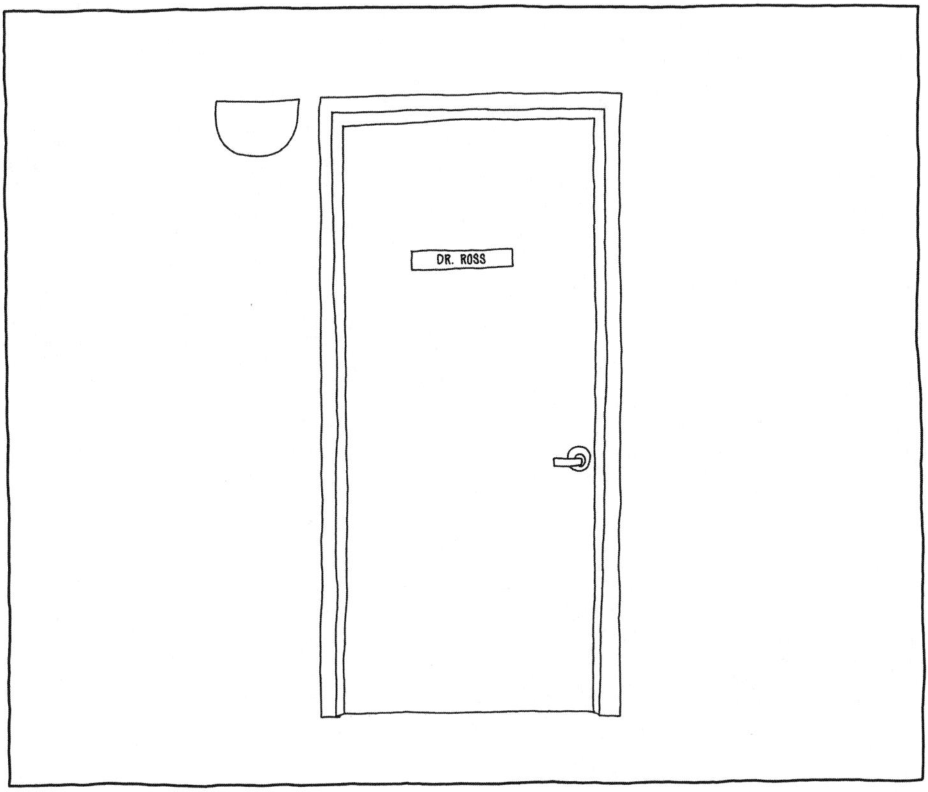
DR. ROSS

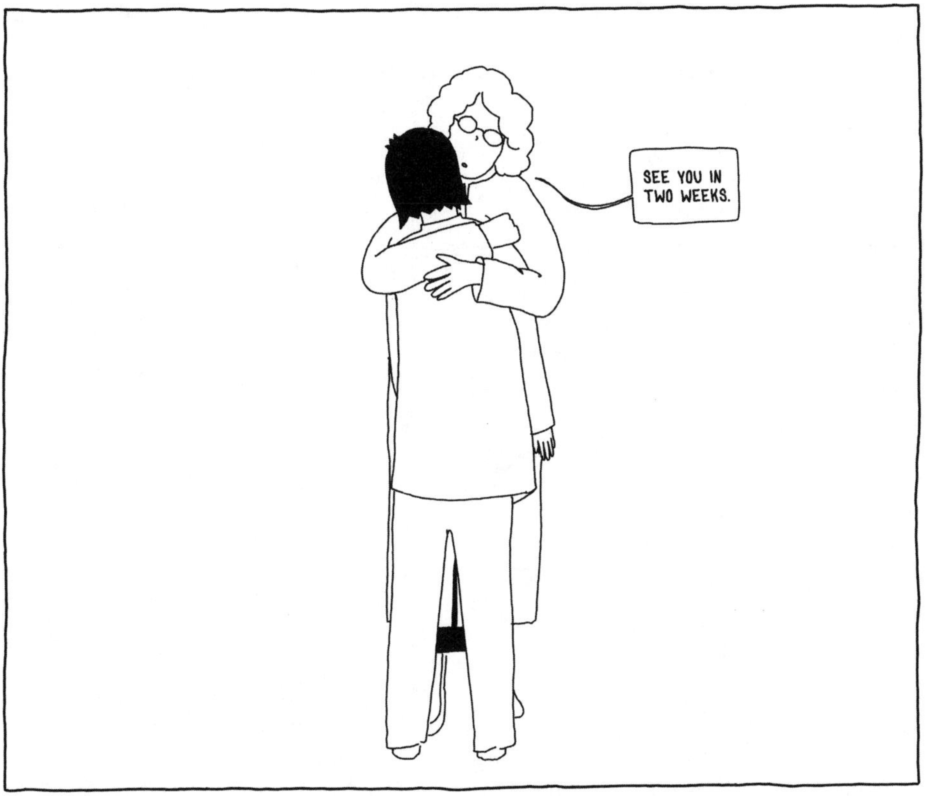
SEE YOU IN TWO WEEKS.

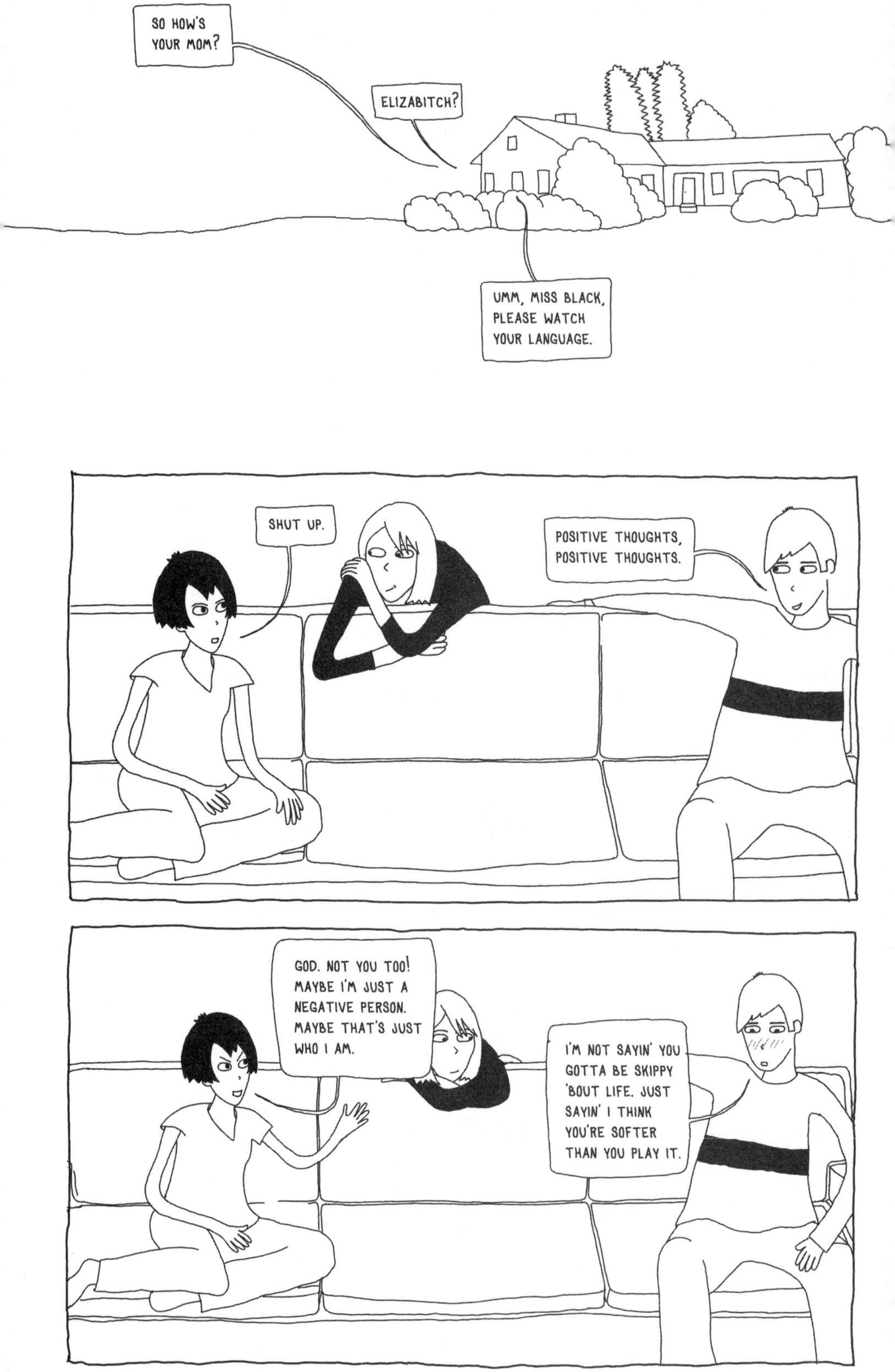
SO HOW'S YOUR MOM?
ELIZABITCH?
UMM, MISS BLACK, PLEASE WATCH YOUR LANGUAGE.
SHUT UP.
POSITIVE THOUGHTS, POSITIVE THOUGHTS.
GOD. NOT YOU TOO! MAYBE I'M JUST A NEGATIVE PERSON. MAYBE THAT'S JUST WHO I AM.
I'M NOT SAYIN' YOU GOTTA BE SKIPPY 'BOUT LIFE. JUST SAYIN' I THINK YOU'RE SOFTER THAN YOU PLAY IT.

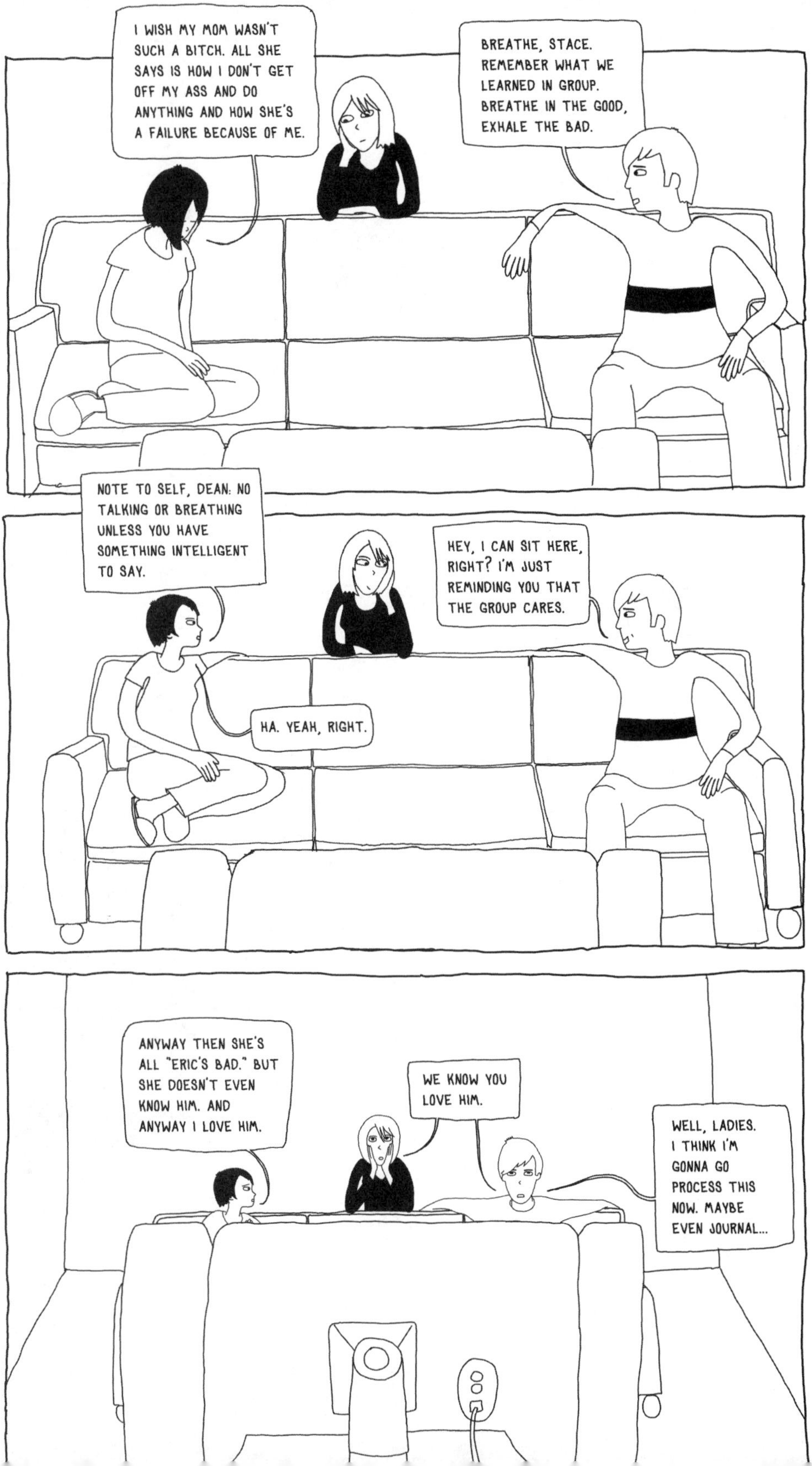
I WISH MY MOM WASN'T SUCH A BITCH. ALL SHE SAYS IS HOW I DON'T GET OFF MY ASS AND DO ANYTHING AND HOW SHE'S A FAILURE BECAUSE OF ME.
BREATHE, STACE. REMEMBER WHAT WE LEARNED IN GROUP. BREATHE IN THE GOOD, EXHALE THE BAD.
NOTE TO SELF, DEAN: NO TALKING OR BREATHING UNLESS YOU HAVE SOMETHING INTELLIGENT TO SAY.
HEY, I CAN SIT HERE, RIGHT? I'M JUST REMINDING YOU THAT THE GROUP CARES.
HA. YEAH, RIGHT.
ANYWAY THEN SHE'S ALL "ERIC'S BAD." BUT SHE DOESN'T EVEN KNOW HIM. AND ANYWAY I LOVE HIM.
WE KNOW YOU LOVE HIM.
WELL, LADIES. I THINK I'M GONNA GO PROCESS THIS NOW. MAYBE EVEN JOURNAL...

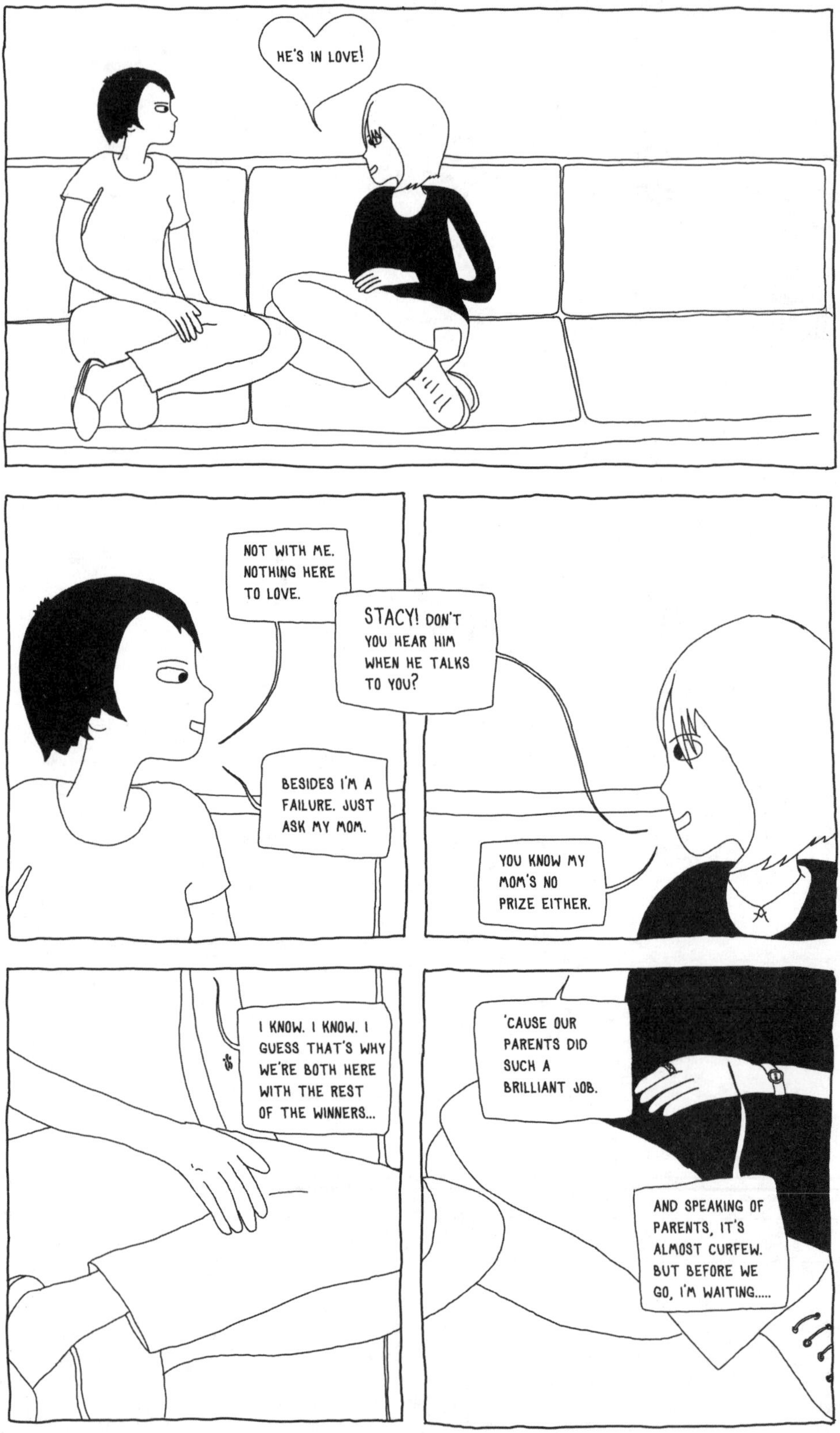
HE'S IN LOVE!
NOT WITH ME. NOTHING HERE TO LOVE.
BESIDES I'M A FAILURE. JUST ASK MY MOM.
STACY! DON'T YOU HEAR HIM WHEN HE TALKS TO YOU?
YOU KNOW MY MOM'S NO PRIZE EITHER.
I KNOW. I KNOW. I GUESS THAT'S WHY WE'RE BOTH HERE WITH THE REST OF THE WINNERS...
'CAUSE OUR PARENTS DID SUCH A BRILLIANT JOB.
AND SPEAKING OF PARENTS, IT'S ALMOST CURFEW. BUT BEFORE WE GO, I'M WAITING.....

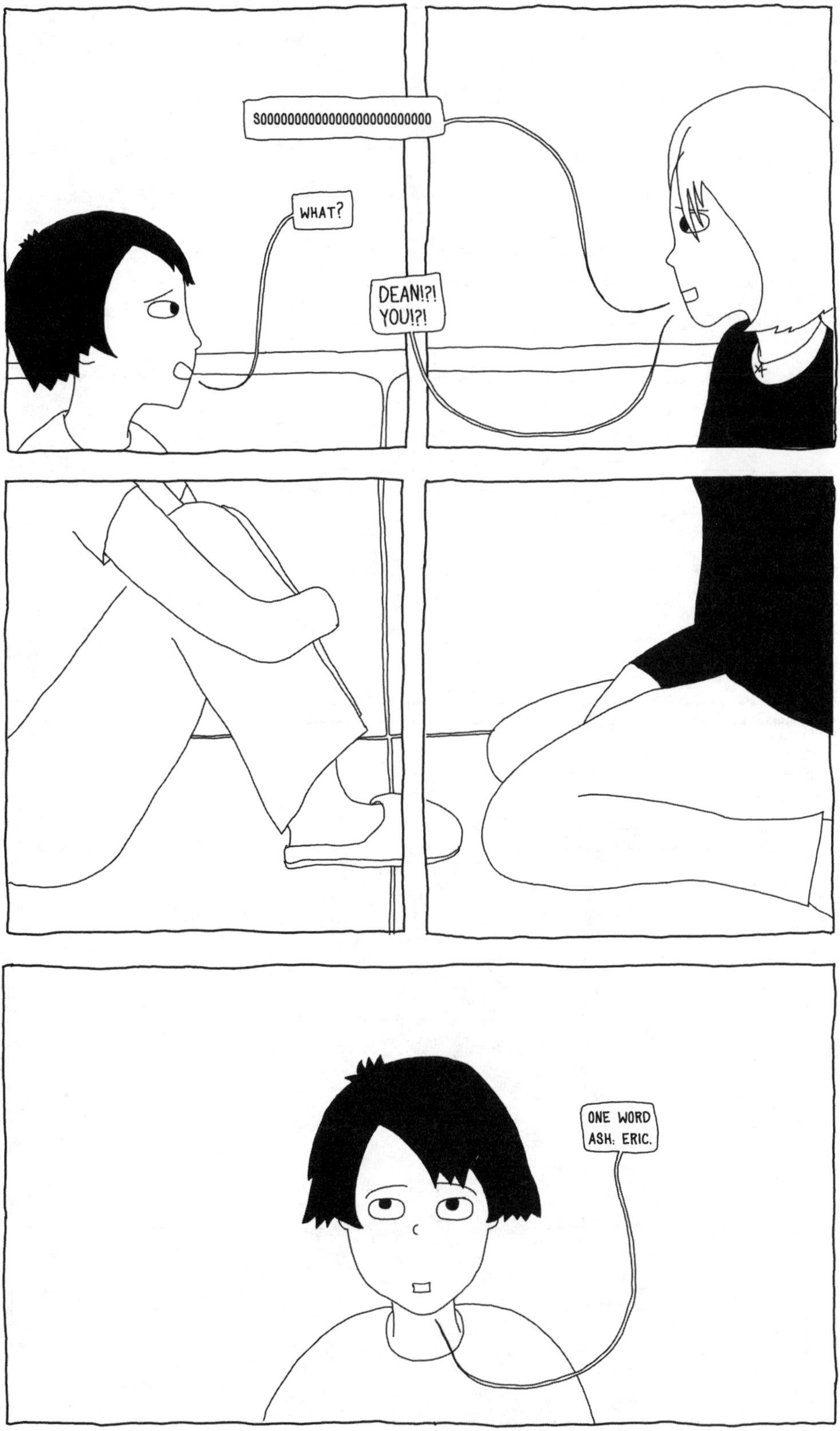
SOOOOOOOOOOOOOOOOOOOOOOOOOO
WHAT?
DEAN!?! YOU!?!
ONE WORD ASH: ERIC.

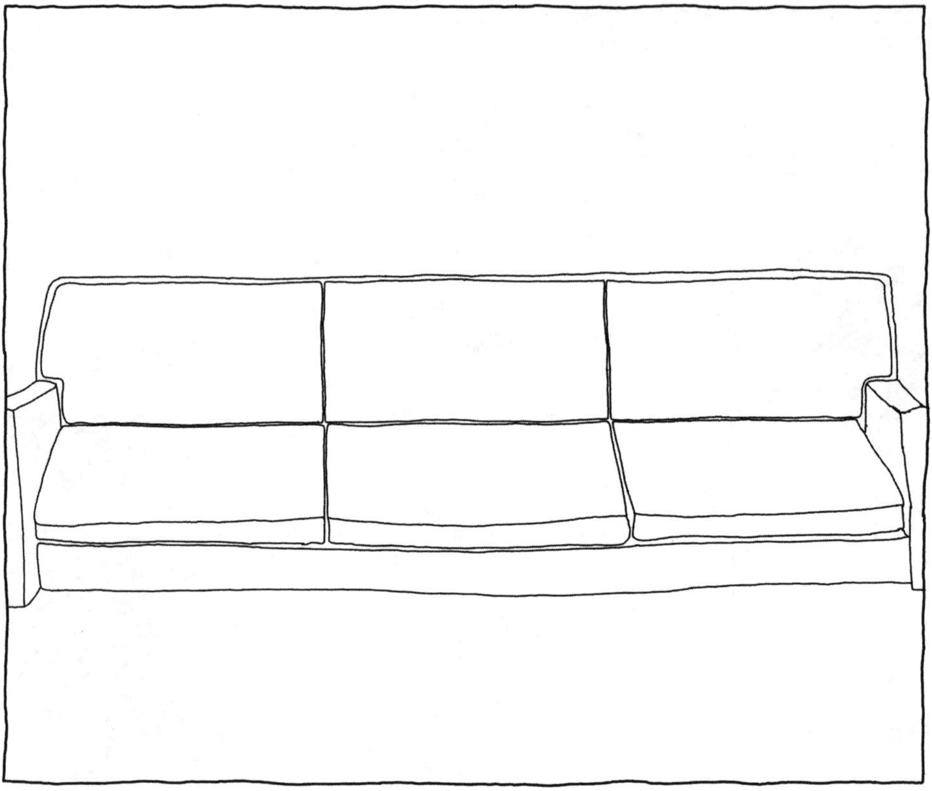

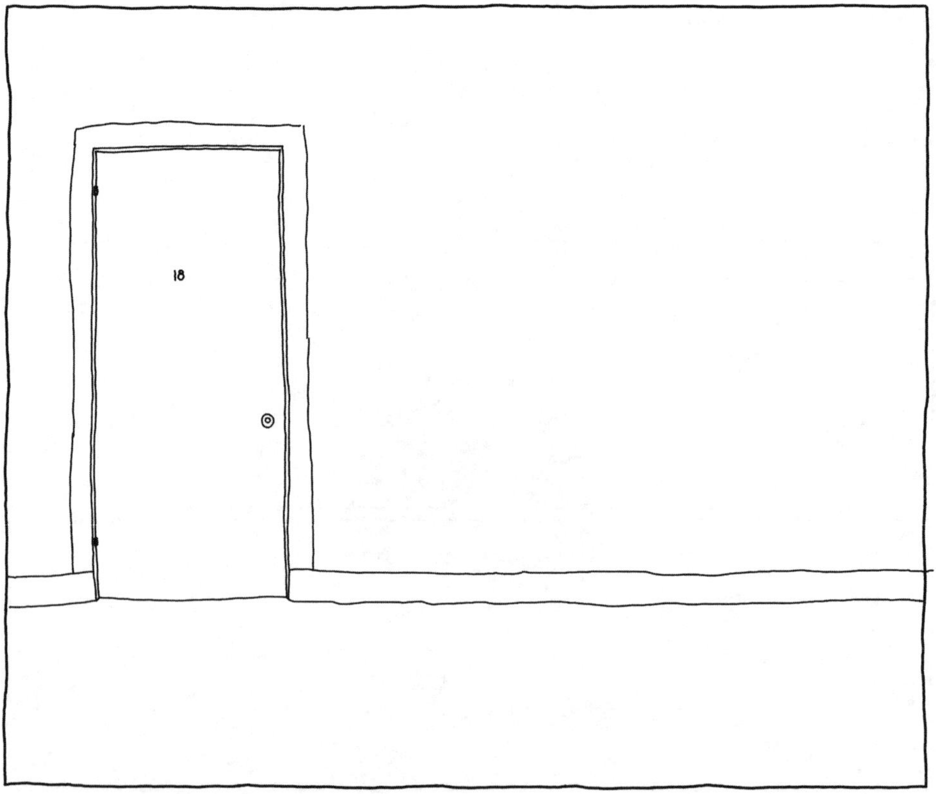
18

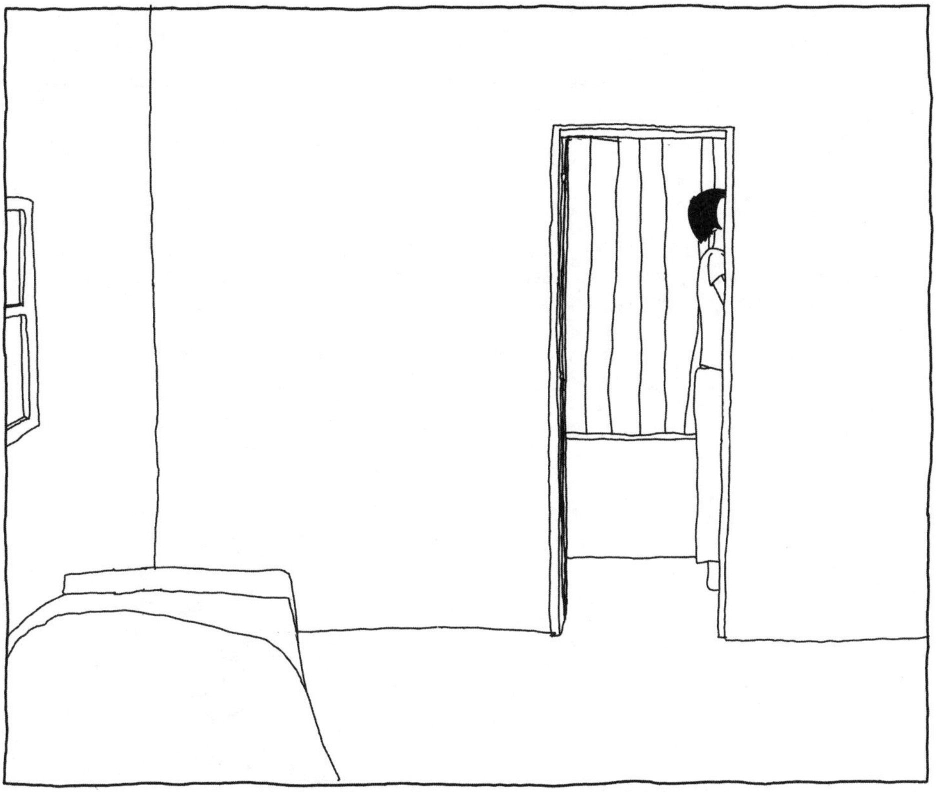

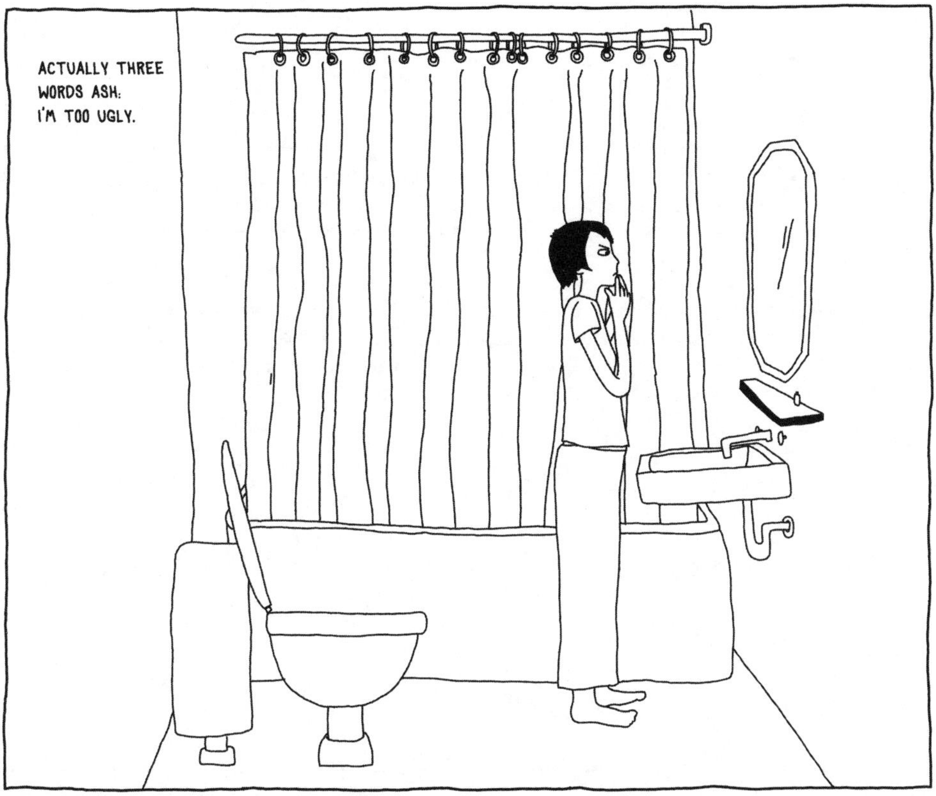
ACTUALLY THREE WORDS ASH: I'M TOO UGLY.

How do you think Stacy's relationship
with her mom has affected her?

MARIA

STACY KEEPS THINGS TO HERSELF.

I CALL HER MOTHER A SMOTHER. THEN BECAUSE STACY NEEDS SPACE SHE DOESN'T SAY MUCH, BUT THEN HER MOM'S ALWAYS WONDERING WHAT SHE'S GETTING INTO. BESIDES MRS. BLACK ONLY HAS HER TO FOCUS ON. IF SHE HAD SIBLINGS LIKE I DO, I BET IT WOULD BE DIFFERENT.

ALSO BECAUSE SHE DOESN'T TALK HER MOM DISRESPECTS HER PRIVACY. STACY USED TO PUT PIECES OF PAPER UNDER HER DOOR BEFORE SHE WENT TO SCHOOL SO SHE'D KNOW IF HER MOM HAD GONE INTO HER ROOM WHEN SHE WASN'T THERE. SHE DID.

VIOLET

I THINK STACY AND HER MOM, WELL, IT'S JUST SAD. STACE AND I USED TO CALL HER BITCH, SHORT FOR ELIZABITCH AND IT SEEMED FUNNY BACK THEN. I'VE BEEN TRYING TO REPAIR THE RELATIONSHIP I HAVE WITH MY MOM — MY SISTER FELL OUT OF A TREE FIVE YEARS AGO AND IS PARALYZED FROM THE WAIST DOWN SO SHE'S REALLY OVERPROTECTIVE OF US BOTH.

SHE USED TO FOLLOW ME TO SCHOOL — DRIVE BEHIND THE SCHOOL BUS TO MAKE SURE I WAS OK. RIDICULOUS, RIGHT? NOW I KNOW SHE DID IT BECAUSE SHE LOVES ME, WELL MOST OF THE TIME I KNOW THAT. I THINK THAT THE LACK OF CLOSENESS STACY HAS WITH HER MOM MEANS SHE RELIES A LOT ON HER FRIENDS, WHICH IS GOOD, UNLESS HER FRIENDS ARE BAD.

LOLA

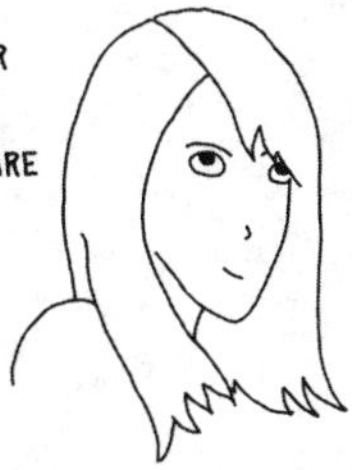

THEY'RE NOT CLOSE THAT'S FOR SURE. MRS. BLACK IS HYPERCRITICAL. GOING TO HER HOUSE FOR DINNER IS A NIGHTMARE. HER MOM IS VERY PARTICULAR ABOUT TABLE MANNERS AND STACE WILL BURP AND EAT WITH HER HANDS AND HER MOM WILL GLARE AND I'LL SIT THERE TRYING TO HOLD MY FORK CORRECTLY HOPING THAT THE MEAL WILL END QUICKLY.

I'M NOT CLOSE TO MY MOM EITHER. AND WHY WOULD I BE? WHO IS? I MEAN WHAT GIRL OUR AGE IS GOING TO TELL HER MOTHER INTIMATE DETAILS OF HER LIFE? AND WHO WANTS TO HEAR THE "WHEN I WAS YOUR AGE SPEECH"...I MEAN, WE'RE INDIVIDUALS NOT COPIES OF OUR MOMS.

STACY TOLD ME THE FAMILY THERAPY SESSIONS AT GOLDEN MEADOWS USUALLY END UP BEING YELLING MATCHES. WELL, WE DO YELLING EXERCISES IN ACTING CLASS AND THEY ARE GREAT THERAPY. IT GETS THE FRUSTRATION OUT.

ASHLEY

FROM WHAT STACY SAYS I THINK HER MOM IS CONTROLLING AND IT MAKES HER ANGRY. I GET THE ANGER. MY MOM AND I ARE ADVERSARIES. MY PARENTS HAVE BEEN GOING THROUGH A DIVORCE FOR THREE YEARS AND SHE WANTS ME TO TESTIFY AGAINST MY DAD AND I WON'T DO THAT.

I DON'T TALK TO HER ABOUT ANYTHING. DON'T WANT TO GIVE HER THE SATISFACTION OF KNOWING PERSONAL DETAILS, SO BELIEVE ME WHEN I SAY I CAN RELATE TO STACY. I THINK NOT BEING CLOSE CAN MAKE YOU STRONGER BECAUSE YOU HAVE TO DEPEND ON YOURSELF. LIKE STACY SAID, WHY ASK YOUR MOM SOMETHING WHEN YOU CAN GET ALL THE INFORMATION YOU NEED FROM YOUR FRIENDS.

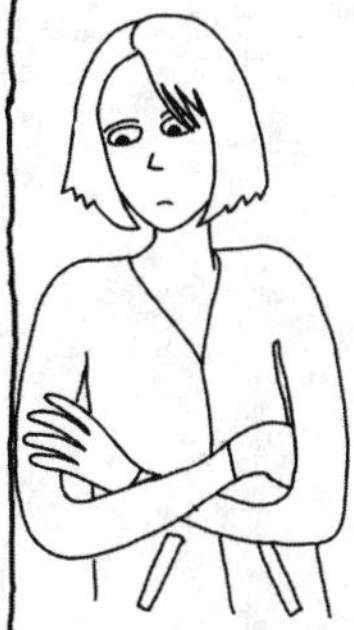

CURRENT LENGTH OF STAY:

*twelve weeks,
one day*

"The depth of Stacy's depression has gotten more obvious as she has begun to be in touch with her feelings and adjust to the new medication levels. Her degree of participation has increased and her appetite has improved. Apparently she has spent a good deal of time on the telephone talking to her boyfriend Eric, who seems to struggle with his own emotional difficulties. This is a very symbiotic relationship and the group is trying to help her get some distance. Stacy is caring and giving to her peers and offers sensitive on-target feedback while having a very difficult time recognizing positive points about herself. Given support, it is hoped that she will feel safe enough to open up."

From the group therapy files of Stacy Black

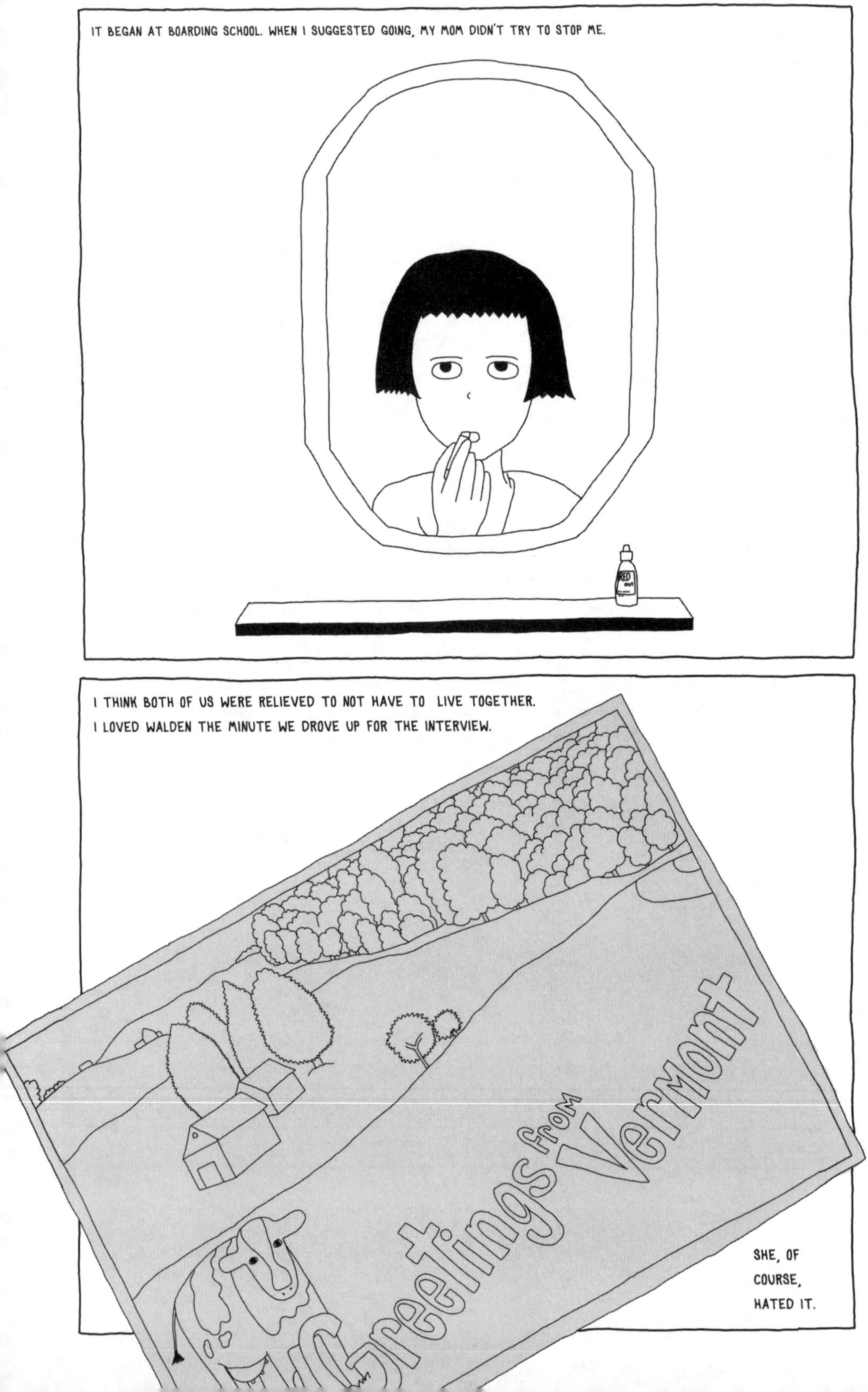

IT BEGAN AT BOARDING SCHOOL. WHEN I SUGGESTED GOING, MY MOM DIDN'T TRY TO STOP ME.
RED out
I THINK BOTH OF US WERE RELIEVED TO NOT HAVE TO LIVE TOGETHER.
I LOVED WALDEN THE MINUTE WE DROVE UP FOR THE INTERVIEW.
Greetings from Vermont
SHE, OF COURSE, HATED IT.

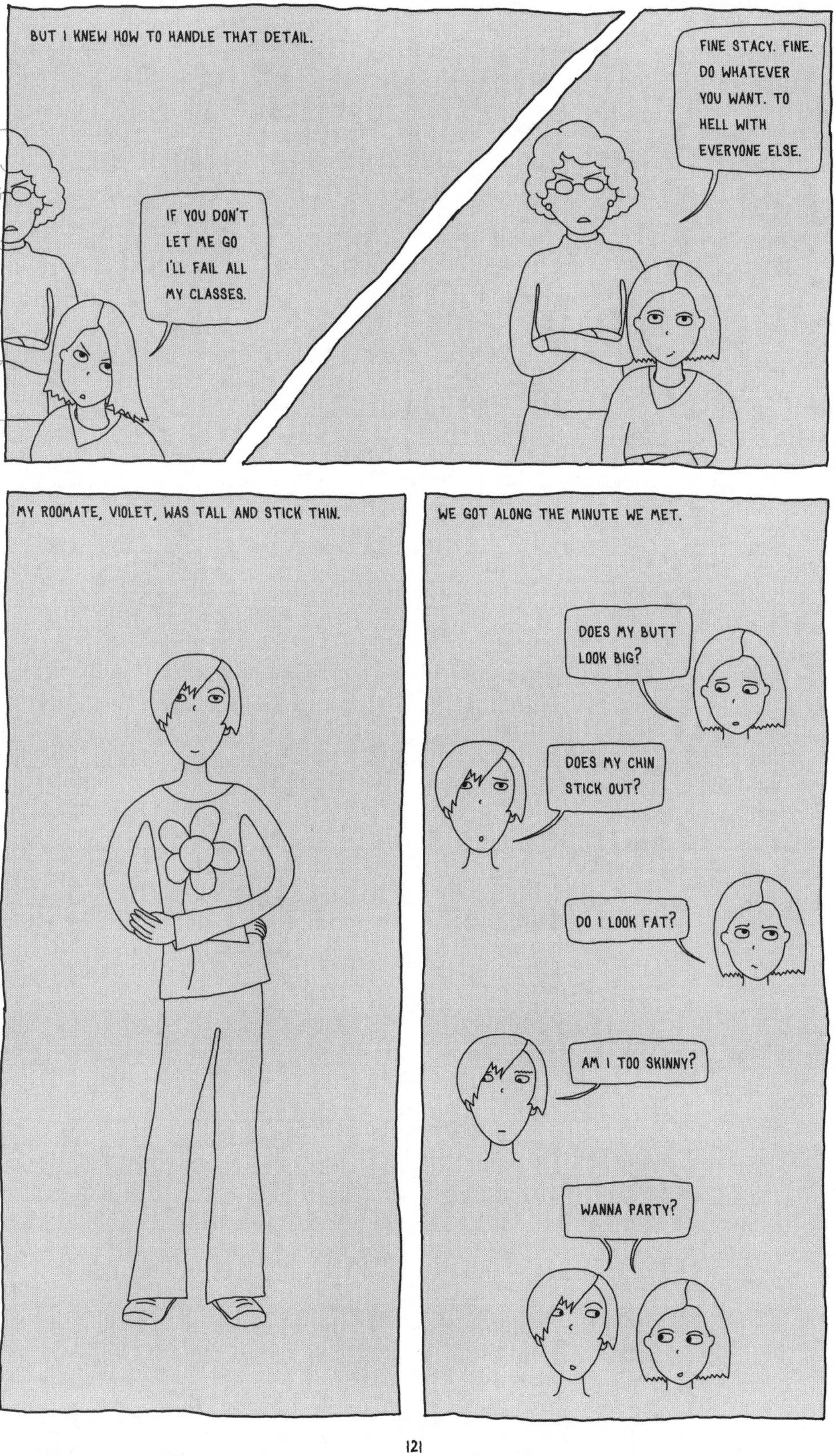

BUT I KNEW HOW TO HANDLE THAT DETAIL.
IF YOU DON'T LET ME GO I'LL FAIL ALL MY CLASSES.
FINE STACY. FINE. DO WHATEVER YOU WANT. TO HELL WITH EVERYONE ELSE.
MY ROOMATE, VIOLET, WAS TALL AND STICK THIN.
WE GOT ALONG THE MINUTE WE MET.
DOES MY BUTT LOOK BIG?
DOES MY CHIN STICK OUT?
DO I LOOK FAT?
AM I TOO SKINNY?
WANNA PARTY?

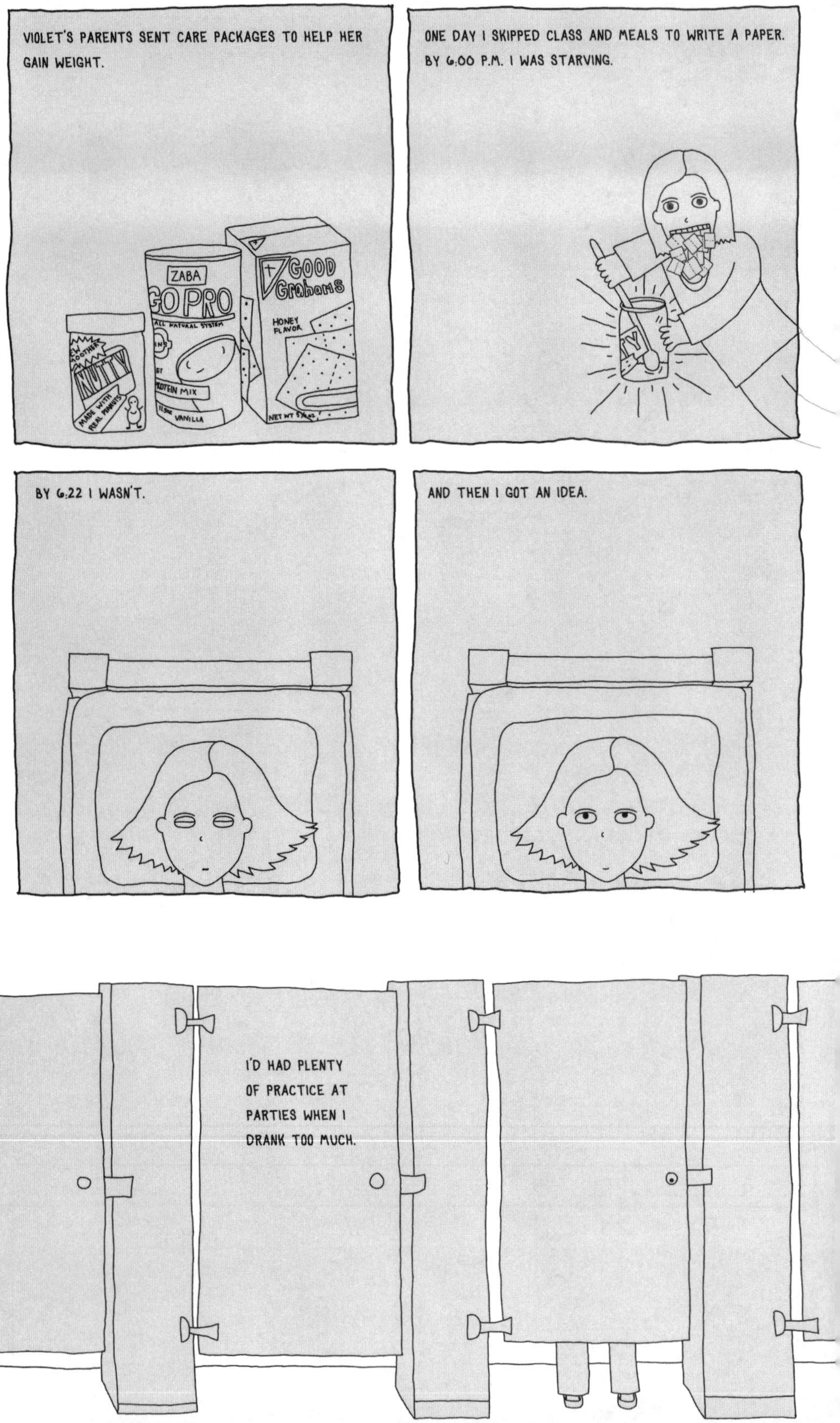
VIOLET'S PARENTS SENT CARE PACKAGES TO HELP HER GAIN WEIGHT.
NUTTY
MADE WITH REAL PEANUTS
ZABA
GO PRO
ALL NATURAL SYSTEM
PROTEIN MIX
VANILLA
GOOD Grahams
HONEY FLAVOR
ONE DAY I SKIPPED CLASS AND MEALS TO WRITE A PAPER. BY 6:00 P.M. I WAS STARVING.
BY 6:22 I WASN'T.
AND THEN I GOT AN IDEA.
I'D HAD PLENTY OF PRACTICE AT PARTIES WHEN I DRANK TOO MUCH.

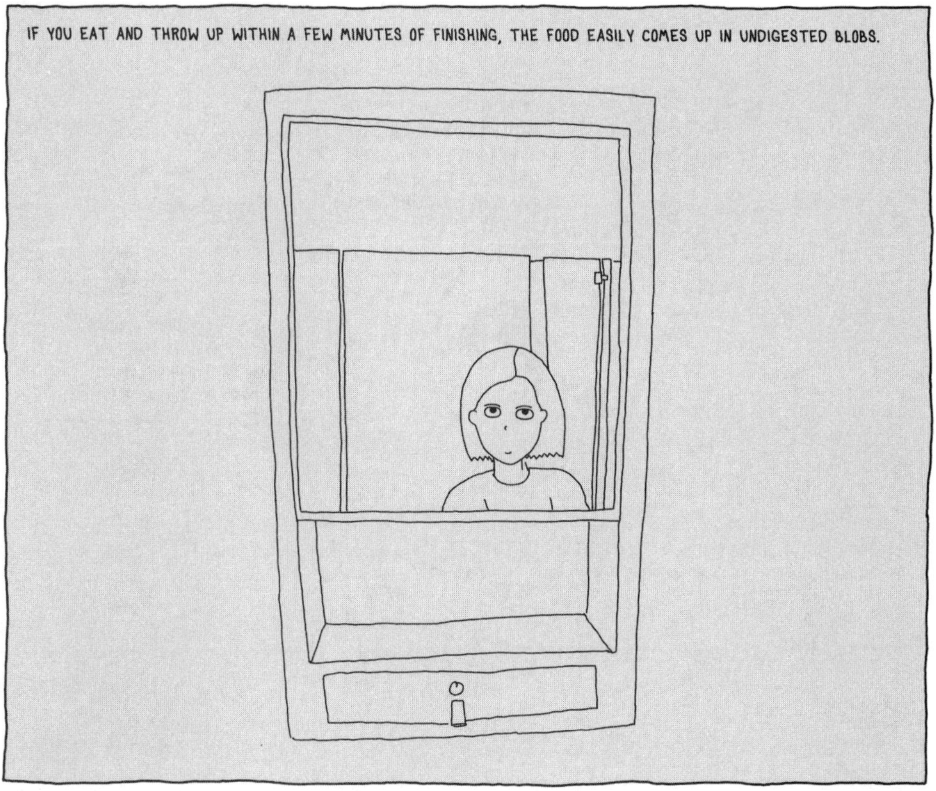
IF YOU EAT AND THROW UP WITHIN A FEW MINUTES OF FINISHING, THE FOOD EASILY COMES UP IN UNDIGESTED BLOBS.

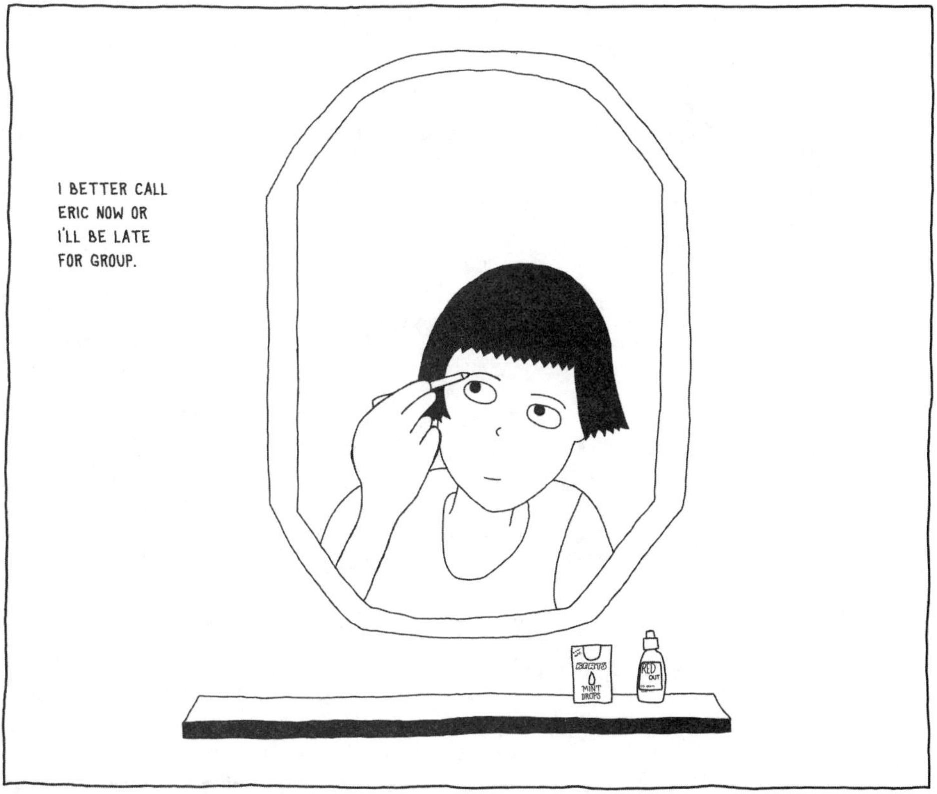
I BETTER CALL ERIC NOW OR I'LL BE LATE FOR GROUP.
BERTS
MINT DROPS
RED OUT

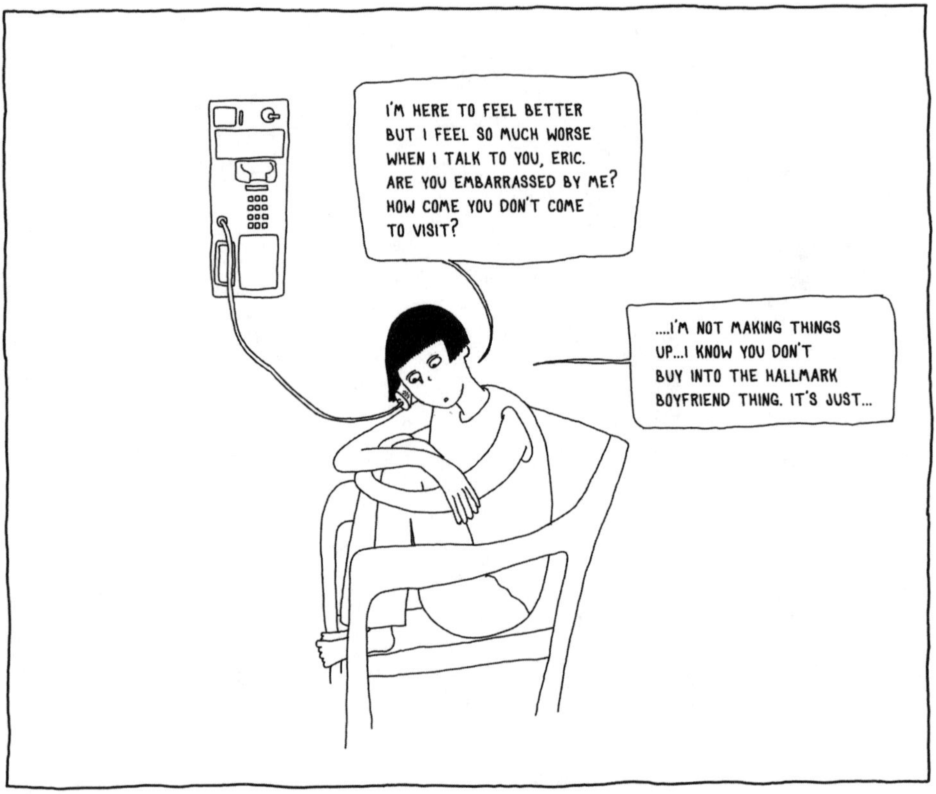
I'M HERE TO FEEL BETTER BUT I FEEL SO MUCH WORSE WHEN I TALK TO YOU, ERIC. ARE YOU EMBARRASSED BY ME? HOW COME YOU DON'T COME TO VISIT?
....I'M NOT MAKING THINGS UP...I KNOW YOU DON'T BUY INTO THE HALLMARK BOYFRIEND THING. IT'S JUST...

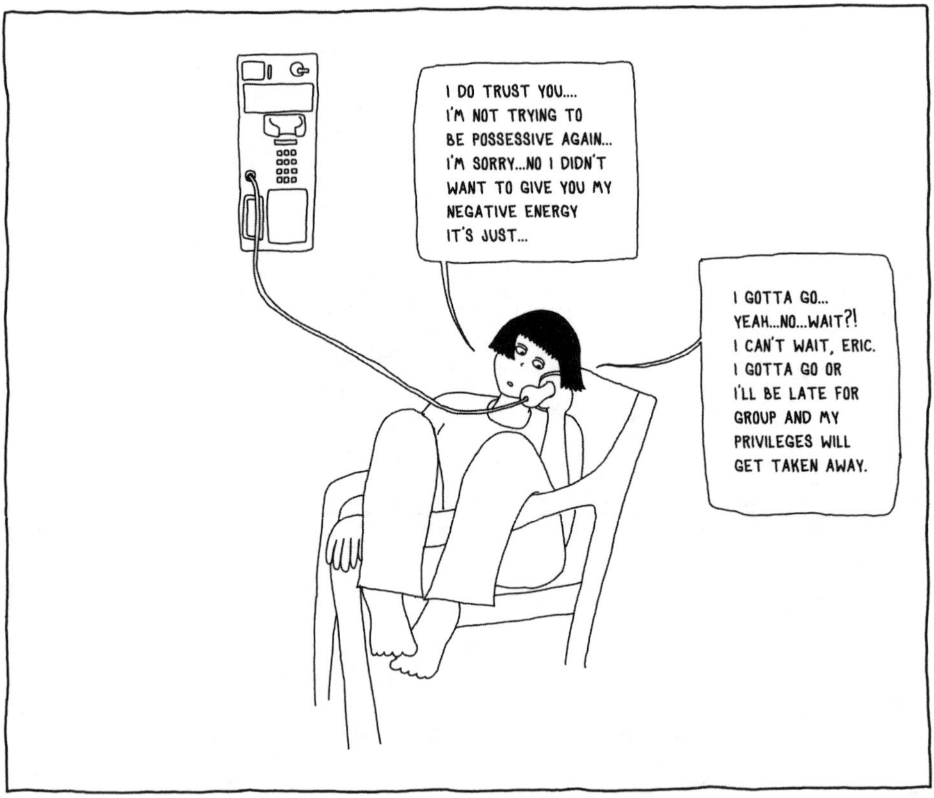
I DO TRUST YOU.... I'M NOT TRYING TO BE POSSESSIVE AGAIN... I'M SORRY...NO I DIDN'T WANT TO GIVE YOU MY NEGATIVE ENERGY IT'S JUST...
I GOTTA GO... YEAH...NO...WAIT?! I CAN'T WAIT, ERIC. I GOTTA GO OR I'LL BE LATE FOR GROUP AND MY PRIVILEGES WILL GET TAKEN AWAY.

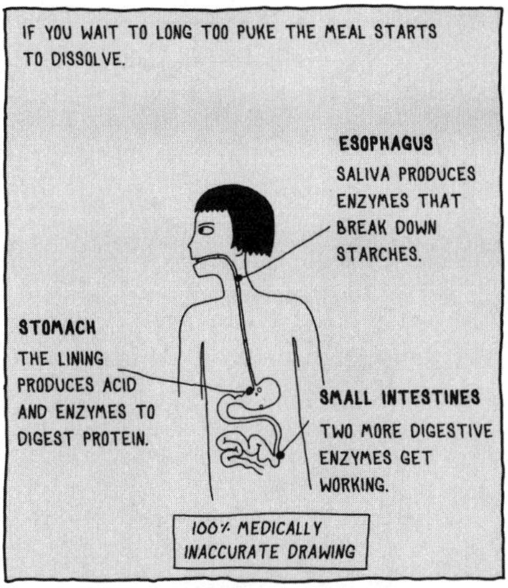
IF YOU WAIT TO LONG TOO PUKE THE MEAL STARTS TO DISSOLVE.
ESOPHAGUS
SALIVA PRODUCES ENZYMES THAT BREAK DOWN STARCHES.
STOMACH
THE LINING PRODUCES ACID AND ENZYMES TO DIGEST PROTEIN.
SMALL INTESTINES
TWO MORE DIGESTIVE ENZYMES GET WORKING.
100% MEDICALLY INACCURATE DRAWING

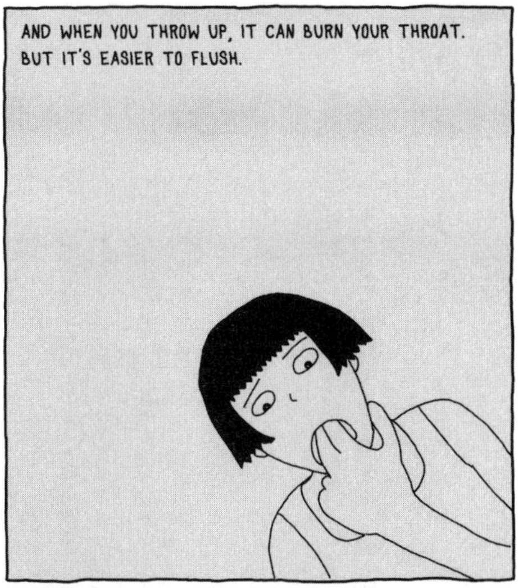
AND WHEN YOU THROW UP, IT CAN BURN YOUR THROAT. BUT IT'S EASIER TO FLUSH.

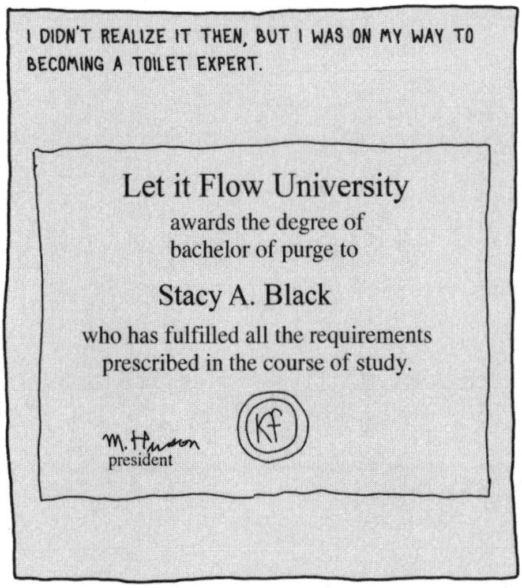
I DIDN'T REALIZE IT THEN, BUT I WAS ON MY WAY TO BECOMING A TOILET EXPERT.
Let it Flow University
awards the degree of
bachelor of purge to
Stacy A. Black
who has fulfilled all the requirements
prescribed in the course of study.
president

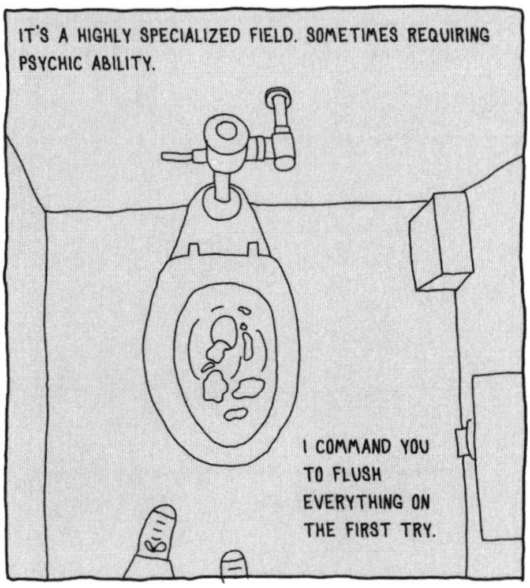
IT'S A HIGHLY SPECIALIZED FIELD. SOMETIMES REQUIRING PSYCHIC ABILITY.
I COMMAND YOU TO FLUSH EVERYTHING ON THE FIRST TRY.

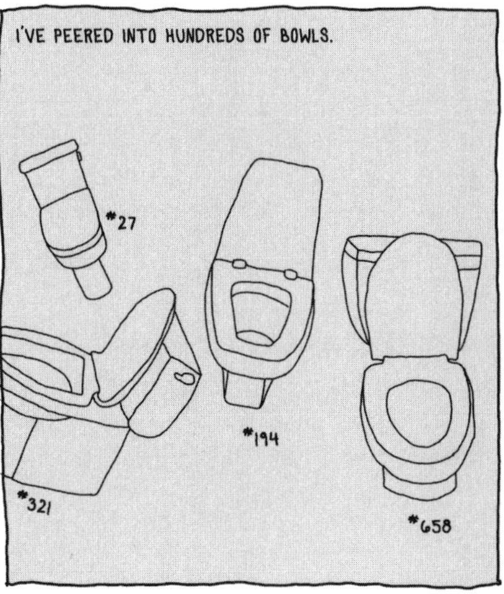
I'VE PEERED INTO HUNDREDS OF BOWLS.
#27
#194
#321
#658

MORE THAN A FEW TIMES I'VE LEANED OVER AND SEEN THE TELLTALE SIGNS OF A PURGER BEFORE ME.

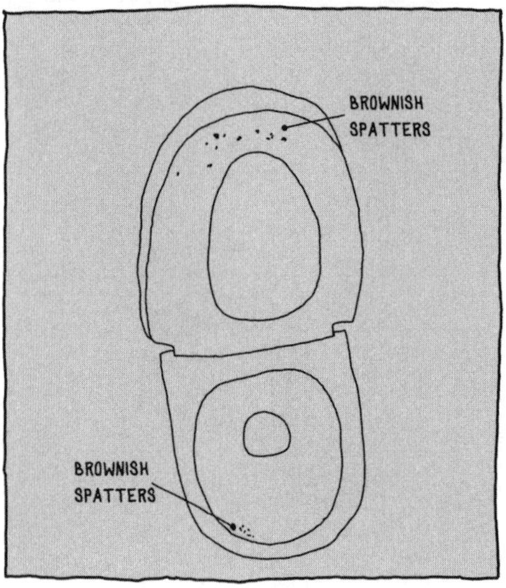
BROWNISH
SPATTERS
BROWNISH
SPATTERS

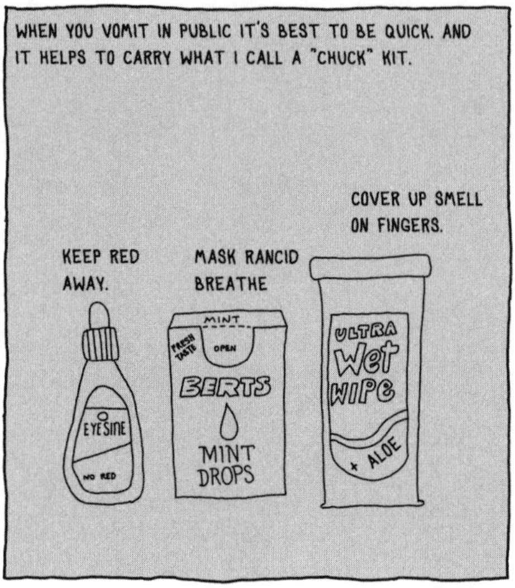
WHEN YOU VOMIT IN PUBLIC IT'S BEST TO BE QUICK. AND IT HELPS TO CARRY WHAT I CALL A "CHUCK" KIT.
COVER UP SMELL ON FINGERS.
KEEP RED AWAY.
MASK RANCID BREATHE
EYESINE
NO RED
MINT
FRESH TASTE
OPEN
BERTS
MINT DROPS
ULTRA
Wet
WIPE
+ ALOE

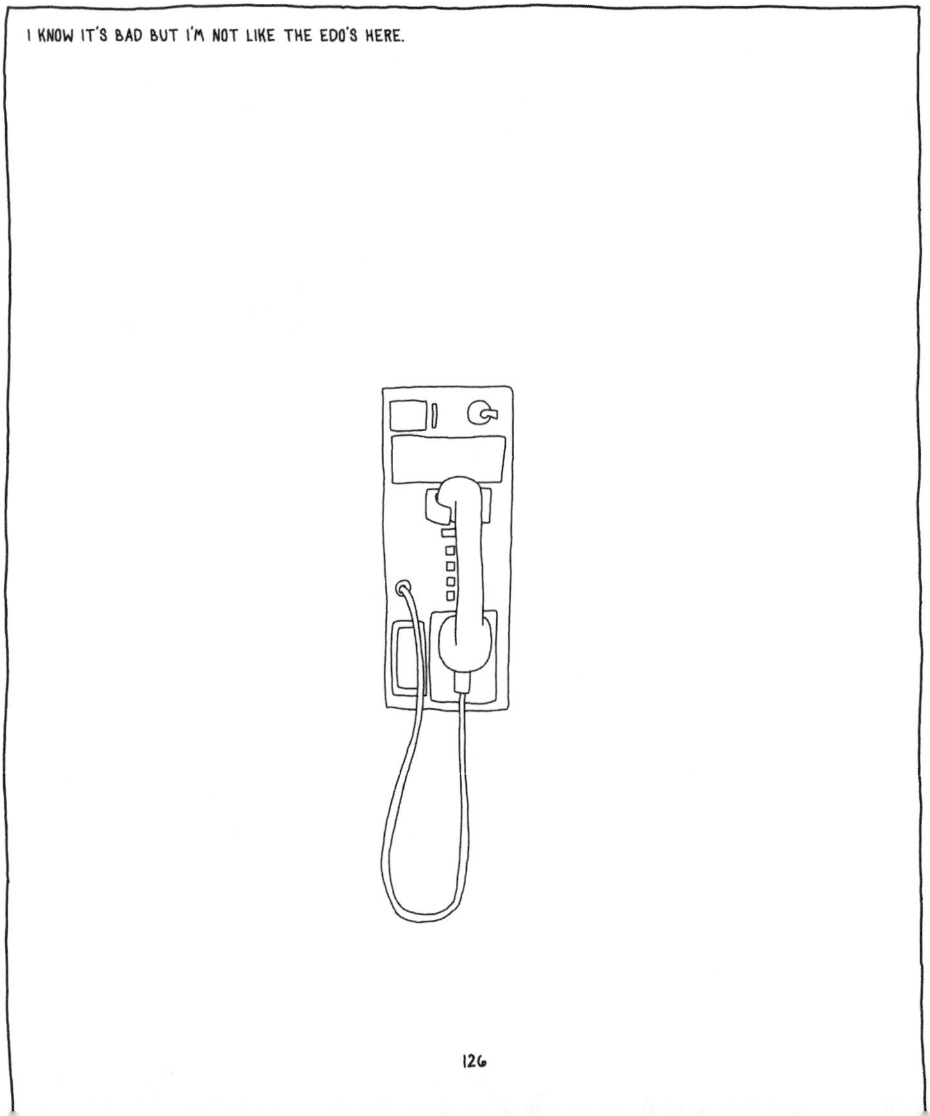
I KNOW IT'S BAD BUT I'M NOT LIKE THE EDO'S HERE.

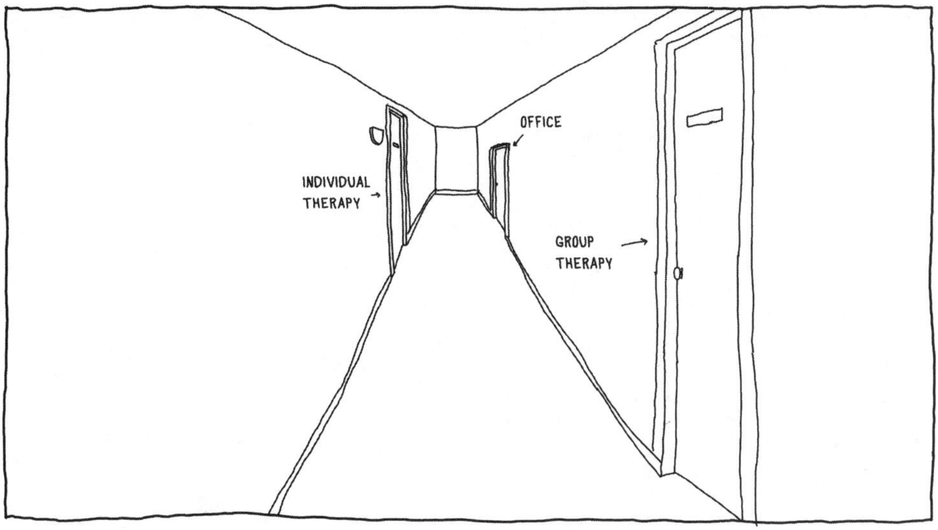
OFFICE
INDIVIDUAL THERAPY
GROUP THERAPY

I'M NOT TRYING TO LOSE WEIGHT, I JUST DON'T WANT TO GAIN ANY. THAT'S A HUGE DIFFERENCE.

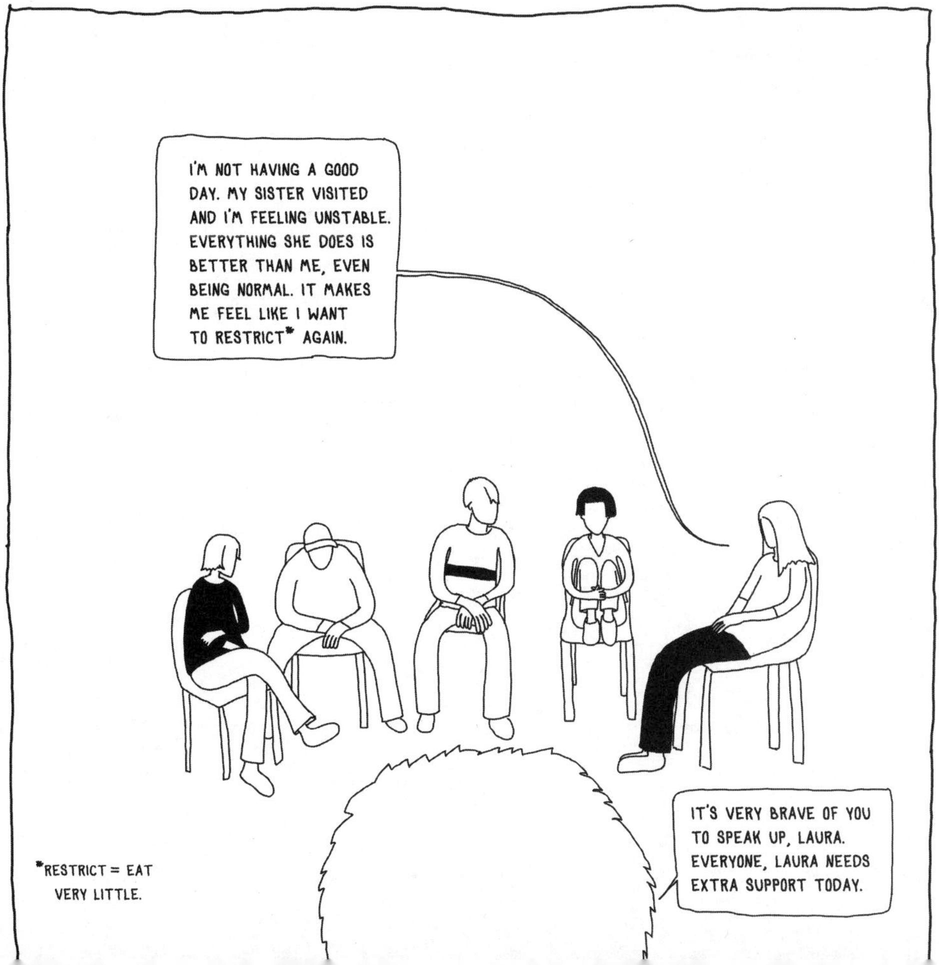
I'M NOT HAVING A GOOD DAY. MY SISTER VISITED AND I'M FEELING UNSTABLE. EVERYTHING SHE DOES IS BETTER THAN ME, EVEN BEING NORMAL. IT MAKES ME FEEL LIKE I WANT TO RESTRICT* AGAIN.
IT'S VERY BRAVE OF YOU TO SPEAK UP, LAURA. EVERYONE, LAURA NEEDS EXTRA SUPPORT TODAY.
*RESTRICT = EAT VERY LITTLE.

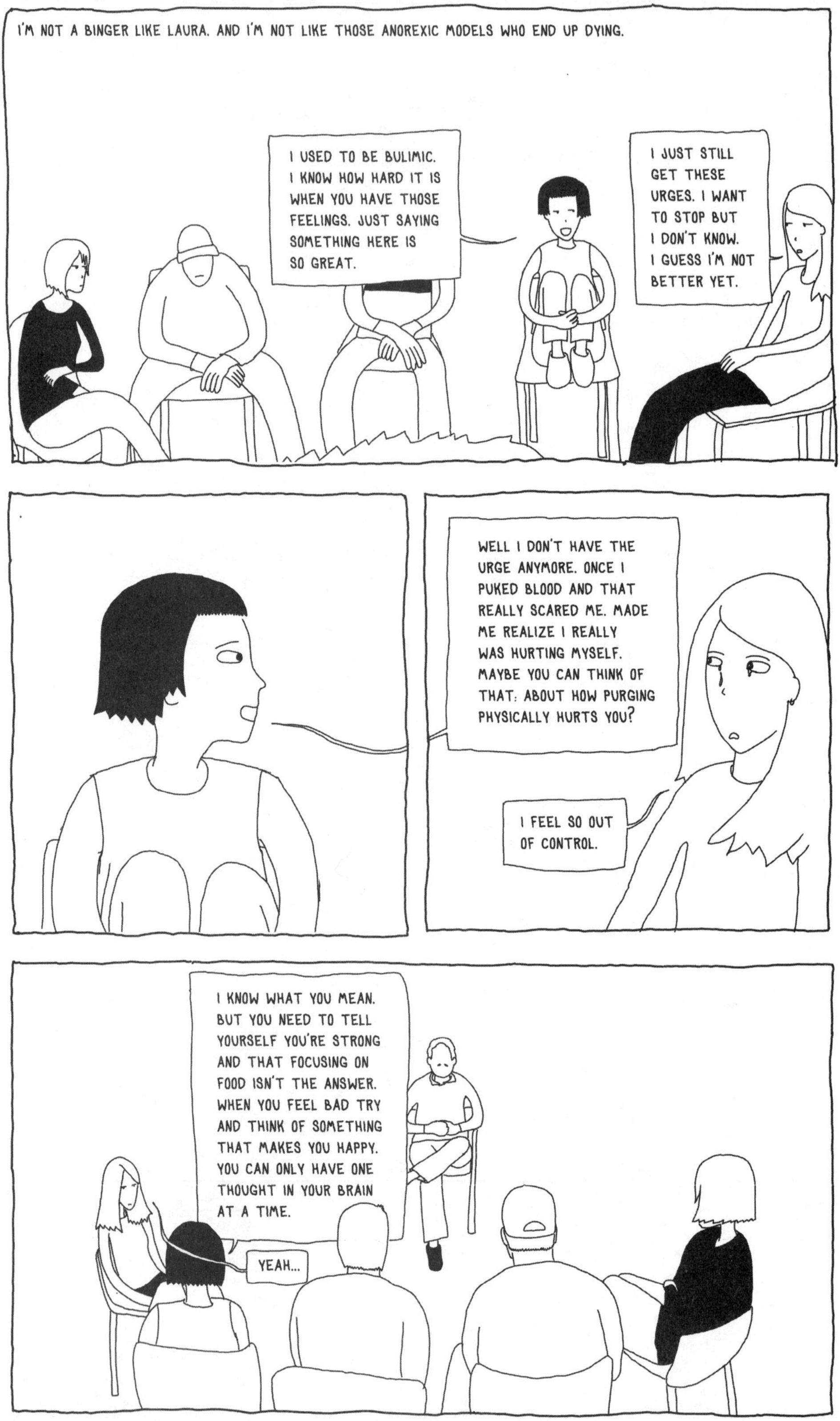

I'M NOT A BINGER LIKE LAURA. AND I'M NOT LIKE THOSE ANOREXIC MODELS WHO END UP DYING.
I USED TO BE BULIMIC. I KNOW HOW HARD IT IS WHEN YOU HAVE THOSE FEELINGS. JUST SAYING SOMETHING HERE IS SO GREAT.
I JUST STILL GET THESE URGES. I WANT TO STOP BUT I DON'T KNOW. I GUESS I'M NOT BETTER YET.
WELL I DON'T HAVE THE URGE ANYMORE. ONCE I PUKED BLOOD AND THAT REALLY SCARED ME. MADE ME REALIZE I REALLY WAS HURTING MYSELF. MAYBE YOU CAN THINK OF THAT: ABOUT HOW PURGING PHYSICALLY HURTS YOU?
I FEEL SO OUT OF CONTROL.
I KNOW WHAT YOU MEAN. BUT YOU NEED TO TELL YOURSELF YOU'RE STRONG AND THAT FOCUSING ON FOOD ISN'T THE ANSWER. WHEN YOU FEEL BAD TRY AND THINK OF SOMETHING THAT MAKES YOU HAPPY. YOU CAN ONLY HAVE ONE THOUGHT IN YOUR BRAIN AT A TIME.
YEAH...

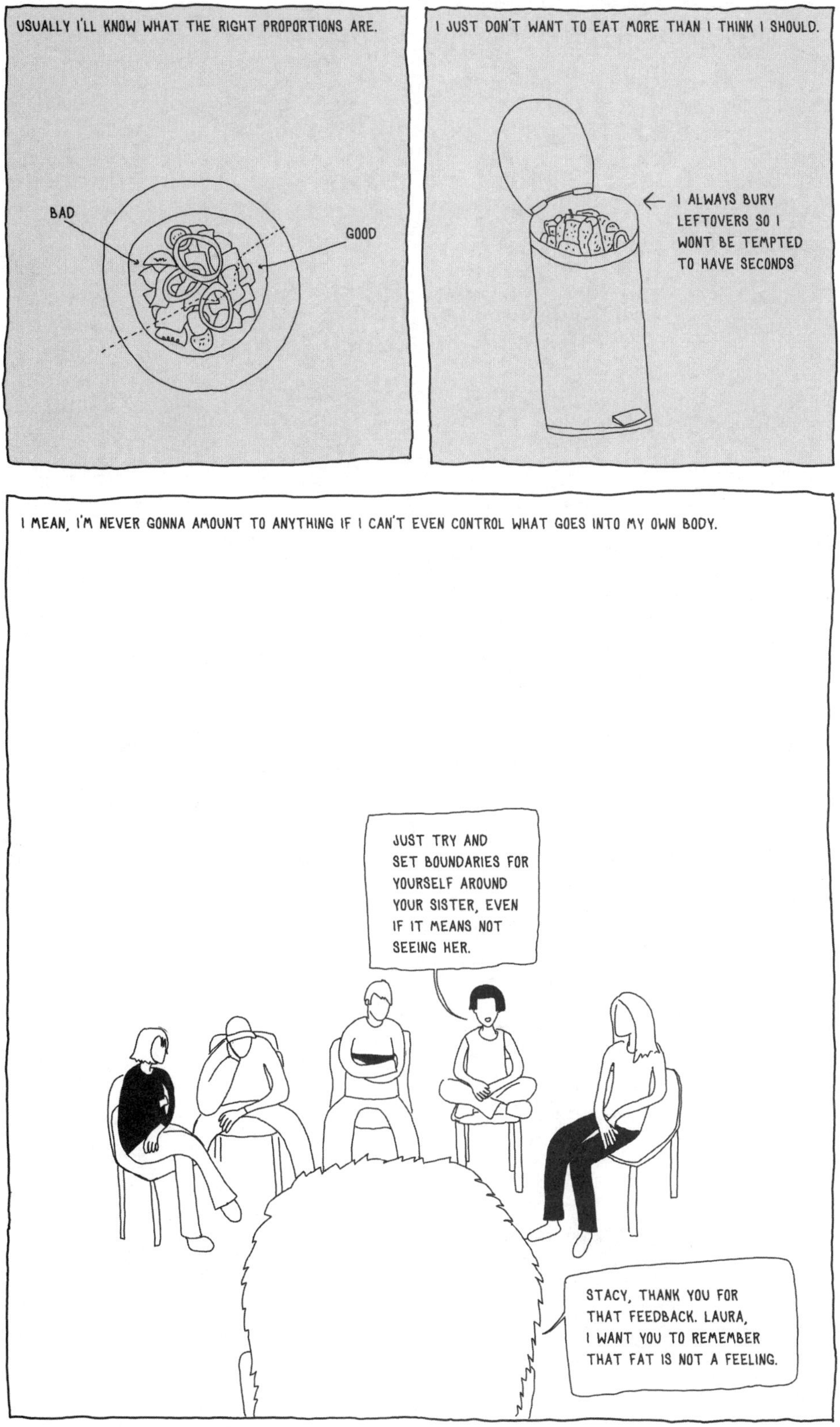
USUALLY I'LL KNOW WHAT THE RIGHT PROPORTIONS ARE.
BAD
GOOD
I JUST DON'T WANT TO EAT MORE THAN I THINK I SHOULD.
I ALWAYS BURY LEFTOVERS SO I WONT BE TEMPTED TO HAVE SECONDS
I MEAN, I'M NEVER GONNA AMOUNT TO ANYTHING IF I CAN'T EVEN CONTROL WHAT GOES INTO MY OWN BODY.
JUST TRY AND SET BOUNDARIES FOR YOURSELF AROUND YOUR SISTER, EVEN IF IT MEANS NOT SEEING HER.
STACY, THANK YOU FOR THAT FEEDBACK. LAURA, I WANT YOU TO REMEMBER THAT FAT IS NOT A FEELING.

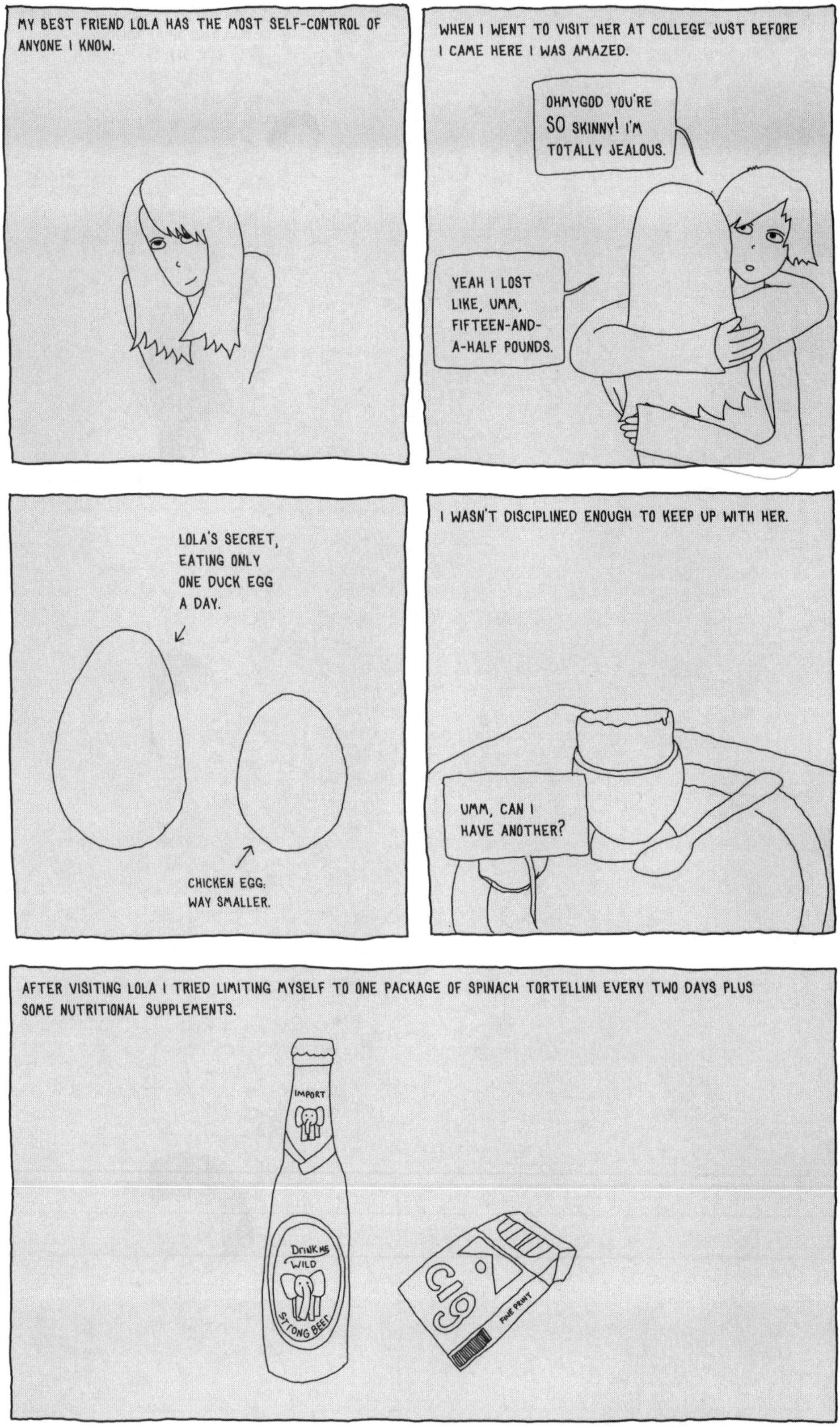
MY BEST FRIEND LOLA HAS THE MOST SELF-CONTROL OF ANYONE I KNOW.
WHEN I WENT TO VISIT HER AT COLLEGE JUST BEFORE I CAME HERE I WAS AMAZED.
OHMYGOD YOU'RE SO SKINNY! I'M TOTALLY JEALOUS.
YEAH I LOST LIKE, UMM, FIFTEEN-AND-A-HALF POUNDS.
LOLA'S SECRET, EATING ONLY ONE DUCK EGG A DAY.
CHICKEN EGG: WAY SMALLER.
I WASN'T DISCIPLINED ENOUGH TO KEEP UP WITH HER.
UMM, CAN I HAVE ANOTHER?
AFTER VISITING LOLA I TRIED LIMITING MYSELF TO ONE PACKAGE OF SPINACH TORTELLINI EVERY TWO DAYS PLUS SOME NUTRITIONAL SUPPLEMENTS.
IMPORT
DRINK ME
WILD
STRONG BEER
Cig
FINE PRINT

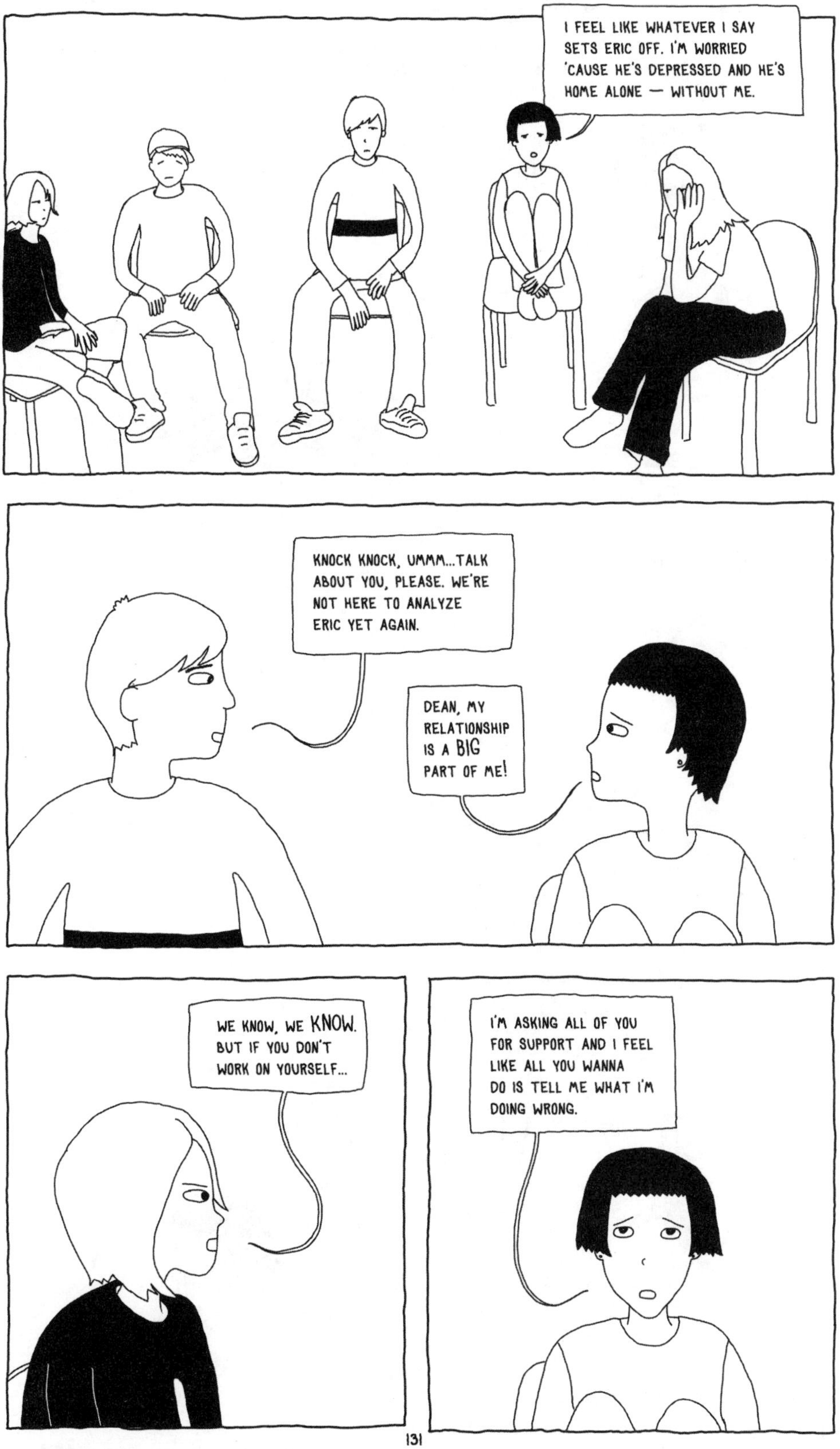

I FEEL LIKE WHATEVER I SAY SETS ERIC OFF. I'M WORRIED 'CAUSE HE'S DEPRESSED AND HE'S HOME ALONE — WITHOUT ME.
KNOCK KNOCK, UMMM...TALK ABOUT YOU, PLEASE. WE'RE NOT HERE TO ANALYZE ERIC YET AGAIN.
DEAN, MY RELATIONSHIP IS A BIG PART OF ME!
WE KNOW, WE KNOW. BUT IF YOU DON'T WORK ON YOURSELF...
I'M ASKING ALL OF YOU FOR SUPPORT AND I FEEL LIKE ALL YOU WANNA DO IS TELL ME WHAT I'M DOING WRONG.

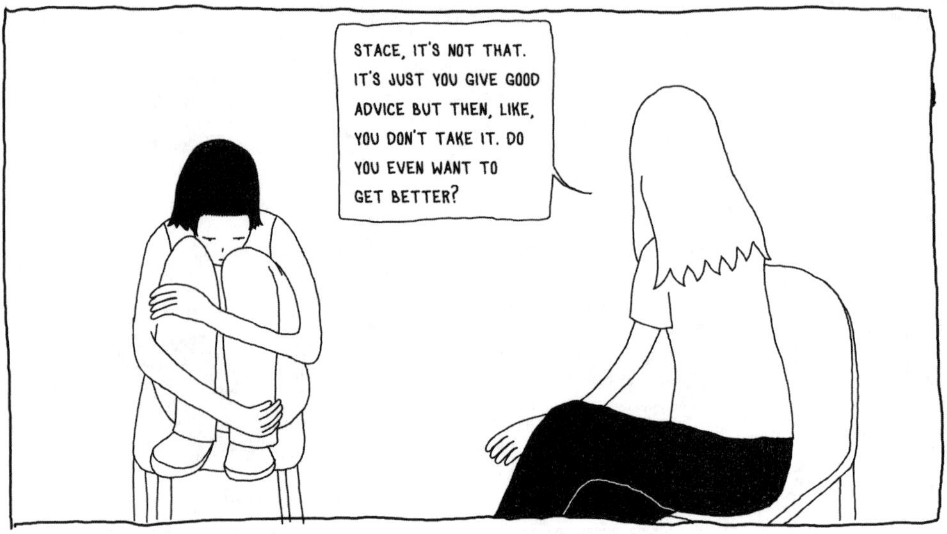
STACE, IT'S NOT THAT. IT'S JUST YOU GIVE GOOD ADVICE BUT THEN, LIKE, YOU DON'T TAKE IT. DO YOU EVEN WANT TO GET BETTER?

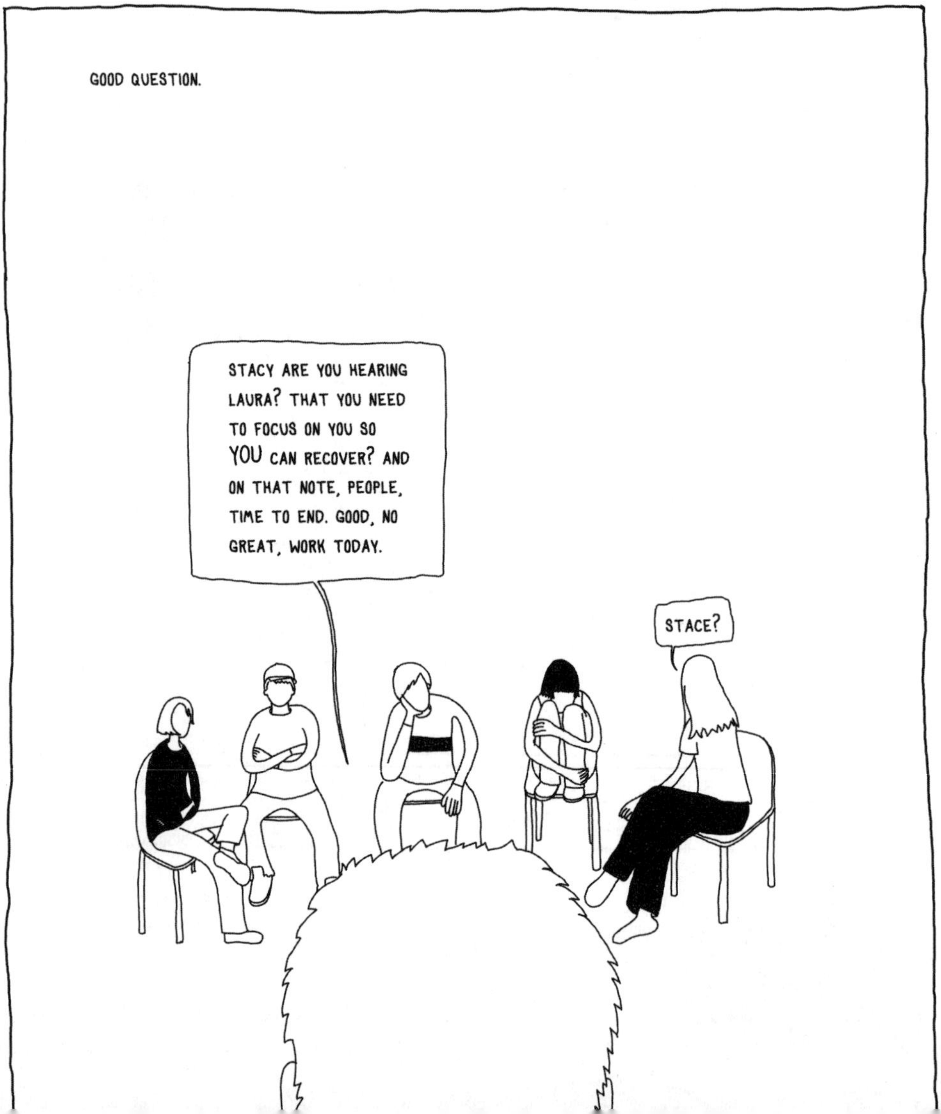
GOOD QUESTION.
STACY ARE YOU HEARING LAURA? THAT YOU NEED TO FOCUS ON YOU SO YOU CAN RECOVER? AND ON THAT NOTE, PEOPLE, TIME TO END. GOOD, NO GREAT, WORK TODAY.
STACE?

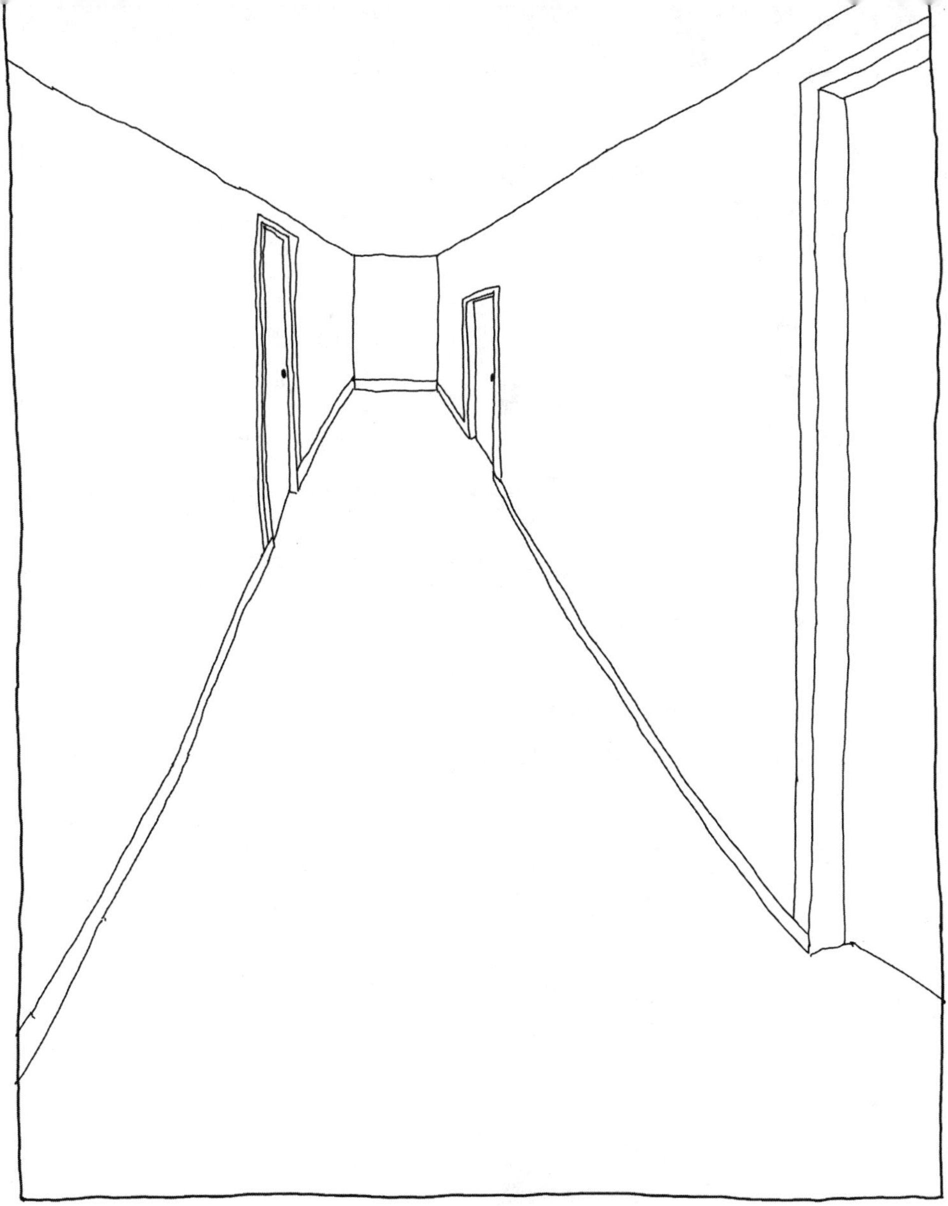

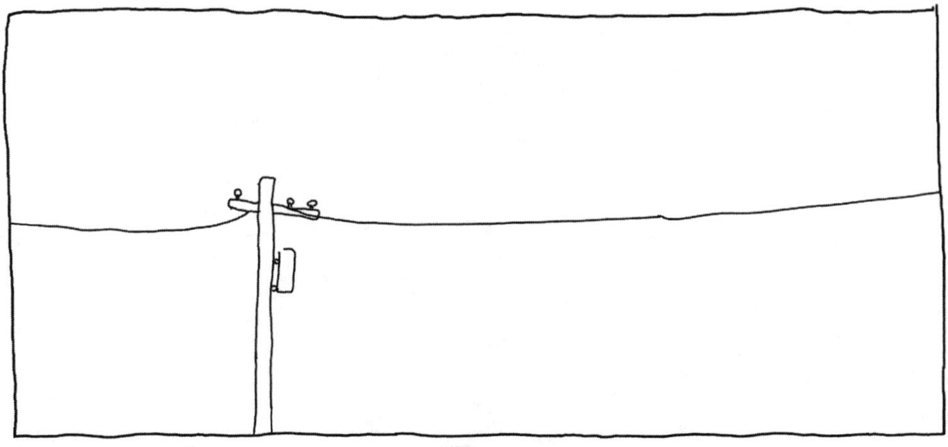

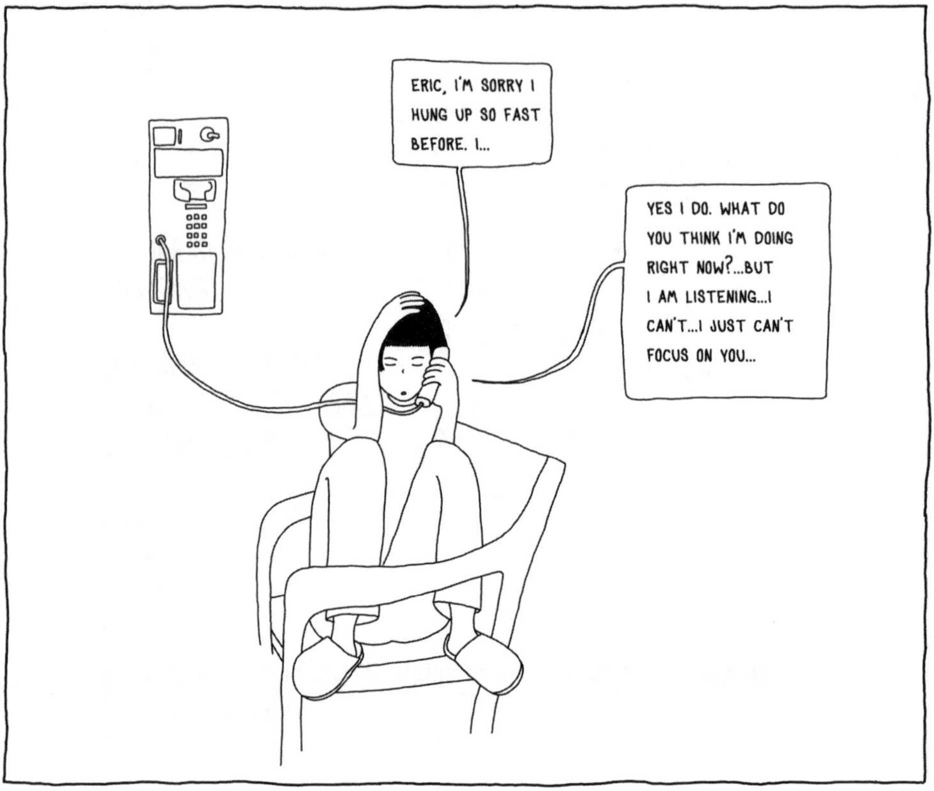
ERIC, I'M SORRY I HUNG UP SO FAST BEFORE. I...
YES I DO. WHAT DO YOU THINK I'M DOING RIGHT NOW?...BUT I AM LISTENING...I CAN'T...I JUST CAN'T FOCUS ON YOU...

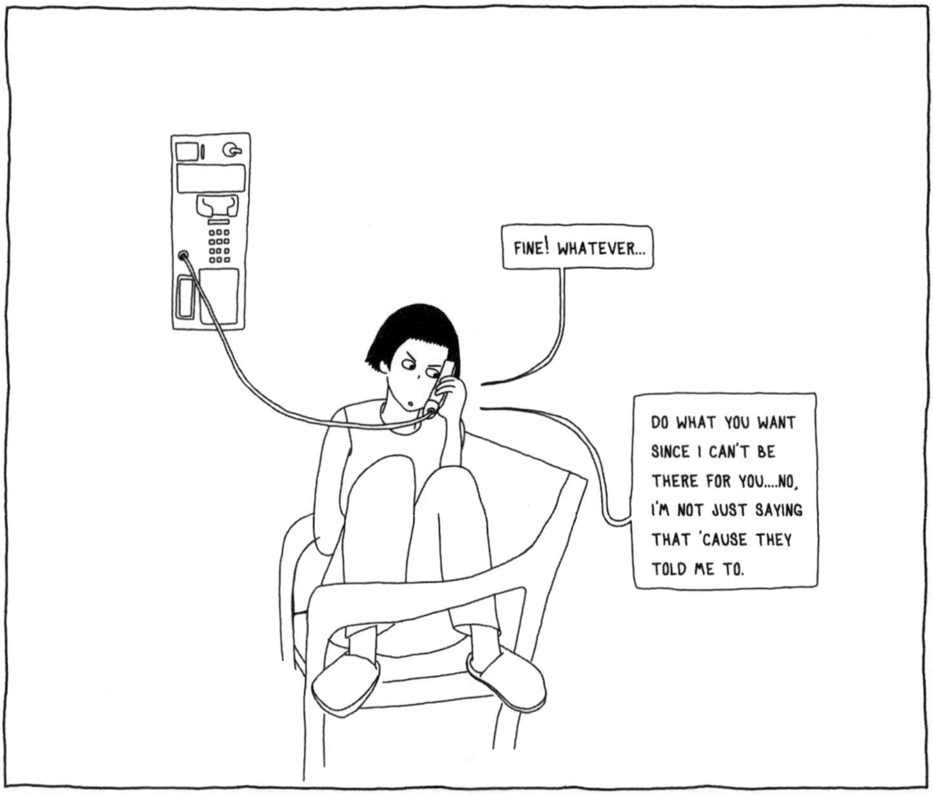
FINE! WHATEVER...
DO WHAT YOU WANT SINCE I CAN'T BE THERE FOR YOU....NO, I'M NOT JUST SAYING THAT 'CAUSE THEY TOLD ME TO.

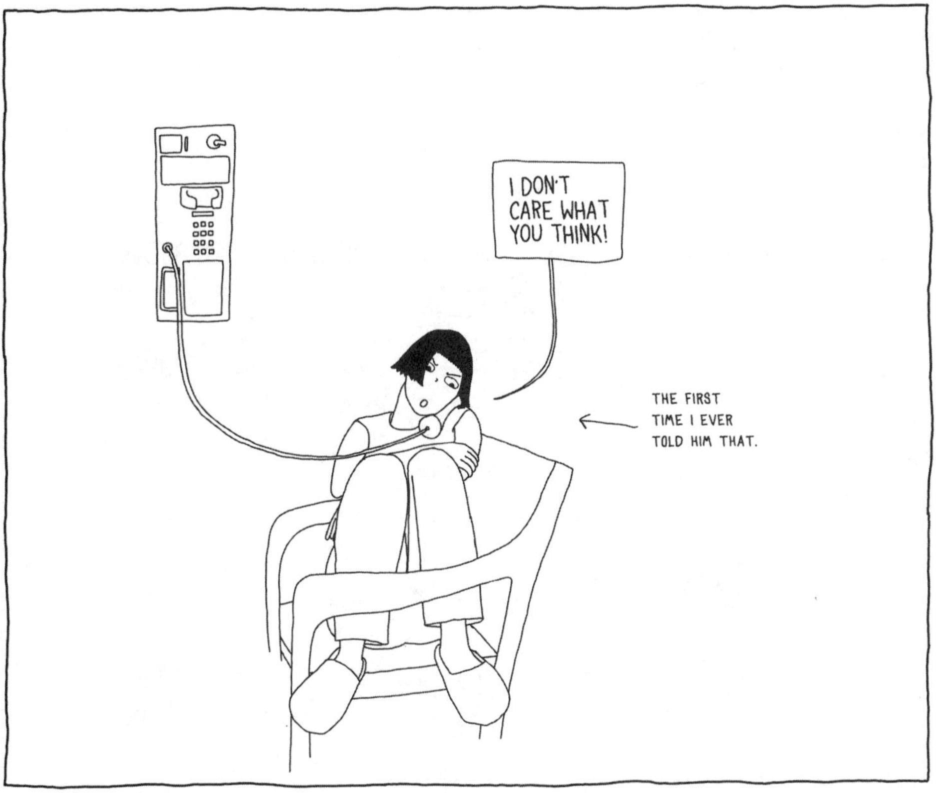
I DON'T CARE WHAT YOU THINK!
THE FIRST TIME I EVER TOLD HIM THAT.

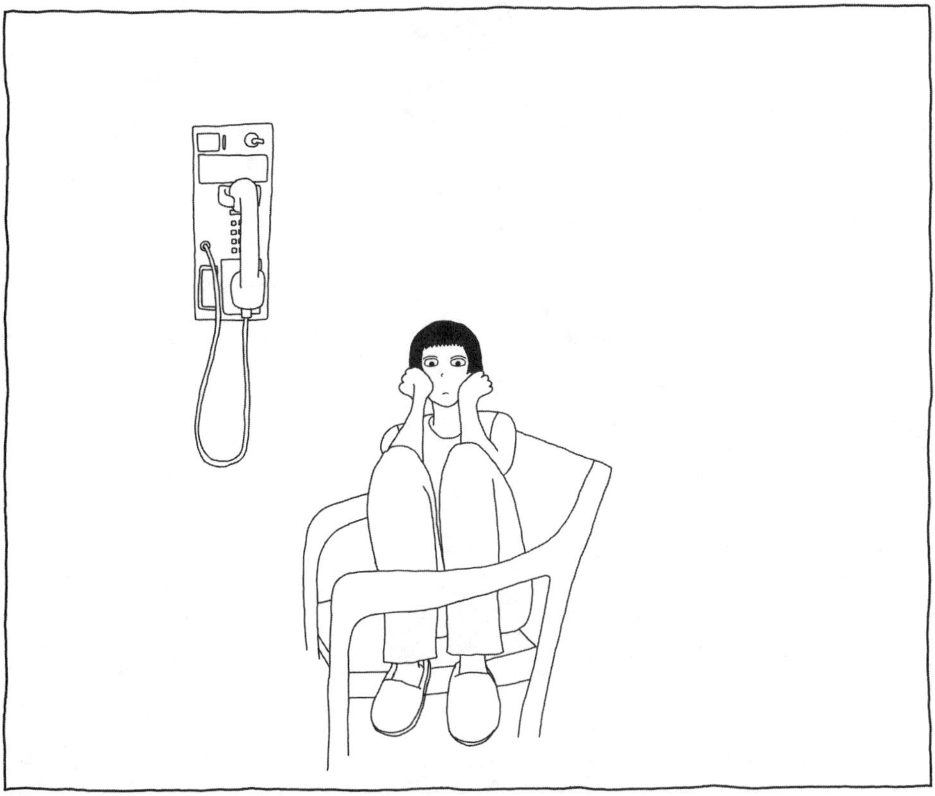

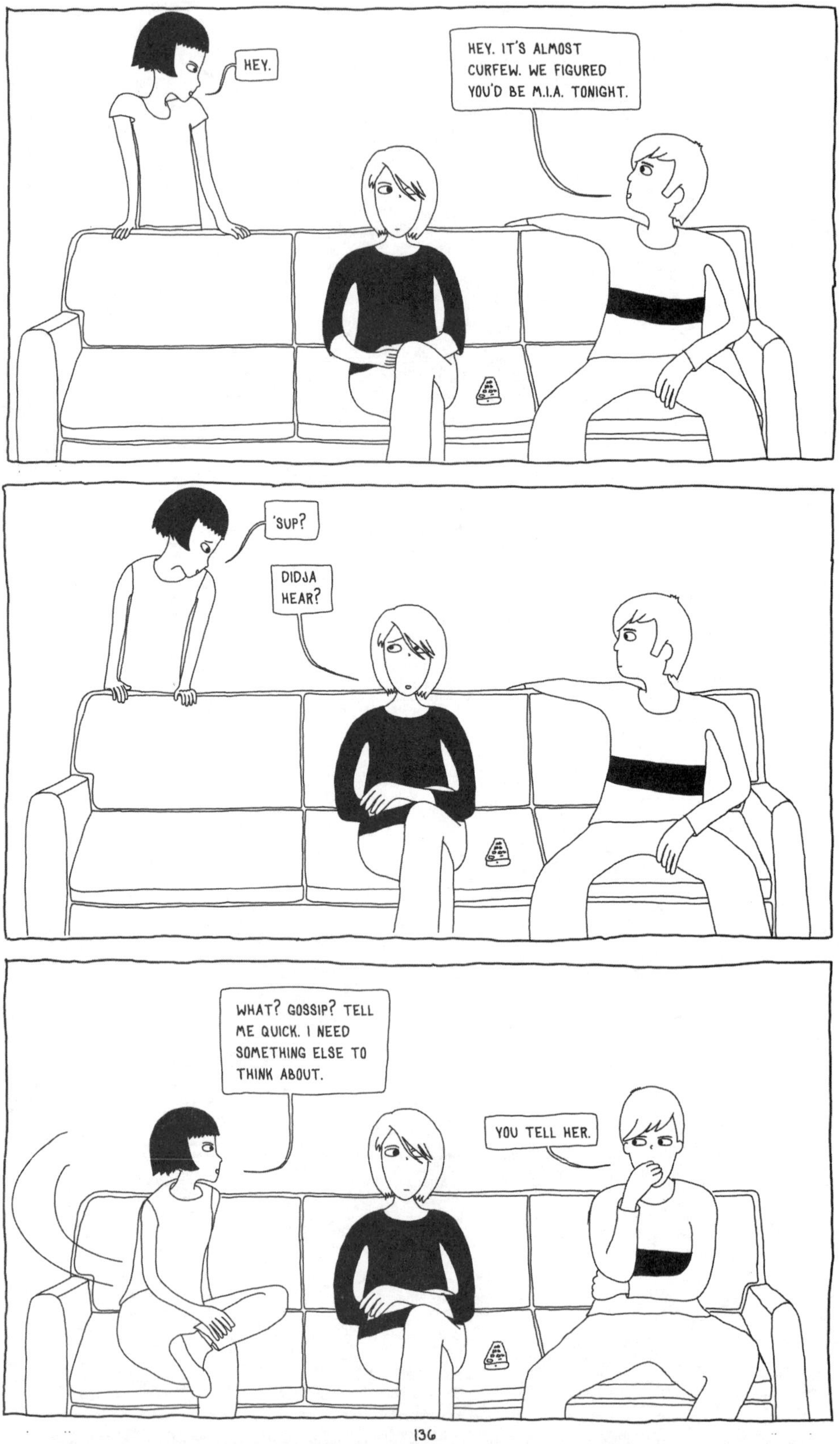
HEY.
HEY. IT'S ALMOST CURFEW. WE FIGURED YOU'D BE M.I.A. TONIGHT.
'SUP?
DIDJA HEAR?
WHAT? GOSSIP? TELL ME QUICK. I NEED SOMETHING ELSE TO THINK ABOUT.
YOU TELL HER.

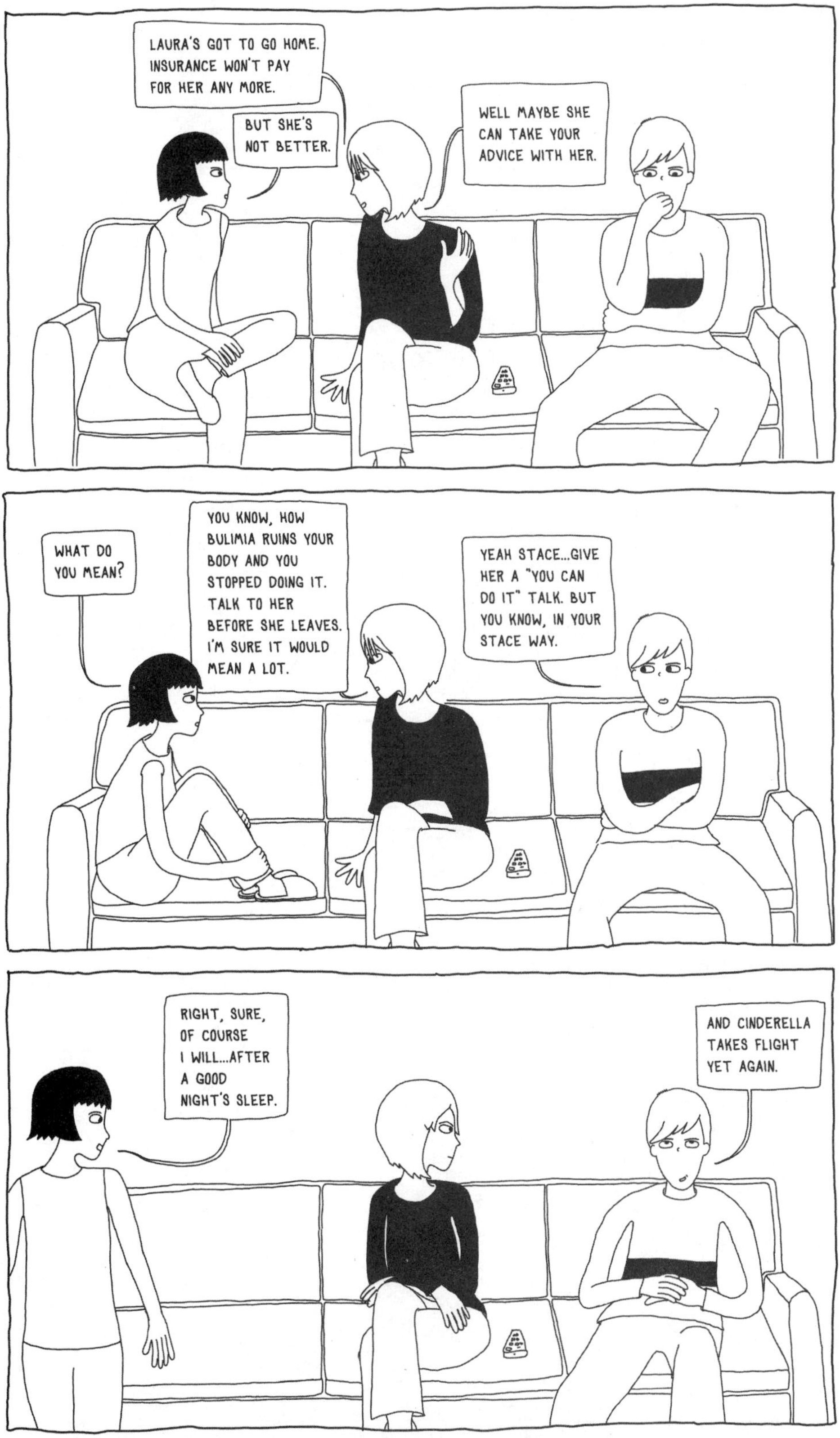
LAURA'S GOT TO GO HOME. INSURANCE WON'T PAY FOR HER ANY MORE.
BUT SHE'S NOT BETTER.
WELL MAYBE SHE CAN TAKE YOUR ADVICE WITH HER.
WHAT DO YOU MEAN?
YOU KNOW, HOW BULIMIA RUINS YOUR BODY AND YOU STOPPED DOING IT. TALK TO HER BEFORE SHE LEAVES. I'M SURE IT WOULD MEAN A LOT.
YEAH STACE...GIVE HER A "YOU CAN DO IT" TALK. BUT YOU KNOW, IN YOUR STACE WAY.
RIGHT, SURE, OF COURSE I WILL...AFTER A GOOD NIGHT'S SLEEP.
AND CINDERELLA TAKES FLIGHT YET AGAIN.

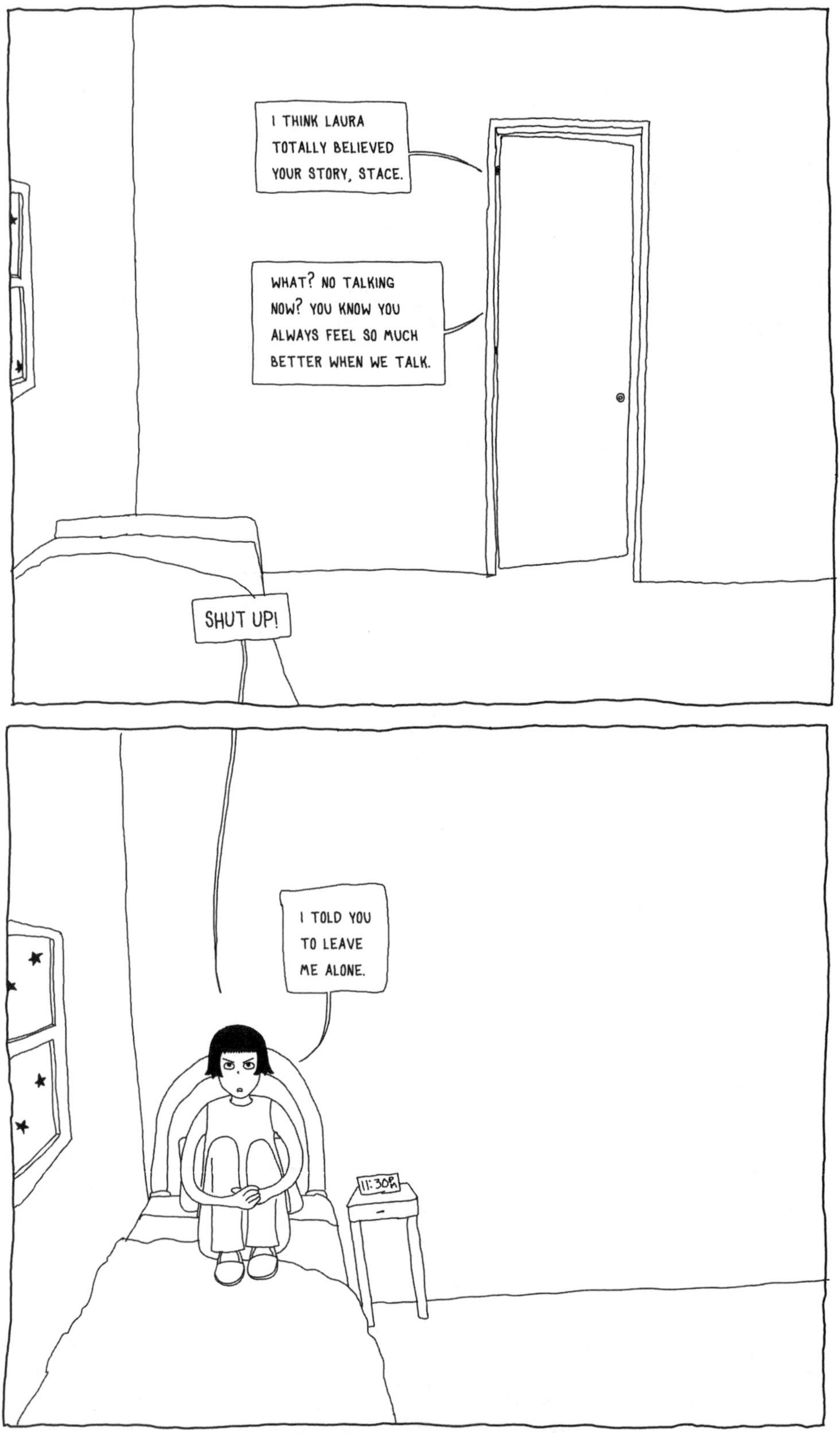
I THINK LAURA TOTALLY BELIEVED YOUR STORY, STACE.
WHAT? NO TALKING NOW? YOU KNOW YOU ALWAYS FEEL SO MUCH BETTER WHEN WE TALK.
SHUT UP!
I TOLD YOU TO LEAVE ME ALONE.
11:30PM

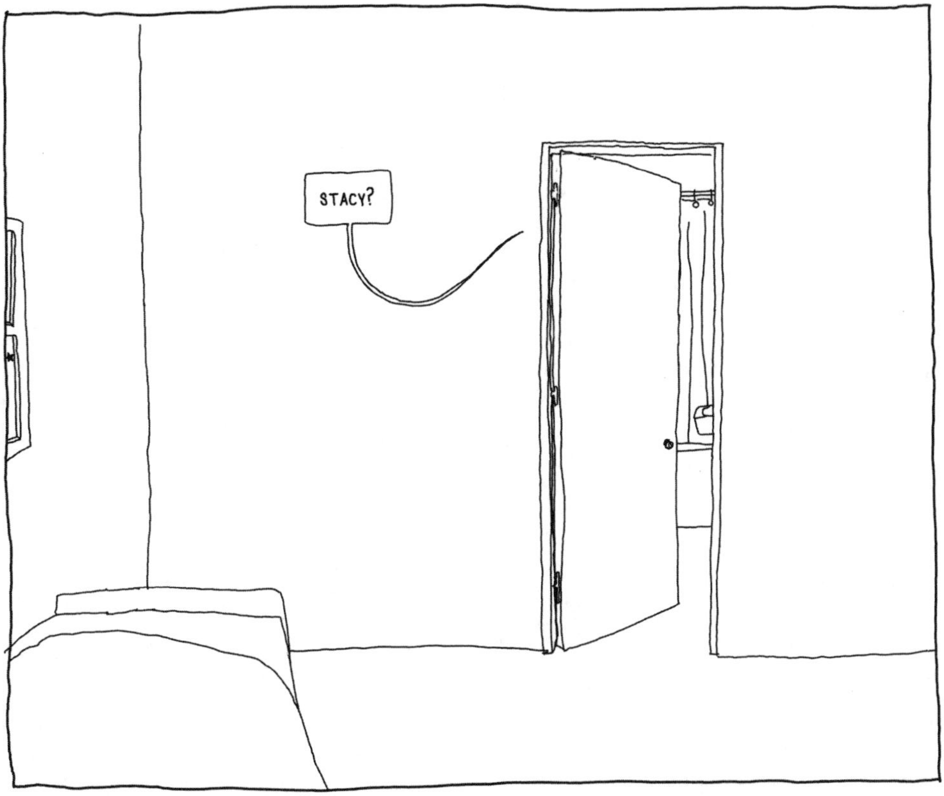
STACY?

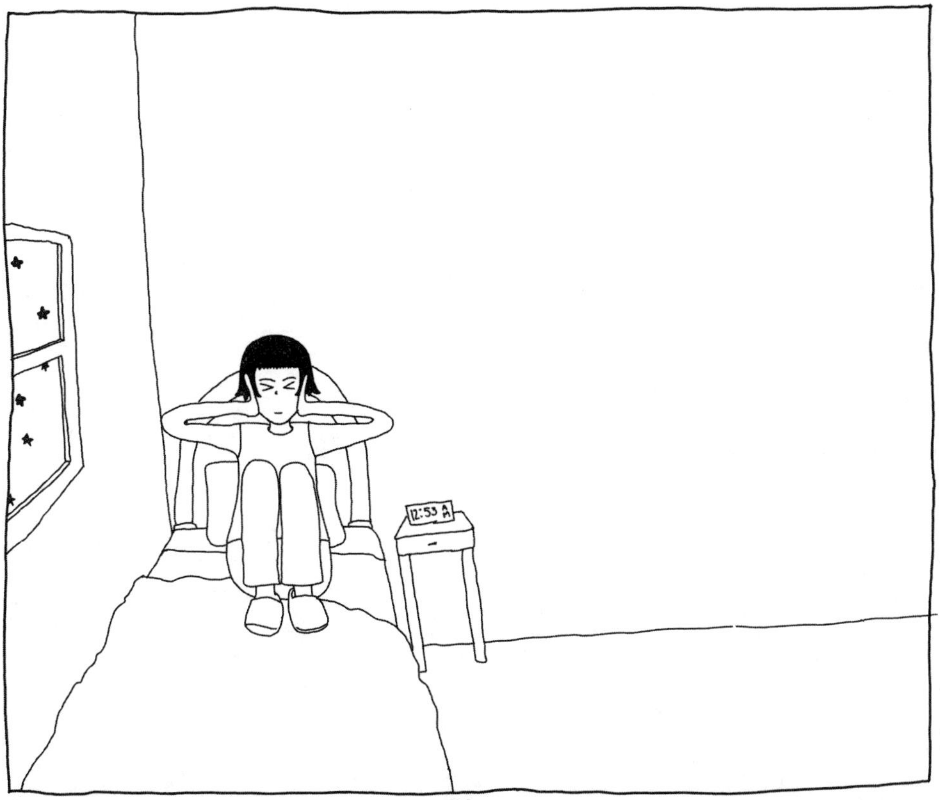
12:53 AM

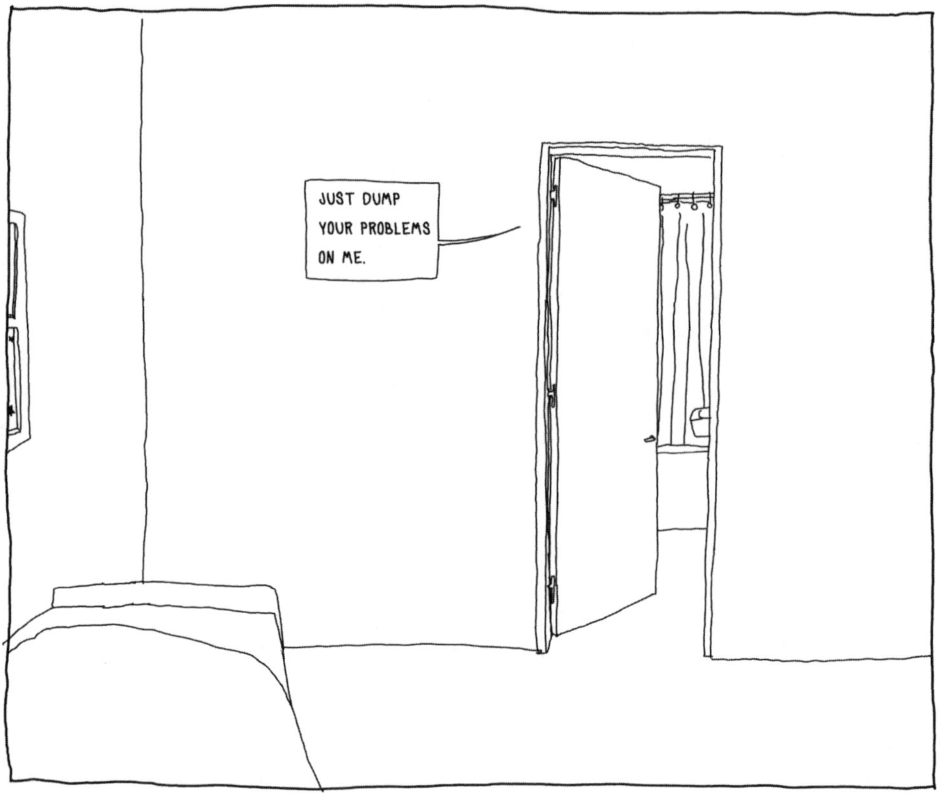
JUST DUMP YOUR PROBLEMS ON ME.

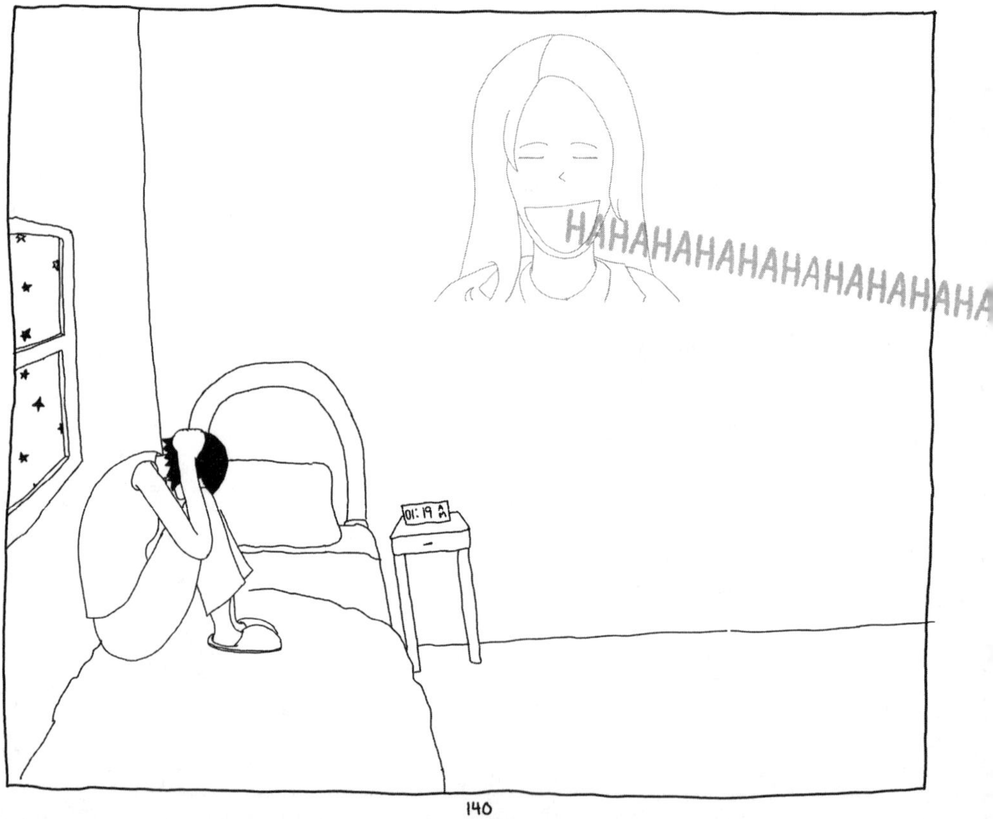
HAHAHAHAHAHAHAHAHA
01:19 AM

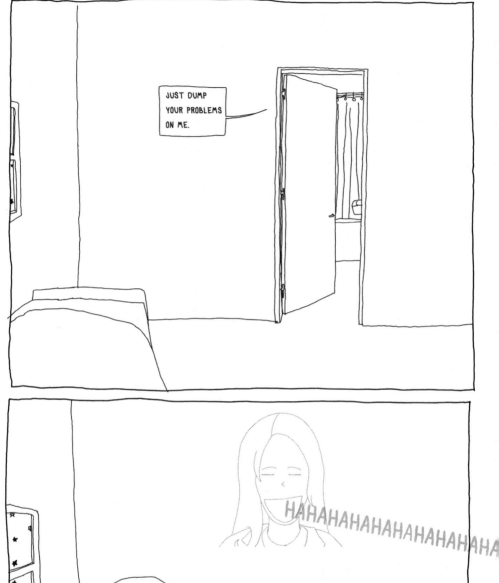

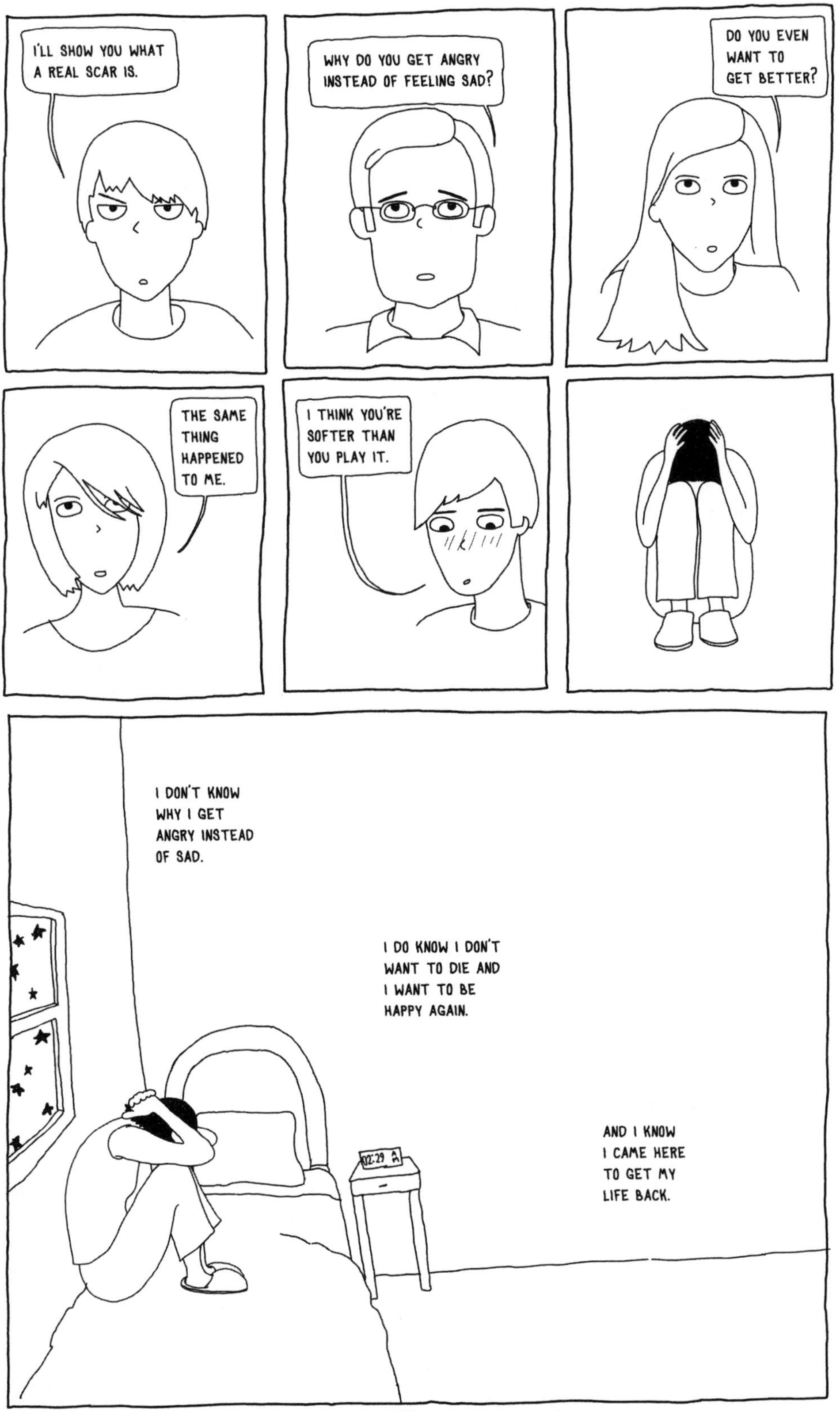
I'LL SHOW YOU WHAT A REAL SCAR IS.
WHY DO YOU GET ANGRY INSTEAD OF FEELING SAD?
DO YOU EVEN WANT TO GET BETTER?
THE SAME THING HAPPENED TO ME.
I THINK YOU'RE SOFTER THAN YOU PLAY IT.
I DON'T KNOW WHY I GET ANGRY INSTEAD OF SAD.
I DO KNOW I DON'T WANT TO DIE AND I WANT TO BE HAPPY AGAIN.
AND I KNOW I CAME HERE TO GET MY LIFE BACK.

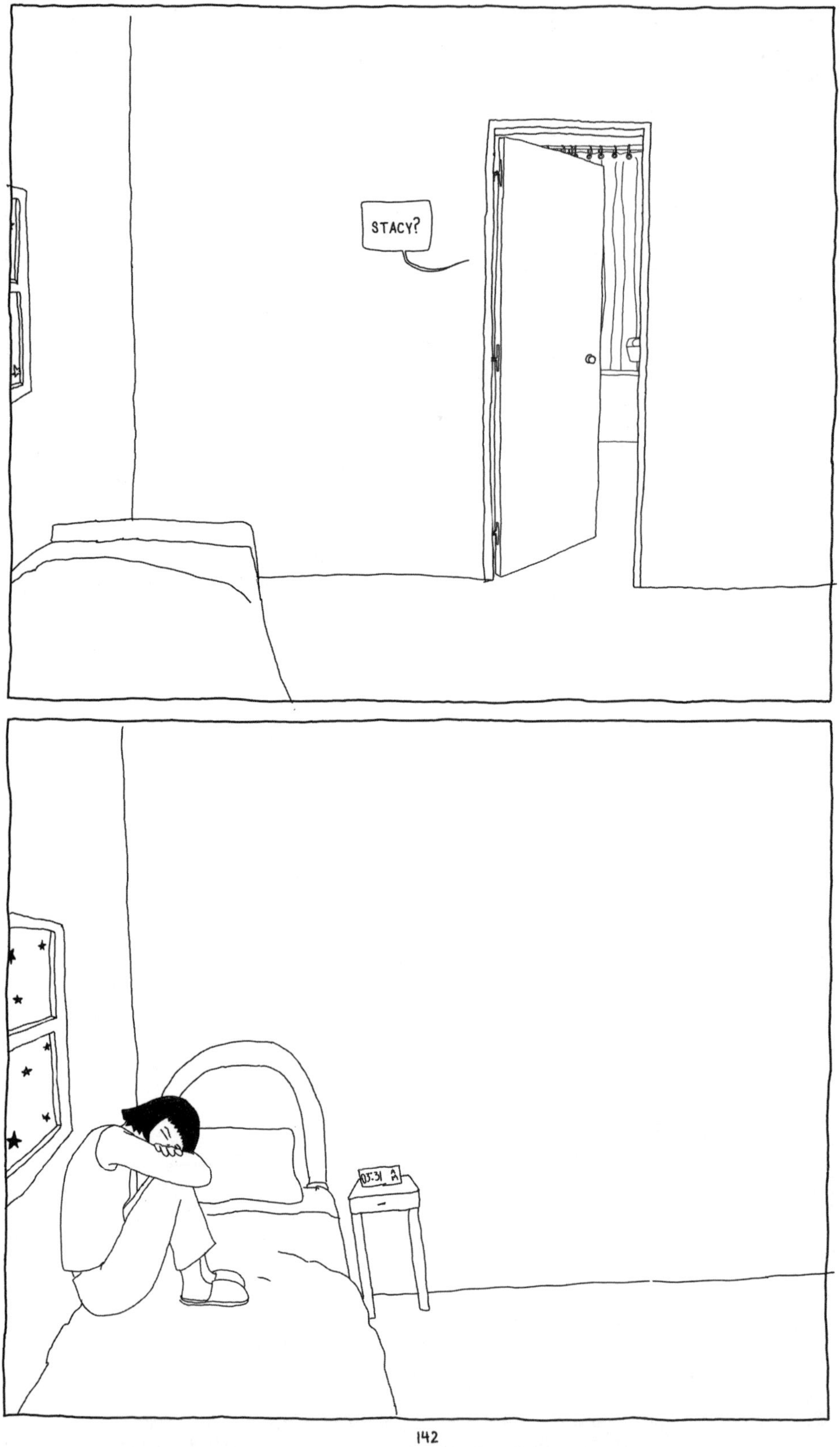
STACY?

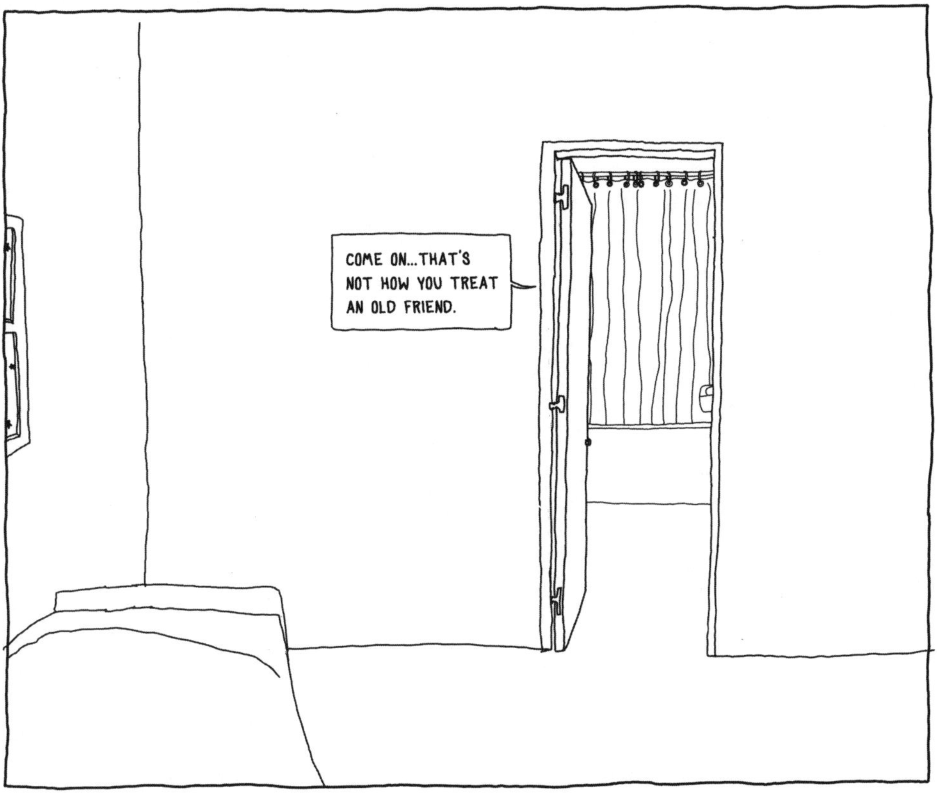
COME ON...THAT'S NOT HOW YOU TREAT AN OLD FRIEND.

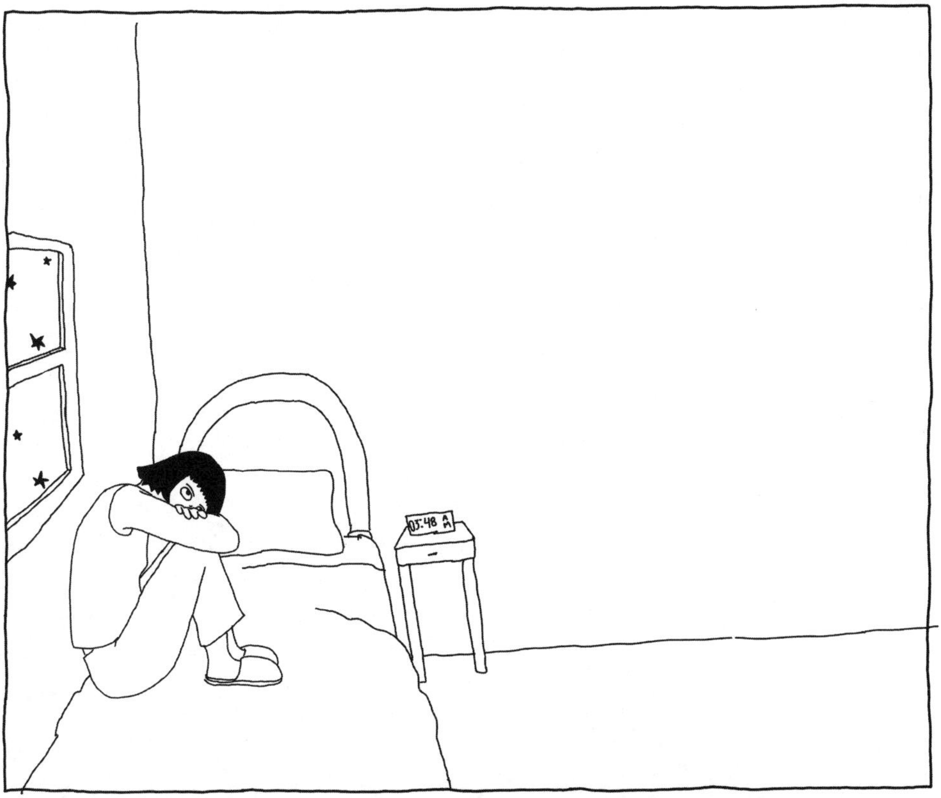

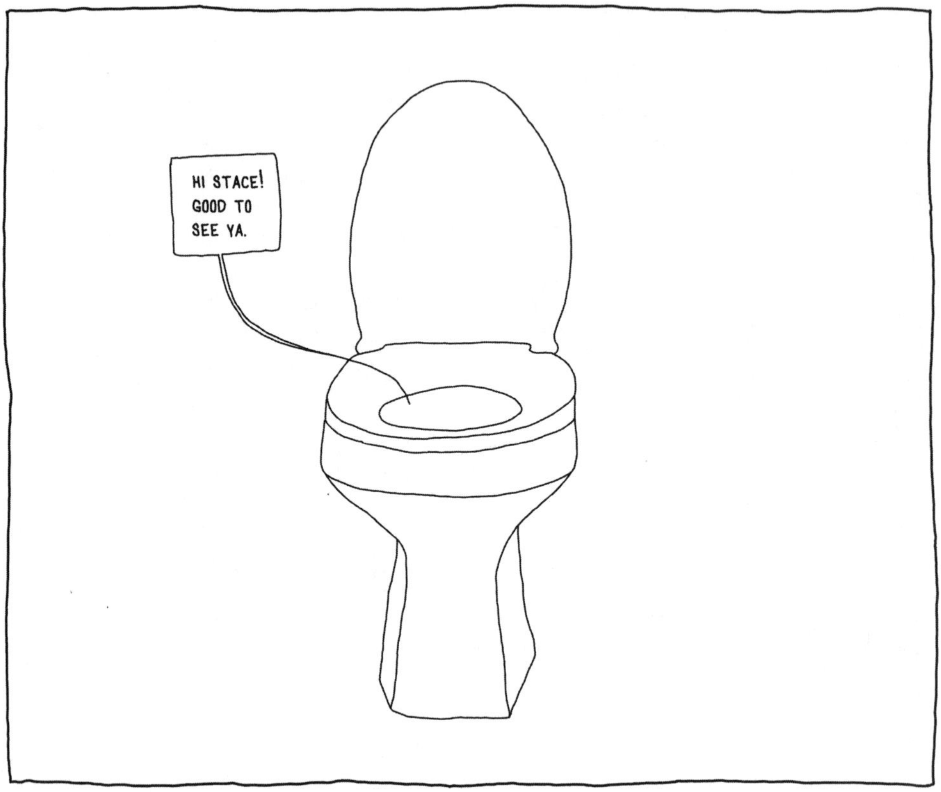
HI STACE! GOOD TO SEE YA.

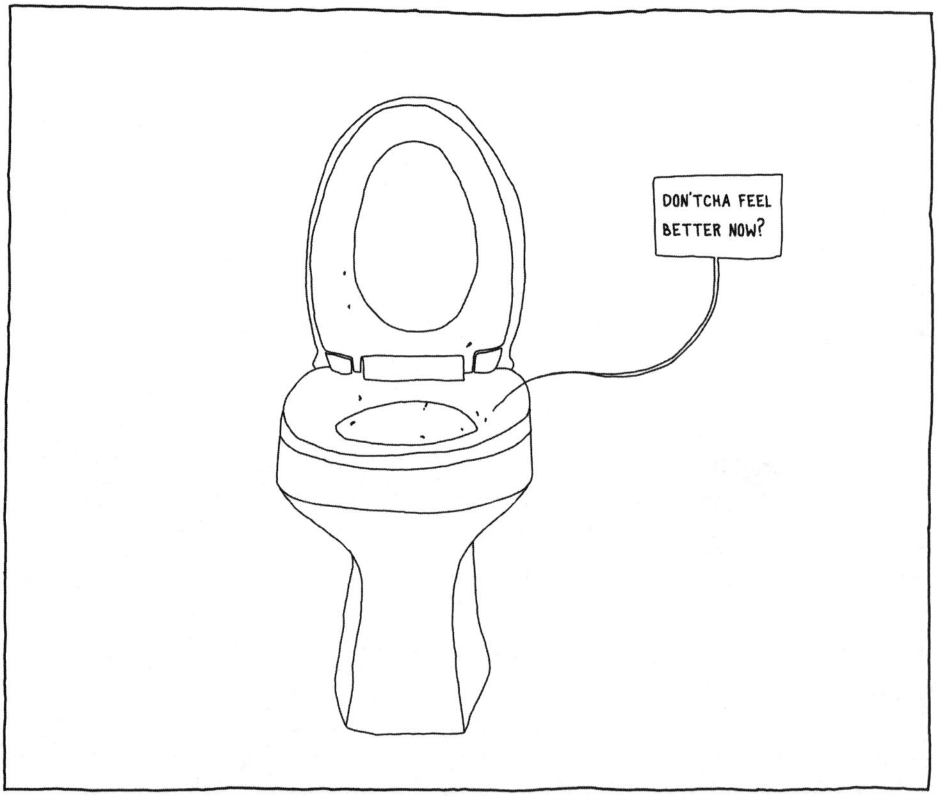
DON'TCHA FEEL BETTER NOW?

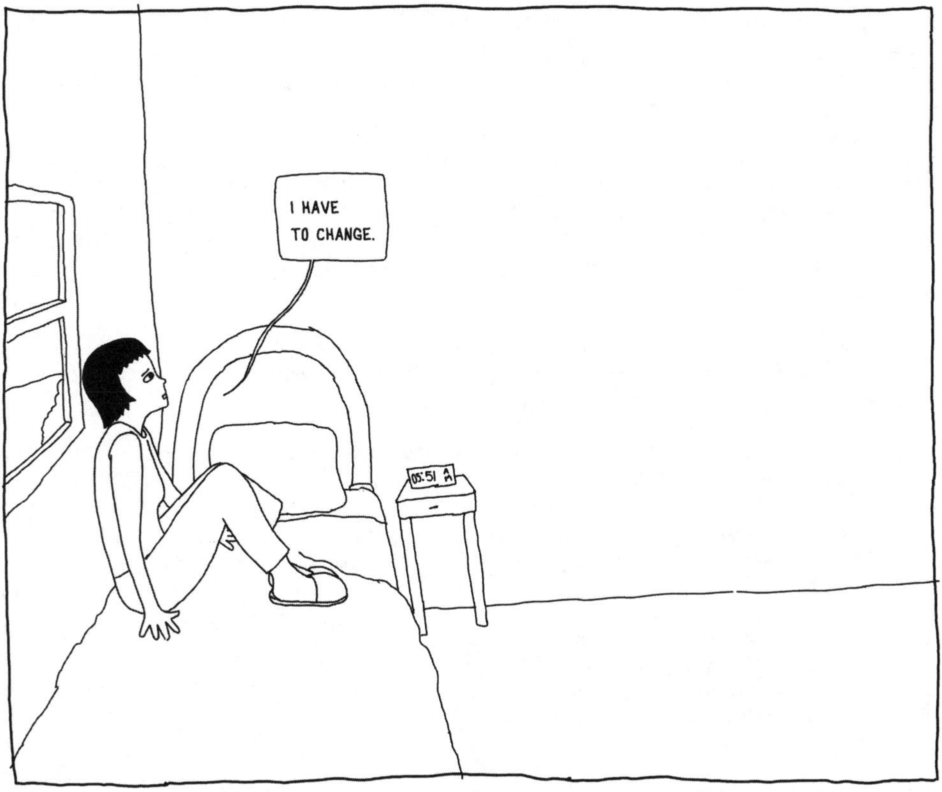
I HAVE TO CHANGE.
05:51 AM

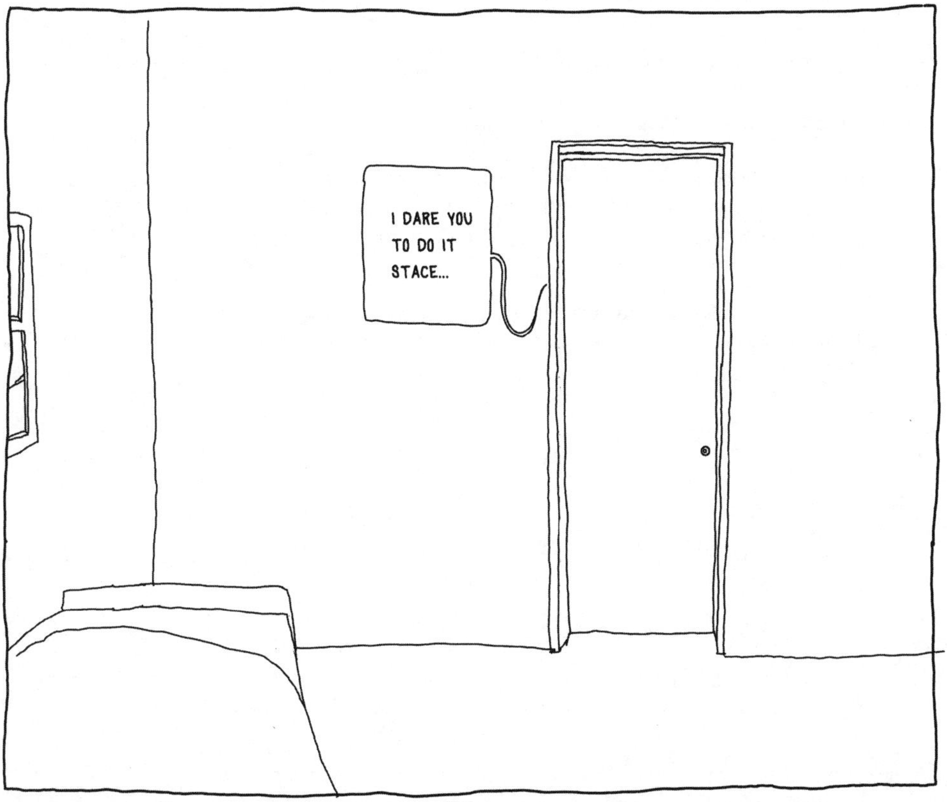
I DARE YOU TO DO IT STACE...

Is Stacy serious about getting help, and did you know she was bulimic?

MARIA

I'D LIKE TO BELIEVE SHE'S SERIOUS. SHE CALLED ME FOR THE FIRST TIME SINCE SHE'S BEEN IN GOLDEN MEADOWS LAST WEEK AND TOLD ME SHE'S BEEN DOING A LOT OF THINKING, AND THAT SHE KNOWS I TOLD HER MOM ABOUT THE DRUGS BECAUSE I LOVE HER. AND SHE SAID SHE LOVES ME TOO, AND THAT WE WILL ALWAYS BE FRIENDS BUT THAT SHE'S NOT SURE ABOUT TRUSTING ME. I CAN UNDERSTAND THAT. I MEAN I DON'T KNOW IF I TRUST HER EITHER.

MAYBE SHE'S BEEN BRAINWASHED OR MAYBE SHE'S JUST SO SICK OF THE HOSPITAL SHE WANTS TO GET OUT, SO SHE'S DOING AND SAYING WHAT THEY WANT TO HEAR. AND YES I KNEW SHE WAS BULIMIC BUT I THOUGHT IT WAS A PHASE.

ON HER FIRST BREAK HOME FROM BOARDING SHE WAS LIKE "MARIA I HAVE THE BEST DIET FOR YOU." SHE TRIED TO TEACH ME HOW TO PUKE BUT I'M ONE OF THOSE PEOPLE WHO CRIES WHEN THEY VOMIT SO IT DIDN'T WORK.

I MEAN, I WOULD LOVE TO BE SKINNY. ALL MY LIFE I'VE BEEN THE BLOND BUT MY THIGHS RUB TOGETHER AND MY BOOBS JIGGLE WHEN I WALK AND THE POPULAR GIRLS WERE ALWAYS MEAN TO ME.

MARIA DIARRHEA IS WHAT THEY USED TO CALL ME IN SCHOOL AND MY BROTHER'S FRIENDS CALL ME CHUNKY. WHAT CAN I SAY, I HAVE WEAK ANKLES, AND FLAT FEET AND I'M SHORT AND ROUND WHEN EVERYONE WANTS TALL AND ANGULAR.

VIOLET

I KNEW STACY WAS BULIMIC, NOT THAT WE TALKED ABOUT IT EVER. IT'S SOMETHING EVERYONE DID AT SCHOOL. PARTY, EAT A TON, AND THEN VOMIT. IT DIDN'T SEEM LIKE A BIG DEAL. I WASN'T PART OF THAT. MY PROBLEM IS NOT WEIGHING ENOUGH AND NOT HAVING ANY BOOBS. NONE. I'M LIKE A NEGATIVE SIZE. I HATE IT, BUT I'M TRYING TO BE OK WITH IT. IT'S HARD.

IF STACY SAYS SHE'S SERIOUS ABOUT GETTING HELP SHE PROBABLY IS. I THINK RECOVERY IS DIFFICULT. SOMETIMES WEEKS GO BY WITH NO PROGRESS AND THEN ONE LITTLE THING HAPPENS AND THE FLOODGATES OPEN.

146

LOLA

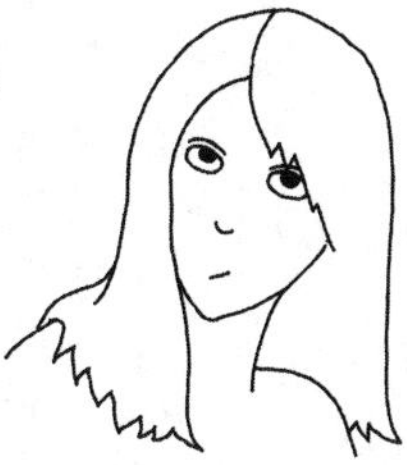

STACY WANTS HELP, TRUST ME. THAT'S WHAT I MEANT BEFORE WHEN I SAID I HOPE SHE TELLS THEM EVERYTHING. I'VE KNOWN THE ENTIRE TIME THAT IF SHE DIDN'T DEAL WITH HER BULIMIA SHE'D JUST BE COASTING AT GOLDEN MEADOWS. I DIDN'T SAY ANYTHING BECAUSE, WELL, SHE HAS A LOT OF ANGER IN HER SO IT SEEMED MORE IMPORTANT TO JUST BE A FRIEND THAN TO TELL HER WHAT TO DO.

AND I'M GLAD THAT'S WHAT I'VE DONE. STACY SHOWED ME HOW TO PUKE BUT I NEVER LIKED IT. I'D RATHER JUST NOT EAT A LOT AND EXERCISE. I DON'T KNOW, LIKE DOING A FEW HUNDRED JUMPING JACKS OR JUMP ROPE WHILE I'M WATCHING TV.

YES I HAVE SOME CONTROL ISSUES, WHO DOESNT? BESIDES, I'M WORKING ON THEM. I SEE A THERAPIST, I'M UNDER CONTROL.

ASHLEY

I HAD NO IDEA STACY WAS BULIMIC UNTIL A FEW DAYS AGO. I REALLY THOUGHT, LIKE EVERYONE ELSE IN GROUP, THAT SHE USED TO BE BULIMIC. I MEAN, SHE WAS SO CONVINCING WHEN SHE WAS TALKING TO LAURA ABOUT IT.

IT'S BRAVE OF HER TO GO TO DR. ROSS AND TO TELL EVERYONE IN GROUP SHE WAS LYING. THAT'S THE REAL PROOF THAT SHE'S SERIOUS. SHE DIDN'T HAVE TO SAY ANYTHING. I THINK SHE'S JUST TIRED, I KNOW I AM.

WE'RE ALL LIKE BIG WALKING WOUNDS BLEEDING EVERYTHING.

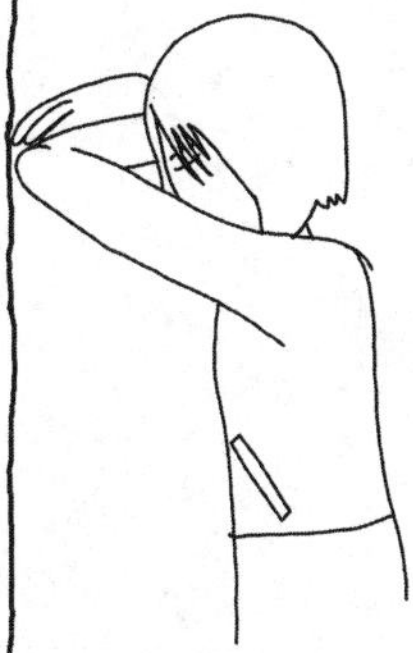

TOTAL LENGTH OF STAY:

twenty-four weeks,
five hours

"Stacy has made considerable progress in the hospital. Her revelation, during the middle of her stay, about her bulimic activities has allowed us to delve deeper into her emotional instability and she has begun to make the connection between her present emotional state, her past history, her substance abuse, and her eating disorder. Stacy will be transferring to Hill House, our off-grounds facility, to continue individual, group, and family therapy. She is currently involved in putting together college applications. Stacy seems to have the intelligence and capacity to benefit from continued psychotherapy. Based on these attributes, the prognosis is fair to good."

From the discharge summary of Stacy Black

In case you are wondering what happened, all I can tell you is that these events occurred last year and I stayed in the hospital for another three months before moving to Hill House. (Ashley is here too, which means I'm not lonely.) We're planning a trip next weekend so I can visit my dad's grave. I've never been before but I think now I want to see it. It's not something I was able to face before, but I'm trying to go back through my life and see what makes me feel bad. It isn't easy to just allow myself to be sad instead of turning to anger or negativity or wanting to purge. I know I've got to keep asking "why" till I have an answer, but sometimes it's easier to just not ask.

What else? I applied to college for next year and got in so it really is never too late because I'll be almost twenty when I go, which is old for a freshman. They say life gets easier—we'll see.

From the desk of Stacy Black

Acknowledgements

I got from then to now with help from Dr. W. (shrink), H.P. (another shrink), and H.S. hospital—a safe place when nothing felt safe.

Meghan Baier, Cybele Pascal, Gail Shafer, Katharina Sandizell-Smith, and Elizabeth Warner—friends through everything—you helped me remember what I didn't realize I'd forgotten.

Thanks to Charlotte Sheedy, my agent, who saw what I could not (and to her fabulous assistant Meredith Kaffel). Nancy Mercado, editor extraordinaire, is the person who encouraged me to write in the voice of my (Stacy's) eighteen-year-old self. Danica Novgorodoff's design input made everything that much better, Gina Gagliano's smart ideas were welcome, and the eagle eyes of Manuela Krueger have kept this book free of creative grammar and spelling.

Cindy Abramson, Melissa Dallal, Ken Grobe, Bruce Ledbetter, Jeff Madrick, Maria Moratis, Scott McCloud, Bryan Nunez, Sam Roberts, Alison Schlanger, Sharleen Smith: your support, time, and feedback with the myriad permutations of this book, and my storytelling in general, have been invaluable.

Finally, thank you, Lakshman and Suniva. ILYMTYK.

This book was written with the aid of 85% dark chocolate. I ate three squares every day while writing and drawing it, and that's 100% true.

TRACY WHITE GREW UP AND STILL LIVES IN
NEW YORK CITY. THIS IS HER FIRST BOOK.

FIND OUT MORE THAN YOU MAY WANT TO
KNOW ABOUT TRACY AT WWW.TRACED.COM.
ALL STORIES GUARANTEED 95% TRUE.